Cover by Airicka's Mystical Creations
Edited by Sara Johnson

Staccato Publishing
Zimmerman, MN

First US Edition: December 2010
Second Edition: May 2012
Third Edition: June 2013

ISBN: 978-1-940202-51-8

Printed in the USA

Bonded
by HK Savage

Ch. 1

Snow was falling gently when I walked out of the lecture hall a free woman. It was a beautiful day despite the low skies. My last final was finished and the next term didn't start until the second week in February. Henry, my boss at the library, head of the Minneapolis coven of vampires and mentor to James, hadn't scheduled me to work in hopes of reducing my exposure to other vampires. Specifically, those who decided I made for useful leverage. So as a result, I was obligation free for the next five weeks. The only thing that could raise my spirits further greeted me as I walked outside of the building.

At the bottom of the steps going down to the sidewalks and forming a maze of paths crisscrossing the quad, stood James. He had told me when we first met that the myth of vampires sleeping during the day wasn't true. Not only did they not sleep at all, the sunlight wouldn't physically damage them as the legends foretold. The myth was rooted in some amount of truth, however. The young vampires, or "newly turned," were hypersensitive to almost any sensation and, as a result, felt a horrible burning in their skin from the sun. I had only recently learned that the vampires closer to the Equator had to stay indoors during the daylight hours due to the sun's intensity. Exposure was too painful to attempt even for the oldest and most powerful.

James was turned almost one hundred fifty years ago, and we lived far north of the Equator so he was able to walk outside during the daylight hours with relative ease. His only holdover, he had confessed, was his eye sensitivity. He wore sunglasses whenever the sun was out. I didn't like it because I couldn't see his moods when he wore them; his eyes had become my compass and I found it disconcerting to lose that.

Feeling my pulse quicken at the sight of him in his black wool coat and dark blue scarf, hair wet and dark brown from the snow had been pushed back off his face. I laughed at my ridiculousness. Seeing James without his ever present sunglasses during the daylight hours, I loved the heavy clouds all the more.

Without thinking, I waved hugely at him like a complete idiot. It didn't matter; I was rewarded with a flash of his pearly whites. He was calm and his fangs were retracted, only slightly longer than human canine teeth. A perfect predator, his kind was camouflaged to fit in with their prey until they chose to reveal themselves as a nightmare come to life. But not him. Not for me.

I skipped down the steps, tossing my backpack over my shoulder and threw my arms around his broad shoulders with a final hop. He leaned down to kiss me, wrapping his arms around me to catch me with ease. The lack of a heartbeat and cool skin didn't bother me, they made him more him. It was only because of habit that he went through the motions of breathing. All of those human body functions were superfluous to the reanimated dead.

"I take it you did well?" James chuckled at me and took my hand as we started back to my dorm.

"I think I did." I shrugged. "Either way, I'm done and officially have nothing to do until February.

James twisted his neck to look down his nose at me, his expression severe. "What are we going to do with you until then?"

Walking became a challenge demanding my complete focus. Frowning at my shoes, I walked beside him without answering. For as much thought as I had put into it, one would think I could have made a decision. I hadn't.

3

His protectiveness required us to be in close proximity at all times, though without any sort of structure on my part to keep me occupied, that left him with very little free time if he was babysitting me. And he most likely had work obligations to consider. Most of the time he worked from home, although there were the occasional meetings with office staff or his editor.

If I were to be honest, I would have to admit that my doubts had little to do with his obligations and more to do with having uninterrupted time together and my own insecurities. I was relatively sure of "us" for now, yet I was nervous to find out how "us" would work when he didn't *have* to be with me anymore; when he no longer had to uphold his oath to Stephen's family. When we first started working together, he promised that he would protect me and he'd been taking it very seriously. Maybe when this whole situation with Bradley, the sociopath who liked using me to manipulate James blew over, James and I would spend less time together. That might be more normal than what we'd had thus far, but I wasn't looking forward to it.

At the same time I was fearful if we spent more time together without all the distractions, he would quickly see that there was nothing exceptional about me; nothing that could keep him entertained once his initial physical interest wore off. Maybe it would be wise for me to accept that and make the best of it while I had him. That had been a nagging thought since he'd first told me he loved me. I believed him that he did, I just didn't believe him that it meant the same thing to him as it did for me.

"Um, I don't know." Uncertain, my gaze shifted to the snow falling at my feet, melting to leave the sidewalk dappled in its wake. Reaching my threshold of manageable discomfort, I changed the subject. "I have some last minute Christmas shopping to do. Would you like to go with me? Otherwise, if you have to work I can call Stephen."

4

James' sudden stop made him an effective anchor, pulling me up without warning. Taken by surprise, I looked up to see his face twisted into a dark scowl, something I didn't often see and his eyes had gone nearly black, revealing a depth of anger at the innocuous remark that came as a surprise.

"Why would I send you off with Stephen when I have been waiting patiently all this time to have you to myself? Don't you think *I've* got some ideas for our vacation?"

I forgot sometimes how possessive a vampire could be, we had such a comfort level I often neglected James' true nature and the complications that came with it. My flushing neck and cheeks betrayed my embarrassment. "I'm sorry, did you have plans?" Living without a lot of interaction with other people made me somewhat socially retarded.

His true nature receded, I saw it in the relaxing of his jaw and his eyes cooled to midnight. "For starters, what would you say to a small holiday gathering at my house this Friday night with our nearest and dearest friends?" His broad grin betrayed his excitement.

James had never looked so human. His cheeks had a flush to them and I knew he'd fed within the last hour before he came to campus. That wasn't unusual for him to do before he put himself in such close proximity to so many humans. Fortunately for me, James had a conscience and he obtained his "food" from a contact he had at the local blood center. As Stephen had pointed out when he first told me about it, giving blood really did save lives.

"That sounds great! When did you decide to do that? Who all are you thinking of having over?" I'd been developing a real taste for people since Stephen and James had taught me to shield myself from the unwanted parts. I was eager to make up for lost time and there hadn't been many

5

opportunities what with all the chaos and death threats around us these past few months.

"Stephen's decided we've been too serious lately and wanted an opportunity to kick up his heels. I volunteered to host so I could reel him in as much as possible." The crooked lift at the corner of his mouth hinted at his doubts of that possibility.

Stephen was a force to be reckoned with, as anyone who knew him would agree. The idea of anyone reining him in was a joke.

"Henry will be there and I know Stephen is bringing a date. I'm not sure about Tara or Tonya, but Troy is currently unattached."

"Well, the only people I could add to that would be Heidi and Ben from work. Ben has a girlfriend and Heidi could scare up a date, I'm sure." In working at the library I had grown close to my two favorite coworkers. I think Henry scheduled us together on purpose since we all seemed to get along and he was very generous to me. Whether that was his or James' doing I wasn't sure; I appreciated it regardless.

James was nodding; of course he would have thought of those two already. He knew me well and it wasn't just because of our romantic involvement. We were linked psychically by what vampires call "marks." Normally marks have to be from a bite; three marks and the human would become a vampire. Vampires used marks to bind humans to themselves as servants. We had all of the signs of the connections that come with marks only without the bite.

James had fed from me once, in an emergency and he swore he didn't mark me. It had to be intentional on the part of the vampire to differentiate it from a feeding bite. He had to inject some of his venom into me to make a "mark." Due to the unusual circumstances of our bond, we were as yet uncertain what would happen to me as a result of the psychic mark or how close to a vampire I was already. According to the vampires, a situation like ours hadn't happened in a very long time and no one knew if, when, or how it might change my mortality or mental status without the usual blood exchange. I had been experiencing decreased healing time, something I'd made use of since meeting Bradley, as well as some hypersensitivity and mood control issues. It was a challenge I tried to downplay while attempting to learn to manage it.

James, on the other hand, was experiencing a revival of his humanity, a fact that further increased the difficulty in remembering what he was. He had a predisposition toward human feelings. His ability of sensitivity to others' "talents" made him different than other vampires. This sensitivity seemed to help him to maintain his humanity a little better than most of his kind, though he was still capable of a vampire's coldness; a side of him I had caught glimpses of despite his careful attempts to guard me from any such displays. It hadn't been directed at me and had only come out when we had been threatened and, as such, I had been able to keep his vampire self compartmentalized and out of my daily conscious thoughts. He had warned me at the very beginning that this was dangerous, yet I found myself doing it more often lately despite my efforts to remind myself otherwise.

Ch. 2

Arriving at my room, James shut the door and leaned against it with his hands in his pockets. He didn't unbutton his coat or make a move to unwrap his scarf. It still struck me as strange sometimes, his lack of human discomfort. Why would he need to take off his coat when he didn't feel a temperature change coming in from the outdoors? He merely wore the coat as a means of blending in. It wasn't physically necessary for him to regulate his body temperature because he didn't have one.

I had an acute awareness of James' attention as he watched me move about my tiny room. Ignoring his scrutiny as best as I could, I unpacked my bag and sorted through the heap of books I'd accumulated during the last four months putting the few I wanted to keep on the shelf over my desk and leaving the others on top to be returned to the bookstore. I might be able to get enough back to cover one book for next term. My family wasn't wealthy and every little bit helped.

James made a small coughing noise, a vampire's equivalent to throat clearing. "Claire, you never said what you were planning on doing for break. Are you thinking of staying here?"

There it was, the question I had been wondering about myself without having the wherewithal to ask it. "I don't know. They're keeping the dorms open so I could stay here." I shrugged. "And Mom and Dad invited me to go home, too." My voice trailed off, weak and undecided. I hated that. I made sure to maintain steady eye contact and took a breath to sound less like a deflating balloon when I continued, "I guess I figured I would stay here at least most of the time. Why?" I watched his eyes and face very carefully to gauge his intentions, dropping my shields to better feel what he really wanted. He was going to decide this, not me. If it ended badly I didn't want it to be my neediness that caused it.

The corner of James' mouth twitched as he felt me open myself up to him. With his ability he could almost always tell when those around him were using their own talents; they had to be really good to hide it from him, and I wasn't really good. Blue eyes went darker as he used *his* shields to block my efforts. I felt the wall between us solidify and set my chin stubbornly. Frustrated and hurt, I stalked over to the closet to get a bag. The thought that I would *not* go with him was never an option. I was weak.

"I was hoping you would want to stay with *me* again." I heard his voice grow husky with the feelings he was otherwise hiding.

That he offered made me giddy. Still, I shrugged nonchalantly, "That sounds good to me. I'll pack a few things." The prospect of us alone for even a fraction of that month, while exciting, also carried with it the potential for a lethal dose of reality. If James were to rethink his interest in me and decide to end things, with the vampires' need for secrecy, I would lose more than the only love I would ever want. I would also lose my life.

Pushing away from the door, James took one smooth stride, putting himself between the closet and me, bringing me up short and leaving me staring at his chest. His hand came up to finger the opal necklace he'd given me. Eyes on the stone, he spoke softly, "I was thinking you should stay the *whole* time."

Glad for the lack of direct eye contact, I ducked my head to hide my unease. Living together again. This time it would be for almost as long as we'd known each other, that would be a lot of time for him to decide I was uneventful and not worth the bother it took to keep me safe and alive.

I kept my voice even despite the honesty he could hear in my hammering heart. "I would be happy to stay with you. If you don't think it would be too distracting from your work." I peeked up at him. "Have you had someone stay with you that long before?" Thinking about it as I said it, I realized I wasn't sure I wanted to know the answer to that question. So far I had limited what I knew of his past relationships. It wasn't fair since he was my first boyfriend and I knew he'd had women before me. That was a rabbit hole often best avoided, but again, I was not adept at social nuances.

I felt a tingling of electricity dance along my senses as he dropped his shielding enough for me to feel the truth behind what he said. "People have stayed with me while in transit or in times of need." He looked down at me, "But no, I have never invited a woman to live with me before you."

Drawing a blank on what to say, I reached up to kiss him and wrapped my arms around his back. Afraid or not, there was no point avoiding it, I thought with a tentative surge of hope. We would know better where we stood in five weeks, good or bad. I squeezed him tighter, making my wish for where that would be.

Ch. 3

Friday night arrived and James' house was awash in Christmas cheer. We'd spent the last few hours putting up decorations. It surprised me how well we'd adjusted to our living arrangements. When I'd stayed over before, the Andrews had been around most nights, lending a sense of communal housing. This time it was just James and I acting the part of a normal couple, watchful of danger, but nothing like before. With our last encounter, we had sent Bradley on the run and we figured he was holed up, licking his wounds for the time being. We felt relatively confident he wouldn't come out for a while. James' overprotective tendencies left nothing to chance, so he continued his vigilance regardless of whether anyone else thought it necessary.

"Come on," I hopped up and down excitedly grabbing his hand and heading to the front door.

He eyed me quizzically letting himself be towed along. "Where are we going?"

"Well we have to go outside and see it like they will. We have to walk up and get the full effect."

He nodded his acceptance, a hint of a smile playing at his lips. "You know you're a little nutty about this whole Christmas thing; I never would have guessed."

A little embarrassed, I gave a half smile and rolled my shoulders. "Christmas has always been my favorite holiday. Everyone is so happy and kind to one another, anything seems possible. It just feels good to be around." We walked down the short herringbone paved path to the curb. "When I was little it was the only time I liked going out in crowds. The mall the week before was great, especially watching the kids waiting for Santa. It was probably my empathy, but I would be giddy for hours after leaving. It must be what getting high feels like." In my mind's eye I could see my parents watching me, actually looking relieved to see me comfortable and happy. It was the closest I'd ever let them get to feeling like the parents of a normal child. The memory was bittersweet. I wished I could have given that time back to my parents with me the way I am now. Let them have a child that gave them joy, not just doubt and pain.

Sensing the melancholy turn in my mood, James touched my arm as we reached the curb and turned me around to face the house. When he did, a small sound escaped my lips. I let myself pretend this was *our* house and *our* first Christmas together, daring to imagine that this was for keeps. I had to breathe deeply and blink my eyes clear before I gave myself away. The way he affected me caught me off guard at times and I didn't want him to know how silly I was. Often times I wished he wasn't so worldly, I probably seemed simple to him half the time.

His arm came up to wrap around my waist. Looking up at him, though I couldn't see his eyes in the dark, I was sure he could see mine glistening in the glow of the white twinkling lights. Leaning down to kiss my cheek, he pushed my hair back where it had blown into my face. "Come on, we have more to experience," he mocked playfully.

Not trusting my voice, I held his hand as we walked up to the house and James opened the door. Glad to have something to focus on other than my emotional reaction to Christmas lights, I surveyed the results of our labors.

To the left of the entry lay the stairs, the top rail of the wooden banister had been wrapped in simple green garland and a wreath hung on the wall beneath the stairs between the railing and the closet at the end of the wall. To the right was the couch, separating the entrance from the living room. In the living room, we'd put cream colored candles in clear glass hurricanes, small sprigs of evergreens lay wrapped around their bases and through to the dining room was a larger hurricane on the square table, draped in holly complete with berries; all of it real. The scent was amazing.

It was simple and elegant, perfectly matched to his house design. As I had noted before, the house was exactly what I would have designed and decorated for myself if given the chance. My favorite touch was the mistletoe hanging in the kitchen doorway. I hoped to trap James there a lot tonight. I felt my suspicions at the temporary nature of my stay slipping away under the optimistic spell the holiday was casting.

"Well, what do you think?" He squeezed my hand gently.
"It's perfect, we make a good team." I smiled and squeezed back.

James' reply was thoughtful, "Yes we do." He stiffened for a quick second and then relaxed. "The girls are here." Clarifying, he added, "I asked them to come and help with the food since they're better at that sort of thing than I am and I didn't want to put it all on you."

I had to giggle at that. James was a fabulous cook situationally. He could follow any recipe to perfection. However, he hadn't eaten human food in so long and it had changed so much, he sometimes had trouble making a go at modern pairings. It would make sense then that party snacks for humans and the Andrews, a clan of werecats who could out eat any human, would confound him. When he let the girls in, my jaw dropped.

The Andrews had a lot of physical similarities such as their honey blonde hair, hazel eyes and high, broad cheekbones allowing them to pass easily as a normal family of humans. Troy and Tonya were the oldest, appearing to be twenty-two. They were also the tallest, measuring a full six feet tall apiece. The two of them were the most similar and were sometimes mistaken for twins. The next was Tara. When I first met Tara, I had thought of her large, athletic frame as formidable. While we might be on friendlier terms lately, I continued to think of her muscular build as imposing.

Tonya was wearing her favorite color, a jewel toned jade satin halter dress and could have just walked off a Paris runway. But Tara was the surprise beauty. Dressed in a striking bronze satin top with three quarter sleeves and gathered at the sides, she had paired it with cream trousers and heeled brown boots. Her attire was as understated as Tonya's was over the top. They both looked amazing, each in a way that suited her personality and body.

"Wow, you too," I gushed, genuinely admiring. "You look incredible. It isn't fair that I have to be here with you. I'm glad more humans are coming, I look dull next to you."

James was back at my side and pulled me close. "You never look dull."

Blushing, I had to push away. "If you guys can start on the food, we have to get dressed." I looked over at James expectantly.

Tonya laughed lightly. "You two better dress separately or we'll never get you back down in time for the party." My blush deepened at her mention of the reputation we'd built for ourselves.

Tonya had been standing in front of us and as she spoke, she playfully put a hand on James' arm. The cats were very touchy, much like their animal counterparts. It meant nothing and had never bothered me before, yet when I saw her long, tan fingers touch his body I felt an uncontrollable surge of jealousy rise up within me. A growl erupted from my throat and a snarl curled my lip.

James reacted in an instant, throwing his arms around me, pinning my arms to my sides and holding me back just as I lunged for her. I felt the insulation of his shields coming up reinforcing mine. Within seconds, guarded by the addition of James' shields, I was back to myself, breathing heavily from the shock and shame of my violent response.

Catlike reflexes brought her and her sister both out of the way at the same time as James' intervention. "What the hell was that?" Tonya snapped at me, anger replacing surprise on her gorgeous feline features.

I shook my head, thoroughly embarrassed and perplexed at such an overzealous response to what I knew was nothing. "I don't know what came over me. Tonya, I am so sorry. Please believe me, I didn't mean it," I pleaded for her forgiveness.

Before she could reply James cut in, an edge to his voice. "Claire, love, that was a *vampire* reaction."

The Andrews knew about the marks, there was no need to hide any of this from them other than for the sake of my pride. The clan was bound to Henry as his animal to call and was as compelled to help him as he was to them. They could be trusted with any of our secrets.

"We are far more possessive and jealous than humans," he went on through gritted teeth. "That was too strong to be human."

Mortified, I had to agree with his deduction. "Is it getting stronger already? It's too fast." I genuinely feared losing my humanity and becoming a vampire without my consent. And now it appeared I had moved farther down the spectrum toward *his* kind with a sudden leap in transference happening through the marks. The reality settled heavy in the pit of my stomach. The question of "turning" had, of course, been one I'd asked myself a few times since becoming involved with James and I'd always assumed it would be my choice. However, it was rapidly becoming clear that I was *not* going to have that choice available to me; it was happening whether I wanted it to or not.

James' expression was dark. "I'm not sure what it means but we'll have to speak to someone soon. Maybe during your vacation."

He might not have meant anything by it, yet I couldn't help noticing that it was back to being "my vacation," not "ours" and I felt a sinking loss. I tried to pull away from James to go upstairs. He hesitated, not releasing me until he took a second to verify that I was under control. Whatever had happened, it had passed for now.

My voice sounded funny to my ears when I spoke, "I'm going to get dressed." I trudged up the stairs, wanting to be alone and wishing, not for the first time, for some amount of control over my life.

Ch. 4

James was kind enough to play host as I heard Troy arrive, making the clan nearly complete, though not quite. I hadn't heard Stephen and his date yet. They were probably fashionably late, as was Stephen's style. That brought my mind back to focus on the night ahead of me. I had no idea how I would get through the next few hours without humiliating myself, or potentially hurting someone. Not everyone due to arrive that night was as quick or as able to defend themselves as Tonya.

I let myself wallow for a few minutes as I slowly got dressed and put my dark, wavy hair up in a clip. It was James' favorite way for me to wear my hair and I found myself wearing it that way lately for his benefit. The style complimented my dress well. Slender straps led down to a gathered bodice and fitted skirt. The sleek material was accented by sparse gold patterning. I wore those colors frequently because they were mixed into my otherwise ordinary light brown eyes and when I dressed for it, it made my eyes more interesting.

With the reality of the party upon us, I was regretting our decision to make it a dress up occasion. I wanted to fade into the background so no one would notice when I ran off to hide. It was harder to sneak away in heels. I harrumphed as I slammed myself down hard on the bed in a mini tantrum.

Hearing a knock at the door, I sat bolt upright and watched the door ease open. James stepped into the room and shut the door with a soft click. We looked at each other for a moment, testing. I had my shields up tight. I knew before I checked that he'd done the same.

"Do you mind if I change as well?" he asked me quietly.

Closing my eyes to keep my illusion of privacy, I nodded. It was his room after all. The sounds of him dressing were second nature to me now. It actually made him seem human because, unlike his fluid movements, the fabrics he wore made sounds as he slid them off or on and I could track his movements about the room.

As I sat motionless on the bed, I heard his shirt slide off before his belt unbuckled. Down went his pants and there was a soft shuffle as he removed his socks. It was only due to my personal turmoil, that I was able to keep myself under control. Knowing he was down to his boxers just a matter of feet from me would normally have me tearing off my own clothes. My remembrance of Tonya's statement about our lack of self-control stung me again, more than it should have.

Meeting the Andrews clan and the vampires, James and Henry, had been the start of the best part of my life. It had also been the start of the scariest. Being abducted hadn't been the most terrifying part. I was more afraid of the fact that I was losing control again and it brought back the feelings I'd had my entire life until I'd learned how to block out the people around me. Helpless to control myself when other people's emotions were strong, I would unwillingly channel them and lose myself in the process. It was a time I never wanted back.

And here it was, happening again because of James; the one person I couldn't be without. He was the other part of my soul and I knew if I walked away from him, I would never be the same. I would stay, I *had* to stay, but at what cost to my humanity? The potential consequences of my decision were paralyzing and yet I was unable to decide any other way.

The bed depressed beside me and I realized with a start while I'd been lost in my own head, James had finished dressing. His cool hand took mine from my lap and brought it to his lips, brushing my knuckles lightly against them.

"I had meant to surprise you."

Unable to face him I opened my eyes and kept them on my lap. I felt my stomach flip over, it didn't seem like I could handle any more surprises today. My nerves were already frayed.

He continued in his deep, rich voice, giving me goose bumps. "But we have found someone with experience in," he paused, "bonded individuals. I was going to surprise you as part of your Christmas present. We are going to see her after we see your family for the holiday next week."

My spirits lifted and I felt grateful tears well up. When had I grown so sappy? I never used to cry and now I did it all the time. I'd learned how to block everyone else's emotions and, as a result, I was starting to feel my own clearly for the first time without interference and it was hard to dial them back. Sitting here, and knowing that James was trying just as hard to control what was happening to us, it was too much. I put my head in my hands.

James slid his arm around my shoulders and pulled me close for a kiss. "No," I nearly shouted, pushing myself away. His confusion made me want to cry more, though I knew from the sounds downstairs that I needed to get a handle on myself. "I'm having enough trouble controlling myself; we don't need to make this more complicated and now a human is here. I just heard Heidi walk up."

Cocking his head he stared at me. "You can hear her?"
"Yes, she's just walking up the path. Why?" It didn't seem like a big deal to me and I was pleased to divert his attention from my recent development of bipolar tendencies. The house wasn't that big, nor was the yard. It was a two story

Tudor; nice, but not large. They weren't in this area, they were all built back before houses got supersized.

James' sudden stillness alerted me to his concern. I had to remind myself to breathe, reacting to his apprehension automatically with a defensive posture while I waited for him to speak. "Claire, she's walking up from the street."

It was my turn to be confused. It wasn't uncommon to hear someone on the street walking up, especially in winter when the sound carried, echoing off of the frozen ground. I used to hear it all the time when we had company at home with my parents. Seeing my lack of concern, James added, "She parked about forty yards away by my guess. Human ears cannot hear her, it's impossible."

My shoulders slumped at the blow. This expert James and Henry had found who could help us was starting to feel like my last chance to keep hold of my humanity. I clung desperately to that last thread of hope. It was becoming too difficult watching myself disappear just as I was starting to find out who I really was.

Standing up, I kept his hand in mine and met his eyes, trying to appear more pulled together than I felt by a mile. "Let's get down there, people are waiting."

James stood with me and kept my hand. Bringing it to his lips again, he brushed them against the back of my hand. "We can worry tomorrow. Tonight I hope you can enjoy yourself. I thought we all deserved a night of no worries." He offered me a smile, one that usually had the effect of weakening my knees. "I will be right here with you all night."

Knees too stressed to be weak, I wished I knew if that would be a good thing or bad.

Ch. 5

James and I went downstairs together holding hands. It was probably a good idea for us to stay close tonight what with my emotions being overrun by the marks. James' ability to help me shield could be my last line of defense. We'd had to resort to it in the past and it had worked as a temporary solution. The first person I saw as I looked to the bottom of the stairs was my boss and James' closest friend, Henry. If anyone could help us, it was Henry.

Henry would never pass for an ordinary Head Librarian, his human role on campus, to anyone who saw him like this. Dressed flawlessly in a chocolate pinstripe suit with a caramel colored shirt, a very good look with his pale skin, combed back brown hair and brown eyes. Whenever I had heard stories about vampires, I had always heard about the young ones, those turned before they were past their mid twenties. I would guess that Henry had been in his early thirties when he was turned.

"Claire," his smile was reassuring. When I had first met him at work, I'd considered him a fatherly sort of influence. Then, once I had seen his scary side, never again. Yet I continued to trust him with my life because of those very attributes that made him frightening. "I've given you the entire term off. Will you find enough to do with yourself now that you are entirely without any cares?"

Without any cares? I felt my eyes well up and James let go of my hand in favor of wrapping his arm around me to pull me in close. To the humans, it was a loving gesture. The supernatural set at the party knew, as I did, that the more his body touched me, the better his ability to supplement my shields. Immediately, I felt his fuzzy layer of insulation wrap around my raw emotions making them easier to manage.

Henry's voice was low, his brown eyes speculative. "Has something else happened?"

Taking a shaky breath I started to speak and before I could say anything Tonya came up and casually threaded an arm through Henry's. Staring as I was at his eyes, I saw a spark of something when she touched him. It was gone in the next breath, as was my limited clarity, when she told him.

"She nearly clawed my face off when I touched her *dear* James." Through her forced smile, I could see Tonya remained upset by my misstep.

"Tonya, I really am sorry." I knew that it was inadequate for my transgression, yet it was all that I had to offer her.

James spoke at nearly the same time, losing no time reporting to his mentor. His voice drowned out the end of my apology. "The marks flared, Henry. Her reaction was not proportionate." Henry knew without James going into detail that he meant I'd acted more like him. Like a vampire.

Henry's eyebrows rose, his interest piqued. He was a quiet thinker and would not speak unless he had weighed his words carefully. "That is certainly something new. I have something I would like to speak with you about after everyone is gone tonight. Would that be possible, or do you have plans?"

We both told him we had nothing beyond this.

"Hey, Claire!" I heard a friendly, human voice shouting from the kitchen. Looking toward the source, I saw my friend Heidi coming through the kitchen doorway, her short brown hair cut into a shag a la Pat Benetar. This week the tips were not orange as they had been when I met her, but a bright red. Coming close enough to talk, Heidi noticed the direction my eyes had taken. She flipped a colored hair tip at me with her fingers, nails painted like flames to match. "Very seasonal. Like it?"

As I was starting to say yes, she grabbed me into a tight hug. Hurriedly, I braced for it. Releasing me, she grinned, the tiny diamond in her nose glinted in the light. "Claire, this is a great soiree!" Shrugging at her empty arm she laughed. "I had a date for tonight, then he cancelled on me so I'm here stag." She widened her eyes in false excitement glossing over the fact that it bothered her. "He had practice and you know, basketball comes first." Her eyes lost a touch of sparkle for just a second before she effused pure false joy again, "Anyway, I got Ben to come with me since his girlfriend has a family thing tonight."

I looked over her shoulder and saw Ben talking to Tara in the doorway. My work friends, James, and Stephen had gotten to know each other quite well these past few months with Stephen escorting me to and from work when James couldn't. Tara had come in a few times as well. They all seemed to get along, Stephen and Heidi especially. I think if Stephen was straight, he would be the perfect guy for Heidi and she knew it. She always looked at him with regret in her eyes, even though there wasn't a chance for it to work.

"Heidi, have you ever considered dating someone outside the athletics department? How about a nice chess player or someone from a book club for a change of pace? Maybe a musician?" I joked, awkwardly attempting to disguise my honest opinions as playful ribbing.

She pinched up her mouth sourly, goggling at me like I had grown a trunk. "Athletes happen to be strong. I like how well they take care of themselves."
Taken aback, I was unable to disguise my disapproval. "Are you so superficial you only need a great body?" No wonder her relationships were short lived.

She rubbed at the tip of her nose, a nervous habit she had when she was thinking. "No, I mean they can take care of themselves; like if there was some sort of trouble or something. You know, like self-defense."

I worked to keep my surprise from showing. By the sound of it, she would fit in very well with my new crowd. All the guys in this house could defend her against anything short of the apocalypse. "Are you worried about something happening?" Or *had* something happened I wondered, quickly checking to make sure I wasn't going to feel anything from her if I accidentally triggered some sort of emotional memory.

"No," she replied looking embarrassed. "I would just like to know that someone *could*." Adding quickly, "Who doesn't, right? That's what we have them for."

Her reasoning made sense to me except it didn't fit my previous perception of her. "I don't understand, you always struck me as so sure of yourself." She was ever the picture of confidence to me. If Heidi was unsure of herself, how could *I* ever hope to believe in myself? I felt a fracturing in my fragile armor.

A cool hand slid into mine just then and gave a small squeeze. I had forgotten James was standing nearby, speaking to Henry. He had given me sufficient girl time, now I took the hint that he wanted to discuss something. I felt the smile creeping into my features while I kept my eyes on Heidi.

Her return smile failed to reach her eyes and held a hint of bitterness as she switched her dark brown gaze to the man at my side. "Not everyone can get a bulls-eye with the first arrow." She turned on her heel and headed back to the kitchen. Holding her cup high above her head so I could see it, she shook it, announcing, "refill," and danced back the way she'd come. Tara laughed from the dining room, welcoming her back into the fold.

Turning back to James, I sighed. I still wasn't very good with people. My talent had so retarded my social development sometimes I felt much younger than my real age. I guess you always needed something to work on. Now that I was mastering my ability, I needed to work on my interpersonal skills.

His silky words broke into my reverie. "What's wrong with Heidi tonight? I thought she liked me." He didn't seem upset by her remarks, merely curious.

I shook my head, "No, I'm pretty sure I offended her." It was impossible to hide the chagrin I felt for upsetting probably my closest human friend.

"She's fine. You've just gotten her thinking about things she would rather forget." James looked after her for a moment, considering what had been said between us girls.

It shouldn't surprise me when his excellent hearing picked up on conversations he wasn't a part of. He'd told me once that he was so tuned in to my voice he could pick me out of a crowd of people at a distance. The lack of privacy was minor compared to the protection it afforded me. Stubbornly, I ignored the nagging doubt at the back of my mind warning me that when trouble passed and left us to build something normal, I might find it to be too much.

"Yes, I guess so." A thought struck me. "Do you know anyone we could hook her up with? She likes strong guys, I guess, and I'd like to see her with someone outside her usual circle of bad picks."

A chunk of his wavy hair fell forward onto his forehead touching his eye. "I could introduce her to someone *very* unlike her usual kind." His eyebrows rose to exaggerate his meaning.

I sucked in a breath and smiled nervously. "I don't think she's quite ready for *that* kind of commitment." A human consorting with a vampire required a life long commitment. The problem being that the vampire chose how long that might be.

I didn't think Heidi wanted to commit to a life bond just yet. Frowning, I gave him a look. "Never mind, I guess your choice would be trouble in a whole new way. We'll have to leave her to make her own mistakes." I turned as I heard him chuckle beside me. "What?"

His hand reached out, brushing a few loose hairs back behind my ear. I was struck by the sadness in his tone. "You worry too much about everyone else. You would have made a good mother."

My hand caught his as it came back down, clamping it tightly within my fist. "I am not giving anything up, you know. By the looks of everyone around me, I have more than most people ever dream of having."

His eyes were dark as he lowered his head bringing our faces inches apart. I had a hard time trying to remain focused when he was so close to me. "You will never have the chance to have a family. I have taken that from you."

"But you gave me a family already," I whispered. Surprise colored his features as I spoke. "I have you and Henry, and the Andrews. My family is huge and wonderful and I love them all. I would never have had this if it wasn't for you."

"Remember, Stephen brought you in. Not me," he deflected the credit.

"Yes, he *found* my ability. But if it weren't for Henry's bond with them, he wouldn't have pursued me."

Last fall, the threat of Gaston's band of violent, human hunting vampires coming into our area had driven Stephen to reach out to me. They tried to teach gifted humans to use their abilities and Stephen, thinking that mine could have been paired with his own ability to keep Bradley's hired gun, Gaston, from wanting to come to Minneapolis, had an ulterior motive to bringing me in specifically. Things had changed before we could test his theory. I had ended up bonding with James almost immediately and our symbiotic abilities had merged us to our current inseparable status.

My ability had come in handy for me when I used it in conjunction with my bond with James to "tell" him where I was after being kidnapped. That was the battle which had led to Bradley and his cohort Gaston going underground where they had remained since.

That would have been bad enough, but they had taken a human boy none of us had seen. We'd been told the boy could manipulate the majority of vampire society, making them do whatever he wanted. Only those with abilities and the knowledge of how to block out others could protect themselves from the boy. Bradley intended to use this boy in conjunction with loyalists to unite the vampires to rise up and wipe out the entire human race, except for some to be "farmed" for food. We were still trying to find and defeat the bad guys while hoping to save the boy, but had had no luck thus far in our efforts.

I could see James thinking about this, too, and he started to open his mouth to speak when the front door opened behind me and I saw his eyes tighten infinitesimally. If it wasn't for how well I knew his face, I would never have seen it. Curiosity made me turn around to see the source of James' annoyance. I was confused when I did.

27

"Stephen!" I shouted, seeing my best friend walk in the front door. He turned and said something to his date before dropping his hand and striding forward to grab me up in a hug, kissing my cheek in the process. It struck me as odd that James would be irritated with Stephen. He liked Stephen, despite the fact that he was the most immature of the clan and was more preoccupied with "chasing tail" as they liked to say, than the other more serious members.

Stephen was looking especially boyish tonight. I noticed he played that up when he was on dates. His small stature of 5'6, shaggy, honey blonde hair that usually hung over at least one eye and his large hazel eyes set atop broad, smooth cheekbones lent itself easily to the allusion that he was a teenager barely old enough to drive.

Turning me with his arm still around my shoulder, Stephen smiled, exuding his perpetual charm. "Claire, James, have you met my friend Brian Peterson yet?"

"I have not." James coolly stepped forward to shake Brian's hand, any hint of displeasure gone. "I'm pleased to meet you Brian. Please make yourself comfortable. Stephen knows his way around and can get you anything you need." Someone called James' name from near the kitchen, "Excuse me, I will be right back." He glided smoothly off toward the kitchen.

"I haven't either, but I think I've seen you around campus." I stuck my hand out, unnoticed by his date who was currently preoccupied with watching James walk away, his expression unreadable. It didn't take telepathy to imagine what he was thinking. I'd done it a million times myself. Stephen sniggered. I cleared my throat to bring his attention back to us.

Brian's face flushed briefly as he shook my hand firmly. "Yeah, I'm captain of the soccer team and we've done well this year so our pictures are up all over school." His soft but deep voice was well suited to his handsomely athletic body. He moved with a grace one didn't often see in humans. I was willing to bet he was amazing to watch on the field. His black hair and brown eyes, golden tan and nearly six-foot frame didn't hurt either.

Stephen stepped forward holding out his hand. "Brian, let me take your coat and we can grab some drinks. James should have plenty, he's used to having people around pretty much always."

Brian nodded and shrugged off his black leather coat, taking a few steps after his date as Stephen took their coats to hang in the closet beneath the stairs. The snugly fitted black wool sweater's v neck outlined his broad muscular chest which was very nice to look at, as were his well-muscled arms leading up to a strong neck where I could see his pulse in his throat. It was fast, he was nervous. I watched his strong pulse with fixed fascination. I could almost feel my tongue on his skin, my mouth on his throat. Licking my lips, I took a half step after him.

A vicelike hand clamped down on my arm above my elbow. James had snuck up on me, though I had to admit with some embarrassment, that I'd been more than a little distracted. "You aren't his type," he whispered in my ear from behind so low only I could hear it. The silky smooth voice had a dangerous edge to it.

Jumping in surprise, I leaped to defend myself. "What are you talking about?" As I turned around, I saw that he was staring over my head at Brian. He caught Brian's eye; I saw him incline his head slightly as Brian obediently followed Stephen to the kitchen, catching the hint that we wanted to speak privately and shuffling dutifully behind his date.

"Love," his voice still held an undercurrent of something dark not far beneath the surface. "You forget our link. I know what you are feeling toward him. Though I do not

29

think anyone watching would need a special connection to know what you were thinking just now."

"James!" It came out louder than I had anticipated and I dropped my voice glancing around to see if anyone had heard. "Are you jealous?" I whispered hotly. He had released me and shoved his hands in his pockets, continuing to glare over my head. "Would you look at me when you accuse me of lusting after someone?" I heard the anger rising in my own voice.

He tipped his chin down so that we were nose to nose. His hands remained anchored and his body was eerily still. His body language was screaming "furious," but it was his eyes that sent a shiver down my spine. They were completely black, lending his face an inhuman quality. The only times I had seen him like that were when he was hungry and when he thought someone was going to die. It crossed my mind that someone might.

My hands stayed at my sides, curling into fists. "Yes, I noticed he was attractive, that is all. Have you not noticed another woman since we've been together?" I was failing to keep the sarcasm out of my voice.

"You may notice anyone you would like. What I felt was your desire. That is what disturbs me Claire. Your desire was…"

In a flash the reason for my initial wanting came back to me. My hand went to my mouth, anger forgotten in an instant. "James," I whispered. "I was watching his pulse. It wasn't him I wanted, it was his blood."

He sucked in reactively, his head jerking away from me. His eyes scanned the room. As quickly as he had looked up, his eyes found mine again as if he was afraid something was going to change if he didn't keep watching. They remained dark but worry had crept in displacing the anger that had ruled him just seconds before.

James was not alone in his fear. Now I was scanning the room, not sure who exactly I was looking for. For a heart stopping moment, I thought James had sensed Bradley in our midst. He saw my eyes grow large and heard my heart. His strong hand came up to the back of my neck, pushing my face forward into his so that I alone could hear his whispered reassurances.

"Love, we need to get you under control." But as I started to pull away and defend myself again, he hissed at me causing my immediate shocked silence. He had never hissed at me. "Your impulses are more severe than you are equipped to handle."

His shirt muffled my choked denial even as I realized that he was right. It had not been an easily thwarted sexual desire that had enraptured me, it had been blood I craved. It was as urgent a call as food to a starving man and one I didn't know if I could resist alone. My fears rose to the surface in that instant. I was turning into a vampire. I was slipping away completely into him. It wasn't fair. Neither of us had chosen this. My thoughts spun out of control, as my breathing accelerated rapidly toward hyperventilation.

As my respiration increased, I felt the room begin to spin. James' other arm wrapped around my back cradling me against his body as my legs failed me. Instantly, another being was beside us, the voice easily recognizable.

"What's happened?" Tara had a hand on each of us, her head in close to us as though we were all sharing a private moment. They were so practiced at hiding the reality of their lives it would have been admirable were I in a better position to focus.

James quickly explained that the marks were flaring and that he would take me to his office upstairs. Tara mumbled she would be right back with Henry. James said something I couldn't make out and wheeled me toward the stairs.

On our way up I looked down and saw Ben watching us curiously. Tonya looked up at us from a few steps away. She immediately understood the situation in a glance and took Ben by the hand to the MP3 across the room to decide what to play next. Ben was more than willing to follow Tonya anywhere. Girlfriend or no, she was a beautiful older woman who was paying attention to him. Who could blame him?

In a heartbeat, Henry was sitting in the desk chair facing me. My head rested on James' shoulder while we sat side by side on the small bed, sharing space with his office equipment. I had lain many a time on this bed and watched James work. Those were better times than these. Henry laid his hand gently upon my arm. "Claire, can you look at me please? I need your cooperation for a moment."

Raising my head up, I turned to look at Henry. His chocolate eyes were black. I searched his face looking for hints of what was coming, only to be drawn back to his eyes. Obediently, I stared more deeply into them. The bed moved next to me as James extricated himself from me. Our bodies no longer touching, I felt his shields fall away; mine offered no resistance. The marks opened wide and in that moment, James couldn't shield himself from me. I could feel everything.

Startled at the discovery, I felt his trepidation at my further descent into his nature. He was fearful that it would tear us apart and that he might lose his new and unexpected link to humanity as well as our bond. He needed me to remain human. The fear he felt about the possible loss was enough to cement our commitment in my mind. Henry saw all of it, his strength easily overpowering both of our defenses.

Henry's gaze intensified, calling my attention back to him. His face was immobile as well as his body as he let his human façade fall away and his vampire nature come forward. I had never experienced the powers a vampire was capable of, but I had heard about them. It was completely beyond my control what happened next.

My perceptions shifted, it felt like I was on a rolling ship as I lost track of present and past. I was reliving my memories as they flew past my periphery. Then, as rapidly as I had felt my world shift, it snapped back.

Feeling myself come back, I gasped as though I was coming up from underwater. It was a physical imperative to get air into my lungs. Each ragged breath cleared my mind as I took one after another. I wondered how long I had been holding my breath. I was dizzy.

"What the hell was that?" I choked out, hanging my head.

Henry spoke up matter of fact. "I apologize Claire. It was time to get an honest assessment of the situation before it got entirely out of control."

"Oh my gosh, Henry. I didn't know you could do that. Could you do that this whole time? Why do you even bother to ask people questions when you can just see into their heads like that?" I was torn between anger that he had just read everything in my mind and relief that he might be able to help us.

Henry sighed, "I do not usually do that because it is quite taxing and often I find out things about people I choose not to know." Gone forever was my last remaining image of gentle, paternal Henry. He was much more powerful, much more frightening than I had suspected.

"Oh," I didn't know whether to be offended or grateful.

James remained silent and unmoving, allowing Henry to continue. He seemed to be unsurprised by what had just happened. "Your marks are advanced far beyond where I had assumed. You are channeling James' bloodlust when he is hungry or angry. We had known that but it is becoming more pronounced, the boundary between the two natures is becoming more blurred. James, you will need to feed more often. That will help keep both of you protected. Claire, your emotions are hypersensitive. We will need to treat you like a newly turned vampire. As soon as the holiday is past and you have fulfilled your family obligations, I will make arrangements for you to see Miranda. She is the only one who can help you."

I froze, thinking of the female vampire from the high Court we had met in Edinburgh last month. Looking to me, Henry continued evenly. "She has the most experience of any of us, James and I have been searching for some time. You were both to go there after Christmas for a week. It is now imperative that you go as quickly as possible." Henry turned to James, "I think you should drink as much as you can this evening. It will make things go much more smoothly for us all. For now, let's mingle and be merry." He finished with a smile and a gentle rub to my arm, though it could not comfort me. "You will be okay, try to believe that." With that, he rose from his chair and left to return to the clan and humans mingling and having a good time downstairs, blissfully unaware.

James tried to quell my unease. "He really doesn't do that very often. Don't worry, he'll respect your privacy and keep your thoughts to himself." He shifted uncomfortably. "I'm going to the cellar where I've relocated my beverage supply for the evening, away from prying eyes." Standing, he held out a hand to me, "Can I help you up? I believe you are missed by our friends, my dear. It is your home as well, therefore, your duty to help me host." The effects of his smile were dulled both by his distraction and mine.

Under normal circumstances, his declaration of co-ownership in the event and place would have left me giddy with pleasure. At present, it was lost to the out of body experience I was having. In a daze, I took his hand and let him pull me to my feet. He pulled me in close to kiss my cheek in passing and we returned downstairs, deep in our own thoughts.

Ch. 6

Walking away, he reluctantly let go of my hand and headed to the cellar whose entrance was around the corner from the kitchen, taking him within feet of where Troy was leaning against a dining room chair talking to Heidi. Without delay Troy's overly warm hand wrapped around my shoulders and he walked me into the crowd, drink in hand. His reinforcing of my defenses barely registered in my consciousness.

It wasn't until a few minutes later that awareness and surety flooded back into my being. James was feeding; Henry had been right as usual. I wondered not for the first time how old Henry was. As far as I knew, a vampire had to be several hundred years old to do what he'd done to me. He had rolled over even James' shields. That had to be difficult to do unless he was pretty ancient.

My head cleared and I leaned into Troy's side, giving him a little hip bump to let him know I was doing better. Given his height, my hip didn't meet his, but he felt it, glancing down at me and winking good-naturedly.

Tonight Troy seemed unusually jovial and loose, even his hair was out of its usual short ponytail. As the head of the Andrews clan he was typically serious. I had to admit, I'd only known him through the past rather tense few months. I'd never seen him so lighthearted. Now Troy had a drink in hand, something clear and, given the glass type and green olives inside, I was going to say martini. Maybe Troy was tipsy; that would be a first. Giggling a little, I found myself beginning to loosen up and enjoy the conversations around me. They were perfectly normal, casual, non-vampirey conversations about regular life that didn't involve anyone dying. It was refreshing.

With my sense of control restored, I dared to look over at Stephen and Brian again. Brian's attractiveness didn't bring about the same physical reaction as before. I was able to let my glance slide over him at his perch behind Stephen's chair and move on, though not before I noticed he had been looking curiously at me. I must have weirded him out ogling him before. I felt my face flame hotly.

Tonya and Ben had their arms loosely around each other's waists and I couldn't help but notice they were so relaxed together. They looked like they were more than casual friends. With a twinge of guilt, I wondered how solid Ben's relationship with his girlfriend was, realizing I would be happy to have the two of them together.

Tara was standing next to Brian listening to something Heidi was saying. I wasn't sure what Heidi had said, I was too distracted by how Troy watched her so closely. While I was mulling this little detail over, Stephen stood up abruptly forcing Brian to hop out of the way to avoid getting hit.

Brian shot Stephen a look of vexation, probably compounded by the fact that Stephen had been ignoring him to that point. It was clear from the way he was positioned with his back to Brian that Stephen hadn't been attentive. However, Stephen looked back at Brian for the fastest moment and I watched Brian's face relax, then shift to adoration when their eyes met. It had been like the flip of a switch.

To a casual observer, it would have been only a curiosity. To me, someone who knows that Stephen can insert thoughts into people's heads, I found it reprehensible. I assumed he had just manipulated Brian's feelings, something he swore he never did. Stephen heard my angry snort, staring straight across the table at me.

We watched each other for a moment; he saw that I was angry with him. Before I had time to say anything, he turned his attention to Troy beside me. "Troy, do you still keep your guitar in your car?"

Troy made a sound. "Never leave home without it."

Stephen had obviously expected that. "I was thinking, what is a holiday party without carols? Who wants to sing?" His eyes scanned the small gathering expectantly, skimming right over me.

"Heidi sings." Ben spoke up from the corner, his arm still entwined with Tonya's.

Heidi flushed, mildly self-conscious. "Just a little." She was smiling, even though she narrowed her eyes at him and faked a scowl. "Thanks Ben."

He guffawed. "A little? You were in a band last year and you guys were good. I saw you play twice at Auggie's." Ben seemed impressed and I had to admit that now I was curious to hear her sing.

Troy raised an eyebrow at Heidi and I could hear the bubble of excitement in his voice. "I'm game if you are."

Heidi nodded, pink creeping up her neck. I didn't know Heidi *could* blush, she didn't seem the type but Troy was bringing it out of her now. Leave it to a supernatural creature to shake up a human on the very first meeting, I thought wryly. I certainly never had a chance from the first moment I'd laid eyes upon mine.

James, where was he anyway? I had felt him feeding but that had been some time ago. Had he been shaken by Henry's pronouncement of our situation? Was he feeling shackled by the constraints and permanence of our bond? With so much interest in us now as a couple, the pressure would be greater for him to stay with me. Unlike other human vampire pairings, where killing the human is an option, for us it was not. I had considered it unlikely but a possibility. The question was how would James react to losing his escape *and* himself.

Ch. 7

Our caroling started out with the two person group singing "O Come All Ye Faithful." Troy was playing guitar seated on the chair on the far side of the living room, Heidi stood with her hand on his shoulder. They were good, really good. Then again, Troy had probably been playing guitar forever. And I meant that literally since he was close to immortal himself. Heidi's voice was well suited to acoustic accompaniment and they were having a lot of fun judging from the way they kept looking at each other, smiling and laughing as they performed. It was a pleasure to be in their audience.

The second song, "Jingle Bells" was a crowd favorite and everyone sang along. Glancing around at the partygoers, I noticed Stephen was intentionally avoiding my gaze. Not that it mattered, Brian was now glued to Stephen's side thanks to Stephen's "suggestion" I was sure. I wouldn't be so juvenile as to chastise him in front of his date, even if I felt it was warranted.

It wasn't right that he messed with people's heads. He'd done it to me only when necessary and he hadn't done anything harmful or false. He had merely kept me in the room and somewhat calm while he showed me his other form. This, what he was doing tonight with Brian, was wrong. He was messing in Brian's head for his own selfish purposes. He had promised me he didn't do that sort of thing. I'd never considered that my friend would blatantly lie to me. Now he was going to avoid me tonight, so I didn't even try to get close enough to talk to him. We could talk about it later.

It was the third song, and my personal favorite "Silent Night" when I felt James slide up beside me behind the couch, leaning on it with a ginger ale in hand. Heidi's voice suited the song well, haunting as she crooned the lyrics with

39

Troy's flawless pairing. James and I didn't speak as we stood listening, close enough to touch while being careful not to.

It was comforting to have him close and I wanted to reach for his hand, but I was being prideful. I was thinking that somehow not taking his hand would make me more independent, that I would be able to distance myself from this strangeness all around me. That I could hold on to *me* a little while longer.

At the close of the song, Tara spoke up from her position on the couch in front of us, raising her glass. "Heidi, can you sing anything from the Beatles? I was kind of hoping to hear something non-Christmasy. What do you think? Could you do 'Yesterday'?"

Heidi gazed down at Troy, the expression on his face in return verified my suspicions. Their attraction was readily apparent to anyone in the room. I found myself torn. How could I warn her, even if it wasn't my place to do so? She was a big girl and capable of making her own choices. I did have to hide my grin upon thinking of her comment earlier about wanting someone strong. He *was* that. I watched her nod her assent and Troy shrug his guitar into his shoulder more firmly, beginning to strum the familiar chords.

Somewhere between the first verse and the chorus, I found myself leaning against James' firm side. His arm slid around my waist and I snuggled into him. How could I question that our fates were intertwined?   My doubts were so easily overcome when I was here with him.   There might be inconvenient challenges to overcome, but I wouldn't extricate myself from him, even if I could.

Ch. 8

After we said good-bye to the last of the guests and shut the door, James took my hand and spun me out in front of him. He moved slowly to the music now playing. It was heartbreaking and sad although I couldn't place it, maybe Nina Simone. We moved to the music, my head on his chest, listening to the quiet around me, broken only by the music.

"Did you enjoy our party? You are a fine hostess I must say, Ms. Martin." I was soothed by his deep, rumbling voice as he held me close.

Not moving from his chest, I responded in kind. "I never mind helping out, Mr. Thomas. It was fun to see everyone so happy. It was a good mix of people."

"You didn't answer my question. I asked how you liked *our* party. Did you not consider it yours as well?" His tone was different, expectant.

"Oh, that part." I pretended it wasn't a big deal. I wasn't sure I was ready for this talk, not tonight.

And now, the fact that James was clearly my "mate," as the vampires called it, begged the question. Could we be seriously involved? And *would* he want to be tied to me so definitively? He hadn't had a meaningful relationship before me, despite having had some long lasting trysts over the decades.

Now, here he was, asking me point blank how I felt about co-hosting and hinting at much more. I wasn't sure how to answer.

He continued to dance me around the house, and mid-twirl, I saw the food still out on the table. I made an effort to pull away and he stopped me with his immovable arms. "James, I was going to clean up some of this mess."

Spinning me back toward the stairs he responded dismissively, "It can wait." He lowered his voice and face. I felt his lips on my ear and the vibration of his voice on my body. The combination was hypnotic; I felt myself melt back against his firm body.

His skin was malleable like my own, although tighter and tougher than a human's and the muscle underneath like steel cabling. Instead of finding it strange, I found it incredibly reassuring. Maybe it was because of my inexperience with physical contact, I found that I liked his feel, knowing that he was gentle with me yet he could take on the world if necessary. I couldn't help but feel safe with him.

His voice was soft, his words hesitant. It sounded strange coming from someone normally so self-assured. "Claire, love, how would you feel about living here with me for longer than just the holiday?"

My heart and breathing stopped. I wasn't sure if my stomach was flipping for excitement or fear. I wanted this, except now that he was asking, I was scared. This was risking so much and yet how could I not want to be with him as much as possible? I pulled away to look up at him and his arms loosened to allow it.

When I saw his face, I sucked in my breath and held it. He was flushed from the blood he'd consumed over the course of the evening, his eyes a deep blue with fear.

Reacting to his apprehension I both saw and felt, I guessed at the cause of his offer and, feeling deflated, exhaled in a rush. "James, you don't need to offer that. You're protecting me well enough with the safeguards we have now. You don't need to do this. We have to think beyond this situation. What do we do when this trouble passes and you find me

42

still in your house? If it isn't where you see us going long term, I would rather not take this step. Moving in is really serious for me." My forthrightness surprised me.

Eyes glued to his features, I was watching him for a reaction and lowered my shielding to feel it. Vampire emotions are more fleeting than those of humans, so they'd taken some getting used to; although I preferred them because they were more clearly differentiated whereas humans' tended to be muddled and layered to the point of confusion.

What I felt from him before he slammed his shields down against me was rejection, and it burned. It both shocked me that I had the ability to hurt him, and shamed me that I had assumed his offer was other than genuinely what he wanted. Mentally, I kicked myself for letting my self-doubt get in the way yet again.

His hand went to my cheek and he trailed his fingers lightly down my face to settle on the light silver chain hanging around my neck. I felt terrible for hurting him, I could see him struggling with what to do about it. Finally with a voice raw with emotion, he did speak and I felt like the fool I was.

"Claire, why do you continue to doubt my love for you? Have I not told you how I feel and proven it over and again?"

Coming clean in a moment of either bravery or stupidity, I admitted the source of my fear. "I have never doubted that you love me."

He snorted.

"Okay, I haven't doubted it for a while. What I am afraid of is that we want different things. I want forever and I don't know what that means to you. Don't get me wrong, I'm not issuing an ultimatum by any means. You know that until you, I'd never loved anyone." Too exposed to look him in the eye, I stared at the top button on his shirt. "I'd like to live here with you, your house has felt like home from the very beginning. I just want you to know that I eventually want more. If that's possible," I finished, mumbling uncertainly in a rush.

He wasn't letting me feel him anymore so, painfully aware of his silence, I flicked my eyes up to see if I could tell anything that way. I wondered if my full disclosure would turn him off, if it would sound too needy and human, and yet I was proud of myself for having the courage to put it out there.

When he did respond, it took me aback again. Chuckling, he shook his head and closed his eyes. "You never fail to surprise me, Claire. I have sworn an oath to protect you, pledged a life bond with you to the Court, and I have repeatedly told you I love you as I have never loved another in all of my existence. Now, I ask you another thing that I have never asked any other woman, to share my home, and still you question my intentions?"

It did sound ridiculous when he laid it out like that without taking into consideration everything else like his immortality, my being a neurotic human and all of the limitations a life with me presented for someone like him. I defended my point. "Call me silly, but I was raised that way. We are putting the cart before the horse and my parents will probably be upset." I attempted to lighten the mood. "Maybe they'll be happy to save the money for my room at school."

James pulled me close. A little too tight. I squeaked and he loosened his embrace with a chuckle. "So you will?"

"I would love to." I squeezed him back.

"You *are* getting stronger," he gasped in surprise.

44

The comment reminded me of my fears, though my happiness in the moment overshadowed the worry. For the time being, I was able to fend off any panicked thoughts about "going vampire" although it stubbornly nudged its way into my consciousness.

Impulsively, James swept me up and carried me up the stairs, kissing me all the way. I felt his excitement in his kiss and it matched my own. No matter what our future held, I knew that I would meet it at James' side.

He carried me into what was now officially "our" room. I'd been elated to learn that I was the first woman he had invited to live with him. When your boyfriend is over a century old, it is hard to be a first anything for him. He set me down on our bed, still kissing me. His lips moved down my neck and to the top of my dress; his tongue swirled on my skin, making me shiver and raising goose bumps on my arms. I heard his soft laughter. He loved it when he could make me react like that.

Rolling over to face him, I kissed his neck and nipped at his jaw. He groaned and let his head loll back, exposing his throat. I reveled in knowing I could induce such a response from him. As I found his mouth again, his hands wrapped around my back and pulled me over on him. His hands rubbed my back and I felt the zipper release.

Ch. 9

The next morning, James made me Belgian waffles with fresh strawberries and cream. I drank my tea leaning against the counter, watching him work. Feeling my eyes on him, he turned and smiled at me. It was hard not to do a little dance for the joy I felt having him in my life.

"You're going to spoil me," I teased.

His playful reply drifted over his shoulder. "That's the idea. You'd be a fool to leave." He turned to wink at me.

My heart skipped at his simple gesture and I saw his amusement when he caught it. "You heard Henry. I couldn't leave if I wanted to."

His features clouded and cleared in rapid succession, making me wonder if I had really seen it at all. "That isn't bad, is it? You don't regret getting involved in all of this? With me?" The human still inside him peeked out for only a brief flash before he hid it behind the strong, cold vampire; the monster inside him capable of destroying everything human that he held so dear, and was yet so vulnerable by comparison.

Of course that was something I had considered in depth and was able to answer truthfully. "No. All couples have their challenges. Granted, ours are more life threatening than most." Seeing his jaw tighten, I hurried to add, "But I think what we have is more special than what most people have as well." I was rewarded with another of his smiles and watched his eyes cool to blue.

I took in the sight of my lovely breakfast, following him out to the table to take my seat. "Is there anything you aren't good at?" I whined playfully, laying my napkin on my lap.

Snorting, he took a drink from the cup holding his much more basic meal. "If you had eternity to practice, you would be good at more than you are now, too."

When Henry pointed out the blurring of our natures, I'd begun to wonder things. "James, will the marks lengthen my life? Will I share your immortality, do you think?"

Brow furrowing in thought, James took a long moment to answer. "We aren't sure. Human servants," he smiled as I cringed at the word, "that *is* what they're called, Claire." He continued, "Human servants have been known to live significantly longer lives than normal humans. The only way to truly become immortal is to be completely turned, however, like the weres. They can live the duration of several normal lifetimes without any significant signs of aging."

Mention of my friend reminded me of a puzzle from the night before. "Why were you angry with Stephen last night?"

His cup froze halfway to his mouth. "What do you mean?"

I put down my fork and placed my hands in my lap staring directly at him, knowing I'd caught something I wasn't supposed to. "You may be the best liar I've ever met, but I know you better than you think. I saw your face when he walked into the house last night."

James smiled wistfully. "I forget sometimes how perceptive you are." Growing more somber, he took another drink and set his cup down. "Stephen has asked the clan to release me from my oath of protection."

I was glad to be sitting down. "Why would he do that? *Can* he do that?"

James shrugged. "I asked the same of him and of Troy. Troy says because Stephen asked that the oath be taken, he can also ask that it be broken. As for why, that is a puzzle to me as well; Bradley is still a very real threat to you."

I tried to think of what would have happened that would have led Stephen to ask such a thing, possibly leaving me to fend for myself. Was he testing James' commitment or was he sorry he had brought me into the family? It was impossible not to be offended by Stephen's request. It added to my growing temper with my friend.

"So, did you?" I asked, watching my hands carefully.

His quiet response rang loudly in my ears, "Yes, I had no choice."

"Oh." I didn't know what to say.

"Claire, I relinquished my oath three days ago. As you can tell, it has changed nothing between us."

Interestingly enough, it did make me feel better. That had been one of my concerns about our longevity and it appeared to be a non-issue. I glanced up at him and smiled before turning my attentions back to my tea; my appetite had faded.

While we were both quietly thinking about that one, drinking our respective liquids, we heard a car door slam and I felt a familiar person. She was happy, delighted even, about someone else I knew.

"Oh my gosh!" My back straightened suddenly, eyes opening wide.

James was instantly on alert. "What?"

Shaking my head, I smiled as I grew more comfortable with the shock of what I had learned. "Heidi is getting dropped off at her car."

He wasn't surprised. "Troy."

I nodded.

"I thought that might happen. They seemed to hit it off."

I remained mute.

"You wanted Heidi to date someone different. Troy couldn't be more different."

"Yes," I muttered under my breath while I continued to think about Heidi now entering into our strange world and all that that entailed. "But can she handle it?"

"He didn't necessarily tell her anything you know," James informed me calmly. "Weres can fit in smoothly with humans, more so than us. Older weres have enough self control that they don't have to change, even during sex. If Troy were younger, there might have been cause for concern. A young wereanimal doesn't have enough control over his beast and the rush of emotions that goes with sex can cause them to change during the act. At best, it is messy and terrifying for the human. At worst, the beast takes over and kills the human."

I'd been thinking of the shock that it had been for me to learn that myths sometimes are reality. It hadn't even been a consideration that Heidi would have been in physical or mortal danger with Troy. My naivete gave me perspective.

It hadn't been that long ago that I'd been anxious at the prospect of being alone with James. How quickly I had forgotten that fear. I would have to try to keep it in mind when dealing with any supernatural beings aside from my own mate. If I wasn't careful, someone could get hurt; most likely me, but there could be collateral damage such as friends and even family.

"Oh, I'm really glad I didn't know that last night."

His hand found mine resting near my teacup on the table. Covering it with his own, he spoke softly, "Not everyone has as much luck as we do."

I glanced up at his teasing tone to see his eyes twinkling. "Are you making fun of me?" I asked, my tone matching his.

"No," he shook his head, "I'm making fun of me." He grew severe. "Sometimes I forget as well that we cannot grow overconfident in our relationship just because of our bond. I am still what I am and you are still what you are. We have merely been fortunate thus far not to have had any serious complications."

"Lucky?" I was incredulous. "How can you say that we have been lucky not to have any *complications*? I would say that our bond is one big damn complication. We've made things work despite that, but by no means have we been without our 'complications'."

"Claire, you know that is not what I meant. I meant that we have been able to work through many issues that plague the few relationships such as ours. If anything, the marks have forced us to work through any doubts either of us might have had; much like being married or having children makes human couples work through their differences instead of walking away when things become difficult."

I laughed a short, snide laugh that sounded cynical even to me. "Don't you watch the news? People don't work through anything, they make plans for how to get divorced before they even get married. Have you heard of a pre-nup?"

Bewildered, James cocked his head and stared. I shifted uncomfortably. At last he spoke cautiously. "I thought that you wanted to marry. How can you hold such a low opinion of marriage and yet want to enter into it 'in the future'?" he quoted.

Defending myself I clarified, "I told you that until I met you I didn't want to get married. Sure, part of it was my ability making it unlikely I would ever get to, but part was watching the people around me and feeling the awful things they felt about each other. They fought, they cheated, they were mean to each other and even used their own kids to manipulate each other all the while feeling justified and self-righteous. It gave me some unique insight on the subject and I have to say I became more than a little jaded." Self-conscious, I looked down and withdrew my hand to rest in my lap with its mate. "When I met you, I saw the other side. I saw what it was people were hoping for, what they *wanted* to have when they first started out with someone before all of that other stuff crept in and poisoned what they had. I wanted that with you." We had crossed into the excruciatingly personal and I could not meet his eyes, keeping them on my fidgeting hands. The words coming from my mouth, giving him a view of my deepest feelings, coming in a surreal stream. I couldn't believe I was sharing so much and yet I heard my voice telling him exactly how to hurt me the most. "It's hard to describe for me how it all fits together. Our bond is a physical need now. I don't just want to be close to you, I *have* to be. It aches," I laid my hand over my core where I felt his loss when he was away, "when I'm not with you. But marriage or a relationship is a *choice*, something that says we *want* to be together forever, not that we're obligated to do so, but that we choose it. That's a big difference." Finishing my gutsy and potentially fatal outpouring I heard nothing but silence so heavy it pressed in on my ears.

Subdued, he broke the absolute quiet. "I understand your feelings. I have also seen many a relationship end badly. People conducting themselves shamefully, in affairs of both the heart and the wallet. Those who cannot see beyond their own greed can cause far greater collateral damage than they comprehend."

James was good at being patient and still. I wondered sometimes if he was like that before, or if it was a result of being immortal. I had noticed that I was growing less frenetic in my time with him and I wondered if it was due to our marks, the shielding or if he was merely a calming influence. Either way, it was times like these that I welcomed that soothing balm on my raw, freshly exposed inner thoughts. The lack of judgment coming from him let me regain my composure and repack my vulnerability away where I kept it hidden as best I could from him.

I had become so tied up in my own thoughts, I jumped when he spoke. "I was thinking we could go out today. Didn't you need to do some Christmas shopping?"

Welcoming the opportunity for distraction and to do something perfectly human, I latched on gratefully. "I do need a few things that I think I could get downtown. How does that sound to you? Or would you prefer the mall?"

His disgusted look was answer enough. I laughed.

"Downtown it is then. Just let me clean up. I can be ready in a few minutes." Patting his hand to indicate he needed to take it off of me so that I could stand, he did. I rose and turned to kiss him before going upstairs.

I had an ulterior motive for shopping with James. It was true that I still needed to buy a present for my parents, and I wanted to get something for Stephen. I also needed to get James to some stores and see what he looked at. I had no idea what to buy for him. Buying for a boyfriend was hard enough, factor in that he was immortal and had enough money to buy himself anything he wanted, and it presented a uniquely daunting challenge.

Ch. 10

Nicollet Mall was one of my favorite places to go during the Christmas season. It was on what could be considered the main drag of downtown Minneapolis. The sidewalks were pavers and all of the stores were on the first and second levels of the tall buildings making up the city's skyline. Sporadically along the street were trees wrapped with twinkle lights, as were the rod iron streetlights, reminiscent in design to Victorian gaslights. The only downside of our visit was that it was the middle of the day and the lights wouldn't be on for a few hours.

The sky was overcast, the clouds hung heavy and dark with the haze of unshed snow. Normally it would be a gloomy day leeching at my good spirits. However, because it meant that James didn't need to wear his eye protection and would not be fighting the faint, yet ever present physical pain of being in the sunlight, I delighted in the gloom above. He looked dashing as always, his eyes accented dramatically by the blue of his scarf and dark coat. His choice of jeans matched my own casual look and black work boots, though I doubted he wore his for the traction they afforded as I did. My Doc Martens were a prerequisite for tromping around on a snowy, icy street. I didn't have the grace of a vampire and it was highly likely that I would fall and break my neck if I tried to wear less weather appropriate footwear.

We wandered, window shopping and holding hands the same as a number of other couples who caught my eye as we walked toward a great Irish pub, the Local. They had a tremendous shepherd's pie there and I mentioned we should go there if we got hungry later. I laughed at the bemused expression James aimed at me.

"Oh yeah, sometimes I forget." I waved dismissively. "You just don't seem different most of the time."

He stopped me with a hand on either shoulder and leveled a steady somber stare at me. "Because of my age, I am able to overcome a number of our outward differences to blend in. But make no mistake, I am different." James' tone was very no nonsense and I decided to let that go, not wanting to put a damper on our day by pointing out how our differences were shrinking.

While I was avoiding his severity, the wall of the building next to where we'd stopped caught my eye. True to the nature of downtown advertising, there were flyers stapled up all over the phone pole on the street side and glued to the brick of the building on our other side. They were both layered with old posters and flyers that no one bothered to take down, just stapling or gluing the new ones over the top. One in particular caught my eye. It was a flyer for an upcoming concert at The Myth.

The Myth was a small venue club, redone recently and I had heard the acoustics were fantastic. I hadn't personally been to a concert there. I had actually never been to any concerts. Ability, no shielding; same old reasons. Now though, I could and this was a band that James and I both had a strong affinity for, Snow Patrol. They were going to be at the club just after classes started back up in February. That would be a great Christmas present for James.

I pointed it out to James.

He followed my direction genuinely interested with the added benefit of being distracted from chastising me. "They're a great band. I would love to see them at a small venue though, no one sounds good at an arena. Where are they playing?" He scanned the wall next to us for the flyer.

"The Myth," I replied as he searched. "That's supposed to be a pretty good place, and small venue, right?" I'd found that playing dumb sometimes afforded more answers.

His open interest kept me hoping he suspected nothing. "That would be a good one. Would you like to go?"

Not wanting him to beat me to the punch and buy the tickets I thought fast and tried to deflect him. "I don't know if I can. I think Mom said we have family coming into town somewhere around then and I'll need to find out when I have obligations. Bummer though, maybe next time." I tried to sound disappointed and feared he could tell what I was up to being so suspiciously evasive. Lying had never been my strong suit.

Fortunately his cell phone rang, distracting him. He pulled it from his pocket and answered. Never having made a habit of listening to people's calls, I tried to make my brain go elsewhere and afford him some privacy despite our proximity. It was always difficult to do if in the same room or car with someone, but I tried. My ears pricked though when he switched to German. I wasn't aware he spoke it and I didn't try to hide my astonishment. Winking, he touched my arm and continued to listen. Not speaking the language myself, he had all the privacy he needed.

However, within a few moments, I heard something I *did* recognize in his tone and he walked away from me to stand closer to a large brick planter near the street. He was troubled by something. The pattern of the conversation sounded as though someone was trying to convince him of something and he wasn't easily being swayed. Despite my distance from him, I was able to hear the hum of the other voice. Listening closer, I could hear the voice on the other end without trouble. It was female, and judging from the silkiness of the tone, vampire.

Fighting the jealousy rising up within me, I reminded myself that I trusted James and that he knew a lot of women. Not all of them were threats to our relationship. I pantomimed to James that I was going in the store we'd been standing near. It was an eclectic little shop specializing in this' and that's from all over the world. I quickly ducked inside, grateful for the overhead music helping to muddle my now supersensitive hearing.

The shop was full of hand carved wood crafts that made me think of my parents' gift I was still looking for. Dad loved to carve wood and even made furniture he sold to a few shops. Mom loved stuff for the house, it seemed like a gift they both might enjoy could be found inside.

It was hard to stay focused, yet I did my damndest as I wandered around the store, pointedly ignoring James' voice still humming at the edge of my periphery as he talked to that woman.

I found a beautiful wooden Rosewood bowl with an entrancing swirl spiraling down to a dark knot slightly off center from the bottom. Running my hand over the smooth lip I could feel the warmth of the wood and saw it in my parents home. They had a small table in their entryway they used for keys. Dad put his wallet and pocket watch as well as loose change and odds and ends in it when he came home. Mom had expressed an interest in finding something to put everything in to keep it neat and more attractive than a heap of pocket stuff.

Taking the time to buy the gift and, after seeing James still pacing animatedly out front, also to have it wrapped, I came out to find James off the call and rubbing his temple with his phone when I exited the store.

Seeing me, he spoke first thereby limiting my questions. "Did you get someone off your list?" His blank expression an indication he would not be sharing anything about his call.

Playing equally cool, I tried not to let my curiosity or irritation show. "Yep, I found something for my folks. That just leaves Stephen."

Raising his eyebrows, James teased me. "Have you already bought something for me, then?"

With an almost physical effort I tried to shake off the sound of the voice that had made German sound sexy. Close to failure, I forced a smile and let some venom leak out in my taunt. "Who says I'm buying you anything? Aren't I gift enough?"

Turning serious in a blink, he ensnared, kissing me hard enough to make my head spin. "Yes, Claire, you are gift enough for me."

More than affection was in his kiss. Hard and fast, he only kissed me like that when he was worried. Taking a breath as he released me, I let go of my jealousy and wrapped my hands around his arm, wanting him to know I was still there should he need help.

We walked all the way up and then back down the mall on the opposite side, talking superficially about the different things we passed as we window shopped. At one point I stopped for a tea at Starbucks; I hadn't grown hungry enough for a meal. Remembering what Henry had said the night before I asked him, "Shouldn't you be drinking something yourself?"

James flinched guiltily. "Yes, I should. I've been thinking the same thing. We need to go soon."

"Like I said, I'm done now except for Stephen and I'm not in the mood to shop anymore. We can go." I turned back toward the ramp where the car was parked.

It was three blocks to the car and we walked the distance in silence. James was driving down the freeway the few short miles home before he finally said something about what was burdening us both.

"I have to go to Germany for a few days. I should be back before Christmas." His eyes never left the road and his voice was without affect.

A chill ran through me and I extracted my hand from his. He didn't fight me. I waited for further explanation but it did not come. Staring out the window I counted the exits until we could put some physical distance between us to match the chasm I felt in my heart.

Ch. 11

Before the car was all the way stopped, I got out, stalked up the driveway, and stomped into the house. It had taken some getting used to that he didn't lock the door. When I had asked, he had reminded me of the uses of Glamour. Glamour was a vampire trick used to change humans' perceptions of appearances. He had used Glamour to make the house unappealing to human thieves and ne'er do wells. As he put it, "anything else" could get around the metal locks anyway. It had not set right with me that "anything else" might want to come here. Although I had grown functionally used to it, it no longer kept me up at night. Plus, now it served my interests since I didn't have to wait for him to let me in and I hurried to be away from him.

When I was a child, solitude had been my only source of peace and it continued so that when I got upset I still sought it. With my emotional turbulence, I wanted privacy now without having to expend all of my energy shielding myself from him. I wanted normal.

I was upstairs in his office, fingers running over the box I had given him when we first were dating. It was a wood inlaid box with different shapes and types, each representing the continents of the globe. As had been its intended purpose, it sat on his desk holding the cards and scraps of paper he had collected with names of places, people and restaurants in his travels all over the world. I had never looked inside or pried into his life before, although now I felt tempted to look for any female names in Germany. My resentment toward the voice on the phone surged anew.

I felt him just before he spoke from the doorway. "I'm sorry that I have to leave. Henry is going to come here to stay with you while I am gone. He will keep you safe in case this is a ruse to isolate you." I saw the cup in his hand and wondered if I would be able to feel anything from him while he was gone or if he was drinking to make himself strong and prevent that very thing.

Bitterness kept me from responding beyond a quick bob of the head. My eyes never left the box.

He obviously didn't want to talk about it either. "I need to leave now to make the five o'clock flight. Would you help me pack?"

Shrugging, I followed him out of the office next door to our room in our familiar ritual. I always sat with him while he packed, except we usually went together and discussed what we were going to do while on our trip. This time, there was nothing to discuss. I was staying behind while he went to meet a woman who could get him to run to her with one call.

I sat quietly on the bed while he got out a suitcase and packed formal attire as well as a few pair of jeans hinting at what sorts of venues he would be in. Vampire functions always called for formal, human for casual so as to blend in. Humans didn't usually go out socially in a suit, especially Americans.

He understood my troubled thoughts and offered a minimal explanation as he zipped the bag, "An old friend needs my help. I have to go, I'm sorry."

Eyes stuck on the ballistic nylon of his rolling bag, I nodded my head. I understood yet I was not happy. Henry had told me in what seemed like another lifetime about James' compulsion to help those in need. I told myself that's all this was, nothing more personal than that. In trying not to reveal the extent of my jealousy, though surely he could discern that was partially to blame for my withdrawal, I remained in lockdown and followed him down the stairs to the front door. He kissed me briefly and left, his silence devastating.

I was sure he was hiding something from me, his leaving me so quickly and at Christmas cementing my suspicions firmly in my mind. After the door had closed, leaving me alone, I sank down on the bottom step and stared pitifully at the dark wooden barrier, feeling that all the air had gone from me. His absence left me a half of the whole he had made me.

It crossed my mind to leave, to storm back to my dorm room making the statement that I was my own person but honestly, I liked his house better than my dorm. I had always felt comfortable here and relished in the idea that I would get to have the house to myself for a few days. Correction, Henry would be here. That didn't really bother me, he kept to himself and maybe I would even be able to get some information out of him during our cohabitation.

Ch. 12

Henry was not a cook and had taken over James' office upstairs leaving me alone to manage my dinner. Since I didn't want to cook for one, I thought about calling Stephen. Until, as I flipped my phone open, I remembered that I was angry with him and snapped it shut with a sour grump. Tonight was not the night to have it out with him either, not with the mood I was in.

After some deliberation, I decided on ordering a pizza. It was a favorite of mine and I hadn't had one in a long time. While I waited for the delivery boy, I sat on the couch reading some mindless fiction James had lying around. I would have to tease him about that when he got home. The reminder of him brought with it images of James intertwined with some beautiful woman in Germany, and try as I might I couldn't shake them.

When the doorbell rang I jumped up to answer, eager to put a new face in my head for a reprieve from the movie looping in my mind's eye. Henry materialized out of nowhere, and from the glare he aimed my way, he made it clear James had informed him that I was not to answer any doors lest I be snatched again. It was difficult for me to go from the total independence I'd grown up with, to be disallowed from doing even the most basic things for myself. If his fears hadn't been proven real and justified, I wouldn't have stood for it. Still, I found it irritating being "kept."

Henry sat with me at the table reading a book while I ate dinner. Though we sat together, neither of us spoke until I finished my second slice and set my napkin on my plate. To my surprise, Henry broke the silence, his voice flowing around his book.

"You are right, she is a former lover." He was matter of fact. "Theirs was a strictly physical relationship that made a difficult time endurable. It ended long ago."

His confirming what I knew in my heart about my love's past bothered me less than the hold she obviously still had over him. There was no way I could compete with the woman who went with that voice. "Then why did he rush off like that? Can't someone *else* help her?" I whined stubbornly.

Henry blinked and set down his book, watching me with a mild sneer of distaste. "You are aware that James' ability is unique, and his network of our kind that has taken him the better part of a century to put together and make him a tremendous asset to us. Before you came along James had only recently returned from abroad where he had been of significant help to the Court in numerous matters, the scope of which I will not bother you with the details."

As was Henry's intention, I snapped my mouth shut and sat back to listen. I would have apologized only I didn't think he wanted to hear a peep from me.

Seeing his point made, Henry took a less severe tone. "She did not call him because they were lovers, she called him because she needs his help." It shouldn't have, but his use of the word 'lovers' turned my stomach and my jaw clenched shut to bite back the bitterness threatening to climb up my throat.

"Claire, our kind has needs just the same as your own does. It is impossible to believe that James ignored those needs until he met you." Again he put me in my place and I fought with myself, so far unwilling to cooperate with reason. "Yours is a special bond and by far eclipses any he has experienced prior. You should be more confident in that."

Tight lipped, I nodded once and asked Henry real questions, questions that weren't rooted in petty insecurities. "What does he need to do for her? And why does he think it might be a trap?"

Henry's brows arched. "Did he tell you that?"

"Yes, why wouldn't he?" I was confused.

Shrugging, Henry answered with a furrowed brow. "James does not like to worry you. It merely surprises me that he would tell you that he might be walking into a trap."

Strangely enough, I hadn't thought of it that way. James had said he worried he was being lured away, exposing *me* to harm. I'd been too busy being juvenile to ask him about it. It had never occurred to me that *he* might be the one in danger. He was next to invincible in my mind, I wasn't used to being afraid for him yet my reaction was automatic.

My panic spiked in an instant, my heart pounding. "Henry, tell me he didn't go alone. Did you send anyone with him?" I tried to meet his eyes, it was the first time I'd done so since he'd rolled me. His power had spooked me.

Meeting my eyes, Henry's shifted darker and I felt pulled. There was nothing I could do as he flooded me with a sense of peace. It was like getting a shot; the effects coursed through me unbidden and, at his command, my pulse slowed as well as my racing thoughts. Artificially at peace, I listened.

"Claire, I would not send my closest ally into the hands of an enemy unprepared. He has gone with Tonya." He released me from his thrall, his eyes returned to chocolate as the room came back to me. "You forget, Claire, James is an aged vampire and can handle himself quite well in battle."

My mind rebelled at the thought of James in any sort of a fight, even if I was certain he had been involved in a few during his existence. His self-confidence could only come from having tested himself and coming out victorious. That much I knew from the soldiers I'd met on base growing up.

James' confidence was one of the things that I found so appealing about him. I had never met anyone like him before, the thought of losing him was crippling. As my anxiety crept up on me again Henry spoke in a new multilayered voice, it emanated not just from his mouth but also from his chest. "Calm yourself." It was a command such as I'd heard they were capable of and I had no choice but to obey it. Simultaneously, my body listened and my heart rate slowed.

Vampires, unlike humans, were able to access the majority of their brains allowing them to do things that seemed like magick. James had explained to me that with age vampires learn how to control their increased mental capacity using it to manipulate humans in ways that we had no defense against. It was this manipulation Henry had been using on me tonight, forcing me to overrule my body's natural responses to stress. According to James, a vampire had to be very old to exhibit the kind of control Henry was showing.

"Henry, how old *are* you?" I gaped at him in an uneasy awe.

He smiled without a hint of warmth. "Old enough Claire. That is all you need to know." He looked away toward the living room for a moment as though he was listening. "Would you like to know why he is helping Ursa?"

"Ursa?" I giggled at the foreign name. His glare froze any sarcastic commentary beyond that. It was clear I would need to control myself around Henry a little better. He was not as patient as James. "Yes, please," I answered soberly.

"Ursa," he said her name pointedly, daring me to say something.

Wisely, I kept my mouth shut.

"Was one of the first vampires James met after we fled Canada in the scandal surrounding his turning." Henry referred to James' violent change and waking without guidance wherein he subsequently killed two humans before Henry could get to him.

I was familiar with the story, though its mention sent the same shiver through me that it did when I'd first heard it and saw how its memory continued to haunt James.

"When it became apparent that James had an ability we went to Germany where the Court had someone who could help. Ursa was very good with helping newly turned vampires to come to terms with their existence. She is an empath, not unlike you. Though her gift is not as powerful." He gave me a nod as shock registered on my face.

I was more powerful than a vampire with the same ability, and knowing it was his ex made it all the more sweet.

"James has explained to you, and I believe you have now experienced firsthand, the sensitivities of a newly turned vampire am I correct?" I bobbed my head, rapt. "His were excruciating. His gift became stronger with being turned and he suffered greatly when he was raw."

I felt the tears prick my eyes at the thought of James in that kind of pain. Even Henry was troubled with the memory. He ran a hand over his face to wipe away the image his distant gaze was seeing.

"As a human he had been a compassionate young man, shaped as he was by the death of his mother and the dispersal of his family. When he was turned, his compassion became stronger and shifted into his need to help others. His gift grew from there. Ursa was the one who taught him how to shield himself from his own sensitivity to others' gifts as well as block their effects on him."

"I thought he could just sense other people's abilities. You mean he can take them on, too?"

Henry held up a hand for me to let him finish. "James' gift is a unique one. As I have said before, he can feel others' gifts. Your empathy, for example; he felt you, the way you feel others. He channels others' gifts, which is why he has been able to train them, like you. He feels it firsthand and, knowing how to shield, he shows you how to control and manipulate your talent. That is also why *he* trained you and not Stephen. A detail that bothers Stephen greatly I might add."

"So, there is a newly turned vampire with a gift that needs him?" Without the static of impotent envy altering my senses I could understand why James had left in such a hurry; of course he would want to limit the newbie's suffering. "They have worked together before then?" I filed away the knowledge that Stephen was angry about my training even though it was his idea to pair me up with James. Perhaps he was upset that things had progressed as they had between my teacher and I. That might explain about the oath being rescinded, although the timing still bothered me.

Henry nodded an affirmative. "Yes, they work together on occasion when a young vampire needs help. He can also help weres in much the same way and has contracted with their Council on occasion. They are more of a challenge because their minds don't work in the same way. They are more animal, especially in the beginning when the beast inside them struggles with the human for control. It is only through his sensitivity that he is able to bridge the gap."

"Does it take a long time for the human to learn to control the beast after being changed? What happens if the beast wins?" I had asked Tonya and Tara about the change once and they said it was a struggle in the beginning. I knew they were downplaying it because they didn't want to talk about it; I welcomed the opportunity to learn more about what made them what they were.

Henry answered with a nonchalant shrug and regarded me with a bored expression. This might be old hat to him but to me it was all new and different.

"All changes are different. The timeframe for how long before the man masters the monster varies depending upon the strength of the person. And yes, when the beast controls the body it is truly dangerous for all beings that come in contact with them. Their Council contracts with our own Court to put down any beasts that cannot be mastered by their human side." Henry did not change his expression when my jaw dropped. "They also rely upon secrecy for their safety."

My mind was reeling with everything Henry was sharing so readily. James had never offered so much about what it was really like for them. Henry was right, James was always trying to protect me. He didn't want me worrying about anyone else. I'm sure he meant well by sheltering me yet all I could feel was selfish. I had a new sympathy for creatures like vampires and weres who were turned whether they had been willing victims or not. It sounded like a terrible ordeal and not one to be taken lightly by either creature. The guilt I now felt for being so self-absorbed chased away the last vestiges of unreasonable jealousy which had been getting the better of me all day.

"Why didn't James tell me this? I would have understood." Henry finally smiled. "Would you have believed it from him?"

69

"Is that why he had *you* come instead of Troy or Stephen?" The other two were more logical choices given our closer relationships.

"No, James did not ask me to speak to you, although he is aware that I do not lie to you nor do I spare your feelings as he might. It might have been part of what led him to ask me to protect his interests in his absence."

Once again, he was right.   "Henry, could I ask you something?"

"You can ask anything you would like. I cannot guarantee an answer," was his reply. He was always truthful, even if he knew that it would irritate me.

"You said earlier that your kind has needs. I took those to be feeding and sex. Is that correct?"

"Yes," his reply was slow and guarded. He was obviously waiting for the other shoe to drop.

"Why don't you have a mate or partner, er, a whathaveyou. I've never seen you with anyone like that."

His lips twisted into a wry smile. "You have only known me a short while. We have needs, though we have a different view on how often they need to be filled. A human might think a year without sex is an eternity, yet to an immortal, a year is but a heartbeat. The draw of an affair is of no matter unless one is truly interesting to me. And that, my dear, has not happened in a very long time."

His candor astonished me. "Thank you for being so honest Henry, about everything. It really helps to have someone who will tell me what's what and not always worry about scaring me."

Abruptly gaining his feet, Henry bowed curtly. "Claire, my dear, I must bid you good night. I hope that our conversation eases your mind and gives you some fresh perspective." Upstairs a phone rang and before I could blink again Henry was gone.

Ch. 13

It *had* given me a new perspective. As I lay alone in our bed that night, my chest was filled with a renewal of love for James and respect for what he was doing. He did so much good in this world that it was hard not to adore him. Impulsively, I switched our pillows so I could smell him while I lay there. Eventually I fell asleep, dreaming of sitting across the breakfast table with James for the rest of my life.

Waking up with a start, I was completely disoriented. Checking the digital clock glowing blue in the darkness I saw that it was nearly morning. Rubbing my eyes, I tried to shake the sick feeling that clung to me after waking from my dream. I remembered having a fight with large dogs and a golden cat in a shining collar. My body was stuck somehow and I could see a strange man standing in the shadows, his face hidden. Even awake, I could still feel the lingering effects of too real a dream and the imagined weight of my limbs made it hard to force my hand out of the bed. I willed it to wrap itself around the glass on my nightstand.

Immediately after I took a drink, I felt the sluggishness of the dream shaking free and I felt an undeniable need to feel James. It wasn't enough to call him on the phone. I needed to feel his presence, to dull that ache inside me where I felt him missing. He needed to know that I wasn't angry anymore and I was sorry things had been weird when we parted earlier. I hoped that was all that was behind my unease, just guilt.

Sitting up, I was determined to contact him. It was nearly six a.m. and he had been there for hours unless I missed my guess. I wished I knew what time it was in Germany, then, I realized with a laugh that it made no difference. Vampires don't sleep. I wouldn't be waking anyone.

Tapping into how I had "called him" before, I knew I had to reach in to my head to find where he was. There was a definite feel of him in my head, different from a memory or thought, and I focused on that now. To help make the connection stronger I took his pillow from behind me and pressed it against my face. Closing my eyes, I inhaled his exotic smell while I reached for him.

It was dark. I couldn't see anything at all yet I could feel him. I was confused, something was wrong. Digging deeper and concentrating harder, I heard him whisper my name; I held my breath.

His weak voice was ragged with pain. The ache of his loss was gone in a flash, replaced by the searing agony of my uselessness. James needed me and I was here lying in his bed. I needed to find him, to get Henry and go to him. Hadn't Tonya gone with him? Where was she? James whispered my name again, driving away my questions, and I ignored everything else to concentrate on him. I felt his torment physically this time as he tied in to our connection. He was weak with thirst and his body was stuck, he couldn't move yet he could feel every inch of his body burning in a nightmare of unending pain; I sensed his mind collapsing.

"James, where are you?" Fighting hard, I remained focused, managing not to go to pieces. I "listened" with every fiber of my being. His pillow was still under my nose and I took a deep breath to strengthen my focus.

Coaxing his mind not to push me out but to open up, I felt the membrane separating us thin and, with a pop, I was inside. First there was a flash of a coffin. It was old and constructed of a dark wood that absorbed the tiny streams of light coming in from the few flickering sources on the walls. The details of the room around it were sketchy. The walls were grey stone and I was reminded of the castles we saw in Scotland. I couldn't tell if this was a memory he was showing me or if he was seeing it at the moment.

The vision was crystal-clear and I was temporarily in awe of what his senses were like. I'd only had the full effect a few times when he was weak. The wonderment was cast aside with the reminder that I was only seeing this because of his condition.

Twisting my fingers in the fabric of his pillow, I pushed myself. Another flash, this one was of a tapestry on the wall of the castle, his clarity of sight giving me the full scope through the dimness of the cavernous hall. The scene embroidered into the emerald green fabric was a disturbing one. Violence was everywhere as woven men on horseback dressed in armor fought large men with the heads of wolves. The scene depicted a bloody battle with heavy losses to both sides; wolf men impaled by human men, warriors ripped from their mounts and torn apart by wolf men using tooth and claw. It was a horrifying scene, the stuff of nightmares.

The coffin suddenly opened, light from the torches on the wall flared and illuminated a figure. It was the shadow man from my dream. His white face was washed out by the suddenness of the light. A flash of long fangs and James' terror flooded through me, breaking our connection.

Clutching his pillow to my chest, I screamed. The backlash of my fears and James' combined pulling me into a vortex of terror the likes of which I had never experienced even when I was being tortured by a sadistic vampire. The screams kept coming until I was beyond hysterical; I had no power to stop myself.

I don't know when Henry came in my room or when he grabbed me. Eventually I felt his cool, unforgiving hands clasped on my shoulders, shaking me. It might have been gentle for him, but it rattled my teeth. It worked to clear my head enough to allow me to find Henry's face with my unfocused eyes, and in a terrified whisper, I told him, "They have him."

"Tonya?"

I shook my head, "I don't know." It was hard to sort me from the ghost of James still echoing in my head. The return to my body left me disoriented, my inadequate vision blurry after his.

Henry's hand clamped onto my chin and I winced. The pressure eased and he turned my face up to his. My eyes were fuzzy and I couldn't make them work right, limiting my vision to a pale face with a dark frame and two black orbs. Stumbling over the words with a tongue that felt foreign, I stammered nonsense.

"We have to go to the castle, the castle with the wolf men on the walls. He has him in a coffin and he can't move. It hurts so much." The memory of the fire in his veins drove me back into hysterics. "James, oh my God, we have to go." I barely felt the tears on my cheeks or noticed when his hands left my shoulders.

I don't know where Henry went or how long he was gone. The whooshing sound of fabric hitting the bed with a thud came into my peripheral senses sometime later accompanied by the sound of Henry's stern voice.

"Get dressed, we're leaving."

Obediently, I did as I was told. He had thrown me jeans and a sweatshirt. I pulled the top on over my pajamas, one of James' white undershirts. They always smelled like him and because he didn't sweat, they didn't get gross. I'd gotten in the habit of stealing them from him when I stayed over. It had made him laugh when he first noticed me doing it; I think he was flattered.

Hastily dressed, I wandered out into the hall and down the stairs. I stood waiting at the front door for Henry. Shoes, I needed shoes, I finally had a thought of my own. I grabbed

75

my black Converse out of the coat closet and went back to the door. Henry's voice floated to me from the back of the house through the kitchen.

"Claire, come here." He sounded hurried, not annoyed. Reaching him, I looked up in confusion. "There is a flight that leaves in forty minutes. We need maneuverability and my car doesn't have the kind we need." He looked closely at me as I stared blankly at him. I had no idea what he was talking about. "Haven't you ever been in the garage?"

Strangely enough, no, I hadn't. We had always parked in the driveway. A fact that did seem odd now that snow was on the ground and he had a two car garage. Most people in Minnesota made room in the garage if they could when the snow came. It was easier on the people and the cars. James just used his remote starter and the Audi was clear of snow by the time we got in.

Henry grabbed me by the arm and directed me out the door at the back of the kitchen. Not needing the light, he didn't turn it on. I, however, didn't anticipate the step down, slamming my thigh into something, and only saw the car inside when the garage door went up and the light on the opener clicked on. If I hadn't been in such a state I probably would have been excited by the black rearing horse on the hood on the black car. It looked fast sitting still. I felt a mixture of nerves and giddiness at the ride I was sure to be in for if this was what Henry thought he needed to handle the drive.

"Get in the car. We need to go now!" Again, I did as I was told, putting some speed in my step now that I had a direction.

We drove faster than I had ever driven in my life. The power of the car pushed me back into my seat with the need for speed and maneuverability apparent as Henry weaved in and out of traffic, blowing through red lights whenever necessary. We made it to the airport in less than ten minutes and ran. Henry half carried me through the security checkpoint and terminal before we arrived at our gate bound for Munich. The passengers were boarding, Henry let go of my arm and told me to stay. Doing so, I watched him go up to the gate agent, speak to her for a moment and turn back toward me. When he turned away from her, I caught a glimpse of her face over his shoulder and knew by the glazed look in her eyes that he had done something to her. I wondered if I looked like that. A giggle escaped before I clapped my hand over my mouth. Unable to stop myself, I thought about security handling an airport full of zombies like the two of us. I tittered again.

He huffed impatiently and grabbed my arm, walking me to the First Class line. Vampires were wonderful to travel with, no coach for them. I snorted and stifled another giggle. Henry shot me a warning glare. He probably sensed how close I was losing it and didn't want me to wreck anything. Neither did I, and taking a deep shaking breath, I got myself somewhat under control.

After we boarded, I slouched into my seat and felt a terrible sense of dread overtaking me. We were going to have to sit uselessly on a plane for hours with nothing to stop me from imagining the damage being done to James and to Tonya while we were served complimentary champagne in oversized chairs. My pulse took off and my stomach knotted.

Frantic, I looked wild eyed at Henry. "How do you know where he is? What if we're too late?" Again I felt the fracturing of James' mind and the blood pounding in my ears, swept away the sounds of the hum of the people around me.

He stared over my shoulder across the aisle. People must have been looking; I didn't care. My eyes were locked on Henry's face; any hope I'd had was quickly fading. His expression was tight but otherwise unreadable. Only his eyes were giving me feedback. They were black, always a bad sign in a vampire. I felt myself starting to break and I swallowed a sob.

Henry blinked once and said simply, "Sleep."

Ch. 14

I woke when Henry poked me hard in the ribs. We were deplaning. Unbuckling my seatbelt I scrambled to step out into the row, Henry close behind pushing me. Our dash through this airport was just as frenzied as the one through Minneapolis had been. We followed signs I couldn't understand down a flight of escalators, past baggage claim, through sliding doors and stopping when we stepped out onto a curb.

At the curb Henry spoke to a short, fat man with a set of thick, brown moustaches and a very bad combover. They haggled heatedly in German until Henry lost patience, produced a handful of Euros and jammed them into the man's protruding belly. His eyes bulged and the argument was over. The fat man barked harshly into a walkie-talkie and we stood for a brief moment before a silver sedan pulled up to the curb. I wasn't familiar enough with European cars to know what I was looking at. Given our mission, I guessed it too would be fast. Henry opened my door, I sat down and before my seatbelt was buckled, he was tearing out onto the street. Looking in my rearview mirror, I saw the fat man shrinking rapidly as we raced away from the airport, hopefully in time to save our family.

We drove and, trapped in that torturously inert position, I watched the countryside race by my window, wishing to hell it would go by faster. It was hard to tell what I was looking at in any great detail, covered in snow as everything was. The falling shadows confused my eyes as the sun set on the horizon and took the last of the light with it. Soon, it was full dark and I realized something that should have been obvious to me before now if I'd been thinking properly.

"Henry, how do you know where to go?" I stared expectantly at him.

He turned to me, not taking his foot off of the accelerator. I felt a flutter of nerves at the thought of crashing. "You told me." His conversational tone was reminiscent of the Henry I had met long before I knew anything about otherworldly creatures.

"What do you mean, *I* told you?" Blinking, I was trying and failing to remember what I had said at the house.

"It is as we had feared, they have been captured. They are in a castle in a small town in the country not far from here, it belongs to a vampire known as Raymond. We should be there very soon." I could feel his tension though he tried to hide it from me.

"Our connection ended when that thing opened the coffin he's in. Do you think," my voice broke as I dared to speak aloud my worst fear, "Do you think they killed him? Do you think James is dead?"

His voice was unwavering, he'd successfully tucked his nerves away and again become a tabula rasa giving me no input but for his words. "Have you tried to contact him again since then?" I stared, entranced at Henry's white face illuminated by the eerie purple lights on the dashboard and the hairs on the back of my neck went up. I didn't like it when Henry got this cool.

"I haven't been clear enough to try. Every time I try to focus all I can see is him, in that coffin, and I feel the pain he was in." I shook my head. "I can't do it." I was trying hard to control the hysteria threatening to return.

Henry was the picture of serenity. I couldn't decide if I envied him or hated him for not being more upset. "Claire," he spoke quietly, breaking into my thoughts, "do you remember what you said to me when you told me you saw James? Do you remember mentioning an animal?"

I recalled the wolf men I'd seen on the tapestries and shivered.

"I am not the only vampire with an animal to call. Raymond also has one, werewolves."

My stomach knotted. Trying to sound reasonable, I focused on practical things. My overwrought psyche rebelled at any further discussion of harm. "What do we do when we get there? How do you know this Raymond and why would he want to hurt James?"

He sighed deeply. "You are well aware by now that vampires are polarized on the subject of humans. Some like your kind while others do not. It seems simple enough on the surface. Those who do not have been hearing from Bradley about how if they fight as one, if they unite, they can be free of the threat of being hunted by humans forever. That they can finally live free from persecution. Raymond has made several visits to Bradley's nightclub where they spout their rhetoric these last few weeks, and we have heard that he is supportive of Bradley's cause. Bradley has been deep underground since we last faced him. However, he continues to try to establish a foothold in the vampire political structure in order to gain momentum for his cause. The Court does not want a full-scale war and they are fighting Bradley on this, at least on the surface they are, who is to know what undercurrents we are not privy to. He knows he has to overturn the Court first in order to truly have the war he is hoping for. We fear he has an ally there already."

Sucking in my breath, I considered the ramifications of Bradley taking down the vampire's high Court. Without the fear of reprisal the Court represented, the vampires who hated or feared humans, or just those who liked to kill for the pleasure, could devastate humankind. Bradley would get his war in some form, united vampires or not. Just the simple fact that there would be so much wanton killing, humans

81

would realize what was happening and come after the vampires. It would be destruction on a level I didn't want to consider.

Factor in the "weapon" Bradley and Gaston were using to unite the vampires, a human boy who we knew had an ability that works on vampires without psychic abilities, and it would be an epic inter-species war.

"What am I supposed to do when we get there? Are any of the cats meeting us there?" My mind was spinning rapidly ahead as I considered the possibilities of walking into the home of a vampire known to hate humans as much as Bradley did. The potential outcome terrified me. But it was James, what else could I do? I prayed that a small army would be waiting to help us.

Henry growled out his response showing a hint of his fangs in his sudden fury. "I have already endangered two dear to me. I will not allow anyone else to walk into danger on my behalf, allegiance or no."

Minutes later, the car's engine slowed and I looked out the window knowing we had arrived. My heart sank as we pulled up to a modest stone castle built long ago and I watched the iron gates open to allow us passage. When they closed behind us I felt sick; we were trapped. The tires crunched on the crushed rock as we drove slowly up a long driveway through perfectly manicured grounds. The approach ended in an open circle of pale crushed rock at whose center stood a small fountain set within a formal garden filled with foliage unidentifiable in the dark of the night. Atop the fountain was a sculpture of a wolf, its head turned so that his stone gray eyes bored coldly into mine.

"You will remain absolutely quiet and speak only if I direct you to do so. Raymond is old and powerful, but he has no special talents beyond what comes naturally to an ancient vampire. He will smell vampire on you and he has to respect the limits to the liberties he can take with you. I can only hope he will assume that you are mine and not James'. We do not want to give him any indications of the connection between the two of you. That power would be hard for him to let go regardless of the laws." He gave me this to think about just seconds before he stopped the car, opened his door and stepped out. In a flash he was at my door, opening it for me and taking my hand. Too stunned to think on my own, I could only follow Henry up the steps and past a very scary looking vampire at the door.

He was tall, close to six and a half feet and had long, black hair blowing loose in the light breeze, suited entirely in black. Hands clasped in front of him with his eyes trained forward, he looked every bit the intimidating bodyguard I was sure he was supposed to be. When I tested his "feel" I realized my mistake, he was not a vampire. He was entirely different than anything I had felt before. My ability struggled with his undecided nature. It was impossible to pin down his emotions they shifted too quickly. I could tell he was curious about us as I watched his nostrils flare and his nose lift into the air, scenting.

If Raymond's animal was a werewolf, and this man was clearly a were, then this was my first meeting with a werewolf and I was duly impressed. He was thicker through the body than the cats, his countenance more aloof. The sheer physical presence of the wolf was magnificent. On a lighter note, I knew I couldn't tell Troy what I thought of the wolf, he already had a chip on his shoulder about their media hype. He said the werewolves he knew were full of themselves and he wouldn't be happy if I went around talking them up.

The guard stepped forward, hand coming up to Henry's chest as we approached the front door. He was not graceful, I noted with some small amount of satisfaction. His gait was more rolling than the cats, yet still smoother than a human's. Henry stopped and looked at the guard, no sign he had any reservations about our visit. "Hello Paolo, I wish to see Raymond. I have traveled a long way. I hope that he will see me unannounced."

A silver cell phone appeared in Paolo's hand before I even noticed he had moved. He dialed it and spoke rapidly in Italian. He grunted a few times and snapped the phone shut. "You may enter and wait in the drawing room. Refreshments can be sent in if you did not bring your own." He barely glanced at me. "Raymond will join you when he is able." Paolo reached forward and took hold of one of the giant iron doors that looked older than my entire country and yanked it open with ease.

Walking forward, my hand clinging to Henry's arm for safety, we entered the castle and I couldn't help but jump when I heard the door slam shut behind us leaving us alone in the huge empty space. The floors were classic black and white checkerboard tile. The furniture visible from the circular foyer was sparse, what I could see was beautiful and old. I was willing to bet they were all antiques collected during their actual period of creation, not the result of any sort of antique shop foray on the part of the owner.

The chandelier above our heads held my interest longer than the rest. It was a beautiful piece with what had to be a hundred teardrop shaped crystals, each throwing light in a different direction around the room. I saw the stairway curving up and out of sight. My view only extended to the first door at the top of the stairs, the hallway went on from there, how far I couldn't tell. What was up there didn't concern me, I knew from my vision of James that he was downstairs, not up. My eyes roved the floor and walls looking for gapping in the stones or some hint of a staircase leading below. There was nothing.

In front of us stood two heavy wooden doors Henry slid open to reveal a drawing room decorated in a masculine motif of dark woods and leather. Upon entering, Henry released me and turned around to slide the doors closed behind us with a decided thud. Turning back, he motioned for me to sit in one of the two leather wing chairs across the room. I chose the one on the left, Henry chose to stand next to me, far enough behind me he could keep both the door and me within his sight.

We waited in silence, not wanting anyone to overhear any conversation we might have. The silence allowed me to try to reach out again. Now that we were here, I tried to quiet my brain and call upon my marks to find James. It took a significant amount of concentration to slow my thoughts, but I did and then I reached for him.

The pain I felt when I connected was excruciating and I felt the breath rush out of my body with the shock of it. I called out to him in my head, hoping he'd be able to answer, elated that he was alive. If he was in pain, that meant he wasn't dead. We weren't too late. Bringing my attention back to our connection before I wasted another precious second, I listened for his voice and heard nothing. Where I usually felt his presence, there was only a void. Fearing his mind had closed itself off to protect itself, I looked around for signs he was still here noticing that he was in the light now. He was still unable to move, although his eyes were open and focused straight ahead of him.

A large cage stood in front of him, occupied. Tonya lay unconscious, a heavy silver collar around her neck. She was naked and, despite the gravity of the situation, I couldn't help but notice how beautiful her lean, golden brown body was.

From James' perspective I knew he was upright. I didn't understand how that would be since he was obviously restrained in some way. A door opened nearby and I heard it both through James' and my own ears. He *was* here! The door slammed and our connection was broken again. I couldn't hold it for long by myself and he wasn't tying in to it at all.

I gasped and fell back against the chair, frustrated at the loss. Henry put his hand on my shoulder and stepped in front of me lifting an eyebrow in askance. He could tell what I'd been doing and had questions. I wanted to tell him what I had seen, but didn't want anyone who might be lurking to overhear us. A vampire's sneaking skills rivaled his listening through doors skills. There was no guarantee we weren't being spied on right now.

Frightening though it was to have him in my head, I knew it was the only option. Squaring my shoulders on Henry, I pointed to my eyes and rolled them. His lips twitched, amused by my amateurish hints. Taking my chin in hand he held my face, eyes trained on his as he got ready to delve into my thoughts. Mesmerized, I watched his eyes go from warm liquid chocolate to hard and black as jet in a second and felt the world spin away.

Faintly, I felt his hand release my chin and the world around me came back into focus as his eyes let go. I watched him frowning at me as he thought about what he had seen through my eyes. His remained black.

There was no time to even attempt to pantomime a conversation. I heard a whoosh as the doors slid open and the faint rustle of clothing as someone glided in. Henry and I both turned toward the sound and I saw the vampire Raymond before me, the shadow man of my visions. He was everything Henry was not. They were both ancient, of that I was certain. That was where the similarities ended.

Where Henry appeared outwardly to be human, Raymond looked every bit a cold, scary monster. To call him even human*like* would have been a stretch. Small, detached black eyes were set in a skeletal, bone white face. He was short, maybe 5'6" or so, had not a hair upon his head and thin, cruel lips that curved around his prominent canines.

Raymond was robed entirely in black and his clothing appeared to be from a different time. The tunic he wore over his trousers was buttoned all the way down the front and draped to his knees. It was impossible to tell where or when he was from, he had long ago lost any sort of pigmentation or hair color that might have indicated his heritage.

When he spoke, his accent was muddled, most likely a result of centuries spent in countless countries and having spoken numerous languages. As demonic as his appearance, it was his voice that froze the blood in my veins.

"Henry, to what do I owe the pleasure of your visit?" His high-pitched voice and icy words prickled my skin, leaving goose bumps in its wake so tight my skin hurt.

Henry gave a small half bow out of respect. "Raymond, thank you for receiving me on such short notice. I apologize for not giving proper warning, it could not be helped. The reason for my trip was rather sudden." Henry's calm and controlled manner belied any anger he felt. If I didn't know better, I would have thought these two were old friends.

Raymond feigned ignorance, "What was it that brought you here so unexpectedly?"

I wanted to slap the smug right off his pasty face, my sudden inclination toward violence taking me by surprise.

"It was brought to my attention that your soldiers picked up something of mine." Henry let a hint of irritation bleed through his calm façade. "I want it back."

"Would you be referring to your boy or your cat? It seems they were both somewhere they should not have been." He too allowed a taste of the seriousness of the situation to show. "Am I not allowed to police my own lands?"

My fists curled at my sides. Stuffing them under my legs, I hid the evidence of my impotent rage.

"Of course you are Raymond. However, it was my understanding that James had been called to work with Ursa in Munich. The Court is fully aware of their work and approves of it. Together they have saved the sanity of many a vampire for well over a hundred years. Ursa, as you know, has been guiding the young for centuries." Serenity returned to Henry's tone.

"Ah, Ursa. She overstepped this time and had to be dealt with appropriately. She had been warned repeatedly." Raymond feigned sadness, though the emotion was clearly too faded a memory and the expression had more in common with discomfort than distress. Giving up on the fake remorse, he returned to the stoic coldness he was better at. "I haven't decided yet what to do with your pets. I suppose it depends what you can offer me by way of apology." He tilted his head at me for the first time; his nostrils twitched and I felt cold all over again. Raymond chuckled darkly. "Your new dish smells sweet." His eyebrows drew together, he scented a second time, "Marked? Is she your servant then? I thought you didn't do that sort of thing anymore. She must be very tasty indeed to have captured your interest." He advanced a step toward me and I trembled, my pulse quickened. I did not want this monster anywhere near me.

Henry spoke firmly. "The Court will be very unhappy that you have taken matters into your own hands and executed Ursa. She was highly thought of by Anton especially," he referred to one of the three members of the Court whom I had met last fall. I had thought Anton the most intimidating of the three. Raymond must be pretty strong to risk Anton's wrath, or that of any of the Court for that matter.

Raymond merely shrugged, indicating that he didn't find this to be nearly as frightening a prospect as I did.

"I assure you any misstep James might have taken was purely accidental. He was called to help Ursa with a newly turned and my cat was to assist him if necessary. Neither one was doing anything of which the Court or you would disapprove." Henry continued, with slightly more urgency. My body reacted instinctively. I didn't think it could be good if Henry was beginning to worry. Raymond gave no indication he heard my human response.

Raymond lifted his chin and looked back to the doors behind him. "I have business to attend. What do you have to offer me as a replacement for my prisoners?"

Henry brightened. "You have long admired my collection of manuscripts by Emperor Nero's scribe detailing his descent into madness. I would give these to you for the release of my companions." I could only imagine the value of a manuscript so old and rare. The Roman Emperor Nero was not only mad, he was paranoid and would have killed the scribe if he knew about them. They had to be priceless and anyone familiar with antiquities would drool over them.

But Raymond merely waved his hand, "I have lost my desire for the material."

Looking at the countless treasures around me, I found that hard to believe.

"For one as old as I, things tend to lose their meaning. However," he paused and looked again at me, I held my breath. "I *am* interested in something rare you have brought with you. She has an innocence I have not savored in many years."

Henry's response was determined. "She is not for you."

89

The change in Raymond made me blanch in fear. I had thought he was scary before; now as he grew angry, a sinking sense of dread swept through me. My body went rigid. I doubted I could have run if it had come to it.

Raymond's albino skin thinned and his jaw elongated by inches. His fangs lengthened to an unimaginable degree, they were reptilian thin and nearly reached his chin. I would have sworn he grew as he drew himself up in his rage and I watched the blackness of his eyes expand, drowning out all of the whites.

"As a visitor in *my* territory, you must allow me blood from *any* human you bring onto *my* lands. That is the ruling of the Court and it is *my* right. Do you come to *my* home and deny me *my* right?" Raymond's voice rose to a screech, it did not hold any of the silkiness of James' or Henry's as he hammered home his point that we were trespassing.

Henry was struggling to remain outwardly calm, but I saw cracking in his untroubled facade. He did not want to offer me up out of respect for James, yet I knew he needed to if any of us were going to get out of here alive. At the risk of offending Henry, I rose to my feet.

"I will do it, if my Master wishes."

Henry put his hand on my shoulder to stop me, but the damage was done.

Ch. 15

Raymond's body turned and the nightmarish figure focused on me alone. Ignoring Henry's protective shift in stance, his grating voice was directed at me. "The child speaks for her Master?"

"No she does not, she is new and does not understand all of our ways. My servant has not been fully indoctrinated in how she must behave in the presence of other vampires such as yourself."

His face contorting with his distaste, it was easy to guess what the ancient monster felt about Henry's attitude toward humans. Raymond knew what he wanted lay in the balance and he agreed to my offer regardless of Henry's attempts to intervene. "I grant the four of you safe passage, if you allow me to taste the young one. She smells of something raw and strange." The nearly translucent lids lowered over his black eyes, his thin tongue paled to a sickly gray, flicked out to slide up a fang before retracting. "I have not had something so unusual in an age."

Glancing over to Henry I blinked, the only sign I could force myself to make. He saw the fear in my white face and shaking knees. The racing of my pulse roared in my ears and theirs as well. Raymond chuckled wickedly. He knew that he had won and was enjoying my reaction as an appetizer.

My focus returned to Raymond as I teetered precariously on my feet. I had only allowed one other vampire to feed on me and that had been James in an emergency. He'd made it a sensual experience for me, I had been only vaguely aware of his feeding at the time, being more focused on the pleasure.

James had told me it was the vampire's choice how it felt for the donor and I didn't think Raymond would want to make it easy for me. I tried to brace my mind for the pain I knew was coming. Uncertain how to proceed or where he would choose to bite, I stood very still, waiting. Raymond had a definite idea of how this was to go and directed me accordingly.

He remained where he was and raised a finger to point at my chest. "Remove your top." Raymond aimed his comment at Henry. "The blood is best at the source, don't you agree?"

Henry said nothing.

My hands shook too hard to follow his command, I couldn't force my fingers, stiff with fear, around the hem. Henry moved in front of me to help and met my eyes with his own. I felt him enter my mind and a numbing sensation filled my body, insulating my mind from the worst of what was to come. Gratefully, I smiled shakily at him. He gave a tiny nod. He knew Raymond was going to make this unpleasant as well.

Henry's hands went to the bottom of my sweater and undershirt, taking them as one and lifting them over my head laying them on the back of the chair behind me. He returned to my side leaving me standing nearly naked in only my jeans to face the monster before me. I had left the house without putting on a bra and regretted the decision now that I stood bare chested and terrified, presenting myself as his unwilling prize.

Raymond hissed with pleasure and licked his lower lip. I felt my stomach flip and bit back the bile rising in my throat. I tasted blood from my lip. Thinking of James, I stood straight and closed my eyes. I wanted to be brave like him.

"No," his shriek tore at my ears. "Look at me."

Barely restrained tears filled my eyes as I obeyed. "Before you have your taste," Henry cut in sharply, "have your dogs put my companions in the car. When they are safely out, you may have what you want."

Raymond snarled, but Henry didn't flinch. Their standoff ended when Raymond barked out a command. The doors opened and another werewolf with a strong family resemblance to Paolo stood before us. His eyes ran over my half naked form and I saw animal lust in his eyes before Raymond's voice brought his attention back to his Master.

"Bring our guests up and put the bodies in the car." He glared at Henry. "I assume that is acceptable to you?"

Henry nodded his assent and the wolf's head snapped back out, closing the doors behind him. Still frozen in place, I felt a flutter of hope that James and Tonya would be okay, though I didn't like Raymond's use of the word "bodies" when he referred to them.

I wasn't sure about *me* as I watched Raymond virtually drooling in anticipation. Henry did not back up, to his credit. He stood his ground beside me, despite Raymond's growl of warning asserting his dominance.

"She is mine. I will not have you go too far and damage her. I will stop you if need be. *That* is *my* right." His voice was firm.

Raymond flicked his eyes in annoyance at Henry, the only sign he'd heard before he closed the gap between us with a last floating step. His pale hands clamped onto my shoulders, locking me in place and holding me tight, the large mouth gaped and huge fangs flashed in the light. Reflexively I gagged when his eyes rolled back in his head and his face slammed down on my chest, his fangs went into the top of my left breast directly over my heart.

The pain burned intense despite Henry's efforts to numb my mind. I struggled not to scream and give the monster the satisfaction of knowing how badly it hurt. He did not just drink, Raymond tore at my flesh like an animal his long fangs ripping into my breast. I felt each violent rake and pull, every suck of my blood felt as though it would pull my heart through my chest. My body was on fire, his bite igniting every pain synapse in my body and I couldn't help but gasp as I choked back the screams, at one point I tasted blood. The burning began to fade as he continued to drink and mercifully, I finally passed out.

Ch. 16

I regained consciousness on a bed in a room I didn't recognize. Managing to open one eye a crack, I saw Henry nearby with his back to me as he worked on something out of my sight. I cried out when I tried to sit up.

"Claire, drink that." He pointed to a glass sitting on the table beside me. "It will help you recover more quickly." Walking to my bedside, he crossed through the faint sunlight trickling in the dark room via the small square windows and I saw blood on his shirt. A lot of blood. Crossing his arms over his chest, he stared down at me. "They are all right now. We were only just in time."

Feeling the relief flood through me I exhaled audibly, relaxing into my pillow before trying to sit up again. Frowning, I found that my body wouldn't listen. Looking up at Henry in confusion, I attempted to make sense of it.

"You will have to move slowly, Raymond nearly drained you." Henry explained the reason for my weakness. "Once he was on you he sensed your power and was greedy. I had to call upon his honor to get him off of you." Seeing my dubiousness, Henry laughed harshly. "Yes Claire, even the worst of us can hold his honor in high regard. After he released you I carried you out to the car. James and Tonya were already inside and we came here. I made certain we were not followed." He pointed at my bandages. "You will have a rather nasty scar, he was violent in his feeding." I shuddered and was glad for my empty stomach, remembering the feeling of him chewing on my flesh.

I turned my attention to my surroundings, afraid to ask the single most important question in my mind and the one Henry seemed to be avoiding.

It was a small rustic cottage. I couldn't see out any of the windows from my position, but from the sounds of the birds coming in through the windows, I was willing to bet we were in the country. The question was which one? How far had Henry driven last night?

In answer to my silent query, Henry waved a hand at the window nearby. "We are in Austria. This cottage belongs to an old friend whom I can trust. Everyone should rest for another day and we can return home. Christmas Eve is tomorrow which will make flying difficult, but I will see what I can do to get us home."

"Christmas Eve is *tomorrow*? How long was I out?" Again I struggled to sit up. My chest felt like there was someone sitting on it and I was so weak, willpower had nothing to do with it, I had nothing left. I raised my head and searched the room, no longer able to wait for Henry to tell me. "Where is he, Henry?"

He didn't answer me directly, instead coming over and helping me sit up. Supporting my back, Henry pointed to the twin bed across the room against the wooden wall. I felt my world tip as I recognized James' prone figure lying on a bed not ten feet away covered to the waist with a red, green and brown patchwork quilt. What I could see of his skin was white as porcelain, virtually glowing in the low light. In the middle of his bare chest was a large dark spot.

"Henry, what is that on his chest?" Henry didn't answer me and I continued to strain my eyes to see. I gasped. It was a hole in his chest. Finding strength where I had none, I threw my legs over the side of the bed and stood. My head spun as I forced one leg forward at a time, rushing to him before they gave out and I collapsed beside his bed.

I took his cool hand in mine as I surveyed the damage done to his beautiful body and face. My fist could easily have fit in the hole in his chest, which was already healing. I could hardly imagine how large it had been originally. The white of the knitting bones and pale purple of the muscles were visible through the hole. James' entire body was riddled with gashes and claw marks in various stages of healing. I was guessing it to be the work of the wolves. There were a few especially deep bite marks at his neck and stomach.

I wasn't aware I was crying until Henry came up behind me and took hold of my shoulders directing me back to bed. Shrugging him off and wiping my eyes I asked in a hoarse whisper, "What did they do to him?"

His normally placid voice was tight with anger. "They used a wooden stake through the chest to paralyze him. If it had been silver, he would be dead. The stake kept him conscious while Raymond and his pack did this." Henry gingerly touched a particularly deep gash on his friend's shoulder.

"Why?" I whispered, holding James' hand.

Henry growled, frustrated. "I don't know. He hasn't awakened yet for me to question him and Tonya was unable to hear James' interrogation. She's gone out for the supplies you both need to help you to heal more expediently. I will not feel safe until we return home to America."

Tonya, I had completely forgotten about her. "Is she okay?" I asked, embarrassed by my singular focus.

His tone was decidedly lighter, a good sign. "Yes, she was not of interest to them. She will only have a scar from the collar they used to immobilize her. They did not punish her as they did James." I looked up, surprised. "Yes, silver will cause a scar to a were as well as a vampire. If not removed in time it eats through the skin, eventually entering the blood stream and causing death."

The thought of such a torturous end was awful. I couldn't fathom what kind of animal would do such a thing. "Do you know what happened to Ursa or anything about the new vampire they were helping?"

"I am still waiting on the newly turned's identity." Henry leaned down and pried up an eyelid, checking James' status. "Ursa is gone. Raymond's soldiers made an example of her. I am certain he was intending to do the same with James." Leaning back, he set his jaw grimly. "He is looking to send a message to the Court and other vampires. It is time to pick a side."

Realizing how close I had come to losing him, I leaned forward and kissed James' bloodless lips. It sickened me to think of what he'd endured unable to defend himself from that madman. It didn't matter that he was immortal and I was the more fragile being. I couldn't help feel protective of him seeing him lying there so close to death.

Just then, the front door opened and I squeaked before I saw Tonya's golden hair. She was wrapped in a long, faded, green wool coat someone must have dug out of a closet twenty years ago and was partially obstructed by the large brown bag in her hands. My eyes went to her throat, seared red and blistered in a thick line. Dragging my eyes back up to her face, I saw her staring at me, a curious look on her face.

Given the fact that our relationship to that point had been shaky I wasn't sure how to read her affronted expression, nor did I want her to think I was gawking and make her uncomfortable. Tonya handled the awkwardness by ducking her head in an unusual display of unease and hurried inside to set her bag down on the table beside the door.

Henry was next to her at once, resting his hand on her shoulder. A quiet word passed between them and I saw Tonya close her eyes. Her eyelashes sparkled with tears as she turned away, making her way to a hallway on the other side of our little great room, going to what had to be the back of the house and out of sight.

"Claire, I need your help." Henry called to me while he unpacked the bag. The smaller bags he was extracting were clear and I could tell from the red color what was inside them.

Thinking of blood I studied my chest, fingers gently probing. "Henry, why am I not bleeding?" After the fact, I figured by getting up like that I would have torn my wound back open. My bandages were pristine white.

"Your wound has nearly closed." He watched my eyes widen and mouth fall open. "Your healing has been rapid. It appears your marks have saved your life once again. Your blood loss was too much for a normal human to have endured, and by rights you should be dead."

Changing the subject, I looked down at the table full of supplies Henry was in the process of unpacking, mildly curious how they had found access on such short notice. "There's so much blood here. I thought we were leaving tomorrow." I looked up at his face, carefully avoiding his eyes. Never would I be able to look him in the eye again.

He continued without pause and arranged the blood on the table in numerous short stacks. "James will need most of this to recover and heal from his wounds rapidly enough for us to leave. Some is for me. It will make me strong enough to protect us all if it comes to that. Put these in the cooler in the corner." He pushed a larger stack toward me, indicating where with a movement of his chin. A smaller stack remained in front of Henry. "I will prepare more for him now, it's been hours since we ran out."

I wheeled around to return to James' bedside, only I turned too fast and my head spun. His hands caught me under my arms before I hit the floor.

"Sorry Henry." I forced an awkward laugh as I attempted to adjust myself to time and place. Stumbling across the wood floor rolling beneath me I deposited my bags in the cooler and, shutting the lid, sat on top of it panting and mildly nauseous.

Easily seeing my imbalance, Henry picked me up and carried me efficiently over to set me down on a rocking chair near the bed where I had awakened. He proceeded to pick me up chair and all, and carry me over to James' bedside.

"Why don't you keep him company, but be careful not to get too close," he cautioned sternly.

Exhaustion set in as I looked over the mutilated body of my lover and considered Tonya's suffering. In my own weakened state from the blood loss and probably no small amount of shock, my mind walled itself off for protection. I rested my head on my arm and fell asleep.

Ch. 17

I must have slept for quite a while. When I awoke, the filtered sun was gone from the windows and only two lamps were on in our room. One at his bedside cast James in an amber glow, making his pale flesh appear nearly human. I sat up to check on him, still lying unmoving and unbreathing, looking entirely dead. His chest remained uncovered and appeared to be healing. The hole was now much smaller, maybe the diameter of a golf ball. It was amazing how quickly he could heal if given enough blood.

I brought my hand to my chest feeling the bandage there, thinking of my own rapid healing. I was curious if that exhausted any of James' resources, or if that ability was now my own and no longer tied to our connection. My line of thought brought me for the first time to really consider being a vampire, I was nearly there anyway. Going the rest of the way to complete the process would make me stronger and maybe even give us both back our autonomy.

I was startled at the ease with which the idea took hold of me. I hadn't consciously thought of choosing to turn before. Thus far, I'd fought against having the choice taken away from me by the bond James and I shared. My reluctance had been tied to the lack of free will, not necessarily the end result. And now, sitting here and staring at James with the fear of being without him fresh in my mind, it was easy to imagine turning so that I could be with him forever.

While I was considering asking James what he thought about my becoming an immortal, I saw him stir. His arm next to me twitched on the bed and I reached out to take his hand. It was weak as it curved around mine, making me wish for just that second we had the option of having James become human instead of the other way around. It didn't matter as long as I had him. Heart full, I leaned across him to kiss his forehead. In the next moment I felt his hand turn to steel, taking mine and twisting my arm behind my back so painfully I was locked against him, unable to move.

"James, no." I objected weakly, breathless with pain as I lay crushed against his chest, struggling to catch sight of his face. With a start, I saw that his eyes were still closed and it occurred to me he didn't know it was me.

He was operating on instinct. He was a hungry vampire with a warm blood filled human lying on top of him. My mind fought to make my body respond, but I was weak compared to him and powerless in his grip. My face was inches from his when I saw his mouth open and his fangs come out.

Thinking only of my own self-preservation, I swung my free hand and struck a glancing blow off of his jaw, trying to turn his head away from me.
Even half dead, James was too strong to fight. His own unencumbered hand came up and took my clenched fist, pulling my wrist to his mouth. Before I could say, "no" again, his fangs had pierced my flesh and he was sucking hard. For the second time in as many days, I was being used as an unwilling food source.

It was excruciating as I felt the life being torn out of me with each pull from his mouth. Raymond had been intentionally cruel, James had been pleasurable before; this was different from both. This was raw animal hunger and it was agonizing without any Glamour to help ease the searing burn.

The pain was one thing. I could have borne it were it not for the blood lust screaming in my ears and in my own throat as our bond blew wide open. We both were weak, unshielded and hungry for my blood. I craved it and at the same time wanted him to stop, yet also to taste the thrill of feeding through James' mark on me. A part of me, bent on survival, struggled to the surface as the rest of me was pulled under the spell of the blood lust. Summoning enough breath to utter a single word, I called for help before surrendering. "Henry."

A low curse came from somewhere behind me and I felt myself pulled freed and lifted off of James to be sat back in my chair. My wrist was still held in his iron grip as he continued to feed. Thankfully, Henry was stronger and disengaged my flesh from James' mouth without another sound. He took my newly released limb and instead of letting go, raised it to his own mouth. I felt the just ebbing panic swell fresh believing he was unable to control his own blood craving faced with a source so near.

Hyperventilating, I watched him put his mouth over my fresh bite yet instead of feeding he flicked his tongue over the puncture marks and I watched the blood instantaneously clot. I chanced a look in his eyes and although his face was smooth and calm, I saw that his eyes were black with hunger. Despite his age, he still felt the undeniable draw of my blood and I questioned my sanity for being here with them at all. There was no guarantee that they would always be able to fight the call of my human blood. That there would not be a slip and James would not bite and drain me in a moment of weakness was a huge gamble I was taking on a daily basis.

And now I realized that I might not even try to stop him. I might not have the energy or the autonomy to pull away next time. I watched Henry feed James as he would a sick child from a bag he'd magically produced from somewhere while I licked my wounds.

Ch. 18

Incredibly tired, strung out and arguably in shock, I stumbled back to my bed while Henry tended to James. I watched the goings on in the little cottage as a distant observer, disconnected from the majority of my senses since James had gained enough strength back to tighten the wall between us. The lack of a tether left my weaker psyche lost and floating as I listened to Tonya and Henry orchestrating our trip home on their phones.

During the night when James regained consciousness, I heard him say my name, though in my numb fog I couldn't get my answer to go from my brain to my mouth. Instead I kept silent and watched Henry stand at the edge of his bed while they spoke in low tones. Several times I caught James glancing over at me, his face stricken. After a few minutes he hung his head, growing very still as Henry continued to speak. The reason for his upset would not come readily to my addled mind, although I did feel sad for him.

James continued to drink cup after cup of blood, eventually getting up to help the others close up the cottage. Tonya was the one who helped me out of bed and brought me in the shower that afternoon before we had to leave. She cleaned me up, dressed me in my clothes fresh from the dryer, and directed me to the car.

I rode with my eyes open, staring blankly at the countryside on the way to the airport. Upon arrival I leaned heavily on Tonya, my legs had become leaden and were hard to move.

Tonya was my nurse for the duration of our trip. Only when we were on the plane did I sleep. Fitfully, I twitched and wriggled in my sleep until Tonya laid her hand upon my arm. Instantly I was wrapped in the warm cocoon of her shields, falling into a dreamless slumber for the remainder of the trip.

I did not wake again until I was home, alone in our bed the next morning.

My brain was somewhat clearer when I woke. I could feel the connection again though it was guarded heavily, keeping me from sensing James' mood. When I attempted to get out of bed to visit the restroom, I discovered that my strength had nearly returned as well. Groggy and tired, I took my time brushing my teeth and hair. Unprepared as I was to go downstairs and face James, I put it off as long as possible. I didn't know what to say, nor how to discuss what had happened. He hadn't been conscious. He had nearly died and his body was merely doing what it needed to do to survive, I reminded myself. And it hadn't been him that had scared me. It had been me.

Head still swimming and feeling like a coward, I finally could put it off no longer and, forcing myself forward, walked slowly down the stairs. In the kitchen I found him, his back was to me as he slowly chopped up a pineapple. The sweet smell met me at the door. He must have heard me upstairs and already had the kettle on while he made breakfast. Not knowing what to say or do, I went back out to sit at the table and wait.

I watched in silence as he brought out a tray with tea, an English muffin and pineapple. Without speaking beyond a faint thank you, I chewed my muffin while watching him drink his own breakfast. Surprisingly, even in light of recent events it didn't bother me to watch him eat. I was thinking about what that meant when he cleared his throat.

Lifting my eyes up to his, I saw that they were a deep blue and I wondered if he was still weak from his experience in Germany. When he spoke, his voice was thick with remorse and I knew his eyes reflected his guilt, not hunger.

"Claire, I cannot tell you how sorry I am for what happened. Henry told me what you did for us. How you," his voice was rough, "offered yourself to Raymond to save us." His eyes closed and he was silent for a time. I thought he was done and, when he continued, his eyes were still shut. "What I did to you was unforgivable, and for that I am truly sorry."

The memory of his feeding had faded yet at mention of it, I felt my gut wrenching reaction all over again. My heart thumped predictably and I set down my muffin.

"After breakfast I can take you either to campus or your parents' home. I will watch the house from a distance so that Jeannette and Doug remain blind to the situation. You will remain protected regardless of where you live."

His reference to "the situation" hit me like a slap upside the head. I had been so out of it I had lost sight of what the full extent of the "situation" was, the message Raymond had wanted to send with James and Ursa, or who the newly turned vampire with the ability had been.

Swallowing, I found my voice and diverted the conversation to something I *could* talk about. "Henry explained how you work with Ursa." I hated how cold I sounded and that it matched his expression. "Did you meet the new vampire before Raymond came?" There was a tremor in my voice when I spoke the monster's name.

James flinched as well while his expression remained unaffected. "Ursa had begun working with her. She was a young girl, about fifteen years old, her name is Annika. She had been living on the streets in Amsterdam when Gaston found her and turned her. Bradley lost his vampire with true sensitivities to others' gifts when I killed Gina and Gaston apparently has a hint of the gift himself. That's why Bradley is sending *him* out to seek those suited to their needs. He's building an army." He traced the lid of his cup preferring to keep his eyes down. "Annika was able to get away from Gaston after he turned her; I would love to have seen that."

106

He couldn't help but smile briefly before growing sober again. "She was discovered by one of ours after she attacked a night watchman at the canal. The vampire knew to bring her to Ursa and when she felt the child's gift, she called me. It seems that Annika can manipulate humans to give her things. She utilized her gift while on the street to fill her stomach and find somewhere to sleep each night. She never thought of it as a talent, only that she was lucky to be one of the few on the street to be safe and not starving. Now she knows differently.

Ursa thought the girl could use a mentor. She had lined up an older vampire in Annika's familiar city, Amsterdam, to find someone who could foster her after we helped her get started. *Someone* told Gaston and he told Raymond. He knew he couldn't take us himself and he wanted us out of the way. He knew Raymond didn't like vampires with special abilities." James shrugged. "With us so close to his home he was able to retaliate using all of his thugs."

Confused, I leaned in frowning. "Why would he care about any of that? He's so old and scary he doesn't need to worry about a threat from anyone else."

James dipped his chin, "He doesn't worry that we're a threat, he believes we are an abomination. Raymond, just like any of us, was shaped by the time he was born in. He sees having special abilities as witchcraft. Against the natural order."

"And that's why he was going to kill you both? Because you were helping this poor girl get a handle on her ability?" I asked, incredulous.

"Raymond believes all vampires with abilities should be 'put down'. He has hated my training and Ursa's encouragement for as long as we have been doing this. For all their power, the Court has been unable to stop him from exacting his vengeance on those like us when the mood strikes, although he's never been so bold as this. The Court *must* answer now. They have no choice."

"How long have you been doing this?" My curiosity peaked at his mention of a history with Raymond. "Henry said you have been doing it since you were turned. Is that true?"

"Yes, I've been working with Ursa and the newly turned since she finished my training. She had been able to work with me to a point, but my abilities were much more in line with teaching those with mental abilities than her own talent. We decided I would take over that aspect of training, allowing us to work in tandem. We usually kept very quiet about our work. We did not want to draw the ire of Raymond or the others who share his opinions. The Court encouraged us only in private, sending us out with no formal notice, only on call now and again. This time though, Gaston told Raymond that we were training the girl to help the *humans* when war breaks out. That we had our own army of specially trained soldiers. Raymond knows that we are friendly to humans and is paranoid. It was easy to deduce what he would do."

Covering my mouth, I asked in a whisper, "What happened?" I wasn't sure I wanted to know.

His eyes narrowed, the first hint of emotion he'd shown. Inside my head I felt a flicker of heat coming from him. "We had been working together all night and Annika had gone up to her room to prepare for the sunrise. Ursa and I were in the study when they came. They came through the window where I was standing, I did not have time to react before I was staked." His hand drifted to his chest remembering the hole there.

The wall between us came down. He couldn't hold me out of his mind and I felt how he blamed himself for his failure to protect them both.

"One of the wolves staked her, they used silver. She was unable to move or speak while she burned to death. Tonya had been elsewhere in the house, coming when she heard the windows shatter. The bigger of the two vampires he sent struck her in the face, knocking her unconscious. If she were human, he would have snapped her neck with the blow. When she was down he put a collar of silver on her rendering her helpless. They knew how many of us there were, that there was a were among us. Only the members of the Court knew that I would be there, or that Tonya would be with me. They would have kept that information quiet. Someone close to us betrayed us to Gaston."

James' voice remained hollow. "Annika must have slipped away in the commotion. We have people searching for her as does the Court, but so does Gaston and I am concerned whoever it was that betrayed us will get to her before we do. If *he* finds her first, I fear for her. She will be used much like they have used the boy." He wiped a hand over his face.

The spell broken, I felt him retreat once more behind his renewed barriers.

"No one has seen the boy, we don't even know if he still lives or if they've destroyed him by now."

I didn't know what to say, I felt impotent. What chance did I have if a vampire and were together were unable to stop them? "Do you think they'll come after you?"

Shaking his head, James stared into his mug. "Raymond does not leave his home territory, he will not follow. But Gaston and Bradley will continue to come for us as long as they perceive us as a threat to their plans for war."

An idea came to mind, a way that I could help. "What if instead of wasting our energy searching for them we drew them out? We can use me as bait, they can't resist that." His eyes flew to mine flashing with alarm.

"No!" James came fully back to life and shouted as he stood, sending his chair flying backward. "It's impossible, there is no guarantee that I could stop them. They could use you; they could kill you, Claire."

Swallowing the fear I felt as he put a voice to my own worries, I willed myself to be strong. Taking a deep breath I forced myself to be calm and make him listen to me. "I will not just stand by and watch them kill any of you while it is in my power to stop them."

"How do you think *you* can stop them? What makes you so certain they would not kill you on the spot?" He was still angry, but at least he had stopped shouting. "Look what happened to you in Germany. If Henry hadn't been there you would be dead."

"They want humans with abilities, right? They know I have one and, judging from Raymond's reaction, it's a good one, too." Hearing no objection I went on. "I could give them a taste. If I can get in front of Gaston, he won't be able to refuse." The idea made me shudder as I thought of the short, hairy vampire touching me.

"But Claire, they know you are with me." Uncertainty flickered in his features.

"James, you went to your ex-girlfriend's house and left me behind. It would be pretty easy to convince *anyone* that I was jealous." Less certain I added, "I was, you know."

"But that's over, isn't it?" The thinly veiled hurt I heard in his voice pained me. "You are afraid of me now."

I had been shutting out what had happened in Austria, unable to deal with it. Yet now that decisions were upon us, my mind was clear. My response was visceral, coming from my very core.

"No." I stood to face him on the same level. He refused to look at me. Feeling he was turning away from me for a second time, I felt my tension escalating. Memory of his previous withdrawal fresh in my mind brought my anxiety rocketing to the surface.

"James I was scared when you bit me," I shook my head, "but that wasn't the problem. *You* weren't the one drinking, *I* was. *I* wanted my blood no matter the cost. I was willing to let you kill me I wanted it so badly." His lips were pulled tight enough I could see the beginnings of his fangs, still I pushed on, needing him to understand. "Since then, I have been trying not to think about it, but I can't. My attachment, my bond, everything we are to each other won't let me shut you out. It killed me when you pulled away from me in Austria." My cheeks felt wet as I finished. "James you're a part of me I can't be without, I don't *want* to be without. Good *and* bad, I'll take it all if that's what it takes to be with you."

In the entirety of my life I had never been as honest with anyone as I had been with him. The exposure of my innermost feelings combined with my fluctuating nature had me shaking where I stood. I put a hand on the table edge to steady myself for the sake of my wobbling knees. It was just like Henry had noticed the night of the party. I was in a hypersensitive state, constantly on edge, and it was only getting worse. Most likely the bond was moving me further toward becoming a vampire and my ability was reacting accordingly. So be it. I could endure anything as long as I had him; even becoming a vampire.

It felt like forever that we stood there facing each other without making eye contact, neither one of us speaking or moving. My eyes were trained on the fingers keeping me upright, following the pattern of blood flow under the surface of my skin as it danced between pink and white with the shifting of my weight against it. If he looked at me I didn't know it, I was too self-conscious to even sneak a peek at him to see how he was taking my confession.

Movement out of the corner of my eye caught my attention. I watched him round the table and was ready to receive him when he wrapped his arms around me, turning me carefully so that I could return the embrace. Feeling me return the gesture, he tightened his hold only barely and kissed the top of my head before letting me go. His lukewarm reception burned after my soulful outpouring. Horribly embarrassed, I let my arms go limp, falling back to my side, and tried to step around him intent upon leaving the room.

Except as I took a step to leave I felt the firm flesh of his hand touch the top of my arm. Stopping, I waited and listened to my foolish heart flutter with wasted hope. "What?" I asked thickly.

"I want to give you something."

"Why?" My hand went to my necklace, the last gift he had given me. It had been a constant reminder of our happiest time together. The last thing I wanted was a gift to remind me of what could very well be the beginning of the end.

"Because I've been trying to think of the best time to give it to you and I think that now is that time."

Finding my gaze drawn to his, needing to see his heart in the only way he couldn't hide, I let my eyes climb up to search his. They were dark. I saw that much before he turned them down, trying to keep them from me. He'd closed me out of his head as well. Thrown off balance, once again adrift, I didn't know what to expect.

"Claire," he reached out and took my hand in one of his. I let him, uncertain what else to do. "I have taken so much from you and given you so little in return. I have no right to ask any more of you and yet I can't stop myself." James lifted his eyes allowing me a look into his thoughts. "My existence has been a lonely one with nothing but the promise of a lonely decline into insanity to look forward to until I met you. You have saved me from a bleak fate and you have given back my joy." His other hand had slid into his pocket and came out holding a small black velvet bag. "Claire I would like the opportunity to do the same for you. Will you marry me?"

Gaping stupidly, I raised a hand to cover my mouth. Beyond our bond, beyond the Court's requirements for secrecy, James was choosing a life with me. Everything we had been through together raced through my mind. Memories reminded me of a life with him so far being dangerous, terrifying and uncertain.

And I also remembered the way I felt the first time I touched him and the peace he had helped me find in my heart. My memories flashed by showing me our intimate times together, how he made me laugh and danced with me for no reason at all in the kitchen. James taught me to protect myself and he liked taking care of me whether I needed it or not. Having him in my life had made it infinitely better, danger, strangeness and all. That he didn't think he'd added anything to my life was laughable. If he'd asked, I would have argued that it was *he* who was being cheated.

There was never a question what my answer would be. It didn't matter our differences or complications. We were bonded, in every sense. Our fates were joined and had been decided from the start.

My cheeks were wet again and I couldn't find my voice. I took my hand from his and closed the short distance between us throwing my arms around his neck and pulling his face to my own kissing him enthusiastically.

"Is that a yes?" He pulled back, smiling broadly.

"Yes," I breathed as I reclaimed his mouth.

Ch. 19

We lay on the couch wrapped in a blanket. My head lay on James' chest and I was tracing shapes on his stomach, enjoying the feel of him against my body and knowing now it would be like this for the rest of my life.

"Did you want to see your ring?" His voice broke into my quiet thoughts.

The corners of his eyes crinkled as he smiled at me. It was hard to believe he wasn't human but for the silence of his lungs and chest to remind me. "I guess I should have looked, huh?"

He chuckled and reached behind his head taking it from the side table at the head of the couch where he must have placed the bag when we were celebrating our engagement. Producing it, he set it on his stomach in front of my hand and shook out its contents.

"It's perfect." I reached out to touch it. The ring was a simple design. The center stone was round cut and stunning in its clarity. The band was unique; different from any I had seen with intricate patterns cut into it. The effect was one of timeless elegance. "I've never seen this pattern, where did you find it?"

There was pride in his voice as he slipped it onto my finger where we both admired it. "I had it made. That is an old Celtic design my mother had on her own ring. It's meant to bless the wearer with happiness and long life."

I was touched to find him linking our lives to his long passed mother. I knew she had meant so much to him, wanting her to be a part of us was absolutely human. "What was her name? Tell me about her."

His brows drew together as he thought back over a century and a half to his human childhood. "Her name was Sophia. She was small like you, even before she got sick. She was little but she was always the strong one. It was her strength that kept our family together." James ran a hand over my arm, the touch seeming to bring him comfort. "I was the youngest and the least help in the fields so I was the one who cared for her when she was too sick to do things for herself anymore. She would sit at the table telling me what to do while I was her hands in the kitchen. When she was gone my father gave up. At least he was able to apprentice all of us out before he lost the farm." Touching the design on the ring he went on, "You remind me of her. I think you two would have liked each other."

"She sounds like she was hard to forget."
He nodded, "She is one of the few things I still remember after all this time."

Unable to resist, I had to ask him. "Making a ring must take some time. When did you know?"

"I started it after we came home from the hospital this fall."

Jerking my face up to his I stared, stunned. "You've been planning this all this time? Why did you decide now was the right time, because of the holiday?"

He shook his head. "No, because I was reminded of how much you mean to me. And if you would still have me," he paused, "after everything, I wanted to make sure you knew that you are my choice as well."

"Well," I tried to joke, "I hope that all of our big decisions aren't going to be brought on by me almost getting killed."

James growled and slid his hand from its perch on my hip up my body. One long cool finger traced the fresh pink scar on my chest. It was the size of a large gumball, the scraping from Raymond's fangs had produced a sunburst effect. James' hand rested on the smooth skin and he leaned his head down to kiss it. I felt his tension in the tightening of his skin and muscles, the vampire stirred within him.

"Claire, I have never wanted to kill anyone in my life more than I want to kill Raymond for what he did."

The thought of him facing Raymond in a fight sent spasms of fear coursing through my body. "No! You can't go back there." I objected, my happiness evaporating around me.

His eyes closed when he spoke. "As much as I want to destroy him, I cannot. He is too strong and his army of wolves too great. Raymond has chosen his soldiers carefully and trained them for over a thousand years, I wouldn't stand a chance against him. All I can do is keep you away from him. That is your only protection now that he has tasted your power. We can never go back there."

The adrenaline slowed its pace in my veins. "Henry mentioned that too, what do you mean now that he has 'tasted my power'?"

James' hand lightly brushed my cheek, pushing my dark hair back behind my ear while he watched the course of his fingers against my skin. "You know you have your own power Love, it isn't all from me. I tasted it when I fed from you." I averted my eyes, awkward. "Those with abilities taste of them, like kissing someone after they eat ice cream. You can taste it, can you not?" Silently I nodded, bringing my face back to his. "Your ability has a unique flavor and the marks amplify power. It is intoxicating; I must admit it was hard to stop when you allowed me to taste you."

The way he spoke of *that* time, it was so intimate I couldn't help but be embarrassed. I remembered him biting the inside of my thigh with a blush. It *was* intimate, I guess. "How did you stop yourself if it was intoxicating?"

117

"Would you rather I had continued?" he asked, bemused.

"No, of course not. I'm just curious how you had the control to only take a small amount. Now that I've felt what it's like when you feed, I realize how hard it is for you to make yourself stop." I felt a pang bringing up the unfortunate incident so fresh in our memories and I saw the pain cross his features before he masked it.

"Yes, it is a very strong urge and you felt it at its worst when I was desperate. But more than that, I love you and have a bond to you as well as having had an oath to protect you at the time. It physically pains me to have you in danger. I would like to *think* that I would have stopped the second time but am glad Henry was there. I would not have wanted to trust my senses the state I was in."

We were lost in our own thoughts for a few moments then I swore suddenly, covering my face with my hands. "It's Christmas Eve and my parents are coming for dinner tomorrow. What are we going to tell them?" I was all of a sudden panicked about their response to our engagement. As far as they knew, James and I were just dating and had only been together a few months. They couldn't possibly understand our relationship. This would seem way too fast for them.

James shrugged coolly. "If you would like to take the ring off and wait to tell them that's fine with me."

I checked his blue eyes, confused. "It wouldn't offend you if I took off your ring?"

"No," he ran his hand over my shoulder. "We are just as engaged if your ring falls down the sink as if you have it on your hand, are we not? It is only a symbol." Glancing at the clock, James rubbed my arm. "We should get up soon. The Andrews clan and Henry are coming by to discuss some things."

Hearing mention of the clan brought thoughts of Stephen to the forefront of my mind. I hadn't even spoken to him since the night of the party. Thinking about the impending confrontation with him I groaned.

"What, don't you want to see everyone? It will give you a chance to show off your ring. Isn't that what women do?" he teased.

"James, I can't wait to announce our engagement." I put my hand to his cheek. "What I don't want is to see Stephen."

"What happened? You two have been best friends since I met you." He wriggled a pinched brow teasingly. "I even thought you were an item when I first saw you two together."

"You know he doesn't like girls."

"I know that, but sometimes the right person isn't in the right body and unusual matches happen. Look at me. I'm in the wrong body for you." His voice had taken on a sullen tone.

"Are you kidding? I can't imagine a better body." I kissed his chest for emphasis.

He frowned at me, far too serious for my mood. "You know that isn't what I mean."

"James Thomas," I raised my head to glare down at him severely. "You are more perfect for me *because* of what you are. I wouldn't have been able to be with anyone *but* you because of your abilities. Plus, if it wasn't for your being different I would be dead right now." He bristled at that. "Stephen was determined to bring me in and train me, sure that I would go nuts without some guidance. I hate to admit I was pretty well there already. The world I live in now is the one I choose and you are the man I *choose* to share it with. I won't hear any more negative commentary from you about my choices."

Shock at my outburst was replaced by a smile. "Claire, I love you." Cool arms drew me back to him and held me close.

My hands started tracing lower on his stomach, Stephen forgotten for the moment. "How much time did you say we had again?"

He groaned and grabbed my hand. "Sadly, not enough. Now behave and go get in the shower. They'll be here very soon."

Grumbling, I extricated myself from his arms and wrapped the blanket around my body under my arms. Sashaying as temptingly as possible, I made my way up the stairs, smiling when I heard him sigh.

Ch. 20

Troy arrived first. He and Tara were having a minor spat on the porch when James let them in.

"What happened?" James asked the "siblings" when they stopped long enough to walk inside.

Tara answered hotly. "Apparently after decades of protecting it, our secret is now no longer of any concern. Humans have proven over how many of our lifetimes that they cannot handle what we are." She shot a look at me, "No offense, Claire."

"None taken."

"Who are you thinking of telling about yourself, Troy?" James asked innocently. I felt his amusement tickle in my head and had to bite my lip to keep from smiling. We both knew who Troy meant.

Troy confirmed it, "Heidi." He raised his voice over Tara's exasperated sigh. "She is a strong woman and I believe she could handle it." Lowering his nose at Tara, he continued in a pointed tone. "It's not something I plan on sharing immediately, I merely commented that I could see telling her *if* things continue to progress."

James aimed his comment at Tara as well. "That seems reasonable to me. Nothing is being decided today so you have plenty of time to be certain of your choice before making it final." That quelled their argument for the moment, although I had the image of a tail twitching as Tara continued to stew.

Tonya and Henry arrived together. Oddly enough it didn't surprise me. They had been pretty close lately. I wondered in passing if anything had happened in Austria or since, not that I'd ever ask. Even with my limited social skills I wouldn't be so bold as to ask such a personal question of those two. I would hate to make *one* of them angry, never mind both.

Stephen was last to arrive. I had been standing facing the front window and saw him get out of the passenger side of a red car, waving as it drove off. I opened the door as he came striding up the walk. Being the closest, it made sense. James shot a warning straight into my brain that made me stutter step when my hand touched the knob and I rolled my eyes, twisting my neck to give him a look. "It's Stephen, I watched him walk up. I'm fine."

I heard a choked snort from the other room as someone found humor in my disobedience. Stephen walked in before any more could be said.

"Hey." I looked at his face, his hair holding my eyes as he removed his hat.

His moppy hair had been cut short. He looked years older and it wasn't just the hair. He stood straighter and let more of what I would say was his animal's power lend him a hard edge. He'd gone from a gentle kid to Neo-Nazi overnight.

"Hey Claire, do you like it? Brian wanted to see my face," he ran his hand over his hair grinning. There was a passing glimpse of my friend in the temporary softening of his features, then he was gone.

The reminder of why I was angry with him came back. "Brian? You mean the guy from the other night?" I couldn't resist the urge to goad him. "Your toy *this* week?"

He had breezed airily in past me, whipping around at my comment, pink flooding his tanned face and ears as he took a few steps toward me. A flare in my mind came from nearby, warning that even Stephen wouldn't be allowed trespass much further. I sent back an attempt to soothe James, Stephen wouldn't hurt me.

"What's that supposed to mean?" he seethed, hackles up at once. "I told you I don't *play* with people."

"Then what did I see the other night? One minute he's irritated with you and then you look at him." I snapped my fingers. "His mood flips like a switch." I was aware that we had drawn everyone's attention now but it was pointless to whisper; they could all hear it anyway.

"Claire, what the hell are you talking about? I told you a long time ago I don't do that to people unless it's absolutely necessary." His hazel eyes were hard and narrowed. "I did see you shooting me a death stare at the party and I wasn't sure why. Brian and I were having such a good time I didn't feel like ruining it by getting into it with you. I figured you were having another one of your 'episodes'."

"What do you mean by that?" I thought, not for the first time, about how they must all be seeing me change with the marks. Did they think they'd wasted their time and energy recruiting me now that I'd gone crazy? Or was Stephen really telling the truth about his innocence?

Stephen furious was a new experience for me. Taking another step and bringing the distance between us to virtually nothing, I felt a ripple of trepidation. James flared again and I held out a hand low to warn him to let me handle this. He backed off, though I could feel his displeasure.

"Claire, we've all been nothing but patient with you and I don't think I'm out of line in telling you it's getting old. I for one am getting tired of having to worry about how you're going to react to something because you can't handle this." He waved a hand, shooting a glare over my shoulder. "Not that you're not spending enough time trying to figure it out." He added sarcastically.

His retort struck a nerve. I felt a similar reaction rising in my head where our bond resided. I had felt like I was neglecting the other parts of my life in favor of spending time with James. But I thought that I had been helping out more and had proven my worth in our last few run ins with the bad guys. James clearly thought so as well, he was wrestling with his own outrage at the aspersion. I bit my tongue so hard I tasted blood. Instead of saying anything and further damaging the only sort of normal friendship I'd ever had, I closed my mouth tight and held up my left hand between us, stepping back to signal that I was done arguing.

"Claire, is that what I think it is?" Tara called out. Her timing couldn't have been better.

Without meaning to, I had flashed my ring when I held up my hand, effectively shifting the focus of the room from Stephen to James. I could see the effect my news I'd wanted to share under far more happy circumstances had on Stephen as he glared at me and stalked out of the room.

The girls were happy for us, full of hugs and holding my hand to see the ring. That Tonya kept her eyes on me when she put her arms around James wasn't lost on me. Fortunately James had fed while I'd been in the shower and I kept myself under control. Troy shook James' hand and Henry gave him a nod. The cats were affectionate, but vampires as a rule were not.

Even amidst the congratulations it was hard to be completely happy, I felt Stephen's disappointment acutely. James caught my eye and smiled warmly at me, guessing the direction of my thoughts either from my expression or what he could surely feel. I forced a smile.

After the well wishing had gone around, Henry gave a quiet cough. With all the super hearing in the room, that was enough to bring everyone's attention back to the reason for our being here. Stephen came back from the kitchen to hover behind the couch where Tonya and Troy sat. Henry stood next to the chair where Tara sat and I chose to sit on the bottom stair behind everyone so that I could hear yet not have to see anyone. I was not used to being the center of attention and between my fight with Stephen and my engagement to James, I'd had too much already, making me horribly uncomfortable.

James had taken up a position leaning easily against the banister a few feet from me. I had the distinct impression that he was standing guard. Given my mood I was reassured instead of annoyed.

When everyone was situated, Henry began filling us all in. "The Court is very angry about what happened in Germany. Raymond has denied any allegiance to Bradley or his cause leaving him unpunishable. On the up side, his return to isolation has removed him from our list of enemies provided we maintain our distance. We can count ourselves lucky, he would have been a formidable foe for us."

I watched James' back stiffen and felt my own stomach knot. Tonya was hidden from my sight by the high couch back. I watched Henry's features soften, even managing a rare reassuring smile for her.

"As you know, they are trying to avoid an all out war. Each time vampires and humans meet in battle, it ends badly for everyone. And now, with the humans' technology and weapons of this century, the damage could be tenfold. The Court wishes to step in and help us in our cause to stop Bradley's movement toward a war between the races. His actions have become too bold; his efforts to collect and use humans are causing some authorities in the human governments to take notice at the corresponding rise in criminal activity. The Court wishes to quell this revolt now, before the situation becomes irreversible."

Henry met James' eyes. "I spoke with Miranda. She suggests postponing your trip until this is settled." He turned his steady gaze back to those around him. "They are sending a Guard to assist us in our search for the enemy."

I didn't know what that meant but was able to assume it was not good given everyone's reactions. The cats collectively sucked in a sharp breath and I felt James' apprehension before he shut me out. Turning his head he explained softly over his shoulder, "A Guard is a team of vampires sent out to investigate and protect the Court's interests."

Troy spoke first voicing his suspicion. "Henry, do you really believe they are *assisting* us, or do you think they have an ulterior motive?" The clan was tied to Henry and trusted James; it didn't sound like that carried over to the rest of the vampire society. From what I had seen, that seemed like a safe position.

"Do you know who they are sending?" Tara asked, looking worried.

Henry shook his head. "All I was told was that they would send a Guard qualified to handle our unique situation. That would lead me to believe that they are all informed we have non-vampires in our numbers. As we discussed," he glanced at Troy, "we suspect that we have a traitor among us. It is the only explanation for how Ursa and James were betrayed. We must be extra cautious now. Whoever our traitor is, he is close to one of us. Aside from those in this room and the Court itself, none were told of James' trip or Ursa's young charge. I must remind you not to speak to anyone about what we discuss in confidence. Is that understood?"

Murmurs of agreement went around the room. Henry regarded each person, searching for signs of a traitor, finding nothing.

"When will the guard be arriving? Where will they stay?" James wanted to know.

"They will be arriving after the New Year and will stay with me. I've explained that I can best handle their needs." He leveled a meaningful gaze at James. "I prefer to keep them close and I think it best to limit their interaction with anyone else."

"Sounds like we're being pushed out," Stephen spoke sullenly from his position behind the couch.

Interestingly, instead of arguing, James agreed. "That *is* most likely what they have planned. They will investigate our ranks first to assess our progress and plans as well as our strengths. From there, I would imagine they will advise the Court and we will be informed of our new directives."

"Doesn't that bother you that they can just step in and take over? This is *our* fight." Stephen had turned, facing James, eyes ablaze with his indignation. "It's *our* blood that has been spilled. We have the right to avenge ourselves."

I was having trouble recognizing my friend. Maybe it was the combined strain of the months of being constantly on guard and the recent attacks, but Stephen seemed unusually quick to violence, a far cry from my cavalier and fun loving friend. Something was wrong and here I was pushing him away instead of offering to listen like a friend should. I vowed to make things right with him, to give him an ear instead of being absorbed in my own world all the time. He was right to be fed up with my selfishness; I wasn't the only one going through changes right now.

James shrugged, unaffected by Stephen's accusations. "We were able to hold our own and fight Bradley to a standstill when he had only a small force at his command. He has been eluding us for months and currying favor with powerful vampires all over the world. If he has even a fraction of the numbers I have heard rumor of, we do not have the resources we need to defeat him ourselves. Not anymore. The Court has been handling revolts like Bradley's for centuries. Although I will not trust those they send, I trust that the Court will do all they can to neutralize the threat."

"James, what do you mean you can't trust those they send? Do you think this Guard intends to harm us?" I felt my stomach flutter nervously.

He spoke honestly, not sparing my feelings. "You must remember their goal is to stop a highly visible all out war between our races. If they must sacrifice a few or all of us to do so, they will. Their soldiers will be limited to assisting only where it coincides with their interests; they will not be here to help us in the way you might think of help. We must keep our own concerns private and, it will depend on who they send, if we can manage even that."

James' words effectively silenced everyone in the room and sent a wave of cold, sickening fear all the way down to my toes. "That sucks."

With that last intimidating bit of information, the gathering broke up and the Andrews left to return to their homes. Stephen caught a ride with his brother. Tonya left with Tara and Henry remained to speak with James about things regarding their kind's politics only they could understand or be privy to. I'd long since grown used to their secrets.

When it was just the three of us remaining, I excused myself to the kitchen to make a tea and give them privacy. I wanted something to do with my hands and not to have to listen to any more talk of war and factions.

It didn't seem right to be sitting in this warm, lovely home just before my favorite holiday on what should be one of the happiest days of my life while we talked of war and betrayal.

Losing one of our family members to the upcoming violence seemed more likely now that we were gaining "assistance" from the Courts. Things were bound to escalate. We'd come close in Germany and I finally saw firsthand that none of them were truly immortal; they could be killed or paralyzed just like me. That realization left me shaken, feeling in far greater peril than I wanted.

I had lulled myself into a false sense of security thinking that I was the only vulnerable one in the mix. They could protect me, but who would protect them? Certainly not anyone sent by Anton, Charles or even Miranda to "help" us.

Ch. 21

Before becoming involved with this whole new life, I'd been a walker and hiker. It had been the only way to clear my head, to get away from everyone else and move. It struck me that I hadn't been able to stretch my legs by myself for a long time. The desire to get out and be alone held a seductive draw, one that started as a passing thought and quickly grew until it pervaded my consciousness.

The thought of leaving for a while to be alone didn't scare me, it was broad daylight and I knew to be on alert. I wouldn't be taken unawares again. Besides, I was stronger than a normal human, healed faster and had heightened senses because of my marks. It would be hard to sneak up on me, even for a vampire. My abilities had developed well enough that I could defend myself adequately, I thought. I wasn't immortal, but I was better than human.

That settled it for me. James and Henry were in James' office upstairs, probably on a teleconference or some other meeting as they often were. I told myself I wasn't sneaking out, I was choosing not to interrupt them. I reminded myself I would be fine, a vampire would not strike in the daylight. The only reason they had before was because they had been able to grab me quickly. I wouldn't make it so easy for them now. Slipping into the kitchen I grabbed a paring knife from the knife block and hid it in my sleeve. Pausing long enough to slide on boots and a coat I walked out the door, shutting it softly behind me. I wouldn't be gone long enough for anyone to even miss me; I just needed to smell some fresh air and feel independent again.

Stepping off the porch, I zipped up my coat and glanced up. There was a movement at the office window. I held my breath for the next few strides, waiting to hear him call me back. He did not. Whether it was the call or Henry or an agreement that I was able to handle myself I could not know but James let me go without a peep or a tremor.

Taking the few steps down to the path, I bounced, feeling elated at my stolen freedom, believing it to be a trial run of sorts. It could be the start of my return to independence, the mere suggestion sending me into a giddy whirlwind that threatened to distract me from my necessary wariness.

The sun was out and I lifted my face to feel its dim warmth as I turned to walk down the block. My boots crunched the small amount of snow that had fallen a few days ago and had been pushed to the edges of the walk by the snowplows. The rest of it was gone by now, it wouldn't really stick for another few weeks if we continued our "warm spell" of 30 degree days.

I was enjoying my walk, feeling alive for the first time in a long time. I could feel my unease subsiding and watched the light glint on my new adornment on my left hand sending a girlish thrill through me.

Engaged. Me! That was something I'd never dared consider until a few months ago and now it was a blissful reality. James had freely chosen me above any necessary obligation our bond caused us. He wanted me as much as I wanted him. I was positively giddy and couldn't wait to tell my parents. It occurred to me that it didn't matter if they thought we were moving too fast. They couldn't possibly know how much we had been through because to tell them would put them in danger. In the end, none of that mattered. They would have to trust that I was making the right decision whether that was now or in six months.

We knew how much we meant to each other. Those bonds had been tested under threat of death and James had declared his feelings to his kind's highest and mightiest. I could not imagine a circumstance that could change how we felt about each other no matter how much time passed.

When I turned to complete the last leg of the circuit home, the sun had begun to fade. The clouds were rolling in for the night and a chill had sprung up in the air making me wish I had worn gloves and a hat. Gusts of wind were beginning to freeze my ears and my cheeks and I broke into a jog. I was jogging at a steady pace, still happy to be out despite the cold when I got within a few blocks of home and the sidewalk curved out, giving me an extended view of what was up ahead.

My pace dropped instantly to a walk when I saw a tall figure up a block in front of me on the sidewalk. He was walking toward me, hands in his pockets, head down with his face hidden in his turned up collar. At this distance his features were indistinguishable, though something about him was familiar giving me pause.

He was too tall to be Gaston. Watching him a little longer I was able to negate any possibilities that he was a vampire, yet he moved too smoothly to be human. I "swept" to feel him and didn't get anything, nothing at all. Whoever he was, he knew how to block.

My heart was still pounding from running and now it felt like I couldn't breathe, couldn't get enough air in my lungs as I fought down the panic. I was trying to appear nonchalant while I looked desperately for an escape route in the maze of fenced in backyards.

The outlook was grim. I couldn't jump the six foot cedar obstacles so popular in the wealthy neighborhood full of people who liked their privacy. I thought if I could cross to the other side of the street I might be able to outrun him the last few blocks home, he couldn't cross too or it would be suspicious. Granted I wasn't as fast as a vampire, but I was much faster than I used to be and, I reminded myself, this was not a vampire. Still, I had a bad feeling deep in the pit of my stomach.

When we were a half a block apart and I began to step into the snow separating me from the street, his head rose up out of his collar and he looked right at me.

I felt the tension in my shoulders ease and diverting back to the sidewalk without being too obvious, I waved. "Hey Brian!" So relieved was I to see a friendly face I didn't question why I wouldn't have recognized his "feel."

He waved back and we watched each other, narrowing the gap until we stood only feet apart. "How are you, Claire?" He smiled charmingly. "I wanted to thank you again for inviting me to the party the other night. It was a lot of fun."

"No problem. We had a great time having everyone. It was fun to finally meet you." I tried for Stephen's sake to do my best to get along with him. It might be a first step back into my friend's good graces.

"Yeah, we've been seeing each other for a couple of weeks now, it was nice to put faces with all of the names I've been hearing. I liked everybody I met." He flushed pink and admitted, "Stephen too, he's nothing like his reputation. I'm glad I got up the courage to ask him out."

My jaw dropped, "*You* asked *him* out?" I felt like a fool, I had accused my best friend of lying to me because of one look I saw at a party. I was glad I hadn't bought Stephen his present yet, it was going to have to be a big one.

"Of course I did," he mocked. "He didn't know I was gay, so he didn't even have me on his radar."

Casting a glance around us, there were very few cars on the street. I didn't see one I recognized and again something waited on the edge of my consciousness to be remembered. "Brian, where's your car?" I didn't see the red car that had dropped Stephen off and wondered if he was walking to kill

133

time. "Are you waiting to pick him up? If you are, I'm sorry but he got a ride with his family a while ago."

Shaking his head, Brian explained, "No, I actually live not far from here and was out for a walk. We don't get many days like this." He cocked his head. "Would you like to join me? I wanted to walk a few more blocks before I head back."

I owed Stephen something. I looked up at the sky and it was overcast, but no sign of snow. It would be warm enough if I put my hands in my pockets. "Sure."

"Great, let's go right." He would know that home would have been straight ahead.

We turned and headed up to the right into another part of the neighborhood I hadn't explored yet. Walking in a companionable silence for a while, I causally studied the houses seeing the details that had been added or kept in all of the renovations in the area. It was so much more enjoyable to walk in a neighborhood with individuality and character like this older one than to stroll past a hundred suburban developments with the same exact house in one of three colors.

The wind was picking up blowing my loose hair into my eyes. I brought my hand up to push a section of it behind my ear and Brian's warm hand caught mine, stopping me from going further. "Whoa, that's new."

I blushed, beaming while he examined it. "Yes, just a few hours ago as a matter of fact."

"Was it a surprise?" He was still holding my hand and though he was warm, I was uncomfortable with his touch. More so since I swore I felt something bump into my periphery when he took my hand.

Attributing my awkwardness to my inexperience with people and newly developed paranoia, I assumed Brian must be touchy like Stephen. Besides, he was gay and human; no threat on any level. I tried to relax except something kept brushing up against my periphery. Distracted, I only half listened as he continued to ask questions about James. Something he said drew me back to our conversation.

"I'm sorry, what was that?" I tried to focus on him and shrug off the unshakable feeling that something was wrong.

He laughed pleasantly. "You must be thinking about him, huh? I asked if you live there already or if you are on campus still."

"Oh, I've moved in recently." Brian seemed overly interested in life with James and my internal alarms were screeching. Trying to appear unconcerned I withdrew my hand, amazed at how much effort it took as he clung to it too hard to be casual.

I looked up at the sky feigning surprise. "It's getting late I should head home, James will be getting worried." That wasn't a stretch. "Thanks for the company." I turned to go back and noted that he had turned with me.

"I should probably get back as well." He looked troubled at my intent to leave him, ratcheting up my anxiety yet another notch.

"No," I said, too loud and too fast. Trying to calm him and myself, I continued, "I was going to jog back since I'm late already."

"Good idea, I need to stretch my legs too." He remained undeterred.

My heart had begun its own race. I couldn't say anything else without being blatantly rude. "Suit yourself," I said and quickened my pace.

We were only a couple of blocks and I couldn't hold it to a jog in my panic. In only a few strides, I was close to sprinting. I was trying to focus enough to call out to James. I wanted to let him know I was coming and something was wrong. Something I couldn't put my finger on.

My pulse was flying and I wasn't able to focus. After the first block, I felt the footsteps beside me speed up as he recognized how close we were getting to the house.

Brian's hand shot out and grabbed my upper arm, jerking me off balance and bringing me up short. "Claire, I have a cramp. Could you stop for a minute?"

Giving him a quick once over I noticed he was barely breathing hard and his face held no traces of pain. I tried to remove my arm but Brian held it like a vice. He was cutting off my circulation and I knew he would leave a bruise even if only for a day.

"What do you want Brian? I told you I need to get home and I meant it." I fought to keep the fear out of my voice. "Let me go."

I felt that *something* bump my periphery again and I took the risk, lowering my shields enough to feel Brian's emotions. As soon as my shields slipped an inch I was slammed with a terrible rush of rage and dread coming from him. His emotional barrage was unfamiliar to me, it was not pure human or vampire but a combination of both. He was something entirely new to me. Raising my face to his I saw that he was looking up the street, wild eyed and tight lipped.

It clicked then that he was waiting for someone. This was a trap. He was trying to distract me for someone who might not want to risk a daylight attack and I was not willing to wait around to find out who that might be. I used my new strength to jerk my arm away from him.

His brows shot up. "What are you?"

He was clearly confused that a little woman like me could pull free from him and I secretly delighted in his bafflement. My pleasure was short lived as I felt his fury building, outweighing his reason.

The violence I felt erupting from its hidden place inside him was staggering. His lust for blood was nearly as strong as that of a vampire and he was projecting his rage at me trying to goad me into a fight. He may not know what I *was* but he knew what I could *do*.

"What are *you*?" I fired back, equally astonished. Raising my shields back up tight, I fought down the anger boiling my blood, wondering briefly if this was the source of Stephen's new rage. He wouldn't shield if he didn't think someone was a threat and he wouldn't use his ability with a lover as he had pointed out before.

If Brian wanted to, he could slip right in under Stephen's guard.

I had been with violent men far more than I cared to admit recently and chose not to be today. Taking advantage of my momentary freedom from his grasp, I made my final attempt at escape. No more polite pretenses of etiquette bound me. I started off in a dead run.

Brian was a great athlete in tremendous condition with a much longer stride, yet I was faster than a typical human. Using that speed in conjunction with my brief middle school track training as a sprinter, I stayed ahead of him for almost the entire second block before his own enhanced speed allowed him to catch up. He caught me by the coat collar and my fingers flew to unzip it and shrug free, my silly knife clattered uselessly to the concrete.

I was able to remain beyond his grasp until halfway up the block when I turned up the walkway to our house. My adrenaline might have been blocking the focus I needed to "call" James to express a detailed message, but it actually helped me to send out a blast for help.

Dropping my shields all at once, I sent out a psychic flare as soon as my foot hit the first paver in the path. At my next footfall the door whipped open and I saw James standing there, his fierce expression comforting only to me. I was safe and Brian was most definitely *not*.

He took in the situation in a second and was down the stairs, waiting for me before I took another step. I didn't slow my stride letting my impetus fold me into the protection that was James. When his arms wrapped around me, stopping my momentum like an only slightly softer brick wall, my fear caught up with me. I was unable to stop my teeth chattering enough to tell him anything. I didn't need to.

James' sharp voice cut through the cool air like a knife. Eyes black and his lip starting to change shape, he stared at Brian. "Is there something I can help you with, Brian?" His words, though genial, dripped with promises of brutality should Brian come any closer.

At the sight of him, Brian had skidded to a halt a step behind me. He barely avoided running into us, not expecting James to appear so quickly, I'm sure. Brian was casting his eyes up and down the street, not even trying to hide the fact now that he was waiting for someone. Surreptitiously, James sniffed the air around Brian and smiled.

"What did they promise you Brian? You know they're not going to turn you." James' eerily calm voice sent shivers up my spine as I remained tucked up against him, happy to be out of imminent danger at least for the present. "I am making this offer to you once out of respect for Stephen." His tone turned hard. "Leave. I will not harm you for what you've done tonight. *They* can seduce anyone with offers of strength and power. However, if you do not respect this warning, if you come for her again, make no mistake, you will disappear."

Brian's panicked glances stopped as he listened to James. Believing every word James uttered, he took a step back preparing to retreat. Before I could speak, I was whisked back up the steps and inside to safety.

Ch. 22

We were in the kitchen. I was perched on the counter not trusting my legs to hold me and James was putting the kettle on. Once the danger was past, I began to shake in earnest. Resting my teacup on the counter next to me, James' hand went to the back of my neck to pull me to him. I let my body lean into his and closed my eyes, drawing strength from his reassuring stillness.

"What did he want Claire?" His voice was carefully controlled, I knew he was holding back all of his guilt and frustration at me for going out. The experiment had failed. I could feel the shackles of my return to captivity closing on me. James would never let me repeat it.

"I don't know. Me? He was waiting for someone."

His growl rumbled against my head and chest as he reacted to the threat again.

"Brian's working with the bad guys, isn't he? He's the one who gave you away to Raymond." It made sense. "Should we call Stephen to let him know?"

James nodded. "Why don't you call him; he'll listen to you. I need to get back to something in my office."

I remembered he was working with Henry up there when I had gone out and didn't question it. Flipping open my phone, I dialed the familiar number and then clicked it shut, remembering something. "James, Brian isn't human. I felt him projecting at me. You knew what he was." I let my question hang.

He stopped with a hand on the doorframe of the kitchen and turned back. "He's a servant now. He wasn't the other night so they've only just marked him again." Rubbing his temple, a human holdover, he went on. "I had sensed something on him at the party only I wasn't sure what it was. Then I was distracted when you became interested and I forgot. It was sloppy of me, I let my emotions get in the way."

I blushed at his mention of my initial reaction to Brian and let it pass. There were more important things to worry about. "Even if he wasn't a servant yet, couldn't you have sensed his ability when you shook his hand?"

"A human servant with no natural ability of his own can channel that of his Master when called upon. Remember, their bond is similar to ours except more one sided. I think that is what Brian is doing. He had no ability when I touched him."

"So Brian is not only working with a vampire, he's a human servant as well? Stephen is *never* going to believe me."

"You must try, Claire. He's in danger now that Brian's been found out." James was earnest in his urging. Any signs of anger toward Stephen had been firmly placed on the back burner in favor of protecting him from our common enemy.

I nodded and again opened my phone, shrugging off any discomfort I might feel in favor of helping my friend and pressed redial before raising it to my ear.

"Yes?" Stephen didn't pick up until the third ring and didn't sound happy to hear from me.

The guilt of my false accusations hung heavy over my head. "Stephen, first can I just tell you what an idiot I am?"

"Yes, you can as a matter of fact. What's second?" A hint of his former self leaked through his new bristly exterior.

I took a big breath and blew it out hard before proceeding. "I should never have accused you of manipulating Brian that way. You told me a long time ago that you wouldn't do that and I should have trusted you. I am so sorry to doubt you. You're right. I *have* been a little too self-absorbed lately and I apologize."

Satisfied, Stephen replied with a simple, "Thank you."

Hearing the levity in his voice, I took heart for only a brief moment, saddened that it wouldn't last. "Forgiven?"

"Yes."

Taking another deep breath I went on, not letting myself think what I was about to do to his happiness. "Stephen, I have some bad news."

On alert, he was quick to shift gears. "Has something happened? Is everyone okay? Is it James?"

"Yes, everyone is fine for now." It hurt that he worried first for me, thinking of my love for James right away. I didn't want to say the words that would hurt him. I had to swallow my nerves. "Stephen, I have to tell you something and I just need you to listen before you make any sort of decisions." "Okay." He was wary.

"I went for a walk just now and on my way home, I ran into Brian." I paused waiting.

Stephen said nothing.

"He was really curious about all of us and asking all sorts of questions. I got creeped out and tried to leave. He chased me Stephen. James had to run him off. He was trying to hold me for someone." Waiting again, I let that sink in. "Stephen I'm sorry, I don't think Brian is one of the good guys. James thinks he's someone's human servant."

There was a heavy pause on the other end before he uttered a soft curse. "I should have known this was about *you*. Claire, what is your problem with my lifestyle? You've been on me since you met me about my casual flings. Now I've found someone I really like and you have to try to break it up." His voice dropped lower and I heard the hurt in it. "I never said word one about your choice and how dangerous it was, or the fact that you drop everything as soon as he calls. That's because that's what friends do, they keep their jealous mouths shut when they see that their friends are happy. Maybe you could try that sometime, you might end up with more friends." The line went dead leaving me staring stupidly at my phone.

Another voice came from the kitchen doorway. "Our visitor has given up on his saviors; he is moving on." I had forgotten about Henry, he was still here of course. James was silent standing between us, watching me. They'd both appeared out of nowhere. I should have found it unsettling, only I was glad not to be alone.

Henry continued his update. "He has been waiting at the end of the block." He shook his head. "He *is* new to know so little of territories. His Master will not come to him so close to us." Henry turned on his heel and strode from the room, his voice floating back to us as the door closed behind him. "I will call Troy about Stephen, he might be better able to talk sense to the boy. I leave you two for the night. Happy Christmas."

I leaned against the counter. "Stephen doesn't believe me. He thinks I'm just being a selfish jerk, which I can't blame him for. I have been lately." I threw up my hands in frustration. "I apologized and he forgave me, and then, when I told him what happened, he thought I was lying to break them up." Close to tears, I got angry. I didn't want to cry; I wanted to scream.

No wonder new vampires were hard to control. If they were all hypersensitive like me I could see why they killed people haphazardly. It wasn't hunger, it was aggravation.

"And, I forgot tomorrow is Christmas. We need to host dinner and I never went to the store or anything. Can we feed my parents some A negative or a can of tuna fish cause I think that's all we have?" I knew I sounded pissy and whiny, but I *was* pissy and whiny.

He came to wrap his arms around me, and I laid my head against his firm chest. Touching him I felt my shields bridge and it brought my tantrum to a halt. "I've taken the liberty of having dinner catered. I thought it would make things go more smoothly with all the other issues we are handling lately." He ran a hand over my back.

"I can't believe you, you never get ruffled. Ever. We are in the middle of this huge *thing* here and you remember to call the caterer for dinner?" I shook my head in disbelief. Without James in my life right now to balance me out, I think I would completely fall apart.

James tapped his temple grinning crookedly. "I don't sleep, remember? I have a lot more time to think about things than a normal human." He aimed a scowl at me. "How can you say I don't get ruffled? Have you failed to notice that since I met you I am perpetually ruffled? When you aren't challenging my self-control, you are trying different ways of getting yourself killed. And now you are surprised that I can remember to cater a simple dinner for my future in-laws whom I am hoping to impress? Claire, you are very observant, until it comes to your own affairs."

His explanation provided a window into his thoughts. "Are you nervous about telling my parents?" I couldn't help but smile at the thought of James actually being nervous about anything that didn't involve someone's death.

144

"Caring for you and having our bond has brought back much of my human emotional range. Right now, I am as nervous as any man asking for the hand of his intended."

My stomach knotted as I thought about my parents' reaction to our news as well. "Do you think they'll be upset? I don't think I can deal with my parents *and* Stephen being angry with me right now."

Wrinkles lined his forehead. "Does it change your mind if they are upset? Would you reconsider your answer?"

"No," I answered from the heart. "I will be with you forever James. Whatever forever means for us, I want it to be together."

We stood together in the kitchen, enjoying the quiet. I never felt calmer than when I was with him. He let me be myself and I had felt the last of my anxiousness about his true desire for me and our future together fade after he asked me to marry him. Now it was a safe haven here with him in our home. It hit me that this was my home too, for real and not just for a few weeks. I couldn't help but smile at the thought of this continuing the rest of our lives.

I straightened and moved to push away from the counter. "What?" He stiffened, a byproduct of being on guard duty for too long.

Putting my hand against his chest, I flashed him a smile as I pushed myself away. "I just wanted to go get something, wait here."

James watched me curiously, surely he heard each step as I jogged up the stairs to our room. It only took me a moment to find what I was looking for and I worried that it was going to be insufficient as I brought the simply wrapped package to the kitchen. When I returned to him, James saw the uncertainty in my expression. I took a breath and set his gift on the counter next to him.

Surprise flickered in his eyes. "Is this for me?"

I tried to appear more confident than I felt. How could my gift compete with his? He had given me his home and himself. Out of nervousness, I felt the need to justify my gift. "It isn't much, I just thought that you would enjoy…"

His lips brought my words to a halt. When he pulled away, he put his hand on top of the small silver package I'd laid beside him and met my eyes. "Love, it's perfect." His hands worked to unwrap the package while he held my gaze until he had to look down to see what it was he held.

Trying to catch him unawares, I lowered my shields as subtly as I could. I wanted an honest reaction from him if I could get it. Though he didn't move to look at me, I saw his lips twitch when he felt my shields come down. Damn, he had felt it.

James' pleasure was genuine when he saw his concert tickets. He let me feel that. "I thought you were busy that night. You must be keeping company with a sordid group these days; your lying skills are improving."

I doubted that I would have fooled him if it mattered, although his teasing made me laugh anyway.

"Thank you, Claire. Am I to assume one of these tickets is yours?"

"If you want me to go with you I would love it, but they are yours so you can give one to anyone you want."

The look in his eyes told me everything I needed to hear. "I know who I want."

Ch. 23

We lounged around the house Christmas morning and James made breakfast yet again. "It isn't fair," I announced as I sat down to enjoy my feast.

He paused before lowering himself into his chair across from me, waiting. "What isn't fair?"

"It isn't fair that you do all of these things for me and I don't have anything I can do for you."

"I enjoy doing these things. It brings me pleasure to make you happy; more than I would have anticipated, in fact." His brow furrowed in thought. "I have not made breakfast for anyone since my mother."

"I'm just going to have to find some sort of special talent you can't live without." I was only half kidding.

His eyes brightened from midnight to smoke and back to dark as I watched. I'd never seen it so rapid and I stared at him, fascinated as he wrestled with his thoughts.

"You have a special talent." His voice was soft and low.

"Huh?" I was distracted by his ocular display.

"You worry you don't bring anything to the table and I disagree. Which actually brings up something that has been requested." James' face had become guarded as he spoke and I felt him solidifying the wall between us again.

I felt my stomach clench, an automatic response to his. "What is it?"

James took a breath, necessary for speech, and in this case buying time before he had to say something unpleasant. "As solitary as we are as creatures, we have found that it is in our best interest as a society to make the transition for newly turned vampires a smooth one. A newly turned vampire left alone can go mad and cause massive destruction, the likes of which we could not readily hide from all the world's modern media cycles. Discovery would be inevitable and catastrophic for all of us." He fidgeted with the corner of the tickets on the counter readying himself to go on.

I waited on edge for the other shoe to drop.

"As you can imagine, Ursa's loss has left a need for our society. Henry and the Court believe that you and I could prove to be a benefit for our kind. We could be better than Ursa and I were because of our combined talents." He paused, his body motionless as he waited for my reaction.

At first I could only stare open mouthed at him, eyes wide in disbelief. I couldn't imagine any member of the Court believing a human would be a benefit to them. When my mind wrapped around what he was asking, I saw a huge problem and wondered how it had escaped his notice. "James, aren't newly turned vampires ruled by their hunger? It wouldn't be safe for me to be around them; I'm human."

Instead of responding, he only stared at me. That was when it hit me. It *hadn't* escaped their notice. They needed me to make a decision that I had successfully avoided until this very moment. Now, here it was. The need to make my choice once and for all reared its ugly head and shattered my newfound happiness. That *James* was asking took my legs from under me.

I tried reminding myself how he felt compelled to help others. This was exactly the type of thing he was unable to refuse and I wondered for the first time if his compulsion was stronger than our bond. If I said no to his offer now, they would pair James with someone else, I thought with a pang. He would be pulled away from me often. The nagging voice at the back of my mind pointed out how selfish I was being.

Here I was with a once in a lifetime opportunity, I had a chance to use my talent to help many in need of guidance. That was something that I had wanted for so long, to truly feel my ability was a gift and not a curse. It had served me only recently in times of fighting, but what about when this conflict had passed? What then? I would just be hiding from who I really was and what I could do.

Wasn't that what had brought me to Stephen in the first place? Stephen had enlisted me in the hopes that I would add something to their world, not just take their time and leave them.

James reached across the table, touching the hand that lay forgotten next to my plate. His touch brought me back out of my head and into the present. He was watching my eyes closely; his own expression remained intentionally unreadable.

I knew if I attempted to feel him he wouldn't let me, so I didn't even try to lower my shields. I thought about reaching through the marks, a desperate move although I knew he couldn't avoid me that way but I felt like that was cheating and I couldn't do it unless it was an emergency. We had to have some privacy from each other. Reflexively I kept my shields up as well. "How much of this was *their* idea?" Forced to rely solely on external indicators, I was operating from a strange place. I tried to read his face for some indication of his involvement in such a pivotal decision.

He knew exactly what I was asking and his expression remained smooth, eyes still watching me while he recited his reply. "I acknowledge the need for our race to have this resource and I will continue to work with them as long as I am able. I do find it difficult to ask this of you. I know the reality of what is involved." It was sterile, completely devoid of any real personal input.

"I'll need to think about it." My own carefully controlled response was mild while my mind reeled out of control, my stomach rolled, and I pushed away my plate.

My sudden loss of appetite did not escape his notice and I knew he felt the depth of my physical reaction. For that he need only listen to the drumming of my heart and see my skin grow pale at his request. It was unnecessary for him to have to tap into our bond or use his ability when he only needed to use his ears.

It would be a difficult decision under normal circumstances. I couldn't get over the timing. "James, when did you and Henry decide this?"

Looking down, he hid his eyes from me. "We were speaking to Miranda upstairs when you went out."

Wincing, I struggled to find my voice. "So you proposed marriage and asked me to turn all in 24 hours? What am I supposed to think about that, that it's some sort of coincidence? How long has this plan been in the works, since you first met me or did it come up more recently? Maybe when Miranda told us we were stuck together?" I could feel the indignation and hurt building inside me as my illusion of a happy future came crashing down around me.

James had closed off any human facades he normally used and stared at me stone faced, he was using his cold vampire persona with me and I didn't like it. I saw him flinch when I suggested his courtship had all been a farce leading up to this moment, yet he said nothing in his own defense. His hand lay lightly on mine and I, not wanting to be so close, slid it out from under his returning it to my lap. James did not take his eyes off my face, no expression showed on his own.

Feeling my tiny, secure world fracturing I sought an anchor to hold me steady. I needed to see how he felt about this, down deep, under his icy exterior. Lash out as I did, I could not believe that everything he'd said to me had been a lie. I had to know how he really felt about my turning. My own feelings on the subject were confused, but it might help if I could at least see how he felt. I was starting to focus, to open up the marks and blow through his defenses when he spoke, distracting me.

"Claire, this decision is difficult, I know, and I apologize for the timing. It couldn't be helped. Miranda is not entirely convinced that this is the best thing for us; she worries we might lose our bond, but you *will* keep your ability. It's strong. And with the influx of new vampires we are seeing, the situation has become urgent. She has appointed someone in the interim but his ability to assist is limited. We need a more permanent solution."

For the first time some of his humanity bled through his cold face. His eye twitched and I felt a ripple roll through our bond as well as something that shocked me possibly more than his question. Blocking me was taking a lot out of him and he couldn't keep it up like this much longer.

"You cannot base your decision on me, Claire. In the end it is your decision, not mine." Once again his face iced over. "If I ask you to turn and I die, you will be left with immortality without me. I cannot be the only reason you choose to turn."

Pushing away from the table, I stood. "My parents will be here in a few hours. I have presents to wrap and I need to get ready. Alone." He sat motionless, watching me go.

Ch. 24

Jeanette and Doug Martin arrived promptly at six, predictably true to Dad's military training. You could set your watch by Dad's timeliness. At the sound of the doorbell I came downstairs in a pair of black trousers, cream v-neck sweater and bare hands. I was not going to put my parents' respect to the test for something when I wasn't sure of it anymore.

I knew James caught the missing ring the second I stepped in front of him to hug my mother. If he had a reaction, he'd hidden it by the time I withdrew from my mom's embrace. We were careful not to touch during the greetings. James shook hands with my father and hugged my mother, all the while looking perfect in a white dress shirt and black dress pants; my favorite colors on him. His shirt was open at the neck, just the way I liked it. He was tempting me and I knew it.

Dinner was fantastic, the caterer he'd chosen had done an impeccable job. We enjoyed a glazed ham and all of the usual fixings. James provided a Petite Syrah from his cellar and his own glass, always refilled in the cellar and not at the table, contained his own special vintage. With the mood I was in, I drank not one but two glasses, raising the eyebrows of James and my Dad both.

Mom held it down to a minimum again. She seemed happier, the tension missing from her eyes and her reduction in consumption reflected that. She and Dad were touchier with one another and smiles between them were frequent and came easily. I couldn't help but feel guilty for having been such a stressor on their marriage for so long.

We exchanged gifts. Mom fawned over the bowl and I responded as expected to the new sweater they gave me.

Mom looked a little uncertain when she produced a thin package and presented it shyly to James.

He looked equally surprised and touched, making me curious about his unusual reaction to receiving gifts. The man always knew what to do in any situation. I'd seen him face down two vampires at once with absolute self-possession and yet he seemed uncertain as to how to accept a gift. Uncomfortable, he reached out and took the box. If he were human he would have blushed.

James opened the box wrapped in simple green paper and a gold bow. I was sitting next to him, and couldn't see what the picture was, though I recognized the side of a silver picture frame. Unable to see what he was looking at, I watched James' face. His jaw moved reflexively, he was visibly moved and I watched a flicker of sadness in his eyes before he brought himself under control. At last, he turned the frame so that I could see the photograph.

He held a picture very familiar to me. It was one of Mom's favorites. It was me as a two year old sitting on the floor of my parents' kitchen when we lived in Birmingham. The morning sun was coming in the kitchen window, flooding the room with light. I had only the vaguest of memories of that house but Mom had told me about this picture a hundred times. She said I had made a habit of sitting on the floor while she cooked nearby. I hadn't been a touchy child, but that particular year we'd moved three times and for six months I didn't let my mother out of my sight. That time had meant a lot to her, I'd felt it. That she chose tonight to open up and share that special memory with him touched me unexpectedly.

In the photograph, I sat in a little white summer dress scribbling on a sheet of paper, head bent with just a side view of my tiny four year old face. My lower lip was tucked under my front teeth, a habit I still have when I'm concentrating. Dark waves of hair swirled around my face with a thin section tucked just behind my ear.

"Thank you, it's perfect." No one could doubt his sincerity or that he'd been moved. My mother's eyes glistened and my father gave James an approving head bob. "I believe we need another bottle, something special." He swept away from the table to disappear again into the cellar under the stairs.

While he was gone I picked up the frame and examined it. I couldn't think of it as a simpler time; I was already sensing others' emotions. The torment of my lonely life came back to me in a rush. Because of James I had my independence.

He'd given me the skills to have a life of my own. When we had first met he'd said I couldn't be left alone with no ability to protect myself. He'd said that regardless of whether I could help them he would teach me to defend myself and I'd seen him operate from that same altruistic place countless times.

James' selflessness defined him and was one of the main reasons I loved him. He was asking me not to turn, but to help. He was as conflicted about the impending change to my nature as I. I'd felt it; he wanted me to stay human.

I was seriously considering breaking "our" news to my parents when James reappeared in the doorway, a bottle of champagne in his hand and four glasses clutched in the other.

He set the glasses down on the buffet against the kitchen wall, the bottle beside them. Without a word he disappeared again, this time upstairs. Only affording his disappearance a curious frown, my parents and I picked up some minor chatter about Mom's new book group she had joined at the library. Mom changed her hobbies as often as some women changed lipstick shades.

When James returned he carried an envelope with him. Setting it down beside the champagne on the buffet, he popped the cork. No flow of liquid, only a sigh rose up the neck of the bottle. I wondered how many magnums of champagne he had opened in his "lifetime."

While he poured and handed out the flutes I had to focus to keep track of his movements, I could tell I was tipsy and welcomed the warm fuzziness the wine afforded me. It was a nice break from the seriousness that had become my norm. My parents were talking about some old friend they had run into at the grocery store and were arguing mildly about whether or not Dad liked her husband or if he was a boor.

James coughed, capturing our attention and raised his glass. Following suit, we raised ours as well. He set the envelope in front of my parents.

"Doug, Jeanette, in honor of Christmas and your upcoming anniversary, Claire and I thought that you would enjoy a special gift." I looked up in surprise at James. I had totally forgotten my own parents' anniversary. Normally, I would have been grateful for his thoughtfulness only this wasn't normally. Overly sensitive to his hiding things from me, I felt the rekindling of my anger with him. For the sake of my parents I kept quiet.

He gave me the quickest of winks making my body react independently of my mind. That part of me was sensitive too, in a whole different way. He could probably light me on fire and I would still want to sleep with him. Bodies were lucky. They weren't bogged down by the troubles conscious minds found themselves embroiled in. My poor conflicted half vampire mind, however, was another thing entirely.

Continuing, he smiled easily at my parents. "I could argue that *I* have gained the most from your marriage." He tipped his glass to me. "I owe you my happiness. Thank you." He raised his glass higher as did we. The bubble in my chest was hard to breath around and I took a deep drink. He was turning on the charm on purpose. James sat down as Mom opened their card, Dad reading over her shoulder. His arm went around my side and I leaned into him without even thinking about it, the wine was simplifying my decisions. I was startled back upright by my mother's gasp and my father's surprised exclamation.

"Oh James, this is too much!" Mom's eyes were shiny when she looked at each of us. They knew my budget, so it was no surprise when they accurately put this mystery gift squarely on James' wallet.

"James, we can't accept this." Dad was choked up and I wished I knew what it was "we" had gotten them. It was obviously good.

Coolly taking a sip from his glass, James smiled at my parents. I stared at his profile wondering why this all had to be so damn complicated. "We insist," he emphasized the "we" and I felt a sting again of having forgotten their anniversary. Was it their twenty-fifth? I knew it was a big one now that I was thinking about it. Stephen was right, I *was* self-absorbed. I was almost twenty and, thanks to my fiancée, I had no more excuses for my lack of social skills. Right then I promised all of them that I would be a more thoughtful person in the future.

Mom finally revealed the mystery. "France? Oh my God. I can't believe we're really going."

"Claire remembered you two saying that was the place you would most like to go if you could and that she would love to send you one day. It made it easy."

That part was actually true. We'd had that conversation months ago, only I hadn't realized I was planting the seed for this.

"We thought you would like to spend your anniversary there. We've arranged for a room at the Hotel Ritz in Paris for three nights. If you want to extend your stay or go out to the countryside let me know. I have contacts throughout France who can find you appropriate accommodations even on short notice."

Mom came around the table to hug James and he rose to receive her, back in his comfort zone being the one giving and not receiving. My dad stood to shake his hand around Mom's clinging hug. I watched my family embrace the love of my life and felt a wave of sadness grip me as I resolved that I wouldn't be sharing my special news with them tonight. It was too confusing still, there were so many things that would change and I wasn't sure I wanted them to. Still James was so natural with them, it was easy to see all of us having years of holidays with them. The being with him wasn't the issue; no it had only gotten tricky with his second question today.

What would I tell them when they noticed I hadn't aged? I couldn't tell them why I was different, that meant I would have to leave. The real question he was asking was would I give up my world for his. Could I walk away from my life and wait for everyone who knew me to die so that I could walk the world without fear of discovery? It had been posed by the bond, blurring the lines between us and I knew it was coming, yet I wasn't ready to give it all up. Not when I had only just gotten a chance to be a real part of their lives. I needed more time and I felt it slipping away leaving me again at the mercy of others' wants. Just once I wanted to be in control of my life and make a decision on my terms, not because someone else demanded it.

We shared the rest of the champagne while James spoke in depth with my parents about France. Things to do, tourist traps to avoid, small out of the way places they had to see. Mom and Dad were both of French descent, Dad more recently through Canada. They both had relations there and now that they were comfortable with the gift, they were excited about the prospect of visiting the "homeland." The tickets had them arriving January 14th, the day before the big day.

He had scooted my chair closer to his after the toast and while they talked I leaned into James, my head resting against his shoulder. The vibration of his speech soothed me and let me be here, enjoying this night possibly as one of my last with my family as I wavered in and out of the conversation. The cadence of their dialogue was comfortable and homey and I was moved to a peaceful place when James changed the subject and brought me back with a jerk.

"Seeing the two of you preparing to celebrate twenty-five years together makes me consider my own future."

He wouldn't. My hand slid down onto his thigh.

"Doug, I recognize that you have raised a strong daughter and the choice is ultimately hers but I am still a little old fashioned; it's how I was raised."

I sat up abruptly. Unable to look at him or at my parents it left me with nowhere to stare except the tabletop. My hand tightened on his leg, warning him. He bumped against my shields and I refused to let him in.

James' voice never wavered. "We have only known each other a relatively short time comparatively speaking, but I feel a true connection with Claire and I believe she feels the same about me. I would like to ask your permission to ask for her hand."

Enraged, I dug my fingers into his leg feeling a need to hurt him in my borrowed predilection for doing violence and gaining a sense of satisfaction when I was rewarded with a flinch. His hand came down to take my wrist and remove my claw from him. Glancing up, I smiled for show; no joy reached my eyes. I wasn't sure if the disturbance I saw in his deep blue eyes was a result of physical or mental discomfort. It didn't matter. I felt no sympathy for him, not for this.

Mom was aflutter, as I would have expected. Dad was a little more pragmatic, watching me curiously. I twitched my lips in a nervous smile. "Have you asked *her* yet?" He had a strange expression on his face as he watched mine, perplexed by what he saw there, or rather what he *didn't* see. I think he had been sufficiently thrown by the past hour's events and the alcohol didn't help.

"We've discussed it, yes." His silky voice worked to soothe me and I could tell he was layering it with Glamour. I felt his hand slide down my wrist to slip into my palm. The anger within me abated leaving only faint traces in its wake and I was lulled into a lazy dozing state that could have easily come from the wine.

Dad roughed his chin with the back of his knuckles still watching me, and his expression changed. He'd seen what he'd been waiting for. Bobbing his head methodically he gave James his answer. "You two seem to be happy and it doesn't always take years to decide on the right one. I knew Jeannette only a matter of months, much like you two when I decided to ask for her hand." His voice warmed and he smiled at me. Tears pricked my eyes. He had no idea what he was saying yes to. "If Claire wants it, you have our blessing."

Mom was conscious of my silence and showed astonishing lucidity. "Doug, we should leave them. I think they have a lot to talk about and Claire, you look a little tired."

James gave my hand a squeeze. "Yes, we do." He didn't go into further detail and I think my parents thought the alcohol and impending engagement were enough. If only they knew

159

about the last curve ball, they wouldn't be so willing to send me off with Mr. Wonderful.

Dad was the consummate father. "Claire, honey, do you need a ride back to school?"

Choosing for the moment not to comment on my engagement status or living arrangements, I shook my head. "No, Dad. I'm fine to stay." I didn't try to hide my intention to sleep here and in that moment I realized that I fully intended to stay the night in spite of everything. All this touching was working against my tenuous control and my languid mood was making it difficult to separate the fiery feelings still floating below the surface waiting for him to let go and allow them to break free.

"Okay," Mom interjected quickly and patted Dad's arm. "Let's be off then."

They got up, as did we and moved independently to hug and say our good-byes. When the door closed behind them I sagged and James reached out to put his hand on my back.

"You've had a long day, Love. Let's get you to bed." When his hand got close, I attacked.

My first strike landed hard on his jaw. He was so shocked, he faltered a step stumbling forward and landing with his hands on my shoulders. Off balance from the impetus of my swing, I fell against his chest and his arms dropped to my sides attempting to pin my arms without hurting me. Stronger than he was prepared for, I broke his hold and two more swings landed on his face and chest, the last of which produced a satisfying thud before his arms clamped down and I was trapped against his chest unable to move.

Physically unable to hurt him, I hissed, "I might have forgiven you swooping in with the trip, but who the hell said

160

you could ask my dad for my hand? Didn't you notice? I left your ring upstairs."

His serene façade faded away with my parents gone and he could be real as well. He held me away from him, hands continuing to pin my arms to my body. "I was raised to ask a father for his daughter's hand and now I feel better having done so. It doesn't change how you feel. Does it?"

Daring to look into his face I saw vulnerability, not the anger I expected having so savagely provoked him; his eyes were nearly black with feeling. The sight of his more sensitive human side served to further confuse my passions. Having never been drunk before, I didn't know what of my confused thoughts was alcohol, what was the result of the marks, and what was me or what was *left* of me.

Inhibitions properly lowered, I stared at his chest. "I don't want to talk about marriage or vampires or Miranda or anything. If you want to have a serious talk, you're going to have to wait until later." My head felt heavy as I lifted it up to nibble his chin.

"You do realize that you're drunk and I would be taking advantage if I took you upstairs right now." He was trying to ignore my hands which had moved to his belt.

"So don't take me upstairs. We can do it down here." My hands were very busy and his belt was already undone, the button and zipper not far behind. Working to keep his resolve, James' jaw tightened and he trailed his hands down to my wrists pinning them to my hips.

Victorious, I watched his desire to give in to my efforts and nipped at his neck, adding to his ardor. Chuckling, I teased him. "You know I can talk you into it."

At that he held his arms out to push me away from him. "Claire, I don't think this is a good idea tonight; you have a

161

lot to consider and I don't want you to regret anything or feel like I've coerced you." From the tremor in his voice I could tell he wanted it as much as I did.

Tongue too lazy for speech, I went to jelly, oozing forward, my hands slipping behind me. He growled in frustration when my chest lay on his taking all the space out from between us.

"Love, you are not making it easy for me to be a gentleman."

"A *gentleman*?" I guffawed. "It's too late for that. You asked to date me *after* we had sex, my hand *after* giving me a ring. I guess I'm lucky you changed things up on this *last* request for my life."

Even with my limited understanding of all things socially acceptable I knew I had gone too far. His hands clenched and I gasped in pain, feeling a virtual "pop" as his shields firmed to a point I could never break into; even our bond went quiet. I was frightened as I felt "him" leaving me and he withdrew from my head leaving me more alone even than when he'd withdrawn in Austria. My body felt empty with him gone and I lost my bearings once more.

Scared and off kilter, I took the offensive and lashed out. "Why do you hide how you really feel from me all the time? Don't married people share how they feel? How can I marry you if you don't trust me enough to show me how you really feel?"

"I *do* tell you how I feel all the time. Do you know how difficult it is for my kind to have what we have with another being? Much less a *human*, a fragile human I could kill with one bite or break in two if I lost my temper once?" His fury darkened his features ominously.

I had rarely seen him so angry and never at me, not like this. For a second I thought maybe I was making a mistake digging at him. But, my judgment was clouded by alcohol and months of frustration from being under constant stress, and I foolishly pressed on. "Well, I think it's awfully convenient that you proposed the same day that you decided to tell me I need to turn into one of you. How am I not supposed to think that was on purpose? Maybe after you got inside my head and saw how easy it would be to seduce me you decided to take advantage."

Eyes narrowed I leaned in and accused him of the worst sort of treachery. "Did you think I would be so grateful to have you that I would never catch on? It almost worked except you moved too quickly. Even I'm not that stupid." I had lost the ability to control my mouth, taking this moment to clumsily verbalize all of my insecurities.

James was livid. His eyes were black and hard, prominent against his pale skin, his fangs were out and his hands were like iron on my arms. "You're being unreasonable. I can't talk to you like this or we'll both say things we might regret."

My brain was fuzzy and it was hard to concentrate. I knew that I wanted to be with him, that I needed him in order to feel right again and my thoughts went back to my physical desire. Twisting my wrists I felt him relent and he let me get loose. I put my hands up against him, fingers slipping up to touch his neck I traced the line in the center of his chest. His hands moved up my arms and he drew me closer. Tipping his face down he kissed me hard, wrapping his arms around my back and I sighed relaxing into his body. Sure I was getting back in, I pushed myself more firmly into him but stopped when I felt him go still.

Pulling back, I saw his expression. James' fangs had retracted and his face had gone blank. He was still angry and wasn't giving in at all. In the next instant, my feet went out from under me and I was swept up into his arms. He carried me upstairs and placed me efficiently into bed where

he left me.   Fortunately, I was only able to cry for a minute
or two in frustration before I passed out.

Ch. 25

Something was buzzing on the table next to my head when I returned to consciousness the next morning. James had blackout shades in our bedroom so at least it wasn't bright. My head was throbbing, nonetheless. With a wince, I remembered snippets of the night before. Yes, he had done some things he shouldn't, but the blame for how badly the night had ended landed squarely with me. I had been horrible and there was no excuse for it. I owed James an apology, it was becoming a theme in my life and I felt like an even bigger ass because of it.

Groping around on the table for my phone, I tried to recall if I had aspirin in my purse.

"Hello?" It was hard to talk with my tongue so dry and fuzzy.

"Claire?"

"Stephen." I sat upright. My stomach and head simultaneously rebelled and I tasted bile. In my foggy stupor, I tried to recall how our last conversation had ended. He had accused me of making up the story about Brian being a traitor. He had called me selfish. He was right. "Listen, before you say anything I wanted to tell you again that I'm sorry for how things ended last time we spoke. But I am really telling the truth about Brian. You can't trust him."

Stephen's voice was hard to hear, I wondered if there was a problem with the connection. "I know."

The fog was lifting from my brain in a hurry, my panic helping to push it aside. "What's happened Stephen? Are you okay?"

"Claire, dear," the hair on the back of my neck rose at the familiar British accent. "I am calling to invite you to visit my club today. As you've heard, Stephen is already here. Silver is such a beautiful color on him; you should see it. It is nearly enough to bring a tear to the eye."

"You're back?" I couldn't believe it. We'd been looking for them for months; now they held Stephen in silver, paralyzed and frightened for sure. My eyes filled with tears.

He chuckled at my bafflement. "I never left." He turned serious. "I'm certain you can figure out how this part goes. You come alone. Leave your boyfriend at home; we have so much to discuss." Bradley's icy instructions sent chills up my spine. "If you fail to follow directions, Stephen will pay for it."

"When?" I remembered the silver burns on Tonya after Raymond had held her in captivity and the scars Stephen carried from his previous master. He couldn't suffer that again if I could help it.

Bradley's pleasure was audible. "I have some things to attend to, but I think it would be reasonable to expect you at noon. I'll see you soon, Claire." The line went dead.

As my thoughts went to the feasibility of sneaking out, I realized I had another issue. Transportation. If I called a cab, James would see it pull up and stop me from leaving. I couldn't explain to him that Bradley wouldn't be coming to get me because I would be going to him. I could sneak his keys away and take a car. James had two of them here. I didn't know where he kept the keys to the Ferrari, nor did I feel comfortable driving it. The keys to the Audi, however, I knew precisely where they were. They were always in his pocket.

With a sickening lurch in my stomach, I recalled the extent my drunken accusations of last night and was filled with regret and shame. Things were going to be different this morning. Not only would this complicate my ability to get his keys, it would be how he would remember me if I didn't make it back.

My eyes closed and head fell back against the headboard as I considered what Bradley wanted with me. I had proven to be the weak link between him and the vampires, posing the biggest problem in his power grab, I was usable as a bargaining chip. This time though, he knew I had a powerful ability and might want me alive instead of dead. I wasn't sure which was worse.

A plan was piecing itself together in my brain as adrenaline pushed away the lingering effects of last night's trespass. I had to get to James so I could get his keys. He would immediately know when I took the car, which wouldn't give me much time to get ahead of him to the club and to Stephen. It was shaky but it was my best bet.

Bradley was looking for humans with abilities to work with him, that was no secret. He also knew that I had a strong gift and that I was marked thereby making my ability significantly stronger than in a pure human. The thought left me hopeful that he would consider me in trade for Stephen. My friend had been protecting me for months, now it was my turn to return the favor. Concern for my own welfare was suspended in light of the pain I knew he was in. It would be inhuman to leave him to his fate and I wasn't inhuman yet, at least not entirely.

Looking at the clock on the nightstand, I saw that it was after ten already. It sickened me to think that Stephen would be in agony for almost two more hours. On a more practical level, that left me not quite two hours to try to make things right with James, say good-bye to him and leave him knowing that I did love him and I did trust him in spite of my stupidity and big mouth.

I saw that I was in one of James' undershirts. He'd come in and put me into my pajamas after I had been so cruel. His tenderness sent a knife through my heart. He had been honest with me. I knew that he hadn't intended for his proposal to coincide with his "job offer." Once again my raw, overactive emotions and lack of social graces had gotten in my way. Being a vampire *could not* be worse than this. Nothing could.

Rushing, I dressed and brushed my hair and teeth before heading downstairs to find him. The upstairs was silent so I assumed he would be downstairs on his laptop where he often worked if he didn't want to disturb my sleep.

As my foot touched the last step I heard the teakettle whistle and found James in the kitchen. He would have heard my phone call. I hoped he wouldn't figure it out; I hadn't said anything that would have intimated I was speaking with anyone but Stephen. His voice startled me when I walked into the room.

Without turning, he spoke. His tone was flat. "My kind and yours do not often have lasting affairs because of our differing natures."

I could see from the set of his shoulders that he was tense.

"I told you that I coveted you from the first and that I loved you. Last night you made it very clear that you not only distrust the legitimacy of my feelings for you, but also my intentions."

I felt the knife twist in my heart and, feeling this was the end, I let go of my pride and begged. "James, I am so sorry for what I said last night. I didn't mean any of it. I love you and I know you love me. I do trust you; I trust you with my life." I couldn't let those be the last words he spoke to me.

His hands were going through the motions of making a cup of tea, pausing for a brief moment when he was scooping the sugar into the mug. Otherwise, he gave no indication that he heard me. "I have spoken to Miranda and she believes that our bond might lessen with time and distance between us. My paper has been eager for me to travel abroad again and I have arranged to be gone until after the New Year. After the Guard leaves us I will be returning to Europe permanently. I leave in a few hours; I expect that you will be gone when I return. Rest assured, you will remain under our protection until this threat has passed and you can return to a normal life." The coldness in his voice belied any feeling underneath it. "Whether you believe it or not, I *do* honor my promises."

Finished with me, he turned and paused long enough to put the teacup in my limp hand. His other hand wrapped my fingers around the handle and he touched my shoulder softly, lingering for only a brief moment before brushing past me. The silence of the house pressed in on my ears that strained for the slightest sound to tell me where he was. Hearing nothing, I felt more alone than I had ever been in my life.

When I had been untrained and kept myself segregated from the rest of the population, I'd considered myself to be alone. I had been wrong. To miss out on love was nothing compared to having it and then losing it. I felt my heart break inside my empty chest and my soul ached for the loss of its other half.

Ch. 26

I stood in the kitchen, utterly devastated. When I could breathe again, I turned to set the cup down on the counter and a sparkle caught my eye. He had taken my ring from the dresser upstairs and brought it down here. Why, I couldn't be sure. In an impulsive move, I put it back on my hand wishing I had never taken it off. Wishing I hadn't been so foolish and said those terrible things and ruined the best thing that had ever happened to me. And wishing I wasn't about to give myself over to the enemy with the knowledge that he wouldn't even know what had happened if I failed to get Stephen out.

Shaking off my grief, I focused on the problem at hand. Walking to the back of the kitchen, I opened the door intending to see if the keys were in the Ferrari. I stared dumbly into the empty garage. The car was gone.

Now I was really stuck. James was going to leave for the airport and he would take my only means of getting to Stephen with him. I needed to get his keys out of his pocket, only I wasn't sure that he would let me get close enough. Not without some sort of distraction.

I knew from my personal experience that his kind had two needs, food and sex. I wondered if I could appeal to one or both in order to distract him enough to get the keys. It might also give me an excuse to feel him one last time.

I heard his fingers on the keyboard in his office when I reached the top of the stairs. It was easy to let my body go to him. Now that I knew this would be the last time I would see him I was more drawn to him than ever.

The only indication he gave that he knew of my presence was a slight hesitation in his keystrokes. Now that I was facing him, ready to offer myself up as a sacrifice I was afraid to face his rejection. The thought of Stephen, paralyzed and burning in silver was enough to drive me forward. James let me walk up behind him and put my arms around his neck, my hands resting on his chest. I couldn't tell if he was holding his breath so that he didn't smell me or if he was just not bothering to pretend to breathe. His absolute stillness again gave me pause. He *had* to hear my racing pulse and uneven breathing, even I could hear the evidence of my apprehension and my senses were nothing to his.

I leaned in to kiss his neck. When he didn't push me away I used my teeth to scrape his skin eliciting a soft noise from his throat. His hands came off of his keyboard and grasped mine. He dropped them at once as if he'd been burned and I knew he'd felt the ring on my finger.

He kept his eyes forward refusing to face me. "Claire I've made my decision. Whether you wear that or not, the answer is the same. We cannot be together when you don't trust me." His cold rebuke tore a hole in me.

Gulping down the sick feeling that came with knowing he would see what I was going to do as pathetic neediness, I thought again of Stephen and steeled myself to do what I needed to do to save my friend. There was no need to lose them both.

"I know," my voice quavered with genuine emotion, "I want to be with you one more time before you leave me." He didn't react. I cast aside my self-respect and whispered. "Please."

It was not difficult to dig down and find my lust for James. When I found it, I used my ability to amplify and projected it at him as my lips returned to his flesh. I felt his muscles stiffen when he perceived my projection bumping up against his shielding. I'd never done this with a vampire who could shield before so had no idea the outcome. I held my breath hoping it would work. I literally needed to get into James' pants and had only this one chance to make it work.

He remained unmoved and, instead of perceiving it as a rejection, I used it as an excuse to assert myself. Because we'd been lovers I knew what he liked and implemented my knowledge as he permitted. I stood up a little straighter, shifting sideways so that my breasts were on the side of his neck and my left hand was able to slide further down onto his stomach. He remained passive, I took it as permission to continue and I moved around to face him and kissed his jaw, again using my teeth lightly. The move had never failed to inspire passion in the past. It didn't fail now, either. In a movement too fast to process until it was done, he lifted me, put me on his lap astride him and held me tight against his taught muscles as he kissed me with a violence I'd never felt from him.

The metallic taste of blood in my mouth made me cry out in surprise and pull away from his kiss. When I raised my hand to my lip, it came away smeared with my blood. He was making no attempt to hide that he was in a state halfway between human and vampire. His fangs were out far enough that they had cut the inside of my lip and his eyes were dark with his need.

James had never let himself lose control when we'd been intimate before. I could tell he was close to the edge and I wasn't sure which of his needs was stronger in this moment, but so desperate was I to go through with this, I didn't care. If I were truly honest with myself I would have seen that I wanted to save Stephen, but I wanted to be with James even more. He had turned away from me, withdrawn his offer of a life with him and I was possibly going to be dead or indentured to Bradley by nightfall.

The revelation and desperation inflamed my own wanting. I pushed my bloodied lip against James' mouth hard, feeling the blood flow into our mouths. Any need for encouragement of his desire was no longer necessary as both of his hungers combined. His hands were rough and unforgiving. I couldn't stop the whimper that escaped my lips as passion mixed with pain.

He picked me up and kicked the chair aside, pushing me down on the bed against the back wall. I was vaguely aware of my clothing being cast aside as my own urgent hands unbuttoned his shirt and pushed it over his shoulders. He took over and stood up to remove his pants. I lay naked in front of him, breathing hard and trying to memorize every detail of him, enough to last me for the rest of my days, however long that might be. Too quickly he was back, his cool, firm body moving against mine as I felt my eyes filling with tears. I stifled a whimper and felt him pause to look in my eyes.

Afraid he would catch me in my betrayal I gaspingly whispered, "Take my blood. I want you to take all of me this one last time."

Normally he might have argued, but we were both wild with needs beyond our control. His tongue traced my throat, tasting my skin before he brought his eyes up where they held mine. I had an anxious moment wondering if he saw through me before the world shifted. His mouth moved down the line of my neck and onto my collarbone. Right when I felt his tongue brush back up the side of my neck I closed my eyes and, before I could stop myself I whispered, "I love you."

He bit down.

Our last time together had been all too brief. As we lay tangled together afterward, I closed my eyes and tucked my face into his skin. I wanted to remember his smell, his feel and this closeness. It would never be like this with anyone else, assuming I could bring myself to be with anyone after him.

His hand was tracing the scar on my chest. He traced the sunburst pattern gently and kissed me tenderly causing me to question his resolve to end things for good. Touching my scar served as a reminder of what a vampire could do and made me recall my mission, and Stephen. I glanced around to locate James' pants. They were at the foot of the bed. I didn't know how I was going to get the keys out without him hearing the jingle.

James' voice came to me, distracting me from my designs. "Why did you ask me to bite you? You don't enjoy it."

"I told you, I wanted to give you everything since this is the end." I tried not to cry. Still, I felt the warm tears run down the sides of my face as I lay beside him. Too much was happening and my emotions were running too high to contain them. I was going to give myself away soon if I didn't get going, only I didn't know if I had the strength to leave him.

Before I could fail my friend, James' phone rang from its perch on his desk. He growled, frustrated, and kissed my neck gently again before he left me to answer. "Yes Troy." His expression altered and he was instantly focused on whatever Troy was saying. He held up a finger to me to indicate he would be back as he walked naked from the office to grab something from his bedroom.

After his remarkable backside moved out of my view, I jumped up out of bed and dressed as quickly and quietly as possible. My hand slid into his pants pocket and grabbed his keys, holding them tightly to reduce any sound that might result from their movement.

I padded downstairs and tried to open the closet door. I decided to forego my coat as superfluous. My boots were on in less than a half of a minute and I slid out the front door, easing it closed behind me. Uncertain if he would hear it and rush out to stop me, I ran to the car, hands fumbling on the keys.

I was inside the car, starting it while I hurriedly adjusted the seat to reach the pedals before I saw the hint of movement upstairs in the window. Thank goodness for German engineering. I felt the car rumble as it woke up and flew into the street in reverse. By the time the front door opened with James in the doorway in his pants and open shirt wondering why I was taking his car, I was moving forward, accelerating rapidly toward the main road.

Ch. 27

Fifteen minutes and two wrong turns later I parked on the street a block up from Glamour. I saw from where I'd parked that the neon sign imparting the name of the club was still partially burned out, giving it the appearance of being run down and laughably called "lamo." It did not, however, make me smile this time. I removed my ring and necklace, coiling them in the cup holder. If the bad guys didn't dispose of the car, I knew James would find it and I wanted him to have his gifts. Not Bradley or his muscle Gaston.

Scouring the glove box, I found what I wanted. I left a brief note for James, merely stating that I loved him and that I was sorry for what I'd said. Anything more seemed unnecessary. Any disagreements we'd had didn't matter. I knew that what we'd had was genuine and I'd let my lack of confidence and ineffective control over my side of the bond ruin it. My only hope was that if I didn't make it back out, my ridiculous rants would make the loss easier for him.

The club was an uneventful brick storefront from the 1930's, Glamoured to be unappealing to humans. It took determination for me to enter it now, although it was not just the Glamour that made me unwilling.

The sky outside had been overcast and it didn't take long for my eyes to adjust to the dim interior. Because vampires don't need much light to see the club was nearly dark inside. I saw the red rope lighting behind the bar in front of me and stepped up to speak with the bartender.

She was an extraordinarily tall blonde woman, not unusual for Minnesota given our excessive Scandinavian population. However, her gorgeous face and figure would have been unusual anywhere, even in Hollywood.

Putting my hands on the bar, I tried to project confidence as I asked for Bradley. She looked at me like I was an insect.

"Bradley has not been here for months." Her lip curled in distaste. "He is abroad, but I will be sure to tell him you stopped by when he returns." She returned to her duties, disengaging from our exchange without bothering with my name.

"That's odd," I replied. "He called me earlier this morning and definitely asked me to come here by noon. Maybe he wanted me to meet with someone else?"

She eyed me up and down speculatively before turning her back to me. I wasn't sure what to do and stood for a moment, trying to figure out how to continue when I saw the slightest of movements in her shoulders. Glancing around her, I saw she was mouthing something to the mirror. Aha! It was a two-way mirror.

Reassured, I drummed my hands nervously on my legs and stood at the bar trying to appear nonchalant. Because vampires don't have a need to sit, there were few barstools. The tables around the dance floor had chairs, but that was it for seating.

Checking out the few patrons in the bar at this early hour, I tried to determine if anyone appeared friendly. Certainly by now they knew that I was a human. No human moved like a vampire no matter how hard they tried.

There was one small, dark haired woman drinking from a wine glass seated at the edge of the dance floor. While I watched, a slightly taller dark haired woman joined her. In this light the most I could tell was whether their hair was light or dark, subtleties of shade were lost. They didn't make a move to indicate they had noticed me; they were not friendly and I couldn't count on them for help.

At the back of the bar, past the tables, was an alcove I was guessing housed the restrooms. I was wondering if anyone used them when I heard a voice beside me that sent my body into a convulsion of terror.

"My dear, I *am* sorry to have kept you waiting."

Turning slowly toward the voice I saw Bradley's blonde, slicked back hair and dead blue eyes staring at me from less than an arm's length away. I could see each individual hair in his pencil thin mustache. He was dressed in his usual tailored suit with not a single hair out of place.

It wasn't just the fact that he was responsible for causing me so much misery, it was the precision of him that caused the shiver racing up my spine. The efficient coldness and inhumanity that poured off of him was what made me want to run screaming. It was hard not to turn and run out of the club right then; only the thought of Stephen suffering, silver burning more scars into his flesh, made me stand straighter and stare at Bradley's mouth, the closest to his eyes I would dare venture to look.

"What is it you want with me, Bradley? Where's Stephen?"

I watched his lips curl as he chuckled. "Aren't we eager? Don't worry about your friend, he isn't going anywhere." He turned to the bartender and held up a finger to order before turning back to me. "Would you care for anything to drink, Claire?"

Shaking my head, I knew better than to push even though my impatience was difficult to hide.

He signaled for the blonde Amazon ordering for me. "Champagne for the lady." When the drinks were placed upon the bar Bradley grabbed his and handed mine to me. "Please, have a drink with me. We are celebrating."

My heart plummeted. "What are we celebrating?" I didn't want to know the answer. If Bradley was happy then I would decidedly not be.

He took a long drink of his "wine" and for courage, I took a drink of my champagne, tricky with my hand shaking so hard. "Because my dear, my little family is finally all under the same roof. You certainly remember the reason your sweet James was called away to Germany? Well, Gaston returned just this morning with the girl and now that I have you as well, James is certainly soon to follow. My cup runneth over with my good fortune." I watched the glass tip up for him to finish his drink, feeling my hope crumbling.

Mentally, I inventoried the abilities Bradley now had at his disposal. Stephen could sense intentions and interject thoughts into people's heads, the boy could manipulate vampires without the ability to shield, Annika could get people to give her things and I could feel and channel emotions. Bradley knew that I was marked and counted on James' loyalty to bring him running; his strength had to have the sadist drooling. The strength of the bond between James and I was yet unbeknownst to Bradley as far as I knew and, for the sake of damage control, I shared with him my loss. "James left me. We aren't really together anymore."

He watched me carefully, unconcerned as he raised his glass for another drink. "You reek of him. Do you deny he bedded you this very morning?"

I froze. Stupid human, I forgot their sense of smell. "He is stronger than me. I'm unable to deny him his needs when he demands."

That did give Bradley pause. Apparently, it was a feasible explanation for a vampire who would see humans as merely a means to satisfy his physical needs. Noticing that Bradley had finished his drink, I set my own glass down on the bar and looked up expectantly at his mustache.

"Shall we then?" He stuck his arm out for me to take. Breathing steadily through my nose I tried to quash my nerves before I reached to place my hand as lightly on his arm as possible. He ignored my obvious distaste as he led me to the alcove at the back of the club.

Sure enough, it did contain the restrooms. Bradley led me into the empty men's room without pause and directly to the last stall, oversized and marked with the familiar symbol of a person in a wheelchair. When he closed the door he pushed one of the white subway tiles behind the toilet and a doorway made out of the interlocking wall tiles opened to our right, opening onto a stairway going down.

I glanced at him, stunned, and he bowed at the waist, indicating with his hand that I was to enter first. Crouching down, I did so. I was able to stand after descending the first few stairs and had gone down about ten steps when the light from the doorway above disappeared. A foot scuffed the step above me and I knew Bradley was behind me.

We descended two flights of stairs completely in the dark before a faint light ahead illuminated our last few steps. Coming off of the stairway, my feet scraped on what sounded like cement. I wondered if this basement showed up on the building plans.

Guessing the direction of my thoughts, Bradley spoke in the darkness beside me. "I had this built in the '30's during Prohibition when building inspectors were easily bribed to keep secrets hidden from county records. It makes for a handy little hideaway when one becomes necessary."

The corridor we now found ourselves in was twice the width of a normal hallway, had a low ceiling of about eight feet, and was illuminated by sparsely placed torches on the walls. The space felt a lot like the Court's hidden venue in Scotland. I noticed the torches marked doorways. There were six doors that I could see. Bradley was beside me

again and motioned for me to go through the middle door on
the right.

Ch. 28

The room had rough, lightly colored walls of stone and was illuminated by several lanterns placed about the perimeter. On the near side beside the door was a twin size bed and upon it a familiar occupant. Beside it lay another familiar form, except he was lying motionless at an unnatural angle. Brian had met his death violently, judging from the horrified expression frozen on the pale, bloodless face turned toward me.

"Stephen!" I ran to the bed where Stephen lay panting on his side. The collar glowed gold in the sparse yellow light. It was the same as the one Tonya had worn at Raymond's ending any doubts I'd had about the extent of Bradley and Raymond's working relationship.

Stephen cried out when I touched him. I immediately jerked my hands away, becoming aware that my skin was tingling. I stepped back examining him more closely and cried out in horror, my hands flying to cover my gaping mouth. Stephen was stuck halfway through his change. His muscles were clenched and shaking in pain while he lay curled in the fetal position. His tanned hands had broadened taking the shape of paws, his lower face jutted out prominently in the shape of a big cat's mouth and nose. Stephen's body was covered in a light coat of tawny fur and his pupils were mere slits in his large feline eyes, reflecting the stress being placed on his mind as well as his body.

Outraged, I spun around to face Bradley who stood observing from the doorway. "What have you done? You're torturing him!" Tara had told me before that the change became less painful with time because it got faster; that it was uncomfortable as their bones and muscles shifted between forms. I could only imagine how much physical torment Stephen was in while he lay frozen, caught between forms. I didn't give Brian more than a passing glance. He had sold us out and right now, I didn't care that he'd lost his life in his deal with the devil.

Bradley ignored me and stepped outside, closing the door behind him. I heard the bolt slip home and turned back to Stephen to see if I could help him.

Cursing my bad luck for being unconscious when Tonya's collar was removed, I examined it without touching to see if I could try to remove it. My hope crumbled as I saw no sign of a closure hidden in the intricate designs on the metal surface.

"Stephen, I'm so sorry. I don't know how to get it off. Can you help me?" I was mortified to see him in such pain and not be able to even touch him or give him some small amount of comfort.

I looked into his furry, catlike face and saw his mouth moving. The vibration of his voice box must have caused his throat to touch the collar, he was trying to mouth his message to me. Assuming he was giving me what I needed to free him, I watched intently as his mouth continued to move. It was unreadable, his mouth being more feline than human and thus changing the shape of his lips.

"Put it in my head," I whispered, knowing we could communicate simple ideas that way.

The word "key" popped into my head.

"Do you know who has the key?" My heart sank when I heard a crisp "no" in my head.

I still planned to negotiate for Stephen's release, supposing I could convince Bradley that I would be of more help than he. Surely he would see that in his current state, Stephen would be useless to him. Miserable, I sat for another hour at Stephen's bedside hearing only an occasional whimper from him. Mercifully, he seemed to be unconscious most of the time.

The sound of the bolt sliding open drew me out of my thoughts and I looked up to see Bradley walking in, Gaston close behind him. Gaston looked much the same as the last time I saw him. He was partially dressed in green fatigues, his shirt was flannel with the sleeves cut off and hanging mostly open over his hairy barrel chest. He had not been an attractive human and being turned hadn't lessened his ugliness by much.

Wanting to show them I wasn't afraid, I stood to meet them. It didn't help that I trembled.

Bradley spoke before I could. "Claire, you recall our friend Gaston? He certainly remembers you. He was so disappointed that I gave you to Gina last time." Gaston's smile was full of need and fangs making me nauseous, yet I tried to maintain my nerve.

"Gaston," he continued, "is going to be taking care of you from here on. Don't worry, he is more than qualified; he was a mercenary as a human." Bradley gave a snide little chuckle. "He actually *sought out* a vampire to turn him while he was in Poland during the war. Evidently, he thought it would make him stronger and faster so that he could be more efficient at his job. Isn't that remarkable?" Bradley hardly looked impressed, though he did look amused.

Properly unnerved by this point I rushed into my offer. "Bradley, I want to make a trade."

He was silent, the only indication he'd heard me was the raising of a blonde brow.

Boldly, I plowed on. "Me for Stephen. I can do everything he can. Look at him, he's weak and can't help you. I can *and* I won't fight you." I had hoped to be smoother and take my time with my proposal but in the end, I botched it because I was so scared. Lifting my chin, I tried to bluff my way through my predicament.

Bradley shot a sideways glance at Gaston and then to Stephen before catching my eyes. Immediately I looked down to his mustache, but in that brief glance I thought I saw him hesitate and it gave me hope. Shielded as they were, I could feel nothing from either one.

"I will think about it. You might have a point and I do see the usefulness of consolidating for efficiency sake. If one soldier can do the work of two, all's the better." He paused and I chanced a quick peek up, feeling my heart plunge at what I saw. "We will need to test your claim, I'm sure you understand. We will do so over the next few days and make a decision then. Gaston," he looked to his swarthy companion, "take Claire to her quarters and you can begin immediately." Bradley lowered his voice and caught my eye again. "Let's see how *you* do under pressure."

Turning on his heel, Bradley left the room and I was left facing Gaston who would surely be sweating and panting like the pig he was if he were human. As it was, he just stood and stared at me with his too small eyes perched atop a bulbous nose, which had been broken numerous times as a human. Given his incredibly unpleasant disposition, I didn't find it surprising at all that someone would want to hit him.

After Bradley left the room Gaston pulled a surprise out of his hat. Well, his belt actually, he had a pair of leather manacles tucked into the waistband behind his back. Pulling them out, he grinned and thrust them toward me. "Give me your hands." His voice was rough and held a remnant of a French accent in keeping with the origins of his name. It was the first I'd heard him speak.

My hopes sank. What would I have to endure with these monsters I wondered. Keeping with my offer not to fight and not wanting to upset him, I stuck my hands out in front of me for him to tie the manacles on. He did so, tightly, and upon wriggling my wrists I discovered there was less give and slip to leather than I thought there would be.

Gaston's chuckle drew my eyes to his face. I didn't fear looking into *his* eyes, he was not old enough to have any extra power over me. My marks rendered me immune to the younger vampires' mind tricks. I fought to push my memory of James from my mind as soon as thought of him entered my consciousness. Thinking of him now wouldn't help me or Stephen, it would only distract me. It was just us now and I had to have my wits about me if we had any chance of getting out of here.

"Forget getting out of those." He pointed at my bound wrists. "That's why I use leather. They will swell and tighten the longer you wear them, and, they will not cut you. Your blood may come in handy; we don't want to waste it."

The reality of what I'd gotten myself into started to sink in and I struggled to stay positive, reminding myself I could find a chance to escape. I had come here because I was going to get Stephen out. Maybe even the other two, Annika and the boy, if they were down here.

Gaston didn't give me long to think. He grabbed the strap connecting the manacles and dragged me out the door at what was a run for me, a brisk walk for him. My quarters, it turned out, were across from Stephen's. I was glad, thinking that when I escaped, I wouldn't have far to travel to get to him. My eyes perused Gaston's waist searching for keys, though there were none visible. I needed to find the keys to Stephen's collar in order to get him out; it was impossible to even hope that I could carry him in the state he was in.

My quarters were much the same as Stephen's. The room was about twelve feet square and had the same twin bed against the same stone wall and the same low ceiling. One lantern hung by the door providing minimal lighting. Gaston shoved me hard and I stumbled into the room. Just before he closed the door behind me, he gave a chilling hint of what was to come. "I'll be back in a few hours to get to know you better."

The bolt slid into place, echoing in the stillness. Feeling like a fool who had no chance to save my friend but had instead put the both of us in danger, I ambled over to the bed where I curled up and stared blankly at the wall.

At some point, I must have fallen asleep because I sat up with a start, hearing the bolt slide without warning. As promised, Gaston entered carrying a tray with food. By the smell, it wasn't bad food and it was hot, though I wasn't hungry in the least. Food wasn't first on his agenda either, I was soon to learn. He set the tray down outside the door and closed it behind himself as he stepped inside.

"You are brave girl. Coming to your friend's aid, offering yourself in trade." Then he laughed. It was a cold, cruel laugh meant to strike fear. It did. "How did you expect to come out on that one? You can't trade with someone who has everything already? You are a stupid girl."

Bristling at his mockery, I argued back. "I offered myself not as a replacement prisoner, but as a willing employee. Stephen will fight you and what will that get you? You can't force someone to use their abilities. I offer to help willingly if he allows my friend to leave here and return to his family. Bradley is smart enough to understand how that will benefit him."

At that, Gaston seemed to consider my words. "Maybe you aren't so stupid." Shifting his focus back to why he came in, he ordered me to stand up and I complied. I remained as far from him as possible with the backs of my legs touching my iron bed frame, trying to hide my fear, knowing he could hear my pulse fly. "So, show me what you can do."

Wanting to impress the man, I planned to make a good showing. With a gulp I swallowed the worst of my anxiety and focused. The shields I'd used to lock myself up tight came down easily. It was harder to keep them up than let them down when I was so upset. I could see it when he felt the beginnings of my probing into his mind, seeking to find an emotion that I could use to channel him and give him a little shock.

Finding nothing except hate and darker things below the surface, I pressed on; those would not be good to take in or I might suffer his wrath exponentially. I sought a pleasant or at least less dangerous memory. Soon I found it and I bent over at the waist, sure I was going to throw up. Gaston's most recent idea of a pleasant memory involved Stephen, the silver collar he now wore and the violent beating it took to get him into it.

His lips twisted into a sadistic smile when he saw my reaction to his thoughts. Ignoring him and trying to dig deeper, I straightened up and looked him in the eye. I came upon another emotional memory of a young blonde girl, she was a vampire like him. After only a glimpse of her torn and bloody body putting itself back together for what I could sense was not the first time, I tore myself away, repulsed.

Gaston belly laughed. "You aren't much of a soldier, you are too soft. We must toughen you up, yes?" Dark pig eyes glinting in the low light gave the man a demonic mien and I watched him approach with no means for escape. My only defense was to draw my shields up tight and keep him out. I could protect my mind, that much I knew.

Coming closer, I saw his intention the second before his hand flew. He struck the side of my face with the back of his hand. It wasn't hard for a vampire; I didn't even fall down, though I did see spots and I knew I would bruise despite my marks.

His face was right next to my own when he spoke. "Do you know what I am good at? What service I provide for Bradley? What I have done for over sixty years? I break people down. I am very good at what I do and you would be surprised the demand for it." He rubbed his hand over his expansive chest. "If you want to be a soldier you must first be broken down so that we can build you back up to the boss's liking. As you saw, women are my favorite. We have so many more options."

My nerves were taught and I felt my legs threatening to give out at the prospect of again becoming a victim to the cruelty of vampires. If it weren't for my experience with James and Henry, I would think them the evil things of legends. It seemed *my* vampires were the rare exception to the stories. The rest of them resorted to cruelty to humans at their every opportunity. James was right, they did go mad with the passage of time and loss of their humanity.

Gaston wasn't done. Taking my chin in his hand he held my face up for his inspection, making sure I was listening. Gritting my teeth, I kept my expression benign. "I will visit you each day with your meals. If you want to eat, you must show progress. It is relatively simple and if you are smart it should not be long before you are a good soldier. Then, we can talk about letting your friend go." He paused and gestured in the direction of the door where he had left the tray. "Do you wish to eat tonight?"

I shook my head no and held my breath waiting for him to do something. When nothing happened and Gaston walked out, I collapsed on my bed, chest heaving as though I'd run a mile.

Within a few minutes I figured out where he had gone when I heard a woman's piercing scream coming from another room. I ran to the door and put my ear to it, hoping to hear some hint as to who might be down here with us. There were sounds of a struggle and then it went quiet for a few moments before I heard a door very close by slam closed and the bolt slide into place. I waited a long time, giving Gaston ample time to leave the corridor before I spoke.

The doors were wooden and thick, but also old and drafty. It would be impossible for me to tear one from its hinges, though sound could easily come through them.

"Hello?" I tried to speak with the other prisoner, wondering if it was the teen that had inadvertently gotten James wounded and Ursa killed. The one Bradley said Gaston had brought back. "Annika?"

There was no reply although I thought I heard faint crying. "Annika, I'm a friend of James. You met him in Germany. Do you remember?" Nothing; the crying stopped. I didn't know what Gaston had done and imagined it was something awful, shuddering at the memory I'd pulled from his mind and thought it best to leave her alone for the night. I would try to speak to her again tomorrow. I returned to my bed and lay down, pulling the thin blanket over myself but knowing I would not sleep.

Ch. 29

Somehow I did sleep. I knew it only because I was awakened by the sounds of Stephen crying out. Jumping up, I pounded on my door. "Leave him alone! Please, don't hurt him!" Angry tears sprang to my eyes as I felt frustration at my helplessness rise up inside me.

Stephen's cries died to muffled whimpers and I hoped they would leave him alone, for a while at least. They did, however, my relief ended abruptly. I was thrown backward as the door flew open and I discovered Stephen was being left alone because it was my turn.

I sailed through the air and skidded across the floor on my side, my leg going instantly numb under me when my hip crashed into the stone floor. Before I could consider what damage had been done, Gaston's form filled my doorway. He was removing a pair of thick leather gloves; what purpose they served, I could only imagine. His face was dark and his fangs were out. I could see that he wasn't there to talk and I wanted to scream, only the knowledge that he would enjoy that kept my throat closed. He was in a cruel mood and my outburst hadn't helped me, or anyone else, for that matter.

"Do you intend to tell me my business?" His hands went to his belt and he began to unbuckle it. I held my breath.

It was almost a relief when I saw him fold the leather strap over and slap it on his palm, preparing to strike me with it. At the first swing, it cut across my hands and face, held up defensively. The ensuing barrage rained down on my neck, shoulders and back when I tried to turn away. I felt the blood running from a number of cuts, but I had been through worse and took heart that he didn't intend to do more than make me fear him. This was about dominance.

When I saw that, I forced myself to cower. Well, not really forced, but I curled into a ball on the floor next to the bed with my manacled hands up, trying to block the follow up blows he aimed at my head. After a few more strikes he relented and restrung his belt.

"A good soldier never questions her commander." He turned and walked out, leaving me to consider my fate.

He didn't return until long after the blood had caked, making movement painful as my clothing tore the scabs away and the blood ran anew. There was no water in the room, I was unable to clean myself up and could only hope there would be no infection. Feeling had come back to my leg and I was able to hobble around the room in slow circles, trying to keep warm in the dank cold.

What time Gaston came back, I don't know. I had no watch, and there was no indication of time of day down here. It was like being in a sensory deprivation chamber, which was most likely part of this place's charm, considering what they used it for.

When my keeper arrived he was carrying a tray and again he set it down outside the door. Unfortunately, my stomach growled when it recognized the smell of eggs. Hearing my body betray me, Gaston smirked.

"You *are* hungry. You cannot lie to me. Now get up and come here to me."

Stiffly, I stumbled over. My shirt tore the fresh scab off a cut on my shoulder and I felt the blood trickle down my arm. I saw the smell of my blood arouse Gaston and his fangs grew half way. Seeing his want, I stopped short, trying to balance on my good leg.

His ire rose and he growled. "I said come here to me."

As much as I knew I needed to go the last few feet to him to avoid aggravating him, I couldn't make my legs move. My experiences with hungry vampires hadn't been good and I was trying to decide which would hurt worse; being bitten without Glamour or being beaten again. I stood, paralyzed with indecision, watching his face to see which it was going to be.

Gaston made his decision. I saw the change in his face as his fangs grew the last bit and he moved before I could get away. Grabbing my arms, he spun me to face away from him, my leg buckled beneath me. The contact of his hard hands on my abused flesh drew a cry of pain from my lips. I heard him growl in pleasure just before he brought his mouth down on my neck and I screamed as he fed.

He drank for long enough that I thought I would faint, except he didn't take enough to let me pass out. When he pulled back, he stared too long at my shoulder and I realized what he was seeing. He was feeding from the same side James had. It wouldn't be totally healed yet.

Shoving me at the bed, Gaston growled again. "I don't blame your lover. Your blood is strong but don't waste your time thinking he will come for you. No one cares for a whore and that is all you are, even to him." He wiped his mouth with the back of his hand and turned to leave. Before bolting the door, I heard his voice once more. "This is your life now, get used to it."

I tried to curl up on the bed unable to find a comfortable position, my body was sore from his visits already. While I lay in misery, I heard a female voice call out.

"Hello?" She sounded scared.

Carefully, I moved my body off the bed to crouch with my face laying against the door. "Annika? Is that you?"

"Who are you? How do you know my name?" Her voice was high pitched and halting, I wasn't sure if it was from fear or hesitation as she translated to my foreign language.

"My name's Claire. I'm a friend of James." I *was* a friend of James, I reminded myself of the past tense and felt sadness threatening to creep in. Again I had to push it aside for fear it would take away my ability to stay focused on what I had to do to get us out of here. There was still hope I told myself.

"Is he coming? Can he get us out of this place?" she asked in an excited whisper.

Not wanting to crush her hope, yet not able to lie convincingly, I gave her a half-truth. "James and several others are looking for you. They want to get you out of here."

The excitement in her voice fell away. "They'll never find us. No one knows this place is here. We won't get out until they need to use us again or they kill us. That's what they do."

I didn't want to talk anymore and crawled back to my bed to curl up under my thin blanket and shiver until I fell asleep, wishing James hadn't closed himself off to me. Even if he didn't want me anymore he wouldn't refuse a call for help, especially if it led him to Bradley.

Ch. 30

The next day or night or whenever it was when Gaston came for me, Bradley was with him. Bradley called me and I struggled to get up. Stiff and weak as I was, it took a few tries before I successfully gained my feet. He waited patiently for me, not taking more than a step or two into the room making it clear that I was to come to him. When I got there I wavered, which only served to make my efforts to stand up straight and stare defiantly at his chin more laughable.

Bradley surprised me by pulling my shirt away from my neck exposing my bites. He sniffed at them and licked the fresher of the two. He rolled his tongue around in his mouth, savoring whatever it was he tasted in my blood.

"You are right, Gaston. She does taste like something, although I cannot quite put my finger on it. No more feeding from her for now. Do whatever you need to do without drawing blood." The carefully coiffed monster spoke and shocked me. "Raymond said he could taste the power in her marks, but it is *her* power that intrigues me. We will let her recover and then I have an idea." With that, Bradley turned on his heel and exited the room, leaving me alone with Gaston.

I saw the irritation he felt at being ordered by Bradley revealed in his pig eyes as my glance flickered across his face and I felt sick realizing how he intended to prove himself a man now that drinking my blood was no longer an option; he had another need he could feed. "No!" But he already had the strap between my cuffed wrists in his one fist while he grabbed at me with his other. I kicked at his knees and he caught my foot easily, twisting it hard. The pain buckled my other knee. To make matters worse, in my weak and frightened state, my shields were failing me and I felt his excitement when he knew he was hurting me.

When my shields dropped, I felt a new surge of rage and heat. With all of my being I wanted to kill Gaston. Thinking that I was tapping into Gaston, I tried to channel it. Maybe he would beat me instead if I could get him angry enough. I could handle that I told myself. Hard black eyes flashed and he let go of my hands long enough to backhand me. This time it was much harder and the explosion of pain in my brain was blinding. Momentarily stunned, my hands dropped and he pulled both wrists together, tightening his hold on me.

Unable to stand on my twisted knee and sore hip and with my hands firmly locked within Gaston's grasp, my struggles were futile against his superior strength. Rage more powerful than I thought possible flared within me and I felt I would combust with the heat of it as Gaston violated me. I cried out, not in pain but in an impotent frenzy, unable to stop even when I could see the passion my suffering inspired.

When he left, I curled up on my bed and stared at the wall like I had that first day, only I was no longer the same person. My eyes were dry and I was now familiar enough with signs of shock to know that was what dulled my senses. This time I welcomed its protection. Faintly, I heard Annika call to me, yet I didn't answer.

I turned my ineffective anger inward. My harebrained plan to get Stephen out was a failure and I knew that beyond a doubt now. Gaston and Bradley were steadily breaking us all down so that when they got us out of here we would be their mindless drones. When I accepted that, I felt the last of my will drain away.

Ch. 31

My marks were strange things. They caused me to heal faster than a human and soon my cuts were fading to pink scars and the bruises from the first beating were turning yellow. Normally it would take a week or more to heal that much, but lucky me, I would be back to the same person on the outside very soon.

Inside, however, was a different story. My mind was numb and thick from shock and lack of nourishment. Gaston brought more trays of food when he visited me, none of which I accepted. Other than when he came for me, I could not bring myself to leave my bed except to visit the bucket they left me for personal uses. The lack of food and water were giving me less cause to even have to get up for that.

When Gaston visited me and took my body again, I had not been able to shield myself from him at all. I had actually felt his pleasure this time, channeling it weakly. My body and mind were unable to work well enough to be completely willing, yet I didn't fight and my angry growls were misinterpreted as desire in his excitement. He was even more eager thinking that I had finally succumbed to him as he had promised I would.

When he left and I slept, I dreamed of James. He called my name from far away, I heard it only faintly. He was scared I could feel it. I wanted to go to him except I knew that I was beyond his help and I turned away. He roared in frustration but I knew that he would no longer want me even if I could convince him that our argument had all been a misunderstanding. It seemed an eternity ago that I'd been so petty and juvenile.

Time no longer mattered during my imprisonment. Gaston visited intermittently. I heard sounds come from the rooms of Stephen, Annika and another voice on occasion, which I had to assume was the mysterious boy that used to be so important to me. Now, I only wanted to kill Gaston and Bradley if I could. I began to dream of fashioning a stake from the wood in my room. Wood would not kill, but it could immobilize. I remembered that fact well.

The idea took hold in my mind. I knew that in order to fight back, I would need to keep up my strength and the next time Gaston visited, I ate what I could. He gloated believing that I was broken and in a sense he was right. I knew that I could stop at least one of them when the opportunity presented itself and maybe if I was lucky, one of them would kill me.

Searching for a tool to break off a piece of the door, I looked to the bed frame. Instead of springs the frame had metal hooks with bent ends. It took quite some time for me to straighten one enough to work it loose and then I set to work scraping at my door to break off a piece big enough to use as a weapon.

Annika became curious when she heard my scratching. "Claire, what are you doing in there?" She was a fellow captive, yet she was also a vampire. I wasn't sure how she would feel about my plan to stake our captors.

"Nothing. I'm just marking how long I've been here." I decided against alerting her to my plan. If only *I* knew, no one else could spoil it.

"Four days." Her voice surprised me.

"What?"

"Four days. You were brought in the same day as me and I have been here four days."

I had forgotten a vampire can always feel the sun. She would know when it was daytime no matter how far underground she might be. The knowledge that I'd been here so long and no one had found me yet fueled my efforts. It didn't come as a surprise that no one was looking, but I knew that the longer I was gone the less likely it was that someone would come for me.

Trying to make as little sound as possible, I continued to work at the door until my hands went numb. Rubbing them together restored the blood flow and brought back the feeling. I went back to it and before Gaston came again, I had fashioned a small stake. It was about half a foot long and the width of a pencil. I hoped it would be enough though I worried it would break. I hid my prize against the wall under the bed where no one would find it. I was worried that the stake was so thin that if I put it under my mattress, my weight might snap it. The floor seemed the logical choice.

My hands ached and were raw from my work. Taking a necessary break, I laid down to rest before I could begin to produce a second stake.

The thoughts of James I kept at bay while awake came to me unbidden as I slept. This time, knowing that I might die soon, I welcomed the sight of him as well as the feel his memory brought with it. Having him so close was comforting in this hellish place.

At first I thought it might be the bond like before, then dismissed the thought as wishful thinking. Miranda had said it would fade with time and distance and that was assuming he would even *consider* letting me in again. In my dream, I saw and heard him.

He was sitting at his desk in his office. I was touched when I saw he was holding the picture he had gotten from my parents. Setting it down, he sighed and rubbed his eyes like he was tired.

Why don't you like it when people give you things?

We did not have much money growing up. I didn't receive many then nor have I had cause to receive many since.

I told him I thought that was a shame.

James asked me to focus on him. He said that it was getting difficult to find me. He wasn't sure if it was the bond or me, but something was getting weaker.

I explained that I was just so exhausted and having a hard time thinking clearly. I liked that in my dream I could feel him like I used to. Part of me wished I would never wake up, that this would be my last living thought. Only I knew that life wasn't that kind.

Knowing that I was going to die soon regardless, I wanted my conscience clear and used my dream to confess. James, I wanted to tell you that I know you loved me and I did trust you. It was me that got in my own way. I'm sorry for any pain I've caused you.

He frowned and said that we would talk about that the next time we saw each other.

My laugh came out in a rough bark. Maybe in the afterlife. Do you have an afterlife? I rambled on, happy to talk to him again, to hear his voice in my head. I've made a stake and I'm going to get at least one of them, both if I can get another one made in time. I didn't want to make him sad, so I refrained from telling him I hoped that if I failed I could at least provoke one into ending my suffering.

I was embarrassed to be leaving Stephen. But realistically, I knew he could last longer than me, and when they brought him up to use him they would have to take his collar off and then he would have a fighting chance at getting free, I wouldn't. It had been foolish of me to try; a human had no place with them.

James was worried and I tried to explain that it was okay. I had only seen Bradley and Gaston down here, no one else.

He wanted to know where "down here" was so I explained how ingenious Bradley was and he had been hiding this whole time right under our noses. I couldn't remember exactly which subway tile had to be moved. I tried to explain how it worked to find the doorway.

James asked me to wait for him and that we would be together again soon. It would all work out.

No, I said, we can't. Not now, not after... I couldn't tell him what Gaston had done. My subconscious couldn't even admit it. I was too humiliated thinking of what he had done to me. I watched rage contort his features, and told him it was for the best. That I was at peace with my decision.

He smoothed out his features and said that he would see me soon.

Good-bye James.

The eerie sound of the bolt jerked me out of my dream and back to reality. Bradley walked in this time with Gaston and appeared quite smug about something.

"Gaston tells me you are ready to prove yourself. Is that true, my dear?"

I couldn't raise my eyes past his chest or he would see my face and know that I was lying. "Yes, Bradley."

"Good, we are going to give you a chance tonight." I risked a quick glance at his face. He was smiling at me, the hint of fangs pushed against his lips. "As you pointed out when you came to me, I don't need you *and* the cat. Annika could use a good meal and I would like to see your ability in a fight, I have heard so much about it. You and Stephen are going to decide which one of you is stronger tonight, and I get to keep the winner." Bradley turned to leave and spoke over his shoulder. "Don't think you won't fight. He has been so close to his beast for long enough he will attack anything that smells like meat." He indicated the tray Gaston carried. "Eat and rest, you will need to be at your best tonight."

Gaston left a tray loaded with a bloody steak whose broiled smell normally would have had my mouth watering. Today it turned my stomach. When enough time had passed that they must have gone, I was at the door again with a new sense of urgency and a change of heart.

I had been missing something that had come back to me in my dream; there were only two of them down here. I had to get another stake ready before tonight if I was going to go after the both of them and get us loose. There was still a chance if I worked fast and kept my head. Some amount of doubt loomed ahead.

I wasn't sure how I was going to get Stephen and Annika out without being eaten by one or both of them. I was weak myself and wouldn't be able to put up much of a fight. Shoving thoughts of failure and my shortcomings aside, I continued working on my stake until I had a second one in my hand.

Rolling under my bed, I grabbed my other weapon and pushed them both up my sleeves, poking into the cuff of my manacles so I could easily reach up and grab them for a quick strike. I practiced a few times to get the feel down.

All the while I was wondering if I would be able to get the door at the top of the stairs open or make it through the club if there were more unfriendly vampires above. I hoped that I might be able to get help from Stephen or Annika, or even the silent mystery boy for that matter. It seemed desperate yet I didn't have a lot of options. I *was* desperate. We all were. After tonight we wouldn't all be alive if we stayed.

Most likely I would be the dead one and with my renewed will to live, that was no longer acceptable.

My opportunity came sooner than I had anticipated and with far more confusion. A short time after he'd left and promptly on the heels of my finishing with arming myself, Gaston came bursting into my cell, fangs out and his movements frantic. Snarling at me, he reached out and grabbed me. As he began to back out, dragging me with him, I struck.

It wasn't hard to summon the anger I needed to make myself attack him. The stake was in my hand in seconds and I gripped it tightly as I rammed it up into his stomach. I had never seen anyone stake a vampire before and didn't know exactly what to expect. The effect was instant. He froze, dropping like a stone to my great pleasure and surprise. Forcing myself to touch him, I patted around his waist and pockets for keys.

My heart leapt when I felt the lump in the lower leg pocket of his fatigues. I grabbed them and ran to Stephen's door first. The bolt was easy to slide open. Hurrying to his side, I saw that he was conscious.

"Hold still Stephen, I have the keys." His eyes closed in relief and my eyes blurred until I blinked them clear. Feeling a twinge of doubt, I had to ask, "You aren't going to attack me, are you?" His tired "no" sounded in my head.

I looked for the keyhole in the collar and finally found it after accidentally bumping the silver into him and apologizing profusely. Unlocking the horrid device, I gently pried it off of him and held onto it, feeling a small amount more confident with my new weapon. I was the only one down here who could touch it and not be harmed, although I did notice that my skin tingled where I touched it. Curious.

Once the silver was removed from his body, Stephen stood awkwardly, stuck mid change. He was out of sorts as he tried to balance on his stiff legs that were neither human nor cat and I got a glance of the same burn pattern Tonya sported after Austria. Hers was beginning to fade, though she would always carry a remnant of the scar, as would Stephen. After only a moment of indecision, he fell to all fours, quickly changing to a cat and chewed through the strap connecting my manacles for me. I was happy to see that he padded steadily alongside me as we left his cell with no signs of weakness other than thinner than normal flanks.

At the door, he tried to turn toward the stairs and escape to our left, except I put my hand on his shoulder and called his attention to Annika who was on the other side of my cell.

"She's locked up, too, Stephen. We can't leave her like that." I saw his hesitation as he thought about getting out of the hellish place before he gave a little chirp and came with me to set Annika free.

Opening her door I saw the young, forever teenaged girl whom Gaston had turned strictly to be used as a pawn and felt my blood boil at the injustice. Forcing a kind smile, I approached her with the keys in my hands.

The petite brunette had been light skinned before she had been changed, now her skin was nearly translucent and she had beautiful clear green eyes. Catching sight of the keys in my hand, her features relaxed. "Claire?" She guessed correctly and I nodded assent. Her fangs were out and the green of her eyes was quickly being overtaken by the black of the monster within. Knowing she was a newly turned vampire, I considered the risks involved in freeing her.

Her face was sober as she tried to speak around her fangs. It was hard for newly turned's to get used to them, like braces for a human. "I will not attack you. I promise. Please don't leave me here." She wasn't using her ability to make me believe her, I could tell she was sincere. Making my decision, I unlocked her chains and carefully removed the silver which had burned red blisters into the pale flesh of her wrists and ankles.

"There's a boy. I know they have a boy down here."

She agreed, although she didn't know which cell he was in. I asked the two of them to go down the corridor looking for the boy and to bring him back unharmed. Stephen nodded and headed down one side, Annika took the other and they began to open doors, the first one so forcefully it lifted off its hinges.

There was something else that I needed to do. Though I had never taken a life, I did not question my ability to do so now. James and Henry both would have done the same thing not for revenge but for justice had they found this place. In my hands, I held the means to destroy the monster that lay incapacitated in the next room.

Gaston's eyes were wide with panic and he was muttering a steady stream of what sounded like oaths in several languages. "Girl, you let me up or I will kill you," he threatened harmlessly with fear and hatred in his eyes.

Without bothering to answer, I knelt down and stared at the hole where the stake protruded, ringed with blood. While I straightened Annika's chains in my hands, I held it dangling from my fingers. With one hand I pulled the stake out while simultaneously pushing the chain down as he tried to wriggle away. The link went into the wound and Gaston bucked and kicked like a wild thing.

Steadily I lowered the chain, inch by inch, until the entire thing covered his body and he lay motionless beneath it. His eyes were wide with pain and his lips were pulled back with silent screams that, though they did not reach my ears, filled my head. Smoke and liquid burbled out of him as he liquefied into a gooey, bloody mess before drying to ash. The entire process took less than a minute.

I was still kneeling beside the man shaped ash pile when the sound of someone rushing into the room caught my attention a minute later. I looked up to see Bradley surveying the scene and I noticed that for once, he had lost his composure.

His carefully crafted appearance of vampire aristocrat was gone, leaving him looking like a common nothing. Hair disheveled, fangs out, and eyes gone black, he was no different from any other monster and his spell over me was broken.

The stake I'd used on Gaston had rolled out of reach when I'd pulled it out and I hurried to get my other stake out of my sleeve but it got hung up in the stretchy knit fabric. Bradley couldn't miss my jerking motions and after a second when he realized that I, a human, was going to kill him, his nostrils flared and enraged, he bellowed.

I was shaking my arm frantically trying to get the stake unstuck when Bradley crossed over Gaston's ashes to take hold of my arms and lift me up to shake me. The pain made me drop my loosened homemade stake and I screamed before I clamped my mouth shut. Bradley continued to shake me in frustration and rage. I tried to keep my body tight to minimize any brain damage or chance that I might bite off my own tongue. A human shaking another human can give whiplash; a vampire can kill. I remembered the collar I'd tucked in my pants. I had the means to immobilize him but it did me no good with my arms pinned to my sides.

In desperation, I clung to the hope that I had access to someone stronger than me. Someone who hadn't been beaten and starved for five days and could make me stronger if I could focus hard enough. I reached inward to open my marks, hoping I could still find them; hoping they were still strong enough to give me something. *Please be there.* I prayed that he would listen this one last time.

Gasping at how readily I felt the connection received, I latched onto James' vampire nature. Bradley noticed the change at once, stopped shaking me and stared, eyes wide as he sniffed. Never having done this so quickly or so specifically, it was hard to focus on the one thing I needed. But the warmth from the other end when he sensed me, and the guidance I felt when he picked up on what I was looking for let me access and channel his strength, breaking Bradley's grip on me. In that moment when he released me I reached behind me and, hands closing on what I needed, I swung it up and closed the silver collar around his neck.

Instantly, Bradley screamed and dropped to the ground shrieking in pain. I hurried to lock the collar with the key and fell to the ground next to the bed. Stephen, Annika and a small human boy came running to my cell seconds later.

Stephen came in alone, Annika and the boy watched from the door. The boy was shaking, the opposite to Annika's stillness. The child's large brown eyes were open wide under a mass of dark curls; he couldn't have been more than twelve years old. Stephen remained a mountain lion and I saw his tail twitching as he looked over the mess on the floor and Bradley, still cursing but unmoving. Lifting his nose in the air, I watched in disbelief as Stephen trotted over to my bed and reaching past me, grabbed my cold steak off the plate and bolted it down hungrily.

"What do we do with him?" I motioned toward Bradley's prone figure.

Stephen swallowed and hissed, showing a lot of teeth, and Annika flinched at the sound. The boy merely stared and I felt sympathy for him. It was hard enough dealing with this as a grown woman, I couldn't imagine how traumatized he must be dealing with this as a child.

Before we could speak further about Bradley's fate, we heard a screeching sound as the door at the top of the stairs slid open, followed by something heavy tumbling down the stairs. The boy ran in and cowered under the bed, the rest of us looked at one another considering what to do. There was obviously a fight, I wondered if somehow our friends had found us. That would explain Bradley and Gaston's panic. Or was it an ally like Raymond come to take us for himself? I fought down the anxiety threatening to take my air. I was running on fumes. These last few minutes had taken the last of my reserves, I couldn't imagine faring well in a prolonged fight.

Stephen took up a defensive position in front of us humans, laying his ears back and growling in anticipation while Annika crouched at Stephen's shoulder. Reaching down, I removed the chain from the ash pile and held it in my hands, moving to stand at Stephen's other shoulder. We all held our breath as we waited, watching the door.

Seconds before the newcomer rounded the doorway, Stephen's ears pricked up and his growl stopped in his throat. I glanced from Stephen back up in time to see another large mountain lion standing in the doorway. Not having seen any of the others changed, I wasn't sure who I was looking at but Stephen obviously did. He chirped a small sound I wasn't aware the big cats made and bounded up to rub his face on his clansman or woman, I couldn't tell.

Annika looked back at me, confusion clear on her face.

Assuming once one knew about vampires, one was allowed to know about weres, I didn't need to worry about anyone's secrets here. "Stephen is a member of a werecat clan. This is one of his family members." I paused as the meaning of the cat's arrival struck me like a hammer, knocking the wind from my lungs. "We're rescued," I mumbled, too numb to feel relief and sank down on my knees.

I saw the girl relax, giggling in relief. Glancing over my shoulder I saw the boy was by no means relieved, though he was climbing out from under the bed to hover in front of it. I wondered if we would be able to find someone for him to talk to about his experience, maybe a supernatural therapist. I snorted at the thought.

The new cat made a mewing sound and turned to pad out of the cell. I regained my feet and waved for the boy to come too. Our small group of refugees exited into the main hall to see the two cats standing, waiting for us. We followed our feline escort up the stairs, past an ash pile at the base, and out of the bathroom back to the club on ground level. I'd been scared of what awaited us up there when I had thought of escape, although it appeared my concerns were needless. The only hint of vampires was four large piles of ash.

I felt my shoulders beginning to ease a little more when a movement to the right of the bar caught my attention. There stood Henry and James side by side in full vampire mode on the opposite end of the bar. Now that I was out and daring to think beyond pure survival, I felt the shame of what had happened, of what I had *let* happen while I was down there and could not meet their eyes. Looking down, I caught sight of my clothes and realized what I must look like.

Bruises in varying stages of healing were visible on my face and arms and my clothing had bloodstains all over as well as tears in the material where the whip had razed my skin. Several fingers were torn and my nails chipped from my stake carving and efforts at self-defense. My hair was a greasy, tangled mess as well and in a pointless gesture of self-conscious vanity I reached a trembling hand up to smooth it, feeling very little in my bloodless fingertips. Lightheaded, I wondered if I was going to faint. Part of me hoped I would and spare me the anguish of facing any of them in this state.

Stephen couldn't speak to anyone but his clansmen in cat form and I recognized the need to figure out what to do with our prisoner downstairs. The sooner we handled Bradley the sooner we could leave this place. I wanted to get away from here yet I didn't know where I would go. My parents would not be able to know what had happened so they couldn't see me for a while. I was terrified at the thought of being alone and I was terrified at the thought of being around anyone else.

"Bradley is downstairs. We don't know what to do with him." I didn't recognize my voice, it sounded dull and thick to my ears. Glancing quickly up to make sure they could hear me, I saw the vampires exchange a glance I didn't have the clarity to comprehend.

Henry replied coolly, not much rattled him. "Have you taken him prisoner then? What of Gaston?"

I looked directly at Henry's nose. "Bradley is wearing Stephen's silver collar. Gaston is dead."

An animalistic rumble erupted from James, though my eyes never left Henry. I couldn't bring myself to look at my former lover. Our bond had been closed while I was down there but I'd reopened it since. My shame was doubled at the thought that he had sensed even a fraction of what had taken place down there.

Henry turned his head slightly over his shoulder, toward the doors and called out, "Ladies, could you come in please?"

The door opened and our small group of escapees flinched reactively toward each other before we saw who it was. Tara and Tonya entered the building in their human forms, glancing around them, taking it all in. Tara ran to Stephen and fell to a crouch throwing her arms around his neck, he purred loudly. That meant the cat that had come downstairs with us was Troy. Tonya was more reserved but was visibly relieved as she saw her brother with Troy. Not saying a word, her eyes went to Henry, her brows raised in askance.

"Ladies, please show everyone to the truck. I will run down and fetch our prisoner. James, you and Claire can take your car. We will speak later." I wasn't sure which sounded worse, being alone with James or surrounded by a group in a crowded vehicle.

I began to open my mouth to object, but I didn't know what to say so I snapped it shut. I risked a look back up at James and saw that he had his eyes closed and his body was perfectly still. In that moment I felt my worst fears confirmed, he wanted nothing to do with me. He was going to maintain that we were over and why wouldn't he? Nothing had changed for him except for me stealing his car. *Everything* had changed for me. Maybe it was better this way. He would never have to know.

Stephen and Troy changed back to their human forms and I saw that Tonya had a bag over her shoulder. She laid it on the bar with a whump and unzipped it. Stephen dug inside, removed several items and dressed quickly. Turning to face us after pulling on his pants, I caught a glimpse of his bare chest. Long, jagged scars ran like bolts of lightning down his chest on his right side. Catching the direction of my stare, he roughly pulled on his shirt and stalked out of the bar barefoot.

Tara remained crouched in front of the boy, "Don't worry, you're safe now." I noticed she kept her hands to herself and her eye contact fleeting not wanting to spook him. "What's your name?" I'd never thought her capable of the gentleness I heard in her voice.

The boy continued to stare at her, big eyes beginning to quiet as he took in Tara's friendly gestures. He didn't answer her, although he did reach out to take her hand. She smiled and rose, carefully leading him from the building.

Henry had disappeared while I had been watching Tara. There was a bang from the direction from the back of the club and I spun, dropping into a crouch. It was Henry with Bradley's limp form slung over his shoulder. The noise had to have been Bradley's head being slammed into the doorframe because he did it again while I was watching. "Oops," Henry joked without smiling. Surveying those of us still in the bar he asked, "Who killed Gaston?"

Hit by the guilt at what I had done, having taken a life, I mumbled that I had. Henry nodded his head approvingly and James' eyes flipped open to focus on me. I saw that he had hidden the vampire within and yet I wasn't sure how to read his expression, he was hiding himself from me so that all I had to go on was the pale and angry look on his face. Out of sorts and uncertain how to proceed I made my way unsteadily to the door.

Ch. 32

The Andrews had a dark blue Suburban. I wasn't sure which member it belonged to never having seen it before, but they were all able to climb inside. Tonya was in the passenger seat, the middle row held the little boy, Tara and Annika in that order. In the back, Troy sat with Bradley sporting his silver collar and Stephen slumped against the far side.

With our reclaimed freedom, and my need to occupy my thoughts with something other than the next few days, I took the opportunity to look over my fellow prisoners. The boy, who had by some unexplained miracle remained human, had dark brown hair that curled into large ringlets and deep brown eyes, wide set making them appear perpetually enormous even without his chronically alert posture accentuating that feature. He had a slightly Roman nose and I saw that his thin lips were pressed tightly together in his anxious position. To be so young and to have to endure so much must be very difficult for him. I wondered where his family was and if they were looking for him. I realized I had no idea how long he had been under Bradley's thumb. It had been at least as long as I had known Stephen. What kind of damage had been done to him in that time? I shuddered to think.

The small, delicately boned body was clothed in dirty jeans and a ratty Twins baseball sweatshirt and didn't look like he had had a bath in a long time. I watched the way he cringed away from the vampires and imagined he would stay with Tara until we could figure out what to do with him.

Annika, on the other hand, was just a few years younger than I. Her face was thin and long, she had a nose that turned up at the end. It was too sharp for her face. Her eyes were black with hunger instead of their normal green. I felt badly for her as well. I didn't know how much blood they had been giving her and I knew that newly changed vampires needed a lot more than the older ones. She seemed to be in relative control of herself and I figured she couldn't be as hungry as I might have thought given her age.

Her body was petite and lean, too lean from the life she had lived on the streets. She moved with the grace of a dancer, possibly due to the change. All the vampires I'd seen moved like that.

Everyone was seated in the van and Henry was preoccupied with buckling Bradley into his seat between Troy and Stephen; why Henry was doing it I had no idea, but the cats didn't seem eager to fight him for the honor. At first I thought it was far too kind of Henry. If there was an accident I would like to have seen Bradley suffer some painful injuries from which only a vampire could heal. They wouldn't be fatal but that didn't mean they wouldn't hurt like hell. Then I realized it was more likely to keep him restrained so that he couldn't bump into or bite anyone.

I suppose it was the sense of relief everyone felt at having escaped with our full family that made us complacent. But while I stood at the doorway waiting for James, I watched Annika, catching her turning toward the boy. Seeing it when he turned to her, his face going blank. In seconds her fangs had grown to their full length and her hands were twitching nervously as her eyes rolled back into her head, her body rigid. Just as Annika appeared ready to lunge across Tara, I screamed.

Henry turned at the sound and, quick as a snake, grabbed Annika's shoulders to hold her down in her seat. Tara pushed the boy into the wall and twisted, putting her whole back between them. He still had a fearful expression until Tara spoke quietly and insistently to him.

James came out of nowhere to within a hands breadth of me, quickly assessing the situation and swept past me to the truck. Handing the new vampire a dark bottle, he nodded to

Henry and she was released. Tara kept the boy on the inside, away from Annika who was too busy chugging blood from her bottle to notice.

Henry and James were standing between the cars parked against the curb discussing something I caught the gist of, though I didn't really pay attention to the details. I had forgotten about the Guard being sent by the Court.

Apparently they were due to arrive within the next day or so and Henry would not have room at his home for Annika or the boy. Or, I thought sadly, me. Stephen was still holding his grudge against me, further narrowing my choices for housing until I was well enough to call my parents to come get me.

I could feel the last of my reserves failing me standing at the curb and could put it off no longer. Slowly I took the last few steps and got into James' passenger seat as Henry had instructed.

Ch. 33

Once I was in, I could feel the familiar soft leather seat cradle me and I could tell James had turned up the heat while he let the car run. That small consideration caused my eyes to well up. As much as I didn't want to be alone with him and didn't want to talk about what had happened, he was also the thing I wanted most. I had no closer friend in the world than him and I wanted the comfort he represented, his words that soothed me, and his strength that I knew so well. For the moment he was being kind because that was his way but I couldn't take advantage for long, it wouldn't do to confuse things. As soon as I was able, I would leave.

I closed my eyes and tried to bring up my shields. My mental exhaustion was making it nearly impossible. In the last few months, my shielding had become second nature. Now it was taking all of my concentration and I was still doing a crap job.

It made me think of how hard it had all been at the beginning when I met the people I had come to think of as my family, the Andrews, James, even Henry. My lip quivered and I took a deep, shaky breath to try to calm myself. I couldn't break down yet. Not until I was alone.

My eyes were closed when I heard the door open and close quietly. The engine growled as he pulled out onto the road. I held my breath waiting for him to speak, but the only sound inside the car during the ride home was the sound of my ragged breathing, vastly too loud in my ears in the enclosed space. I wished he would turn on the music but didn't want to speak to ask.

The ride was too short. Before I knew it the car came to a stop, I heard the sound of a garage door and opened my eyes in surprise. We pulled into the empty garage and I heard James' quiet voice.

"You were right; it was too flashy and impractical."

The garage door had gone all the way down and I remained in the car, hoping I might disappear and not have to face him. I didn't have the skills to discuss what had happened and that was assuming he even *wanted* to. When I'd left he'd been ready to leave for Europe; I assumed he'd come back as promised to manage the Guard's visit before leaving for good. Then, at the club, it had been quite obvious that he'd been disgusted with me. Why I was here was probably just a matter of logistics. We were tight on space with the new guests coming in and James and I were probably assumed to be on decent terms, though I really didn't know what anyone knew of our situation. Maybe he hadn't told anyone, it didn't matter, they would all know soon enough whether they cared or not.

While I sat, indecision anchoring me to my spot, I heard my door open and his cool hand took mine. I let him lead me inside the house and up the stairs. Without saying a word, he motioned for me to have a seat on the closed toilet lid while he drew me a bath. Staring at the water while the tub filled was therapeutic for me and I hardly noticed when James slipped out.

The water called to me and I stripped off my filthy, torn clothing to slip into the water. The heat of it made me cry out at first, but within minutes I adjusted and immersed myself.

When I was done washing myself thoroughly, I drained the filthy water and refilled the tub. I lay in the water and promptly fell asleep. The chill in the water roused me much later. After toweling off, I saw a pile of clothes on the counter and my dirty clothes had been taken out. Dutifully, I dressed in the light blue loungewear James had set out for me. The soft knit pants and t-shirt felt wonderful on my tender skin, the zippered hoodie promised warmth I'd been without for nearly a week.

Now that I was clean and dressed I was equally torn between eating and sleeping. The smell of food wafting up from downstairs made my decision for me. I felt more human now that I was cleaned up and James' acceptance of my silence led me not to fear being alone with him as much.

True to our pattern, I sat in my place and he of course sensed me. He brought out a cup of tea and I nearly wept. The first sip was pure luxury and I held it in my mouth for an extra long time. He brought out eggs with bacon and an English muffin. My favorites. James sat quietly across from me while I ate, sipping his own breakfast and working on his laptop. We didn't speak, although I couldn't tell him, it was comforting to have him with me. It was like things used to be.

A few times I thought I saw him surreptitiously sneaking looks at me while I took a bite or was zoning out. When I was done eating, I announced that I was going to lie down. James looked up and I saw his eyes were midnight. He was upset about something despite his attempts to appear at peace. I was guessing he wasn't pleased about my being in his house. It made my stomach roll, threatening my breakfast's security. Turning, I made my way deliberately upstairs to lie down. Out of habit I ended up in what used to be our bed and wrapped myself in the fluffy down comforter before sleep took me.

Ch. 34

When I opened my eyes sometime in the night I didn't look at the clock. My attention was immediately drawn to the presence I felt, the cool body lying behind me, not touching me. Having him close was reassuring as was the fact that he was not touching me. He knew when I woke because my breathing changed.

James was hesitant. "You were calling for me." He was uncertain, so un-vampirelike. "I hope you don't mind."

Sighing, I answered truthfully. "The whole time I was down there I thought about being here."

"I worried about you. When you took the car I knew it was bad. It was," he paused again, his hesitation made him sound almost human, "it was unbearable not knowing where you were. We found my car right away with your jewelry inside and no sign of you, even when we went into the club. When you called me I was relieved to hear you alive. Then, when I saw him..." His voice broke off mid-sentence.

Perplexed, I started to turn around and stopped myself. "I didn't call you. My mind was a mess, *is* a mess. I couldn't have called you if I wanted to." I was grateful for the darkness. It made it easier to talk to him.

"You don't remember talking to me? We spoke until they came. Our connection was still there, in the background. I heard them tell you they were going to make you kill Stephen. I felt you, only you were so different." He was trying to tone down his concern though I could feel his upset. Dread settled in my stomach as his words hit me. I had changed so much he could feel it.

"I thought that was a dream." My response was sharp in my agitation. Wiggling forward, I felt the loss of him as a

219

physical pain. "We weren't going to do *this*, don't you remember? We aren't together anymore."

"I told you if you couldn't trust me, we couldn't be together. When you thought you were dreaming, do you remember telling me you *did* trust me? That it was a misunderstanding?"

His reassurances that we could simply go back to the way things were when I knew they never could, infuriated me. I wanted to fight, I wanted to rage. I wanted to draw blood but he was so damned calm it was impossible. Hopping up, I stood facing him while he lay reclined on the bed.

"You're right about one thing, I *am* different now. You have no idea what happened down there. I'm never going to be the same and it's all because of you. I just want to go back to my old life, before I met you and before *everything*." I was on the verge of hysterics.

"Claire, you were miserable before you met me, met *us* and learned to control your gift. I am sorry this happened to you, but I still love you. You can't undo that and I don't believe that you want to."

It gave me a thrill of pleasure to hear him say that he wanted me only to have to remind myself that it didn't matter. He might be saying that but I had seen his face, I had seen how he really felt. His declaration of love was meaningless, he only wanted to make me feel better and I knew the truth. I knew that he couldn't.

"I might have been miserable before, but no one ever did what he did to me before I was involved with you. Since I've met you, I have been kidnapped repeatedly, stabbed, bitten, beaten and, and..." Even in my worst rage, I couldn't bring myself to say the worst.

James was on his feet, his hands came up to grab hold of my arms and I backed away.

"Don't touch me. I don't want anyone to touch me ever again." I turned on my heel and ran into the bathroom, locking the door. The lock wouldn't have kept him out if he wanted in. He could have torn the door off the hinges, yet I had made my point and he stayed out. For the next few hours, I lay curled up on the bathroom rug wondering if I could beg Stephen's forgiveness and go stay with him before falling asleep.

Ch. 35

When I emerged after the sunrise, I had resolved to stay put and to be polite for the remainder of my stay. While some of what we'd said might have been exaggerated and poorly timed, it was still true. My association with the supernatural had been more fulfilling than life with humans, and it had also been far more perilous. This last experience being more than I had the capacity to handle.

As it turned out, it didn't matter what I wanted to say to James; he wasn't there. Instead, Troy and Heidi were sitting on the couch holding hands when I came downstairs.

"Hey Claire, wow, you look terrible!" Heidi came to put her arms around me. "I heard you were mugged. They really worked you over, huh?"

I glanced over to catch Troy shrugging his shoulders with a mild smile. He had seen me looking worse. His blasé attitude rubbed me wrong and I lashed out.

"Are you on guard duty, Troy? Keeping someone out or me in?" Even I thought I sounded juvenile and awful.

Without waiting for a response, I kept walking past Heidi who was staring after me, her mouth wide in disbelief, and continued into the kitchen to find some juice. When I closed the refrigerator door, Troy's stoic face was behind it. I jumped and dropped the bottle of juice, his reflexes allowed him to catch it and set it on the counter before I could move.

Troy barely blinked as he regarded me sternly. "Claire, you are not the only one who has suffered. I am sorry for whatever happened and if you want to leave, do so now. But don't be so quick to dismiss the efforts of everyone who came to your aid or forget the suffering of those who were there with you. It was unfortunate, but it is behind you now.

Do not cheapen yourself with such flip remarks. I am not James and will not tolerate it." With that, he turned and walked out.

Troy projected his voice so that I could hear him when he returned to the living room. "Heidi, let's go. James wanted us to be here in case Claire needed anything when she woke but I think she would rather be alone."

I heard the closet door open and they must have been putting on coats and shoes. Some more quiet mumbling as Heidi said something to Troy and then the front door opened and closed. And with that I was alone, just like I'd wanted. Feeling very sorry for myself, I slid down on the floor and cried.

Ch. 36

I was alone all that night. It was New Year's Eve and I sat alone in bed staring at the ceiling. My phone rang a few times and I didn't answer. I debated whether I should call my parents only I didn't know what I could talk to them about. There were so many secrets to keep now, my safest bet was to say nothing at all.

Before, I had to keep quiet about what I felt coming from those around me. Now I had so many other people's secrets it was hard to keep track of it all, I had to think ahead before I said anything or I might end up saying something I shouldn't. Had this been the life I wanted? Which life was better? A life of hiding behind shields and pretending I was normal or throwing my lot in with others who had loved and understood me and had their own gifts and abilities, while risking danger in a secret world I would never be able to share with anyone not directly involved. And what would I do now that I was alone?

In the morning I woke to the sound of the front door opening and someone padding up the stairs. It couldn't be James, I never heard his footsteps. For a moment I froze before I remembered the threats were gone. Bradley and Gaston were both either captured or dead.

"Hello?" I called out hesitantly.

A light knock on the door preceded Stephen's blonde head peeking in. "Can I come in?"

"Sure." His appearance astonished me. Although he was now in his human form, his face had stayed longer and wider than it had been, he was broader shouldered and he had grown at least an inch.

Seeing my confusion, Stephen pointed at himself, "I was between forms for too long. It messes with our cellular structure and changed my human body. What do you think?"

I could tell he wasn't as amiable about all of it as he sounded. Everyone deals with grief differently and this was his. "You look bigger. More grown up."

"Yeah, I won't be able to play the youngster much anymore. I'll have to say I'm closer to twenty now." He flashed a grin. It was halfhearted and quickly faded.

"Stephen, I'm sorry. When Bradley called I jumped before I thought it through. I went in thinking I was going to be able to outsmart them; it was stupid." I couldn't bring myself to meet his gaze.

He came over to sit next to me on the bed where I was perched. "Claire, what happened was an ordeal for everyone. Annika and little Omar are both going to need some time to be right as will you, and you have to remember something. Our world is not as kind as yours. Ours is a world still rooted in the old ways where existence has to be earned and penalties are far harsher than in this realm."

"How can you stand it? You act like this is not a big deal." It was amazing to me that he could be so philosophical about all of it.

Shrugging, Stephen answered seemingly unaffected. "We survived. Our friendship made you cast aside your fears for yourself and come to help me. I will never forget that. Because of your tie to James we are all here today, able to heal. Knowing that you saved three lives besides your own, would you go down there again if you had to do it over?" He held up his hand to stay my response. "Just think about it. It might help you to put it into perspective."

It hadn't registered with me up to now that my bond again led James to find us and rescue us. My brain was so jumbled up and only slowly starting to straighten out. I knew that he was right. I'd had to save them from their own nightmares even if that meant I would have to endure my own. I couldn't have hung up that phone and done anything except what I had. Thinking about people dying down there, I remembered the body I'd seen in his cell.

"Stephen, who killed Brian? I saw him in your cell when they first brought me there."

He sagged, all at once worn. "You were right, Brian had thrown in with Bradley. They made him a servant after the party once he'd met everyone. They offered to turn him and he wanted the physical strength and enduring youth, but he didn't realize they had no intention of following through with their offer. As soon as Brian brought me to the club, I knew you were right and I had been betrayed. Brian himself put the collar on me and I was done. Did you know he wasn't really gay? He… " Stephen ducked his head to hide his face, "he did all that just to get close to us. They told him he had to for them to consider turning him.

When they led me downstairs, Brian came right along, expecting his reward. Bradley bit him, except he drained him instead. He never fought back. They left him there for a day or so thinking it would bother me. When they saw that it didn't, they moved him. As far as I'm concerned, he ceased to exist the second I saw that club." His hazel eyes blazed with his pain at Brian's treachery.

I felt terrible for him and at the same time felt a pang as Troy's words hit me. None of them deserved to be treated roughly or dishonestly just because I was having a hard time. James had not deserved the treatment I had given him. He hadn't given up on me and had found us after all. I hadn't even said thank you; I was too busy punishing him for

226

leaving me. After the way I'd acted I could see why he would want to.

"You know, vampires are not generally warm and fuzzy. No one understands *why* James is how he is with you, or why you have this connection. But you shouldn't treat it so lightly. It's pretty special and you should have more regard for it than you do." Stephen knew me well enough to peer into my thoughts.

Chastised roundly for the second time in as many days, my cheeks flushed in embarrassment. "I know that. It's just that we broke up right before Bradley and then after what happened, I didn't know what to do. I should have been able to…I should have been stronger."

Stephen understood. "You know, the same thing happened to me a long time ago. Back when I was a human."

My eyebrows shot up in surprise. "Someone did that to you?" I couldn't make myself say the word.

"Yes," he nodded, explaining without feeling, "I was a boy about Omar's age and we had a salesman pass by our shop while our father was out. He followed me to the storeroom and caught me alone. He was bigger than me, stronger than me and there was no way I could have been able to stop him. After it happened, I felt guilty and angry anyway. It was a different time then and we didn't discuss those things, especially boys, so I stayed quiet. When I was changed years later, I found the man who'd done it and I took my revenge, much like you did. The rest comes with time."

His words were healing in an unexpected way. It helped to know that I was not alone and that he understood what I was going through. Grateful for him, I offered him a smile and touched his arm.

"You come off as such a joker and then you shock the hell out of me with a moment of wisdom. Thank you."

He smiled that boyish grin I'd come to love. "I can't let just anyone know I'm smart. It would ruin this whole image I've cultivated." Rising, he held out his hand to me. "Now, I could use some fresh air. Care to go for a walk now that the streets are safe?"

Ch. 37

A walk in the fresh air did wonders. It was a crisp, cold day and we were bundled up. It felt good to be alive and outside. We walked for a long time, enjoying each other's quiet companionship. By the time we returned home and I made us some hot cocoas, something had changed. I felt ready to try to return to the world, at least to take the first step.

"Where is everyone, Stephen?" I hadn't seen or heard from anyone for nearly two days, James for almost an entire day, making my imagination run rampant with the possibilities of what that might mean. I worried he'd left for Europe and I would never get to say good-bye.

"The Guard has arrived and they are dealing with Bradley. Henry has James tied up for probably another day at least. Tara is with Omar at her house. He's scared of the vampires and won't go near them. Tonya is with Henry acting as family spokesperson, and Troy and Heidi can't seem to come up for air so they have been relegated to his house where no one has to watch." He rolled his eyes playfully at this last.

"How much does Heidi know? Do you guys have to apply for consent like the vampires do?"

"She knows that Troy is a nice guy. Beyond that, it's up to him when or if he lets her know about himself. If he shares about anyone else he'll be in trouble with the Council. And if *she* leaks, he has to contain it."

We were being honest so I had to ask, "Why did you have James relinquish his oath?"

Stephen paused, rubbing his forehead with one hand before he replied. "Because I was jealous." He laughed harshly at my look of bewilderment. "I'd love to say it was something more meaningful or honorable than that, but it would be a lie. It bothered me that you rolled onto the scene, got the guy, adapted to the lifestyle so smoothly and were going to live happily ever after. I thought if I had the oath removed you two might have some trouble and it would bring you back to Earth with the rest of us."

Swallowing hard, I had to buy myself some time before I yelled at him. I was able to calm myself sufficiently before responding. "Do you know how hard it is to live with this bond no one understands?" I nodded when he had his turn to be shocked. "Yeah, it isn't all paradise. I have virtually no secrets from him and he can get to almost anything he wants in my head." I ticked his flaws off on my fingers. "He's overprotective, he's overbearing and I can't find a single thing I am better at than him."

"Thank you." He winked at me. "You've demystified him and now I won't think he's such a prick. Things will be *so* much easier now."

Joking, I sneered and went into the kitchen to get some space. I called out from the interior, "Marshmallows or whipped cream on your cocoa?" I preferred simple decisions today.

"Whipped cream, of course."

Ch. 38

Stephen left that afternoon and I was alone in the house through another long day. I saw that James had left the Audi for me to drive. I still had enough bruising that I didn't want to go out in public and have to explain myself so it stayed parked.

My mother had called again and I didn't answer. They were going to call the police soon, I was sure. I didn't want to talk to her until I could answer what was sure to be her most pressing question. As strange as it sounded, I didn't want to say out loud that our engagement was off. My parents were going to be so disappointed and I was going to feel like a failure.

In the meantime, I tried to deal with what I could handle. Like Stephen said, it would take some time for it all to process and the pain to fade; hurting those who loved me wasn't the answer. Several times a day I looked in the mirror to see the visible signs of abuse fading, bringing me closer to leaving. I was lingering because I wanted to see James again. Waiting for him, I busied myself with cleaning the house, reading and walking outside.

By the end of the second day, I could bear the silence no longer. I called James and left him a message to call me back. I wanted to see him and apologize in person for the way I'd acted, it was no way to thank him for his hospitality. He must have been busy I told myself. He wasn't avoiding my call. I hoped I hadn't pushed him away so severely he wouldn't consider friendship in time. Thought of a life without him in it at all was a blow.

There was another apology that I needed to make and I dialed Troy next. Heidi answered at the house and sounded tentative when she heard my voice.

"Heidi, I just wanted to let you know that I appreciated you two checking on me the other day and I am sorry I was mean. The mugging just had me a bit shaken, you know?" It was pretty close to honest.

She warmed at my apology and said she would pass it along to Troy. We agreed to meet for a girl's night soon.

That night, I woke to find I was not alone in bed. Again, he had taken the liberty to climb in bed with me only this time I touched his hand where it lay on my hip. He was careful not to touch me anywhere else.

The darkness made me brave. "I'm sorry for being so awful. It wasn't fair and it doesn't excuse it, I just didn't know how to deal with everything. I'm still not sure, except I promise to try not to take it out on you anymore." I held my breath as I waited to hear his response.

His hand traced the scars fresh on my arm, visible beneath the hem of my sleeve. "I don't know what he did to you, I only see the effect of his violence on you. I also know that nothing could change how I feel toward you no matter what you might believe. You can talk to me about it if and when you are ready; I plan on being here."

A powerful surge of relief washed over me only to be checked when I remembered the reason we had argued originally. Trying to be more reasonable, I kept my voice even. "What about the job offer?"

James sighed before he answered. "I have thought about that and I believe that we can try it without turning you. I saw you with Annika and it gave me the idea. We can figure something out, I'm sure. If you are still interested, that is."

I nodded, knowing he could see with his keen eyesight. "The idea that I can help someone appeals to me. I would like to think this ability might serve some purpose after all."

His arm rested on my hip and I hid a yawn behind my hand. "Sleep well, Claire. Tomorrow we have some people for you to meet."

Ch. 39

The next morning I came awake to feel a tickle at my throat. James had put my necklace back on in the night. With a wiggle of my fingers, I saw that my ring had been replaced as well. It didn't bother me that he had taken the liberty. On the contrary, I was flattered that he'd kept them.

A perfunctory look in the mirror showed that thanks to my super fast healing, I now looked decent enough that a thin layer of makeup would hide my facial bruising. It being sweater and jeans season, the rest of my body would have plenty of time to heal. Time would tell how badly I would scar, bathing suits might be a thing of the past.

Before I could get distracted, I went downstairs and sat down on the couch to call my mother.

"Claire honey, I was wondering if you dropped off the face of the Earth. I've been calling you for days." She sounded slightly miffed, but thanks to our relatively loose relationship, she wasn't surprised that I would be out of touch for a week or so.

"Sorry Mom. I lost track of days. It's weird with no work or school, they all blur together." It was a lame excuse and I hoped she wouldn't question it.

She didn't. "Oh. Well, that's okay. So, do you have any big news to share?" Poor Mom had been waiting to hear my answer to James' proposal for over a week. I wouldn't be surprised if she had pulled all of her hair out.

My mood brightened. This was an opportunity for a perfectly human and normal conversation. "Yes Mom. I said yes."

She was predictably elated. "Did you pick a date yet?"

"No, I guess we are going to see how school and his work go." We hadn't talked about *when* but I wasn't adverse to a longer engagement. Now that I knew he wanted me and I wanted him, I had patience for the rest to play out. I wasn't eager to get married as a teenager and I would be twenty in March.

We talked for a while about their upcoming trip to France and my engagement. We agreed to get together for a ladies' lunch in the coming weeks and I hung up.

When I hung up, a quiet cough sounded from behind me. I turned and saw him standing dressed in a black suit and shirt. It was too soon for me to want to hop into bed with him, yet I was physically affected by him and I felt my pulse quicken at the sight of him.

"Are you ready to meet the Guard? We are due in Taylor's Falls in a few hours."

Assessing his somber mood and more formal attire, I mentally clicked through my wardrobe. "What am I supposed to wear? I can't wear a dress if we're hiking through the woods in January. Humans get cold, remember?"

His smile eased my concern. "Don't worry, I think we can find something. Would you like my help?"

I nodded and we went upstairs. We agreed that black chinos and matched sweater would allow me to cover the necessary hiking boots and with a coat and scarf I could be warm enough for our purposes.

"What are we doing up there anyway? Why can't we meet the Guard at someone's house?" It struck me as a strange place for a meeting. I felt a twinge of anxiety as I allowed myself to wonder about the identity of the Guard. I hoped they weren't the ancient scary kind of vampires that hated humans.

James was slow to answer. "We are meeting there to discuss Bradley's punishment."

I was glad I was reaching in my closet. It gave me a moment to hide my reaction though I was sure he saw my body freeze.

"Do I have to go?" I was hoping he would let me off the hook.

"Yes, you're a witness." He caught my sigh. "And we need to present a united front for the Guard as they are watching us for signs of weakness, non-vampires especially. We are a unique coven in our mixed species composition. It would be best if you were with us."

I let that comment hang while I pulled my shirt over my head. Hearing him growl behind me, I remembered he had not seen me naked since I had come home. I must have looked horrible. Embarrassed, I moved to cover myself.

His voice shook. "I'm going to tear him apart."

For a minute I thought he meant Gaston and I nearly corrected him, then I realized he meant Bradley. He was behind me before I could think and his lips touched my neck. He'd laid with me since I had come back and it hadn't bothered me, but something about his quiet approach from behind called up a raw memory. Without any ability to control my blind terror, I screamed spinning away from him and clutching my shirt against my chest.

James stood, hand hovering in the air where my shoulder had been. I watched the alarm on his face quickly replaced by rage. In a hoarse whisper he asked, "What did he do to you?"

I looked at my toes and answered softly, "Maybe you should wait outside."

Without another word, he left the room and I heard the door close. I took a long time to get dressed. When I went downstairs, James was standing in his black coat at the door. Wordlessly, I put on my own and walked out when he opened the door for me.

Ch. 40

The drive was a pretty one and I tried to concentrate on the light layer on the ground from the minor snowfall the night before. The temperature was above freezing so it was melting, leaving a misty haze in the air. With the sun partially hidden James probably didn't need his sunglasses. I had the notion he chose to wear them to hide his emotions from me. He knew I hated that; how could I blame him today?

We drove without speaking. A cd was playing, Vivaldi's Four Seasons. It was one of my favorites and I sat back to close my eyes and enjoy it. I must have fallen asleep because the next I was aware, James spoke my name and I sat up to see we were parked amongst several cars I recognized at a designated trail head. The connected path quickly led into heavy tree coverage. I was thankful for having worn hiking boots, thinking this was going to be a muddy affair with the melted snow. From the look of the mush leading away from the parking area, I was right.

Before I could, James was around my side to open my door for me. He had kept his chivalry through several lifetimes and I knew there was no way I would get him to stop so I went with it even on the few occasions when it bugged me, like now.

He led the way up the trail and we hiked with relative ease for what I guessed to be two miles. Once walking, the release I always felt at being outdoors eased my mind and I was able to even enjoy the hike. It was reassuring to look ahead and see his broad shoulders just ahead of me. Only a vampire could hike this terrain in dress shoes and make it look easy, I thought with a snort. He heard me and turned. I flashed a brief smile before I looked away. I was discouraging conversation and he got that. Trust an immortal to be patient.

I was busy looking at some deer tracks just off the path when I bumped into James who had stopped suddenly in front of me. Recovering myself, I looked around him to see our party waiting for us. It looked like we were the last to arrive.

Everyone was in what I would call church clothes. I fought the urge to laugh at what we would look like to someone who might happen by. Here we all were, dressed for a formal occasion, standing in the middle of a state park in a Minnesota winter. The situation was laughable if it wasn't for the ball of dread forming in the pit of my stomach.

The area where we had stopped was a small clearing on the edge of the coniferous forest. The pine needles carpeting the area were dry due to it being sheltered by a tall rock face behind the trees.

The Andrews clan stood in a half circle, their backs to the rock. Standing behind Tara were Omar and Annika. The young vampire was next to Troy. Before them knelt Bradley, flanked by two very scary vampires. Henry had come forward to meet James and me upon our arrival.

Henry was about twenty feet from us when he called out pleasantly, "James, Claire. So pleased you could make it."

James responded, leaving me to adjust wordlessly. "We came to see this bastard punished." Though his voice was relatively controlled, I could feel the fury rolling off of him as he glared at Bradley.

Henry turned to indicate the strangers. "James, you remember Lucas and Gabriel."

James inclined his head at the two and I took a moment to study them.

By Henry's gesture, the tall, thin vampire to the left was Lucas. It was crazy but he looked just like an elf. His straight, blonde hair gathered in a leather thong was incredibly pale, nearly white. His features were long and lean with a straight, thin nose, wide mouth and almond shaped eyes the color of spring grass. Absolutely beautiful, he exuded a dangerous air, pushing me to take a step closer to James.

The man to the right, Gabriel, was the polar opposite to Lucas. Gabriel had been of African descent in his human life, his dark features still readily apparent despite his vampire pale skin. Black dreadlocks hung loose past his broad, heavily muscled shoulders. His wide nose and strong jaw were marred by a scar he had obtained in his human life running from the corner of his nostril through the corner of his mouth on the right side of his face. He was the epitome of a scary vampire and I vowed not to make eye contact with either one. I didn't want them knowing any more about me than absolutely necessary.

Finally, I let my eyes fall upon Bradley. He knelt facing us, wearing the silver collar I had placed around his neck in the down in the cells days before. His clothes, normally perfectly pressed and finely tailored were torn, untucked and smeared with his blood. His blonde hair was sticking up in clumps and matted with brown crusted blood. One of his eyes was missing, the dark socket staring emptily into space ahead of him. His face was marred by torn flesh and I saw that one of his hands was missing several fingers. I sucked in a breath of air to try to calm my stomach. James' cool hand slid down to take mine and I was glad to have him standing beside me.

Gabriel spoke a deep gravelly voice I could feel in my feet. It sounded like rocks in a blender. "This must be James' human we have heard so much about. Claire, is it?"

I nodded dumbly, staring directly at his huge chest.

"Our prisoner says that it was you who captured him. He also thinks that you are responsible for the death of his man, Gaston. Is this true?"

Again I bobbed my head in silent affirmation.

Lucas chuckled, an oddly melodic sound. "One tiny human girl was able to take down two vampires after they had days to break her." He turned toward Bradley and smiled benignly. "You are an embarrassment to us all."

At the mention of my ill treatment, James impulsively started toward them. Henry held out a hand to stay him and the Guard was amused. Gabriel turned to James and spoke, undaunted by his posturing, "Anton said you were fond of this one. Strange, I see nothing unusual about her, nothing worth staying *here* in this god forsaken country."

The offense I took must have shown on my face, Lucas' haunting laughter rang again. "See how she doesn't like to hear how ordinary she is." His voice dripped with sex and promise. He looked at me. "Don't worry little one, all humans are ordinary to most of us. James is one of the few to believe otherwise."

Henry redirected the conversation. "Let us proceed with the judgment."

Gabriel and Lucas turned to face Bradley. Lucas spoke and I found his voice entrancing. I could feel myself being drawn to him as he spoke, calling us to him. "Step forward and face the accused."

Lucas' voice extracted me from James' side, drowning out all other sounds from around me until all I heard was his alluring intonations. "Come forward child, look at me. I will not harm you." I wasn't sure if he spoke aloud or in my head, his draw was irresistible. The soft moss color of his eyes filled my vision and I closed the gap between us,

241

captivated by the swirling greens in his eyes. When he spoke, I felt him even through my shields almost as strongly as James. He was different from a normal vampire. I could feel it, though I couldn't readily identify how.

He blinked, breaking the spell and I came to my senses standing less then three feet from Lucas. Around me were gathered the others who had shared in captivity at the prisoner's hands. All but Annika were blinking, just as dazed as I. Annika stood patiently, looking at us in confusion.

Gabriel laughed, a harsh, crackling sound. "Like moths to a flame, Lucas."

I shot a glance over my shoulder to James where he stood glowering at the Guard, fists clenched at his side, Henry's hand on his shoulder. Hearing Gabriel speak I turned back to them.

"Bradley, stand and hear testimony for your treason." He shoved the prisoner roughly from behind.

Grunting with the effort and wobbling, Bradley unsteadily gained his feet.

Gabriel continued, "Who bears witness to this being acting against the Court's decrees?"

Annika spoke for all of us, "We do."

"Bradley Pennington, you stand accused of recklessly endangering our kind's vital need for secrecy to forward your own personal agenda against the wishes of the Court. Do you understand these charges as they are made against you?"

The accused stood up tall, ran the flat of his hand over his wild hair and used his damaged hand to straighten his suit coat all while he stared at me, pure loathing in his eyes. "Yes, I do."

"Do you contest these charges?"

"I do not."

"Do you have anything to add before judgment is passed?"

Angrily Bradley spat his reply, his one eye rolled in his head and landed on Henry, "That you base your decision on the word of humans and the real traitors to our kind," he glared at Henry and James, "is ludicrous. *They* are the real enemy. This war is greater than us all and has supporters at every level. It does not end with me."

Gabriel made brief eye contact with Lucas over Bradley's head and Lucas gave a minute nod of his head. Gabriel reached into his black overcoat and I saw a flash of black leather gloves on his hands as he lifted out a silver stake easily a foot and a half long. He held it high as he raised his voice for all to hear, vibrating the very air around us with his percussion. "It is the decision of the Court that the accused is guilty of the charges against him. The penalty for his crime is death."

Without another word, Gabriel's hand swung down and drove the stake deep into Bradley's chest. His cry was short as his lungs collapsed in on themselves, turning to goo a heartbeat before his body followed suit. Within seconds nothing remained but ash and the silver collar, which Gabriel picked up with a leather cloth that he proceeded to wrap it in and deposited it within a pocket of his coat. Using another cloth, he wiped off the stake and wrapped it up before sliding that back into his coat's inner pocket. No evidence remained that a man had died here. Arguably more tragic was the fact that after centuries of existing, no one argued *for* him or came to mourn him.

My wobbly legs decided at that moment to give out and I landed on my butt in the pine needles. For a long time, I stared at the ash, watching it slowly blow away in the gentle breeze. They were both gone, Gaston and Bradley were now in the wind. I considered Bradley's final threat that nothing would stop what was set in motion and the war would commence without him, wondering what faceless enemy we had to fear *now*.

Sadly, I felt no closure staring at the remnants of the monster staining the snow and rising on the wind. In a strange way I thought I might have *more* trouble sleeping now picturing the faceless monsters waiting for us around the corner.

A pair of hands grabbed me under the arms and lifted me back onto my feet. With a half cry I jumped only to be held suspended inches above the earth, my pulse flying. After my feet left the ground I heard a seductive chuckle and my nose picked up the scent of pine and fresh grass. Done with his little amusement, he let me back down and I lurched forward nearly losing my balance. He caught me again. "Caution little one."

Standing so close, I had to look way up to see his face when I turned around. His mouth was twisted into a smirk as he lowered his face to the top of my head and inhaled deeply.

Lucas took a step back trading his snide mien for genuine surprise. "Now I see what draws you to her." He sniffed again and shot James an amused look. "I can smell her still; you can't completely cover it up by rubbing yourself all over her. She smells of old magic, I daresay; very tempting." When he looked down at me again his fangs were out and his eyes had gone black with hunger; for blood or sex, I wasn't sure.

The thought of another vampire near me drove me to action. With a squeak and a jump I nearly fell backpedaling away from him. James was at my side instantly, his arm thrown about my shoulders possessively, a snarl rumbling his chest. "She's mine, Lucas."

Gabriel's low rumble cut in. "Lucas, control yourself. Remember, she is forbidden."

Lucas continued to ogle me hungrily. "I will not damage her, I only want a taste. She has a magic in her I have not tasted for a long time."

His power pulled at me again and I heard his voice in my head. "James cannot give you nearly the pleasure that I can. Come with me now and I will make you forget." My feet moved on their own carrying me toward Lucas, my desire for him eradicating all other thoughts.

James' arm looped around my waist and swung me behind him, breaking my eye contact with Lucas. As soon as our eye contact was broken, his voice was no longer in my head although the need to go to him continued to echo in my mind. James pressed me behind him and I hid my face in his back willing myself to ignore the nagging drive to follow the tall vampire.

His laugh chimed in my ears. "James let her go, she wants to come to me. Would you deny her desire?"

Gabriel's harsh tone cut in, "No magic, Lucas. You cannot interfere with their bond, it is strictly forbidden. Henry, we will wait for you at your home. Our work here is finished."

I heard a rush of air and slowly my control over myself returned. James relaxed his grip on me only when he felt my tension dissipate. When I was able to face everyone again, I saw that Tara was comforting Omar who was crying. It was a no brainer what had frightened him; Annika stood on the other side of Tara with her fangs out. She seemed to have been affected by Lucas' hunger as well. Tonya had maneuvered herself between Tara and the young vampire and from the expression on her face and the speed at which her mouth was moving, she was working fast to keep her at bay. Troy and Stephen were poised and ready to intervene.

With the Guard gone, Henry took command of the chaotic group. "Tara, take the boy home with you now."

Tara nodded and moved, still protecting Omar with her body as she carried him away from the clearing. Annika's hungry stare followed the boy until he disappeared over the small rise in the trail.

As soon as Omar cleared the hill Henry moved, lightning fast. Annika's head rocked backward and I heard the crack of his openhanded slap. He spoke low and deadly. "You will stop using your ability on *anyone* unless ordered by me. If you draw that boy to you again, I will remove your fangs myself."

Annika flinched at his threat and nodded. Blood flowed from her mouth where he had struck her.

Clearing his throat, Troy addressed Henry. "If we are no longer needed, Henry?"

Henry nodded, thanking him, and the remainder of the clan left.

When just the three of us remained James turned to me, his eyes dark. "I should have known he would be drawn to you, he covets powers different from his own." James cursed and turned to Henry. "His enchantment will pull at her whenever she is in his presence now. I must be allowed the freedom to protect her."

Henry nodded in agreement, watching me closely. "Indeed, her ability makes her far more susceptible to an Enchanter but the Court will not allow you to go against the Guard. You know that better than anyone." Some silent exchange passed between them before Henry changed the subject. "It seems we can expect more trouble from Bradley's lot. I will find out what I can about his alliances starting at the club."

Listening to them talk about more danger coming our way, yet another "special handling" provision for me in regard to Lucas' pull on me, and then the mention of the club; I had enough. The two of them didn't need me and I knew James could catch up. With a shudder and a quick squeeze to his hand, I turned on my heel and headed up the trail looking for peace.

Hiking back along the path I felt my head clear and my stomach unclench. I took deep breaths, filling my lungs with the cool, crisp air. It wasn't so cold yet that it hurt to breathe it in as it would be soon. January and February were historically the worst two months in Minnesota with temperatures sometimes plummeting into the double digits below zero without factoring in wind chill.

Even though I took my time I found myself back at the trailhead all too soon. Looking around me, I was struck by how beautiful the forest was in the fading afternoon light. I stood there enjoying the peace for only a few minutes when I saw him appear on the far side of the parking lot.

"Ready?"

Ch. 41

"What's an Enchanter?"

Keeping his eyes on the road, James took a long time to answer. "They are an old race; very few remain among the living. Lucas was turned when they were more plentiful."

"When was that?"

"It would have been during the reign of Richard I, just before the start of the 13th century."

My mouth hung open. "He's over eight hundred years old?"

James nodded, "Yes, Lucas and Gabriel are the best the Court has in their ranks. They are both very old, and powerful enough to deal with any transgressor. They're only sent out on the most difficult or sensitive of matters. The Court is taking this situation very seriously to have sent them." He frowned at the windshield.

"But what is this ancient race? Are there any more of them living as vampires?"

"You would know his race as Elves. As far as I know, Lucas is the only one that has ever been turned. They were usually able to enchant the vampires, stunning them and allowing the elf to escape unscathed. Lucas must have been caught unaware somehow."

"Oh my gosh, he's an Elf? That explains it. He felt so different than you. It was more." I searched for the word trying to pick the right one, "wild. But not like an animal. It was like he was on a different wavelength, he went straight through my shields."

James turned to me, face grave. "You will have to be *very* careful around him. Elves are collectors in a sense, they are fascinated by magick different from their own. He will try to find a way to get to you if he is able to get around the Court's ban on you."

Watching his profile, I could see by the set of his jaw how serious he was. I gulped. "Miranda is guarding our bond *and* she wants to work with us. I wonder why she is so interested in us."

"I'm not sure either, but she will most likely summon us soon now that those two are gone." He meant Bradley and Gaston, of course, and was being kind and didn't mention their names out of courtesy.

"What about the others he mentioned? Will they take up the charge now?" I felt my chest tense as I considered the implications.

James shook his head. "We don't believe his allies will be so bold though whether that is good or bad, only time will tell. Bradley was overconfident and often came to the Court's attention for overstepping his station. Any allies he has will be far more careful to avoid detection."

"But what about us specifically? Do you think they'll come for *us*?" I wasn't sure I was ready to face another three months of constant wariness; none of us were.

I saw his eyebrows pull down as he considered my question. "We will have to wait and see."

Ch. 42

The sun had set by the time we pulled into the garage. "Are you hungry?" he asked as we walked into the kitchen. "I could make something."

"You know, you haven't let me cook for myself since I've been here. Why don't you have a seat and let me cook tonight?" The idea of having something simple to busy my hands and mind had its draw.

"Certainly. What are you going to make?" He indicated the shelf containing the cookbooks by the pantry. "Do you need a recipe?"

I considered my options. What was I in the mood for? It wasn't like I had to worry about his tastes so it was entirely my choice. "I think I should see what you have around here and let the ingredients be my guide."

He stepped aside and I moved from the refrigerator to the pantry perusing the shelves. It was hard not to smile as I tried to make sense of his organization of the items. Having lost the distinction between flavors had left James with an inability to organize items beyond canned, jarred and boxed. My pantry back home had spicy together, tomato products together, etcetera so it always took me a little longer to make sense of things in here. Now that I lived here, I thought I might ask if I could rearrange. Maybe I'd wait and see how much I ended up cooking before I changed things.

The ingredients lent them themselves well to a vegetarian stir-fry with a spicy peanut sauce. He went upstairs to check his email as I started the rice and I went on to chopping vegetables. I was peeling carrots when his arm wrapped around my waist from behind.

The second I felt a presence behind me I was back in my cell in that hellish place and logic fled my mind. It was Gaston who was once again laying his hands on me. Screeching, I whirled and pushed my back against the cabinets with the knife held out in front of me defensively.

As soon as I was facing him, my mind woke up and I felt my cheeks flush. I looked up at him and saw him struggling to control his own feelings. He was unable to keep his face blank, as would have been his wont.

"I'm sorry, Claire. I didn't think..." His voice trailed off.

"You just surprised me, that's all." Weakly I tried to downplay my reaction, setting the knife back on the cutting board behind me.

"That was not surprise, Love, that was fear, I know the difference." A familiar ring sounded from the other room. He looked relieved, "Excuse me."

Though I wasn't hungry anymore, I went back to chopping vegetables. When the meal was cooked, I put it in a container and set it in the fridge. It would make a good lunch tomorrow, I decided with a sigh.

When my prep dishes were washed and put away, I took a seat on the couch and picked up a book I had been working on before my life had turned upside down. For the first time ever, I *heard* James walk down the stairs. That he felt the need to make noise and avoid any surprises put a lump in my throat.

"Was that work?" I asked him over the back of the couch, trying to sound as though nothing happened.

He didn't answer and I sat up, twisting my neck. James stood at the bottom of the steps, eyes trained on me and not speaking.

Growing alarmed, I tried unsuccessfully to read his expression. "We need to talk."

My heart slammed in my chest. "Why?"

"We have been summoned. We must leave tomorrow."

"The Court?"

He came around to rest on the chair opposite me. "I know that in time you will heal but we don't have that luxury and I'm worried about your ability to handle this visit. We will be underground again and surrounded by vampires. If you show signs of being unstable it could put you at risk."

I didn't ask what kind of risk he meant, I was stuck on the fact that we'd been summoned. The thought of a visit terrified me. Part of me knew it would help to talk to him about what had happened while the other part of me wanted to lock it away for good and hope it would go away on its own. The time restraints forced my hand. "I'm not sure I can talk about it, James." I admitted picking at a stray hair that had gotten woven into the blanket on the back of the couch. "I never want to think about that place again."

Frustration was plain in his aggrieved expression before he looked down at his hands and responded. "I won't make you tell me what happened, although I can tell you that whatever it was has changed you. You *feel* different to me, you even *smell* different. I can see now why I had so much trouble finding you through our connection when we were looking for you. It wasn't until you reached out first that I was able to find you again. I am not naïve enough to believe that no one else will notice the change in you, especially since they will be looking for signs of weakness."

I had thought I was keeping the extent of my distress hidden and gave myself a mental kick for not realizing our bond would give me away. He was right, though; I had to get myself together if I was to meet with the Court again. Miranda was going to want to delve into "us" pretty thoroughly, fascinated as she was with our bond. That *was* the whole reason she wanted to see us. His mention of our bond and remembering what Henry did gave me an idea, not one I was excited about but maybe a way of avoiding having to speak the words. If I could trust anyone with my secret, it was James. Ashamed but sure that he was correct in the necessity, I glanced up at him to see him waiting.

I asked him quietly, afraid to look him in the eye. "I can't talk about it. Could I try to show you?"

He saw what it was costing me and nodded soberly. "I will follow your lead. If we can help you, we will give the Court no cause to question their faith in us."

He was right; I waved for him to come around and sit. When he was seated next to me, I held out my hands to him and dropped my shields. They went down in a whoosh, I was clumsy in my nervousness. Taking my hands, he looked into my eyes and waited patiently. It was just like our first session, totally unguarded, and I flinched when I felt us connect. I gave him a warning, "Make sure you don't go looking around."

"I will stay with you." he promised somberly.

It took a few tries for me to settle and put my memories in order so that they would make sense. In my mind I went back to the night I drove to the club. There was no way to separate my emotions from my memories so he felt everything I had when I was taking off my gifts from him leaving them in the car, thinking that I might not see him again. He also saw my intention to trade myself for Stephen and my hope to get the boy and Annika out when Bradley told me they had her. We wound back down the stairs and into the corridor again. He had never been down there and was seeing it for the first time. As promised, he stayed with me and I kept my eyes downcast so that I didn't have to see his reactions.

I showed him Stephen, suspended in mid-change and Brian dead on the floor. We saw Gaston putting my manacles on and locking me in my cell. Coming closer to the more emotional memories, I wanted to withdraw from him and close off. James felt my discomfort and gave my hands a gentle squeeze. Peeking up at him, I saw that his expression was open and not judging. The last barrier between us went down and with a deep breath I let go, trusting him with all of it.

My mind recoiled when we came to the last days. He felt my frustration at not being able to focus enough to use my ability to protect myself. Trust or no, I cringed when he saw me too weak to protest and accidentally channel Gaston at the last encounter. I let my memory lead him through the staking and final events leading to our reunion.

Exhausted, I withdrew my hands from his and closed my eyes. I leaned back into the cushions, putting my hands over my face. Now that I had shown him everything and it was done, I found it hard to breathe waiting for his reaction, believing at least in some parts of my mind that he would ask me to leave. That he would think less of me for seeing it all there in front of him. I wished I'd been strong enough to tell him and leave out the worst of it.

"My sister was raped."

I opened my eyes to try to read his expression.

He was sitting with his elbows on his knees looking at his hands, rubbing the underside of his fingers with his opposite thumb. It was a human gesture and one I hadn't seen from him until these past few stressful days. I wondered if it was something he'd done as a human, coming back with his humanity.

"She was twelve when it happened. My mother had died already and my three brothers were gone leaving Father, my sister Anne and myself."

I waited for him to go on. Rubbing a hand over his eyes and looking tired he went on.

"Father was sick from drinking and had been in bed for days; it happened a lot after our mother died. I was working in the field, trying to get the seeds in before the spring rains came. Anne took the wagon to town to get supplies like she usually did a few times a month. When night came and she still wasn't back I worried and went out to meet her. I walked a long time before I found the wagon on the trail. I found her crying in the bushes nearby. She said the man from the store that had loaded the wagon asked her if she wanted a kitten. He'd told her one of the barn cats had a litter and they were trying to get rid of them. Anne loved animals and she was so lonely for something of her own. She followed him into the barn and was no match for him when he forced himself on her. What he'd done hurt her insides and she couldn't ride in the bumpy wagon for long without it giving her pain."

"James I'm so sorry. What happened?"

He answered my question without a hint of regret. "I took Anne home that night, we went very slowly and didn't make it home until after breakfast. Two weeks later when we needed supplies, I went instead of Anne. The boy didn't know who I was and followed me willingly enough behind the shop when I told him I needed help with the wagon. I was too small to be threatening and he didn't suspect anything until it was too late. I used the hunting knife my brother had given me. He was the first person I ever killed. I was ten years old."

"Did you regret it?" The James sitting with me was a compassionate person. I couldn't believe he could kill someone as a child. But, I also knew there was a different

255

James I associated with the vampire in him. I wondered if there had been some of that in him before he'd been turned. Then again, I supposed anyone was capable of murder under the right circumstances. There was nothing I wouldn't do for my family.

"No, I was glad I did it every time I saw Anne startle at a loud noise, hide from a stranger, hold her sides in pain when she moved a certain way." James laid a hand on my arm. "Claire, let me help you." His eyes were pleading.

Thinking I knew where he was going with this, I refused. "I don't want to take any drugs. They would make it hard to keep my ability under control." I snorted. "It will be hard enough when I'm down there freaking out."

"It doesn't have to be like that. Now that you have shown me, they are my memories as well. Do you remember how my emotions feel to you? I can erase your memory of your time there and give you back *my* memory of it if you wish it. It will be fuzzier and second hand. It won't hurt you any more."

I felt my jaw drop and my mind tried to wrap around the idea. "You can erase my memory?"

"Yes."

Anxiously I asked him for confirmation of what I already suspected. "Can you do all the mind stuff? Like Henry can do?"

"To some extent yes, though he is older and more powerful than I am. But you and I have things that only we can do."

"Because of the bond."

"Yes. That and our complimentary abilities give us some unique options." He reached for my hand. "Let me do this for you; I need to help you."

"Why do you *need* to help?" I assumed it might be his compulsion driving him beyond regular compassion.

A shadow darkened his gentle features. "I remember my sister. Part of her died that day. She was never the same after that night. Now I've failed to protect you as well. At least I can help you to erase the memory. I never had that option with her."

Not wanting to be this way forever as his sister had been, I made my decision. "How do we do it?"

He reached out to put his fingers lightly under my chin and raised my eyes to his. "Just look at me."

I did as I was told then pulled away thinking of something. "I want them back, my memories. I need to have reference to that time; it's part of me now." He nodded and I leaned in again. Much like when Henry rolled my mind, I felt my perceptions shift and the room swirled around in my periphery. While I stared into his eyes, I felt my burden lift as James did exactly what he'd promised and took my memory of that time away. Relief flooded through me and I exhaled exhausted. It wasn't like before it had happened. It was *better* because the additional burden of stress and fear it created was gone as well, leaving only nothingness in its place.

When he implanted his own memory in my mind, I saw the scenes like I'd watched a movie. The disconnection let me keep the feelings at arm's length, preventing it from hurting.

James sat back and kept my hands over mine, watching me closely to gauge his success. In answer to his unspoken question, I smiled tentatively.

257

"James, I think you saved my life."

Ch. 43

We left for the airport the next evening after a lazy day around the house. Our flight was uneventful as we flew back to Edinburgh.

The clouds were heavy with unshed rain, covering us in a gloomy fog that left my skin wet. The only sound in the car on the way to the hotel was the wipers while I acclimated to the sights and sounds of Old Towne Edinburgh for the second time. As before, we stayed at The Howard, a small, townhouse style hotel that prided itself on its privacy. I smiled as the butler led us to the same room before handing James our keys.

"Just like last time?" I teased.

He opened the door to enter, "It brought us luck before. I hope that it will again."

Entering the beautifully appointed suite, decorated in the same Georgian style as the rest of the hotel, I recalled our first visit to Edinburgh. We had just committed to each other and were here to gain the Court's blessing of our match. It was hard to believe that was only a few short months ago.

I watched James open up his bags, unpacking and hanging out his clothes since I finished first. I loved to watch him move when he was doing mundane tasks. It made him seem more human, more attainable and real and less the mythical creature who might just decide one day to go back to his world and leave me to return to mine. It had come close and I never wanted that again.

He became aware of my gaze and turned around. "What?"

"Nothing, I just like to watch you." I felt my face grow warm.

James closed the distance between us quickly. Than, as he came within an arms length of me, he hesitated.

I knew he was waiting for a sign from me. In answer I took a step toward him and slid my arms around his trim waist. Coming up on my tiptoes, I raised my lips to his for a cautious kiss.

"Are you certain?" His eyes were deep blue, betraying the strength of his wanting.

I nodded my head. "Yes, if we're careful."

He was very cautious and it felt right to be with him again in what I considered "our city."

When we lay together afterward, I enjoyed the feel of his body pressed against me. I had missed his physical absence, only now feeling complete again. "Do we *have* to leave?"

"Actually, we don't. We could stay here as long as we wished."

"No we can't." I playfully slapped his arm thrown across my stomach. "I have school and you have work."

"I can work from anywhere and you have talked about studying abroad. Why not study here in Scotland?"

"That might be worth thinking about. I haven't even started talking to schools, though. It would be hard to get it done before next fall." I rolled to face him.

He looked smug. "If you want to go to the University here in Edinburgh, I can get you in right now."

"I don't need your money to get me in." I bristled. My pride wouldn't allow anyone to give me a handout.

"I'm not saying you need a bribe, your grades could get you in. What I mean to say is that I can cut through some of the red tape for you to speed things along."

"How?"

He lowered his voice to sound mysterious. "I know a guy."

"Let me think about it." I let the idea roll around in my head. I had been thinking of the UK or France. And then I'd come to Edinburgh and fallen in love with the city on my last visit. The idea of living here for a while was amazing. Especially since I would have James here to help me navigate; he had a history here, although I'd never asked him much about it. That was our agreement; what was past was past.

"Did you want to eat something before we have our audience with Miranda? If you do, we should get moving." He ran his hand up my arm, sending goose bumps running down my leg. His lips curve up in a smile. "Although you could always get something take away if we're pressed for time."

I put my head back against his chest. "I'm going to have to take a rain check. I'm not quite up to a repeat performance just yet."

Instantly concerned, his hand tipped my chin to see my expression. "Did I hurt you?" His eyes searched my face as if he couldn't trust what I would report.

"It isn't anything to be concerned about. My body just needs a little time before it's back at a hundred percent." It had felt good to be so close with him again but there was still some bruising all over that would take time to heal. Smiling, I kissed his nose before rolling slowly off the bed. "I'm going to shower before I go anywhere. Help me pick a dress while I'm in there?"

Ch. 44

James had picked a black suit for himself with a black shirt and my light green and gold dress I wore for our Christmas party. Of course, he looked like a movie star. I thought about pushing my body for round two tonight after we got back from our audience. The look he gave me as he helped me into my wool coat told me he was thinking the same thing.

As before, we took a cab to the Frankenstein Pub over the George IV Bridge and entered the gaudily macabre establishment. We had come early enough to eat which we hadn't last time, even if time had allowed my nerves wouldn't have.

Though any time a member of the Court wanted to meet was cause for some amount of trepidation, Miranda had offered me a job so she must see some value to my life and I figured I wasn't in immediate mortal danger. The only thing that gave me pause was that she had asked that I be turned first. We disagreed that it was a necessary prerequisite and intended to tell her that tonight. I was not ready to consent to "life" as a vampire and James was willing to try some different options before doing anything drastic.

The bartender was not the large dark man working the last time. Tonight there was a petite Chinese woman with a bright pink, chin length bob and violet eyes. She glanced up at us when we walked in and I could tell from her seductive smile that she was an admirer of the man beside me.

"James, tell me the rumors aren't true." She was batting impossibly long eyelashes that appeared to have been doused in glitter while she pouted at him.

James' polite response held a hint of irritation. "Amani, what a surprise. Yes, I've been working in the States these past few months and I will be staying there for the time being." He touched my hand where it rested on his bent arm. "Allow me to introduce you to my fiancée, Claire."

Her eyes narrowed at his use of the term and I smiled at her, liking the way he said it. She sneered a less than heartfelt "Congratulations."

Thanking her, we put in an order for "wine" for James, a ginger ale for me. Once we were seated at a table with our drinks, Amani sent over a server to take my order, Grilled Scottish Salmon. While we waited, I took the opportunity to survey the pub and its patrons.

"How many here are yours?" I asked James, eyeing a pale looking couple with glasses of red wine on their table and no food.

Following the direction of my stare, James chuckled and shook his head. "Nope, not those two. They're locals. There's not much sun here, which is one reason why so many of us choose to live in cool climates. Pale fits in."

I tried to see someone who looked "different." Someone who screamed out "vampire" but no one jumped out at me. "I don't see anyone obvious," I complained.

"That's the point," he teased. "We survive by blending in. If we can't, that's it."

Leaving that comment unanswered, I didn't want to think about what would happen if I turned and failed as a vampire.

Amani brought my meal and another drink for James.

"So," she gave me a withering glance. "It's true; you and a *human*, huh?" She rested her hand on her hip shaking her head dubiously. "There must be something I'm not seeing."

When she turned to go, James' mumbled his reply loud enough for her to hear. "There is a lot you don't see, Amani."

It didn't sound like a terribly hurtful jibe to me, but judging from the way she stalked away, it had hit a nerve.

"What's her problem? Is she just mad because you're with a human?" I took a tiny bite of the salmon. It was really good and I quickly took another regular sized bite.

James sighed and took a sip of his drink. "I suppose it has something to do with that, or it's jealousy."

I stopped mid-chew. "You were with *her*?" I ground out around a mouthful of salmon.

He watched the thick "wine" swirl in his glass. "It was a long time ago. We had a fundamental difference of opinion on lifestyle choices and it did not last long." James tried to make his explanation brief.

Unsure what to say I picked at my dinner, saying nothing. After I ate my fill, I looked to James for direction. "When are we due downstairs?"

"We are more informal tonight which allows us some amount of leeway." He glanced at his watch. "Whenever we're ready."

Pushing back my chair I pointed, indicating that I would visit the restroom first. He rose when I did and returned to his seat like a gentleman of his time. I was thinking about what it would be like to live in a time so different than the one I've been raised in when I walked into the restroom.

I was washing my hands when a bright pink wig appeared next to me. I smiled pleasantly at her reflection in the mirror. "Hi Amani."

She stared at me for a long moment before she opened her mouth. "I find it interesting he would choose a human for a mate. His appetite was insatiable as I recall." She moved up beside me, her lips so close to my ear they touched me when she spoke. "I can't imagine you have the stamina."

Meeting her gaze in the mirror, I gave her my best offhanded smile. "A lady doesn't kiss and tell." My twitching fingers caught her eye with the sparkle reflecting in the light and I couldn't resist. "He's chosen me, that should say something."

Pinching her face up in an unflattering way, she spun on her heel and left me shaking at the sink. I had to breathe myself calm before my hand was steady enough for lipstick application.

When I finished, I rejoined James who had come to stand just outside the restroom. "Did she hurt you?" He had an air of tightly controlled anger about him.

I shook my head and managed a weak smile. "Just some girl talk." I heard a snide laugh from the direction of the bar. Of course she would hear me. "Ready?"

He eyed me doubtfully before he took my hand and we walked down the hallway to the door leading to the staircase. We descended down the stone steps into the limestone waiting room. Lit by torches on the walls, it wasn't overly bright. Knowing what to expect, I didn't find it so eerie this time around.

We waited to be escorted into the reception hall adjoining the waiting room.

"Amani can be a very spiteful woman. I'm sorry if she offended you." I had never seen James so ill at ease, he shifted nervously from one foot to the other. "Things ended badly with us and she has never missed an opportunity to take a swipe at me. I apologize she came after you."

It made me feel better to hear it from him, and yet I couldn't help but wonder what their "fundamental difference of opinion" had been. Before I could ask, the door opened and I saw the tiny albino woman would again be our escort.

Her serene greeting cast a tranquil spell. "James, Claire it is a pleasure to see you again. We've been expecting you." I had never seen her smile before. When she did, it lit up her entire face. She was delicately beautiful in an understated way. Because of her demure nature, she was easy to overlook until she spoke in her beautiful voice and smiled so brightly.

"You're beautiful." It came out of my mouth before I had the sense to stop myself. She turned and smiled at me.

"Thank you, Claire." She led us into the reception hall.

The large hall opened before us, roughly the size of my high school gymnasium and just as tall. The hall was illuminated by torches anchored in iron sconces and several large candelabras hanging from the high ceilings.

We were led through a crowd of maybe one hundred or so vampires and possibly a few humans milling about the hall. This time I didn't readily see the three members of the Court. Our guide led us straight to the front of the room past the thrones, for lack of a better word, and through a side door on the right. A motionless male vampire stood guard outside the door. I gave him an anxious glance and tightened my grip on James who slid his arm around me to draw me closer. He, too, had his misgivings.

Our guide led us into the side room. I peeked around seeing nothing, relying upon my ability for an accurate read. I could feel another body in here aside from us. This room was the size of my parents' living room decorated in creams and pale yellows. The décor was feminine and light with a chaise lounge I recognized as the one they had brought for me to lie upon when I fainted unceremoniously on my last visit.

As we entered, movement by the Asian themed dressing screen across the room caught my eye. Miranda was stepping from behind the screen to stand before us.

"Madam, James Thomas and Claire Martin at your request." Our escort curtsied low before taking her leave and closing the door silently behind her.

Ch. 45

"James, Claire, so good to see you again." Miranda's soft mixed accent lent a hypnotic effect to her words.

James bowed and I did my best to curtsy before addressing our hostess.

"Miranda, I wish to thank you for sending your capable Guard to assist us in our pursuits. They were most helpful in the interrogation and subsequent execution of our prisoner." James informed her respectfully.

Miranda turned her eyes to me as she approached in her satin robe, the fabric rustled lightly and caught the light turning the cream to gold and back in a beautiful display. "Yes, they might have helped in the tying up of loose ends, though I hear it was our dear Claire who was responsible for the actual apprehension of our problem children."

I had to swallow and clear my throat to find my voice. "Yes, Madam." I took the hint for address from the albino servant.

Her eyes remained trained on my face, I could feel her gaze burning into me. Still I kept my own eyes downcast. "Tell me James, how did you find Bradley's hidden lair? He has successfully kept it secret for decades, retreating whenever he got himself into trouble."

"It was Claire again."

He squeezed my hand and I knew that I should, but I couldn't look up. Miranda's beauty and poise made me conscious of my inadequacy.

"She was able to use our bond to call to me." I noted the pride in his voice and my chest swelled.

Miranda perked at the mention of the bond. "You have tested your bond at a distance? How great?"

I saw James dip his head in agreement from the corner of my eye. "Yes, we have tested it to approximately fifty miles above ground, ten with her below." That he chose not to mention the greater test, when he'd been in Germany, didn't escape my notice. I assumed he had good reason to hide evidence of our joined strength.

"Interesting," she indicated the chairs and chaise at the front of the room, "please have a seat."

I thanked her and chose the chaise, relieved when James sat next to me. It made me feel more secure to remain near him when in the presence of such powerful vampires. Regardless of her offer of a position with them and her interest in us, I didn't trust her beyond her own ambition. We weren't sure why she was so interested in our bond; I had to assume it was somehow for her own benefit.

"Do tell me more about your bond. Is it similar to a true mark? Claire do you feel compelled to obey James? Do you feel a need to be with him?" She could not hide the eagerness in her voice. "Are you stronger?"

James and I had spoken ahead of time and agreed it was best to share only what could be proven by others. Other than that, we wanted to keep the power of our connection secret to avoid any exploitation by power hungry vampires. And according to the weres and vampires I could trust, that included pretty much all vampires.

Miranda was waiting for me to answer. James applied a small amount of pressure to my hand to tell me. Raising my eyes to her nose I replied softly but honestly. "We can feel each other in times of need. As for the need to obey and the need to be together, I don't think ours is any stronger than any other couple. Though I have to say I don't have any

269

other experiences to draw from. And yes, I am a little stronger."

"Hmm," she eyed us suspiciously, glancing from one to the other. "I told you, did I not, that there was another such bond some three hundred years ago?" She paused waiting for us to confirm she had indeed told us this information. We both dipped our chins as expected. "The parties were mixed, as with you two. One vampire, one human, and they could speak to each other across great distances as well as exist in each other's minds their bond was so great. Is yours so different from that one? Maybe you are keeping something from me? You do not trust me, perhaps?"

I fought the urge to look at James to see if he had known. Being a terrible liar, I kept my own mouth shut. With her ability, she could see through any lies I might tell. I wasn't sure about lies of omission, although I dare not test it. James knew her talents better and took the lead, "Miranda, this bond is new to us and we have not yet had the opportunity to fully explore it. We share with you only what we know to be true, but yes, given time it is possible more could be discovered." I deduced by the fact that she didn't call him on it that her ability did *not* apply to omissions. James had left out a lot.

Miranda continued to eye us both. "Have you considered my request that you work for us? Your combination of talents would allow you to work effectively together, however, your bond could change when you are turned, Claire. That might prove somewhat limiting, though not enough to make me question your usefulness. Times such as these require us all to sacrifice."

The air went out of me in a rush. I didn't look forward to pushing her and I could tell she wasn't used to having to ask twice. Again I left that to James, not knowing how offended Miranda would be if she perceived my answer as insolence. He was far more practiced in Court politics than I.

James intervened quickly. "Miranda, we are willing to accept your generous offer, however, I do not believe it is necessary to turn Claire for it to be successful. As a matter of fact, it might be more effective as things are now."

Risking a peek up at her, I saw her looking at him surprised. "James, certainly you realize the danger of putting your mate in such a situation as a human. They will tear her apart. Are you willing to risk her so recklessly?"

"I do not agree that she will be in danger. Claire has proven to be quite capable of defending herself and, provided I manage their initial hunger, she will be in no great danger."

Miranda looked doubtful and James proceeded, hoping to convince her of the wisdom of our decision. "We have focused on the importance of our connection but what of her ability? When humans are turned, their abilities can become stronger or be lost entirely. It would be a great loss to have her ability disappear *and* our bond with it. I would like to try without turning her if you would agree to the experiment. Should an emergency arise, I would be with her and could handle her turning should it become necessary."

I considered the implications of what he was saying. I had thought briefly about my ability going away and was comfortable with that. What I wasn't so okay with was the loss of our bond with it. It had crossed my mind that it could happen although I hadn't sat down to really think in depth about what that loss would mean. The fear I felt at being around young vampires grew with the images that popped into my head when Miranda mentioned being torn apart.

The reality of what we were going to do struck me as disastrous either way. I didn't want to lose our bond, it had saved my sanity, and my life, and I found it reassuring to have such a private connection with another person. I'd come to think of it as integral to our relationship. Then there was the other risk of me being torn apart. I wished declining the job offer was an option.

Miranda considered James' amendment to her job offer, withdrawing into herself until she was still as stone, as only a vampire can, while she was deep in thought. My patience and nerves were wearing thin when she finally reanimated to speak.

"The human partner in the bond I spoke of all those years ago had also had his doubts about turning. In the end, it was his mortality that ended the bond when a jealous vampire killed him. Our bond was broken and the hole left in its absence was beyond compare." She stared at me and I let my eyes go to hers, sadness lending her a heartbreaking beauty, and she made no move to use her powers on me. "He was my mate for many years. Our bond was all encompassing, having grown more than you can imagine possible. His loss was great and it very nearly destroyed me. I have often questioned whether I should have turned him in spite of his objections and risked his anger if it would have kept him with me." Miranda's heartfelt speech was honestly shocking coming from such an ancient vampire, making me think she had gained what James had with *her* connection; humanity. My respect for her grew and I began to trust in her motivation to help us.

"Thank you, Miranda. You've given me a lot to think about." I spoke from the heart. Her story had inspired me and I had an idea I couldn't wait to discuss with James once we were away from here.

She nodded in approval. "Do not wait too long as I did; being with a vampire brings with it an element of danger humans don't often survive. And yours would be a loss one does not recover from, I assure you." Miranda regained her vampire coolness and rose, signaling the end of our meeting.

272

We did likewise and, as if by some telepathic signal had been passed, the pale girl reentered the room.

"Rose will escort you out. Please, keep me apprised of any new discoveries you might make in your partnership." It sounded like she meant more than just our bond. I shrugged it off, there was already too much to think about.

We followed Rose back through the reception hall and into the waiting area where she left us to find our own way back into the human world.

Ch. 46

Our meeting gave us a lot to think about; I had meant it when I'd said as much to Miranda. And as she'd pointed out, a human's position in the vampires' world was a precarious one. Should any of them come for me again, I would fare better as a vampire, but at what personal cost?

With so much on my mind I wanted to walk instead of taking a cab back to the hotel right away. It was full dark when we left the pub. We were dressed like we'd been to a show or a social event of some elegance, so we drew the occasional stare. Personally, I thought it had a lot to do with the appearance of my fiancée.

The use of that word ran an involuntary shiver of pleasure up my spine. I was still getting used to our new status and when he introduced me as his fiancée tonight in the pub, it had felt good. Even though initially I had worried what others thought of my wanting to marry so young I had let that go and found that it didn't matter to me. What mattered was what *we* thought and it was right to be with him, regardless of age.

"What are you thinking about?" James broke into my reverie.

Playfully, I taunted him. "Can't you tell?"

"Not specifically, though I do know you were pleased with whatever it was." He stopped, and holding my hand as he was, I had to as well. His hand lifted my face and he looked in my eyes. In the lack of light, I could only determine that they were dark. "Let's try something." He instructed. "Focus on what you were just thinking about."

I caught on right away and tried to focus. "James, we can't know if you are messing with my head or if it's the connection if you're looking in my eyes."

He agreed and released my face. I remained facing him and closed my eyes while I returned my focus to my earlier thoughts of our lives together. Concentrating on my choices for mortality and what that could mean to my ability and bond as well as my hoped for marital bliss, I felt a cool brush on my lips. My eyes popped open and I caught the glow of his pale skin under the street lamps.

"Both would be great losses. I hope that we can find a way to avoid losing either one." His tone softened, "Me too, by the way."

"Hmm?" My brain was still struggling with my lower parts for control of my jumbled thoughts.

"I'm surprised that I look forward to marriage as well. It was not something I had considered for myself until only recently."

Cutting in as usual, James' phone rang. He answered by the second ring, "Yes."

James swore in a hiss. "When?" He listened carefully for a moment before snapping his phone shut.

He was instantly agitated and darted his eyes over my head, scanning for something or someone. "We need to go back to the hotel. I need to speak with you in private."

I felt my stomach knot instinctively. "Okay."

He hailed an approaching taxi. It stopped and James held the door for me. Within a few tense minutes we were back at the hotel, locking our door behind us before breaking his silence.

"What is it, James?" The anticipation had my nerves humming with tension.

"We need to stay a few more days. Lucas has been very busy in Minneapolis."

"Didn't we *want* him to investigate? Has he found out something about Bradley's partners? Some alliance?"

Shaking his head, James blew out. "No, not yet. He has been focused on *our* ranks as we had suspected he would."

I was confused thinking that I had been our weakness, and if I was gone, what could Lucas have found?

"We had been hiding Omar's talents when he was rescued, hoping he could remain undetected. Tara has grown attached and feels if we could hide him from the vampires, he could be saved. Now Lucas and Gabriel know that *he* was the weapon Bradley had intended to use to against our kind and they have reported him to the Court. We only barely missed being there for the call."

"They aren't going to let him live." It wasn't a question.

James looked grim as he shook his head again. "No, they can't let an ability like that exist. It's too dangerous to our kind, especially combined with his fear of us. Fear is very easy to twist into hatred."

"So what's going to happen now?" I feared I already knew *their* plans for the boy. The real question was *our* retaliatory measures. If it involved the clan, they would most assuredly call upon Henry to assist. I didn't look forward to pitting us against the power of the Court. We wouldn't win.

"Lucas already attempted to execute the boy but apparently Tara interfered and when Gabriel tried to assist, Tonya stepped in as well. The rest of the clan has now come in and they remain at a standoff. Lucas has called the Court to rule on the case. Everyone is booked on a flight tomorrow night to have an audience so that his fate can be decided. Henry is on his way as well; Troy has asked him to lend a hand."

As I suspected Troy had called upon Henry. That meant James was in, and by association, me as well. Being a part of this family, I had a new understanding of clan warfare. "What about Annika?"

He shook his head, "She hasn't known us for long and has no allegiance to us. She remains neutral and is staying behind."

The thought of Omar's uncertain fate and the domino effect leading to our newest Court drama acted like a cold shower and I no longer had the urge to jump into bed. Instead, I undressed in the bathroom and changed into my pajamas.

When I came out with a clean face and clean teeth, James was already laying in bed. He motioned for me to come lay with him and I did, welcoming his reassuring touch.

Ch. 47

We passed the next day walking all over town and making a definite point of not mentioning Omar. On the surface it was hard to comprehend how a young boy could pose a threat to such powerful creatures as vampires. It was strictly my knowledge of abilities that reminded me they had a valid concern. Still, I could only picture the frightened boy crying into Tara's shoulders when he came to mind.

We successfully passed most of the day without mention of anything vampire while James showed me more of the city, including an introductory tour of the University of Edinburgh. I could see myself living in the city. It suited me, instantly feeling like home.

"So what do you think?" James asked me over a late snack of scones and tea. We were sitting beside the large front window of the bistro watching pedestrian traffic while I rested my legs. James needed no rest, he could go all day. Sometimes I envied him, other times I felt bad for him that he could never shut his mind off and just sleep for a few hours.

I thought about it as I chewed a bite of scone. Not an American coffee shop scone, a real one. More like a biscuit and best enjoyed with clotted cream and jam. It was heavenly. "If for nothing else, I'd live here just for these." I sighed taking another bite.

"This is a city with a lot of history for my kind. I would enjoy living here again."

"When did you live here?" I'd heard enough passing mention of it and returning to Europe lately it had made me curious. The only thing stopping me from asking was the agreement we had about living in just this lifetime. Still, I was getting curious.

James lowered his voice so that only I could hear it. I had better hearing than most humans now so it was doubtful anyone even standing next to me could hear our conversation. To them it would sound like we were humming.

"I lived here during the war and for a short time after. It was just before I returned to America the first time."

Something itched at the back of my consciousness. "Was that when you were with Amani?" I hoped I didn't sound like the jealous girlfriend I was.

His expression closed. "Yes, it was."

Fighting to keep my tone and pulse normal, I pushed. "What war? Did you leave because of her?"

Hesitating, James looked out at the street traffic passing in front of us. "It was the first World War. I had been here for a few years already and was more heavily involved in Court business at the time. Amani had recently come over from China. She'd been turned during the Boxer Rebellion when her village was taken. She was the only survivor and she'd come over to work for the Court, eager for revenge against the West. We worked together on a few assignments. After that, I took my leave of the Court and chose to live far away in America."

"Can I ask what the 'fundamental difference of opinion' was with Amani? Was it something to do with your work or was it more personal?"

"I really don't see why it matters now, but yes, it did come up in our work." James was increasingly uncomfortable with our conversation, shifting in his seat and fidgeting with the small jam jar on my plate.

That a difference of opinion could drive him from someone concerned me. I wanted to know what was that big a deal for him. "What if *we* have the same difference?" I prodded.

He laughed, "It's impossible."

"How do you know? You don't know everything about me." Anxiety gave way to anger.

"I do know that you are *human* and Amani hates you for it. I don't. That is our difference." He sighed, resigned to sharing the last little bit of the mystery with me. "Amani and I were investigating a vampire attack in a small town north of here. She was supposed to interrogate the villagers and erase their memories. No harm was to come to them. Instead, she slaughtered seventeen people before I was able to stop her. We had to burn half the village down to hide the evidence."

I knew she was scary; now the thought of her having been so close to me made me queasy. Superceding my fear of Amani was the realization of what James had been doing for the Court. "You were in the Guard! Why didn't you tell me?" It made sense, why everyone was sure he was wasting his time in America and should return to Europe.

Gritting his teeth, his agitation became more pronounced. "I did work for them for a while but working for the Court required me to set aside my own beliefs for theirs. That's not something I take lightly." James put his hand on my arm, adding. "Don't worry about Amani, she may be angry but she will not touch you. You are forbidden."

I rolled my eyes. "I know, the bond. Miranda is protecting us."

His lips twisted and he welcomed the chance to change the subject. "An approved consort is forbidden to other vampires although it isn't strictly adhered to. And yes, with

Miranda's special interest in us, the penalty of a transgression is greater. I have heard that she has assured the populace that it *will* be enforced."

The inner workings of the Court were fascinating and frightening as well. "How so?"

James shrugged, "Normally the penalty is a year locked starving in a coffin."

I tried to imagine what starving would be like for a vampire and pictured James when he was desperately hungry in my mind's eye. I couldn't imagine an entire year like that.

"For harming you," he continued staring out at the crowded street. "The penalty would be death."

"Hmm." I nibbled on my snack thoughtfully.

Ch. 48

The next day was rainy and cold, keeping us inside for the day. If it weren't for the potential for serious injury to any and all of our ranks stemming from Omar's trial scheduled for that night, I would have relished the thought of a comfortable bed and James to myself for an entire day. As it was my nerves were frazzled and I wished I had a book for distraction.

"I'm going upstairs to take a tub." I announced after breakfast in the hotel restaurant, The Atholl.

"Go ahead and get started." He was reading the local newspaper and didn't look up. "I'll be up in a few minutes."

I couldn't read his expression and he didn't offer any more information. Overall, he was too sedate for my keyed up state of mind and my temper flared.

I sat back down and snatched his paper from his hands, aiming my frustration directly at him. "You can't let them kill him, he's just a boy. You *have* to hold some sway, you used to work for them."

Quelling the spark I saw temporarily ignite in his eyes, James tried to reason with me. "More lives than his are at stake. If someone were to use the boy he could cause countless deaths, chaos, and unnecessary bloodshed. You know that as well as I."

"Are you saying you're going to let him die just because he was born with a gift? Don't you guys have a way of using magic or something to make him promise not to hurt anyone? You can compel him or something. There has to be something you can do." I could tell I'd gotten too loud and I cast a worried look around the restaurant before whispering. "Aren't you supposed to 'need to help' or something? Why don't you help now?" I rose from my seat and offered one last argument before I stalked back to our room. "What if it was me?"

Some time later I heard the lock turn on our door. The shower had helped to take the edge off of my easily inflamed temper, but not as much as the physical distance. Things had grown more volatile with me. Unless I was physically touching him, it seemed my nerves were in constant vibration when I was near him. I wasn't sure how to interpret it or even if I wanted to. So much seemed to point to me turning and I had the same argument as always; I just wasn't ready. And now I was taking it out on him when I knew better.

"I'm in here." I called out from the bathroom where I was brushing out my hair, still wrapped in a towel.

"James asked me to tell you to meet him at the pub at five o'clock. But if you're lonely, I can stay." A rough, Scottish brogue answered from just behind me.

I squeaked and spun to face the new voice, clutching my towel more firmly around myself. "Who the hell are you?"

The young vampire had been younger than me when he was turned. He leaned against the doorframe staring at me. With his jet black hair standing in spikes, purple lipstick, black dog collar and matching leather pants he looked the part of punk rock vampire, something I couldn't picture anywhere but on the cover of a graphic novel. The red t-shirt stretched across his undeveloped juvenile chest was stylishly torn around the light grey outline of a dragon running up his side. Half his mouth turned up exposing one fang. "I'm Iain." He said it like his name should mean something to me. When I didn't react, he went on to explain. "I've known James since he worked here in Edinburgh. Sometimes I run errands for him."

"So, was that all?" I didn't comment on being called an errand.

His eyes roamed up and down my body landing on my thighs, presently far too bare for my tastes with a stranger standing here, staring at me like I was a slab of meat. "If you want it to be." He left the offer hanging.

"Then good-bye, Iain." I stared at him trying to will him out the door.

He didn't blink until I set my brush down with a crack on the counter and added. "I'm sure James would be interested in hearing about your offer of companionship."

At last, Iain started to look uncomfortable. To give him a final nudge I added, "And Miranda."

Throwing up his hands in surrender, Iain backed away still smiling cockily. I heard the door close and rushed to throw the latch and bolt the door. Leaning against it, I let out a breath I hadn't realized I'd been holding.

Standing there, I wondered if James was angry with me for my harsh accusations and if that was why he hadn't come himself. I would be. With nothing else to do, I threw on some clothes and walked down the street to pick up a few magazines to read by myself for the rest of the day.

By three o'clock I had nearly gone out of my mind with worry and boredom. Worry for Tara, worry for Omar and worry for James. I hoped I hadn't pushed James to do something crazy on my account. My new temper issues were becoming dangerous for us both. I would have to broach the subject of taking it to Miranda soon if they continued to get worse, maybe she would have some advice.

When I could stand it no longer, I dressed for the Court and called a cab. At least if I waited at the pub I would have four different walls to stare at and other people to watch. Sitting here was making me crazy.

I had brought a a simple black dress that concealed most of my scars and wore my hair down to cover those on the tops of my shoulders. It showed off my jewelry from James and some small diamond earrings my parents had given me for my sixteenth birthday I'd dug out for the occasion. Meeting with the Court was stressful, and it was helpful to get dressed up in all of my finery, it made me feel more confident facing them. More like the grown woman I was supposed to be now. Maybe I would feel more that way if I could stop acting like a spoiled three year old. Again I chastised myself, ignoring the fact that my mood swings were beyond my comprehension or control.

If I'd been hoping for company I was out of luck. No one I knew showed up at the pub and I was left to wait by myself for over an hour. To add to my growing misery, Amani was tending bar again. When she saw me waiting by myself, she sent over a glass of champagne with a note that read "To the beginning of the end." I sent it back with the note crumpled inside the glass and she laughed.

Finally, it was ten to five and in walked James. He went straight to the bar and ordered two drinks, downing them in rapid succession while standing at the farthest edge of the bar, pointedly avoiding Amani's attempts to engage him in conversation. I watched him, trying to gauge his mood before he noticed me. He was wearing a dark suit and shirt, different than what I'd seen him in at breakfast. When had he changed?

After his last drink he turned around and saw me watching him curiously. By his lack of surprise, I would guess he'd known I was there. He made his way to me and I saw pink claw scrapes on both his cheek and jaw disappearing below his collar. They were already healing now that he had fed.

"What happened?" I jumped up, reaching out a hand to touch his wounds.

He held out his hand taking mine from his cheek and brought it to his lips. "I'll explain later. Are you ready?" His lips brushed my palm lightly as I stood up.

A lead ball of dread dropped into the pit of my stomach and though I tried to hide it, I knew he sensed it. He had consumed his drinks at the bar to avoid having to explain himself to me. That did not bode well in my mind at all. He gave my hand a light squeeze and avoided my curious stare as he led me down the familiar path to the waiting room below. The wall between us was up, yet there were a few faint surges of pain, gone as soon as they'd come. I concentrated on breathing and walking at the same time, clinging to his hand to keep from coming unglued.

Rose, the young albino, led us into the main reception hall where the full Court greeted us. Charles, Anton and Miranda were before us in front of the room, sitting in the high backed chairs that had never looked more like thrones.

Charles, short and doughy with long, wavy brown hair, Anton, tall, whip thin and sporting a thin moustache and goatee, musketeer style, and of course Miranda, dark featured and devastatingly beautiful. All looked far more serious than they had on my previous meetings with any of them and wore black, formal robes. I couldn't swallow the lump in my throat.

We bowed as we were introduced and as I came back up, Tara and Omar entered from a side room. Omar in a dark suit held onto Tara also formally attired in burgundy and black. Only because I knew her could I see her nerves and, as she drew closer, the hair on my arms and neck rose. She was anxious enough to be close to changing. She had told me once that it happened sometimes with heightened emotions, much like a vampire's fangs. I noticed now that she wouldn't look at us, though Omar shot a nervous smile at James. It was the most friendly he'd been with a vampire that I'd seen and instead of being heartening, it only filled me with a dark sense of foreboding.

Anton took charge, broadcasting his voice for all in the hall to hear. "This human you bring before us has a dangerous ability, too dangerous for the majority of our kind who cannot protect themselves from psychic attacks. You have tried to hide him from us, endangering us all. For the safety of our population, we must end his life that others may continue to exist in peace."

The assenting murmurs in the hall from the onlookers gave weight to the ball in my stomach. I watched Anton, the most severe of the three. His vehemence left no room for doubt that he would not be deterred from his decision to put an end to Omar's young life. Charles was expressionless as he gave a slow nod of assent. Miranda remained my last hope and I watched her close her eyes before finally inclining her head. My heart sank for the boy and Tara for what they would both lose, at the same time hopeful no one else would come to harm should Tara get between Omar and his executioner.

When I heard James speak, my heart stuttered, my mind flashing to his scrapes as I watched him. What had he been doing this afternoon? In my head I felt a flutter of nerves echoing my own.

"If it pleases the Court, I would like to offer a third option that does not include the death of the boy."

Tara hissed under her breath and confirmed my suspicions as to where James had gotten the claw marks. From the dangerous look in her eyes I was guessing she would like to take another swipe at him. I prayed no one would die, clenching my fists uselessly at my sides.

Anton didn't move; he only blinked with an exaggerated slowness. "Please, James. Do go on." His was the air of a tired parent listening to a child's imaginations.

James continued confidently; only I could feel the nerves he wrestled. "It is agreed that an ability like this boy's giving him power over so many of our kind cannot be allowed to exist, however, I believe that I have a solution." He looked at Tara who was still glaring down at the feet of the Court members. Omar clung to her hand so tightly I could see his white knuckles. He also stared ahead trying to look brave.

"The fear is that the boy will use his ability against our kind out of fear or retribution. What I propose is a gamble. The boy is young, he has not reached puberty and his ability is not yet fully developed. It is highly likely he will lose it if he is turned."

The muttering in the hall rose to a crescendo while the Court members sat unmoving in their seats, statues of great gods unconcerned with the affairs of mere mortals. It was utterly impossible to predict their intentions.

Charles, the first to move, held up his hand for silence. When the hall quieted, he spoke. "He is young to be turned, it has been difficult for children to tolerate the change in the past. And I ask you, what do we do if he keeps his ability? What do you propose then?"

Tara moved and I saw her starting to drop into a crouch as if to leap and the hair on my neck tingled with the magic she was raising. I knew just as James spoke what his plan was, he leaked a glimpse into my mind as well as his misgivings. I opened my mouth to object but his hand flashed out, taking mine and squeezing tightly, freezing the words on my lips with a steady *no* in my head. Obedient, I held my objections.

"If he keeps his gift after he is turned, I will kill him myself." James' words took the strength from my knees and I fought to keep them from buckling.

Again the noise in the hall rose, only this time the Court allowed it. They were deep in discussion. Tara was mumbling to Omar and stroking his hair. He was flicking his eyes from James to the Court and to me. He was just twelve years old and stood here among a race of beings who had shown him nothing but violence until James and Henry. And now, James was standing here offering to betray him. What must he be thinking?

Now that everyone was distracted, I pulled James' hand to get him to face me and whispered. "What are you doing? How is this helping?"

When he looked at me his confident mask slipped and I watched his eyes flick to his highest rulers and back, his eyes dark and disturbed. "What else is there for anyone to do? He cannot live as he is. This is the only way he has any chance at all."

I knew he was right and I felt it tearing him up inside to put himself in the position of executioner, then I looked over at Tara and Omar. She was holding him to her as tortured as if she'd raised him. My heart clenched painfully. No matter the outcome, they would suffer.

Omar would never get to grow up, never date or marry. He would forever be frozen as a pre-teen and that was a best-case scenario. At worst, he would undergo the painful change only to be killed for good if it didn't turn out, and he would be killed by someone he'd known as a friend.

Miranda spoke, immediately silencing the hall. "James, I have known you to be loyal to this Court in spite of our differences in the past. You have had the most experience with our young with abilities such as this boy's. Do you believe this will work?"

"In my experience, the ability will appear within the first few days if it is to resurface. If it is not in evidence after that time, it would be safe to assume that it did not survive the change. I think that we cannot condemn a child to die unless we are certain he truly poses a threat." He let his eyes wander to the other two. "He is a child. If we blindly kill children out of fear, then we *are* the monsters they accuse us of being. We must try for our own sakes to do this."

"Will you turn the boy?" Miranda was studying Omar who was trying to be brave, his giant eyes in a trick of the light looked black.

Shaking it off, I tried to ignore the impression that he already looked like a vampire.

"If he is successfully turned, he will forever be a responsibility for his maker. James, you know this, do you accept responsibility? To my knowledge you have never turned a human, I must be certain you are capable of handling it."

My head was on a swivel, swinging back and forth between the two. James was nodding an affirmative and I felt him grow more certain, he thought he'd gotten Omar clear of death. "I will accept the boy as my responsibility."

Tara's eyes were wild when our gazes met. I could feel her desperation over losing her charge. They had grown close so quickly. Though maternal for her and not romantic, it reminded me of the growth of the bond between James and myself. It had been strong and sudden, just as likely due to the violent nature of events surrounding us as our abilities. It was only out of fear of repercussion she kept herself together at this point. If she was killed she could never protect him.

290

Without any further ado, James squeezed my hand and bowed to the Court. I took the hint, curtsied thankfully without falling and turned to leave the hall. Tara put her hand on my arm, snapping out of her panicked silence.

Pointedly ignoring James beside me, Tara pleaded with me, her pride gone. "Claire, if you have a heart left, you won't let him do this." She gestured to Omar. "He's just a child."

Omar's thin voice broke in cutting her off. "I'm not scared of 'em."

We all stared at him. He had never spoken to anyone but Tara, as far as I knew. He had no accent, only a hint of the street in his words. Just like James had said, his voice had not changed yet and held no hint of a man, yet his words were more absolute than they should have been from one so young. Children grow up quickly on the street. Poor kid, had he ever gotten a break, I wondered.

"There's no shame in being scared of them." Tara tried to soothe him, rubbing her hand on the back of his. She narrowed her eyes at James. "They are scary creatures; everybody knows that."

Omar put his free hand on top of her other to stop it petting him and continued, "I don't like 'em but I'm not scared of 'em. They're trying to protect themselves, I get that." He raised his face to James and squared his shoulders. "I want you to try."

James dipped his chin and stuck out his hand, a rarity for a vampire. "I will do everything in my power to keep you safe."

Omar set his jaw and drew himself up, his head barely to James' shoulder before he put his tan hand in the pale one.

Ch. 49

James and I found ourselves on the street outside the pub in the cold night air. He cautiously put his arm around my shoulders and I let him draw me to him. I felt his lips kiss my hair and leaned into his chest. I could finally breathe and concentrated on just that until I heard him speak.

"It's the only way, Love. He's dead if we don't try this."

"I know."

"Tara is sure it won't work. She's mourning him already."

"Why doesn't she even want to try?" I couldn't shake the memory of her haunted eyes when Omar had agreed to be turned. "It has to be better than losing him."

He tried to explain. "She doesn't want him to be scared for nothing. So much of his life has been out of his control and frightening, she's trying to save him this last bit of pain and fear because she loves him. And, in case you haven't noticed, she isn't entirely sold on our way of life."

"Do *you* think it will work?" I looked up at him, trusting implicitly his opinion.

He was still staring over my head when he answered. "I don't know. Some do lose their ability with the turn, with others it intensifies and a few times I've seen it shift focus. There is no way to tell in advance, although more lose it if turned young. It has something to do with the changing state of their human bodies before puberty. Once a person is through puberty, their ability is set and remains through the change unless it was weak."

I felt a charge of hope on a purely selfish level. "Maybe that means our bond would stick since I'm older."

"I'm counting on it."

The cab arrived but I wanted the fresh air I'd been cheated out of earlier.

"Let's walk." I suggested.

He looked down at me before agreeing, a curious expression on his face. "Okay." He waved off the cab. "Claire, before you met me, did you get cold in the winter?"

I snorted and gave him a look. "Of course, who doesn't? Okay, what *human* doesn't?"

James pointed to my open coat then held his hands out to encompass the night surrounding us. "You haven't been cold enough to button your coat the entire time we've been here and at home you have been doing the same. I've caught you leaving behind your hat and gloves. You have so many of them I was assuming you bought them to wear, not as props."

My mind spun back to the last few weeks when it had grown colder back home and then here in Scotland, slightly warmer, but by no means balmy. "Oh my gosh, I don't feel it." Throwing my hands up in the air with a dramatic flair, I nearly shouted, "There goes *another* thing I've lost." So much of me was sliding away it was silly to worry about not needing gloves or a hat, I told myself. It didn't help. This was tangible proof that I was changing and it seemed like every day there was a new symptom of me being lost to the more belligerent nature on the other side of the bond from me. Difficult as it was for me to lose myself, it was with a reluctant satisfaction that I watched him regain that which he had feared above all else he would lose; his humanity.

We walked in silence the remainder of the first mile. After the second mile, I wanted a drink. Though usually not much of a drinker, I didn't see a reason why I shouldn't have a glass of something after a night like this one and I was developing an appreciation for the warm, fuzzy feeling it gave me. It dulled the sensations I was feeling more now that we were both struggling with control.

James was reticent but gave in to my request, leading me into the next restaurant we encountered. It was a small Italian affair with red and white checked tablecloths, the works. I ordered a glass of Pinot Grigio, James did as well much to my curiosity.

"It doesn't mean I am going to drink it, but you shouldn't drink alone," he said when I stared at him strangely. "I'm blending, remember?"

We had a normal, casual conversation while I drank my wine, it was very relaxing. After I drank the first glass, I traded my empty for his full one and enjoyed that one as well.

"Are you finished?" His eyebrows rose expectantly.

I nodded, feeling warm and sluggish when I stood up. Once outside I took off my coat entirely, putting it over my arm. James held my hand and I quickly found it necessary for my balance to grasp it more firmly. Heels and wine were not for amateurs, I giggled at my own folly.

We had traveled another block or so when I began to find it hard to put one foot in front of the other. Our progress had led us down a quiet street with few streetlights and no open businesses at this hour. It was the type of area I had been raised to avoid as a young woman. It was far too deserted to be safe.

James heard the footsteps first. I might have heard them sooner if I could focus on anything beyond my own heavy feet. My ears didn't catch them until they were upon us. James spun, pushing me behind him and I saw three young thugs closing in. They were dressed in dark clothing and bulky jackets. My eyesight, like James' let me pick out their numerous tattoos, piercings and human colored flesh in the faint light.

When James pushed me behind him, I lost my balance and fell on my rump. He bent into a crouch and I saw the man on the left pull a gun. I screamed into my hands when I heard the shots.

James recoiled and I knew he had been hit, but I was watching the men in front of us in astonishment. The one who had been holding the gun was on the ground, bleeding from a gaping throat and the man in the middle was laying on his back, unconscious before the echo of the shot had fully died. James faced the man on the far right who had by now pulled out a knife and was advancing with no signs of the fear a human should have facing something so fast and fierce. He had to see James' face at this range.

To my bleary eyes, it looked like James leaned forward to take the man's hand but when he came away, the hand was bent at a funny angle and the man screamed before blood was running down the side of his head and he fell as well.

James turned, scooped me up off the pavement and ran. We were at the hotel in a heartbeat and of course James already knew the location of a back door and service elevator, keeping us out of sight until we reached our room.

Once inside, he set me down and went into the bathroom. "Take off your dress and bring it in here," he commanded.

Still fuzzy from wine, I did as I was told without understanding why. When I came into the bathroom, James was stripped to his pants and wiping his chest with a now bright red washcloth.

"Put your dress in the tub. We have to get rid of these and limit the blood in the room." I did as I was told, throwing my dress on top of his shirt already in there. When I put my dress in, I saw the blood from when he carried me. There was so much. His pants followed over my shoulder. He was so practiced I knew he'd done this countless times through the years. Disturbingly, I realized I should have been more upset by that than I was.

Turning around, I saw he was standing in his boxer briefs and I had to take a few deep breaths to steady myself. His chest was still so bloody I couldn't tell where the bullets had struck him. The back of my throat itched.

"Where did he get you?" I managed to get out, though my mouth seemed minutes behind my brain and I continued to scan his chest for the wounds.

James looked at me oddly and pointed at his chest just below his right nipple. I clenched my teeth when I saw the opening. He pointed again at the underside of his right arm and I felt my stomach lurch.

"What do we do?" My eyes were locked on the blood, there was too much.

Breathing raggedly through clenched teeth, James grimaced. "I need you to get your tweezers and fish them out before they heal inside."

I felt faint, the room spun around me. "What?"

"Claire, I need your help. Go find your tweezers in your bag. Please, I can't get them out myself. I'm right handed."

"Okay." I mumbled, staggering off to find my tweezers. I returned with them seconds later.

Ch. 50

James stood staring in the mirror, hands braced on the counter, exposing his shoulders and back to me. I had to force myself forward. I did not want to do this.

"Turn around." My voice was thick and I tried to swallow the irritation in the back of my throat.

He did so and I was eye to eye with the first bullet hole. I breathed through clenched teeth so that I didn't vomit. My hand was surprisingly steady as I used the tweezers to fish inside James' hard chest to grasp the first bullet and pull it out. I refused to look up at his face and see if it hurt. The second turned out to be a false alarm. The bullet had passed through completely and did not need to be extracted.

James occasionally grunted but was otherwise encouraging of my efforts until I finished.

When it was done, I looked around for some sort of bandage. He stopped me saying it was unnecessary. Sure enough, when I looked again, the skin over the wounds was closing.

He gathered the clothes and put them in a plastic bag he managed to find in the closet holding spare pillows.

We both stood bloody and in our underwear in the bathroom. I was drunk and he was thirsty. I didn't notice he was thirsty until I was washing off my own bloody chest and arms with a damp washcloth and the irritation in the back of my throat grew to a burning sensation I'd felt before.

I heard a low growl from where he was standing and glanced up to see his fangs out and his eyes gone black.

"You're hungry. Don't you need to feed so you can heal?" I was tipsy, but I knew him well enough to know what was necessary after that kind of blood loss. Unafraid, I watched his reflection steadily.

He was visibly torn between answering truthfully and telling me what I wanted to hear. That told me enough.

Grabbing his hand I led him to the bed, pulled back the covers and sat down on the edge. "Okay." I figured we could replace the sheet since there were others in the closet for the pullout couch in the sitting room. The hotel might notice a missing coverlet. Already I was thinking like him. After covering up murder and assault, what was a missing sheet? I snorted.

James dropped to his knees in front of me and put his hands on my thighs. "Are you sure?"

Not trusting my voice, I nodded and closed my eyes. He really needed this if he wasn't arguing.

His hand touched the back of my neck, pulling my face to his. "Open your eyes and look at me, Love."

Experience told me what he was going to do and I obeyed, knowing it would be better this way. He could make it pleasurable or agonizing with only a suggestion. Looking into my eyes, he altered my perceptions and pushed me back onto the bed. His mouth and hands were gentle at first. His needs, both of them, grew more intense and his hands tore the last of my clothing aside.

In moments, I was on the verge and when I cried in pleasure, his fangs sank into my neck.

When my breathing returned to normal, I became aware of my more normal human thirst and my clearing head. I tried to sit up to get a drink but James sat up first.

"What do you need?" He looked at me, oddly out of sorts, and he sounded funny.

I shook my head. "Nothing. I was going to get a drink of water."

"I'll get it." He stood and turned to the bathroom. I watched him wobble as he walked away.

In a few seconds James returned with a glass of water and I sat up, taking it from him but not before he sloshed a little on my leg. He sat heavily back on the bed next to me.

I was alarmed, worried the blood loss or bullets had been more severe than I had first thought. "What's wrong? Do you need more blood?" He was moving like a human, not his usual gliding self, even with our crossover he couldn't have changed so quickly. Could he? I didn't want to think what that might mean should he have to face the full Court as a near human.

But he shook his head in an exaggerated side to side weave. "Nope. No more of *that* blood tonight."

Offended, I started to argue that he needed it since he was stumbling and he couldn't even talk right and then I realized what was wrong and burst out laughing.

"Oh my gosh, my blood got you drunk."

Grinning lazily back he bobbed his head and rubbed a hand over his healed chest. "Yes, it did. It's been decades since that's happened. You know some really like that kind, the high ones. It's the only way we can get that feeling again."

I laughed at the idea of vampires using humans under the influence as a means to get high, suspending morality for the moment. James laughed too. He was unguarded and I didn't know if I should take advantage or not.

My common sense was offline so I didn't use it. Now that I had the opportunity, it was hard to think of things I wanted to ask him without worrying he would change his answers to protect me. "Tell me what it's like being a vampire. Do you like it?"

His expression clouded and he looked serious as he considered his answer. Taking a finger and tracing a pattern of freckles on my thigh he watched his finger while he talked. "It's hard at first and then after a while it becomes all you really remember. Eventually, everyone who used to remind you of your human life dies and you are only left with other vampires for company and most of them are piss poor company, talking about the good old days before everybody was dead." James raised his bare shoulders and let them drop, "It's lonely, to be honest."

"Are you ever sad you became a vampire?"

"Not anymore." A clump of hair had fallen down on his forehead and absentmindedly he pushed it back. "At first it was hard," he stopped tracing and rested his hand on my leg. I watched all but the pale of the vampire fade, his expression no different from a pure human, "Now it's all I know. Being able to go out in the daytime made a big difference. It isn't so bad now. I do still miss some little things I never gave much thought to before." Leaning back on the pillows, he kept his eyes on the wall in front of us and I lay back with him watching him keenly. "I miss enjoying a fine meal and a good night's sleep. I miss waking up with the sun and, not just dealing with it, but *liking* the feel of it on my face. That used to be my favorite part of morning, getting up to feed the mules before we plowed, watching the sun rise." He looked at me, eyes curious. "Did you know prey animals don't like us?" He blinked at me and I shook my head. "Other predators don't either, they see us as competition." He sighed in resignation. "At least I have Henry and the Andrews, even if they aren't always happy with the arrangement. And, now I have you." He took my hand and

301

brushed the back with his lips, crooked grin wrinkling the corners of his eyes. He looked tired.

At last I thought of a question I wanted an honest and unguarded answer to. "James, do you want me to be a vampire too?"

He met my gaze, his grin fading. "Selfishly, I want you to be with me forever. Realistically, I know it is asking too much to take you from your human life; children and a safe future; to ask you to watch your family and friends age and die until it's only us. I guess I don't know Claire. How can I ask that in good conscience? How can I know you won't come to hate me for it in time? I love you too much to know what I want, if that makes any sense."

"I love you, too." It made perfect sense. I felt my eyes growing heavy.

Nothing resolved, we crawled under the covers together where I promptly nodded off and James had to spend yet another night alone.

Ch. 51

The sun came into the room the next morning and I cursed it. I must have forgotten to close the drapes when I went out the day before and cursed myself for that as well. The mumble from behind me on the bed told me James wasn't feeling well either. I wasn't sure if it was the vicarious alcohol consumption or the gunshot wounds, but one look behind me showed me he was also not at the top of his game.

"Do you feel as bad as I do?" I asked through a fuzzy head and the beginnings of a headache.

"I don't know, it's been a long time since I've had a hangover. My head hurts and so does my chest. I'm not sure which one is worse but I hope it passes soon." He cocked his head. "You could stand an aspirin, breakfast and a hot shower I think."

"You even got them in the right order." I smiled weakly in return. "What about you? Do you need to feed again?" I hoped he did not.

Slowly shaking his head he answered. "No, I will last until I return to the pub tonight. They can handle my needs."

The corner of my mouth twitched up at his reference to needs.

He gave me a dark look that tugged at my insides. "They can handle *one* of my needs. The other is all yours."

"Now?" I was surprised and again hoped he didn't want to do that right now.

"No, I don't think either of us is up to it." He winked and I smiled, closing my eyes for a second. I wasn't looking forward to getting up.

I rose to find the aspirin in my bag while he called room service and ordered eggs with a side of green vegetables. He swore eggs were the best for a hangover, greens for blood loss.

He was right. After breakfast I felt closer to human and after the shower I felt loads better.

We had a day in again, not being due back until dusk for Omar's turning.

"Are you nervous?" I asked him while we dressed to go find me some caffeine and stretch our legs.

"Yes, I am." I caught him absently rubbing the backs of his fingers. "I know the procedure, although I've never done it before. It is difficult to stop when one has to get so close to draining the victim; I can only hope that I have the control to stop myself in time."

I walked over to kiss him after I fastened my jeans. "You have more control than anyone I know. You'll do fine."

James regarded me quizzically. "How can you of all people say that? I have had very little control since being with you."

Casting a doubtful glance over my shoulder, I smirked. "If that is you with no control, you won't have a problem."

He watched me, his face unreadable as he finished buttoning his shirt and then wrapped me up in a tight embrace and a thoroughly knee weakening kiss. "See, no control." He set me back on my feet with a wink, seemingly overly satisfied with himself. "Ready to grab a cup of tea?"

I didn't have a third formal dress for tonight's event so a shopping trip was on the agenda for the day. James had a clothier in mind and we cabbed it to the store after our morning tea.

An hour after we walked into the shop, I walked out with a fashionable, dressy lilac top, light grey fitted pants and matching grey heels. James picked up grey trousers and another white dress shirt pressed and ready to wear.

Left with over four hours to kill after we brought our purchases back to the hotel, I was about to ask James what we he wanted to do when he made it clear. One minute I was hanging our bags up in the closet, the next thing I knew, I had been yanked back, crashing into his body.

His mouth was on my neck while his hands raked roughly down the front of my body with a ferocity he'd never shown in our lovemaking. I turned to face him and our mouths met eagerly. James was so urgent, so desperate in his passion it frightened me for the reality of what was going to happen tonight.

Ch. 52

When we arrived at the pub it was standing room only with both vampires and humans. I was guessing at the vampires by how much red wine was going around at the bar and only a few cocktails. I was pleased that Amani wasn't working; I was in no mood to deal with her catty jokes. Too wound up to eat anything, we stood at the bar and I ordered a glass of wine. James ordered two for himself.

"Are you really that thirsty?" I inquired, taking a sip of Pinot Noir.

"I don't want to take too much tonight by accident. This is insurance."
"Oh." I gulped. The true risk of what he was going to do was sinking in and I drank a huge gulp of wine to steady myself. We had enough time for us both to finish a glass and when he started on his second I ordered another.

When James looked askance at my order, I was defensive. "I'm nervous." He didn't look pleased.

"Are they all here to watch?" I wondered if it was considered voyeuristic to watch someone turn. If turning was as intimate as when James fed from me, it was definitely voyeuristic. That thought of this involving a young child made me distinctly uncomfortable and I pushed it aside, needing to be calm in this crowd tonight. My shields were under constant barrage from those around me in their states of heightened excitement.

Anxious and pale in spite of the blood he was taking in, James replied, "Yes, word's gotten out and they're hopeful something dramatic will happen. Maybe an accident or a fight between us and the cats."

Alarmed, I tore my gaze from the crowd. "How possible is it that there will be something 'dramatic'?"

I didn't like the way he avoided eye contact with me or shifted on his feet before he answered. "I told you, it's hard to do this." He was unusually short.

I reached out to put a comforting hand on his arm only he raised his glass to his lips and I retracted the gesture. "You aren't going to do that. Is there some other reason?"

Continuing to glare in the opposite direction, I almost missed his lip curling and the look of disgust on his face. "They are hoping Tara will object. If she interferes she will be killed."

"Oh my gosh!" I gasped. "But she isn't going to do that, right?" The assurance I was hoping for did not come.
Instead he rose from the table and surveyed the room over my head, already scanning for threats. "Ready?"

I grabbed my glass, "No." I rose to follow.

Ch. 53

The reception hall below was as crowded as the pub above. Indignation rose in my breast as my gaze fell upon the eager faces of a crowd of well over two hundred vampires hoping to see the people I loved fail.

"I feel your anger and I agree, but nothing good will come of you provoking the Court with an outburst. It would be considered poor form." His eyes continued to scan the crowd while he spoke beside me.

"Poor form? They're hoping to witness one murder, maybe more, and they're worried about *my* poor form?" I gawked at him, incredulous.

James stopped and stared me down, unusually severe. If it weren't for the anxiety I felt in him that I, too, would be pulled into a fight, I would have been offended. Given my recent behavior I wouldn't trust myself if it weren't for his help with my control. I reached for his hand and for the first time, he jerked it away. His tight lipped speech stopped me from saying anything, though I could feel the barb from the affront and a shadow crossed his midnight dark eyes. "This is a group of immortals. They are bored and hoping for some entertainment; you can't take it personally. As far as poor form is considered, this is our Court. It is the same as human politics, they are less concerned with what happens than they are with who is showing proper respect for their authority. You are human and they will tolerate little interference from you. You *must* control yourself." I barely caught him mumbling when he turned away to lead again. "If Anton hadn't insisted I would never have brought you."

I took another gulp of my nearly empty wine glass and let him lead me by the hand through the crowd to where the Court awaited James' arrival. His nerves were bleeding over, compounding mine and making my skin hum until I felt like I was going to catch fire. If I wasn't still stinging from his rejection before when I'd tried, I would have reached out to touch him and gotten some relief.

Upon reaching the front of the crowd, I was struck by the stage set for the drama that was to unfold. A low black sofa had been brought out into the hall. Irritably, I wondered if leather was chosen for its ease of cleaning.

In the front row I saw three familiar faces, Troy, Tanya and Henry all stood at an angle somberly facing both the crowd of hostiles and the Court and making their own faction.

Pulling out ahead of James I made a beeline for my family. Hailing them, I realized one face was missing. "Where's Stephen?" My eyes continued to search the crowd.

Tonya's lips were tight and her eyes barely touched me. She too was entirely focused on the bloodthirsty vampires. "He was told not to leave the country."

I felt my sense of equilibrium shift. "What? Why?"

Tonya reported without emotion, flicking her eyes down to me briefly. I envied her ability to keep her emotions at bay. "Brian's parents filed a missing persons report and there's an investigation underway. Stephen is a person of interest and he's been warned not to travel and was upset he could not make it tonight. He sends his regrets." Her hazel eyes flicked to James, hard and disapproving.

I knew Stephen and "upset" would not begin to cover it, although with his impulsive nature it might be best that he *wasn't* here tonight. The atmosphere was already charged with hunger and fear and we didn't need anything else added to the tinder. I was starting to feel battered from all of their feelings which had been bumping into my shields since I'd walked into this place and I was, by now, nearly exhausted with the extra effort of keeping them up tighter than usual.

Plus, there was no blocking the shocks coming through our bond. It was rapidly becoming too much. My control was strained already and we had yet to begin. It was looking like a real possibility that I would lose it and make James do something awful.

Realizing the source of the fear I was intercepting couldn't be coming from the vampires, I cast my feelers out for it, searching for the other missing family members. Lowering my shields was dangerous in this crowd; still, I went ahead and did it. I was going mad not knowing where Tara and Omar were and, more importantly, what she might be planning to do.

The animosity I felt toward the weres from some of the vampires was shocking. I didn't dare explore it here by digging into the wrong vampire's mind. The last time I had done that, the vampire had been terribly offended and she had tried to kill me. A few of the vampires in the crowd had brought humans for the purpose of feeding tonight and I felt their hunger building and mixing with their other appetites as they eagerly awaited the start. My stomach turned and I hoped they intended to erase their donors' memories and not drain them tonight. I had a very real fear that this could turn into a blood bath of Roman proportions.

I found what I was looking for coming from a room behind the Court's seating opposite Miranda's quarters. Tara and Omar were waiting there, I recognized their "feel." At least one other presence was with them and it "grabbed" me as I extended myself outward.

I felt the air rush from my lungs. The thing holding me felt wild and my body responded at once, ignited with the mystery he offered. As if in suspended animation, my mind stopped functioning and left me a body without a will of my own as my feet moved forward, heeding the call.

Another force, this one physical touched my upper arm impeding my progress. I didn't fight either force. I merely stood frozen, closer but not enough. The allure continued to beckon. Yet, buzzing nearby and making my skin tingle, something warm touched my arm. Still I remained blank; standing stiffly and staring at the closed door.

Something bumped me in a far corner of my mind. It's familiar pull went deeper into my soul than the other's pull, except it couldn't get through the haze that the wild thing had poured into my head. The cool hand that wrapped itself around my other arm sent a shockwave surging through me pushing the foreign presence from my mind and allowing me to snap back to myself.

Left panting from the battle in my weak brain, I attempted to regain my composure and looked to see who was touching me. Tonya was holding one arm, James the other. Tonya warily searched the crowd for the cause of my confusion. James, however, knew. There was murder in his black eyes as he stared directly at the same door that had captivated me seconds ago. For once I was glad he was blocking me. Then, in the same breath I realized how selfish I was being. I could see what it was taking from him to keep me out. He had to have been as volatile as I in here.

His hand remained locked vice-like around my arm, barely loose enough to allow my circulation and he swiveled his face to Charles a few feet away. In a low, furious tone that would certainly not be considered polite, he forced his words through clenched teeth. "Lucas must control himself. This is neutral ground. If he cannot stop toying with my fiancée, I will take great offense." The threat of what he might do about that offense hung unspoken.

Anton responded in the same tone James had taken. "You will be respectful when you address this Court James. *We* control this hall, do not forget that."

"Then control it." James shot back icily.

The crowd had grown still as only vampires can. They had all heard the exchange. The only sounds in the hall were the breaths and heartbeats of the humans and weres. I could feel the hungry anticipation that the immortals were going to get what they wanted.

Charles took a step forward, making his way toward us. I felt my stomach tighten and pulse speed up thinking he was coming to punish one of us. Then, surprisingly, he reached his hands out and pointed to my left hand. Waiting for the other shoe to drop, I held out my hand so that he could see the proof of James' declaration.

I heard the lighthearted tone though it was in direct contrast to the black eyes and hint of fangs that held my gaze. "I am embarrassed, you have caught me off guard and I do not have a gift prepared. When will the special occasion take place?"

Charles' interest was unusual and I had to wonder at his real intentions. *He* wouldn't be trying to avoid a fight here, would he? I didn't think it mattered to any of them if the whole group broke out into a massive blood fueled orgy as long as they got to stay in charge. Either it was the wine, the stress or I was having "an episode" again, as Stephen called them but I was starting to feel lightheaded. Not now, I thought anxiously trying to focus on Charles' face, I'd never noticed how white he was before. Staring at him now so close I couldn't help ogle his bone white skin so smooth it could have been porcelain, even the flame from the torches reflected off of its opalescent surface.

Charles' madness stemmed from an eternity of being able to do whatever he wanted without consequence, an affliction James said they all eventually suffered from, which caused him to waffle between being a flake and a stone cold vampire who made me think he would tear off my head as

312

soon as look at me. Whether intentional or not the effect kept me more than a little off balance around him.

James had cooled himself outwardly at great personal cost. The holes erupting in his defenses gave me insight into the extent of his distress. I felt his agitation like sandpaper scraping across my skin, no wonder he hadn't laid a hand on me before. James was radiating his disquiet to me. "Soon," was his simple reply to the question I hadn't asked aloud, "when could we leave this place?" To Charles, he maintained a stubborn silence.

Charles considered James and me, his usual foppish mien returning in full force. "This hall remains neutral ground for you, Claire. You are a protected human, safe from unwanted feeding and unwelcome manipulations." His pudgy hand withdrew his lace edged handkerchief to wipe at his nose for no reason but display or habit.

To me, there was a glaring loophole in what Charles said. Unwanted and unwelcome were easily overcome by an older vampire who understands how to alter a human's mind. Lucas could do his magic and make his call both welcome and wanted. I didn't complain, not wanting to be in "poor form" which we were dancing dangerously past. If James didn't calm down, we were actually going to graduate to appalling form or worse in a hurry.

Raising his voice, Charles called without turning away from us. "Lucas, Gabriel, bring the boy."
Gabriel. That explained the unidentified presence I had felt beside the others, a presence that made itself known yet also defied explanation as to what I was feeling. He was like a vacuum; nothing existed there. I didn't want to know what he'd been before being turned.

Lucas strode forward alongside Omar. His self-satisfied smirk was infuriating to both James and myself, I felt James' hand twitch on my arm. Gabriel kept pace with Tara

313

on the other side of Omar. From the chatter I heard around me, the Elite Guard was gossip worthy even among the immortals.

When the entourage stopped before the Court Charles' command rang out clearly. He'd gone back to stone cold. "Lucas, you will interfere no more with this human while in my hall. You are on neutral ground and transgressors shall be punished severely. You may be Guard and the stake doesn't apply to you, however, that doesn't mean you are without consequence. I believe we can find a coffin to fit even you." I wasn't sure if he referred to Lucas' unusually large body measuring at least 6'3, his status of Elite Guard, or super rare Elven vampire. Lucas was a giant compared to Charles and I had to wonder if that might be a sore spot for the vain leader of the vampires.

Lucas dipped his head, never taking his eyes from Charles'. His melodic voice carried to me through the other sounds as if he was standing beside me. My body hummed in response. "My apologies to you Charles, I forgot myself. I meant no offense to the Court. No further interference will occur in this place."

I could tell from the rage emanating from James that he had noticed the same loophole I had. Lucas guaranteed nothing except that he would not bother us *here*. Everywhere else was open season.

"Enough about the human. We are not here for that." Anton's sharp voice raked our ears. He projected his voice to the crowd, though I doubted they needed the extra volume to hear. "This boy's life has been spared conditionally. If his ability survives the turning, he shall not. You have five days to prove he is no longer a threat. If you fail, you agree to execute him. All present stand as witnesses." Anton raised his chin to James. "Do you understand and agree to these conditions?"

James released my arm at once, dulling the emotional maelstrom he'd been sending, before turning to face Anton full on. "I do."

Anton's eyes narrowed and he sneered showing a hint of fang. "Then it is time."

He gestured to Lucas who came forward with Gabriel matching his stride, guiding Omar between them. Tara, pinched out, followed close behind. As they passed him, James put his hand on Tara's arm giving her pause, and drawing a glare of pure loathing.

"I will make it as painless as possible, I promise." They were nearly the same height and James stared directly into her eyes. I could feel his sincerity as well as his apprehension through the patchy shielding he was managing, his exhaustion making him transparent to me.

Tara was also too jittery to block me out and I caught a hint of the nausea roiling her stomach. She was busily berating herself, feeling she was failing Omar. Her shielding was coming and going as she lost focus repeatedly in her distraction and mine was stretched thin. We all were close to our breaking points and my skin prickled with the energy pulsing through me. The only thing keeping me from losing it was that my ability was actually too confused to know which one to channel.

Lucas sat Omar on the sofa and left him, following Gabriel to take up a position behind the Court members. Omar was shaking visibly, his cheeks wet with tears as he stared at the sea of vampires surrounding him. There was no putting it off; to prolong the process would be cruel. James walked forward and crouched in front of Omar. The trust that had developed between the two was not enough to keep Omar from being frightened of what was coming. He leaned back as far as possible, even pulling his feet up under himself to crawl backward and escape. James' hand rested on Omar's shoulder and he stopped moving, frozen in a crouch on the black leather staring at James. To an onlooker it would have seemed as though the boy had been caught at some prank and was being scolded, not forever altering the little boy's future and tying the two together for eternity.

When Omar looked up at James, I felt James push his shielding away just barely and reach out to Omar's mind. All of a sudden, in a dizzying rush, my world shifted and my eyes saw Omar's close up as though *I* was crouching before him as well. I felt his young bony shoulder warm under my hand. Losing my sense of self once more as my marks flared up and thinned the membrane separating our minds, I was pulled into James. He'd been reaching for my ability, the complete merging of our minds was a surprise to him. I felt him startle at my unexpected presence and then his acceptance.

Omar stared into our eyes transfixed as James tapped into *my* ability instead of Glamouring him, thus allowing him to better monitor the boy's reception of what was happening. We conveyed serenity and were instantly rewarded with the glazing over and drooping of his eyes.

When his breathing relaxed and his eyes closed the rest of the way we knew he was close to sleep and we let go of his shoulder to reach for his arm, drawing his wrist to our lips. Our fangs grew, the vibration that should have been disconcerting somehow was second nature and the burning hunger roared up our throats while we watched his pulse, heard his heartbeat and then let go of the tightly clamped control we used to shut it away. Unleashed, the hunger came spilling forth and we struck. Tara's painful groan barely registered over the thrumming temptation that swiftly filled our mouth.

The warm liquid velvet that was his blood poured down our throat with each beat of his heart. As we drank, his pulse pushed less and we had to actively suck on the wound to keep pulling the blood into our mouth. When the pulse had faded until it was nearly gone, we fought the primal urge to keep feeding. The urge fought back; for me it was akin to asking my lungs to stop breathing. The reminder of my human nature pushed back against the vampire's need for blood, my human mind recoiled at the thought of taking Omar from Tara, of killing a child. James tied into my revulsion and our fangs retracted in favor of our tongue that flicked out to seal the wound.

Releasing the boy's hand we gently laid it in his lap, lifted our own and bit down, using our razor sharp fangs to tear our own flesh. The pain was fleeting, a minor annoyance only. We slid over to sit beside him, putting an arm around his neck and cradling the boy's head in the crook of our elbow to hold our wrist to his mouth. His limp body, paled from blood loss, slumped near death and his head lolled against our body.

"Drink," we commanded watching a few drops of our blood drip down on his shirt. Involuntarily the boy obeyed, fluttering his closed eyelids as he latched on. He drank for a few swallows before instinct kicked in and his body recognized the return of life to his limbs. His hands came up to grasp our arm, pinning our wrist to his mouth as he eagerly sucked in our blood.

When he was sated and fell back into a catatonic state, we lay him back on the chaise as we would a sleeping child to rest and swiped our tongue dismissively over the wound on our wrist, sealing in our own blood. Warm and giddy from the blood exchange, we stood to face the members of the Court, the human part of us trying to ignore the feeding orgy going on all around us in the crowd.

Charles, Anton and Miranda had gone completely vampy in the ecstasy they could feel coming from the witnesses and more closely, from us. Their own fangs had grown in the excitement of so much blood and Charles and Anton were monitoring the activities of the crowd, I hoped in order to keep anything from going too far. Miranda, however, was staring at us unblinking, a knowing and very unhappy look on her face. We could feel her wrath burbling under the surface. She had seen more than we'd intended.

"It is done. When he rises, I will return." Our voice was deep and rich, vibrating in a totally different way than I was used to, yet familiar, too. We were strong from so much blood.

Tara rushed forward from where her family had been restraining her to kneel by Omar's unconscious body, stroking his curls anxiously from his forehead and listening for his heartbeat. We could hear it from where we stood and it was strong. Turning to face Henry, we saw me. What was happening to me only became strange when I looked upon my own body staring vacantly at us from ten feet away from where I felt myself centered.

Henry sidled over to the vacantly staring body and spoke rapidly to someone over our shoulder. His mutterings reached me, garbled like he was under water, and Miranda moved closer to us. I became acutely aware of the cold presence that reached into the body I was watching and pulled while something else tugged at the place in my mind tied to James. The pulling sensation crossed over from uncomfortable to excruciating and then with a soul rending snap, my awareness "popped" back to my other body and I felt us tear into two separate entities with another motion sickness inducing shift that left me blinking and adjusting to my new perspective. At the same time, I was filled with a crushing sense of loss at having to flee the proximity of James' more dominant nature.

I gasped as I felt my "self" settle back into my own body now being held by Henry. A glance showed James being held by Miranda, and judging from his stormy expression he was equally unhappy with the separation.

Miranda snarled at Henry. "Follow me, bring her." Agitated, she strode off quickly. James kept up easily while Henry followed, dragging me along with him as I struggled to keep pace with his long legs.

She led us into her private sitting room where we had met with her yesterday. Henry sat me down in one of the chairs and James hovered protectively nearby. Once I was sitting, I heard Miranda call for someone to enter.

The door opened and there stood Iain. He winked at me, hunger still in his eyes and ever-present cocky smile on his lips. Miranda barked and in a flash he retracted his fangs, his eyes clearing from black to bright green, leaving no trace of the nature that had just ruled him.

"Iain, go upstairs. Find food and drink for her, now." Miranda's order was quieter but bode ill for any who would not obey. Iain briskly exited the room with a bow.

She came to stand two feet in front of me, sniffing the air around my head. "Claire, when was the last time you ate?"

I tried to answer but my voice was thick and still not quite my own. "I just did."

Her hand struck the side of my face with a resounding crack, taking me completely by surprise, rocking me back in the chair. James lunged to attack and she pivoted to face him, uttering one simple command, "Don't." He stopped in his tracks, unable to disobey his more powerful elder.

"Your human is weak. She has been neglecting her human body and she is losing control of it. Has she consumed alcohol tonight?" She leaned down to sniff at me. My head was spinning from the blow and the lingering effects of the marks; I was pretty sure the alcohol had been scared out of me.

"She had wine upstairs." James answered, irritated but wise enough not to further inflame her ire. I had no idea where the glass I'd had with me in the hall had gone. Honestly I didn't know where all *I'd* gone in the hall. Between Lucas and James I'd been out of my head for most of it; it was no surprise that I had managed to lose my drink.

She glared at James. "If you value her, you need to be more cautious with her life. Choose wisely your timing when you feed from her. Do not weaken her before throwing her into a situation like this one. It was stupid and reckless." She hissed. "Do not think for a moment Lucas will not pursue her outside these walls. Her ability to go beyond ordinary empathy and channeling makes her highly susceptible to others' minds, a trophy to be collected or destroyed. You would be wise to continue to teach her to shield her mind and make certain she cares for her body or she will be lost."

Her eyes flicked back to me, frightening in her anger. "And no alcohol. It makes you weak. Your shields on your *best* day cannot withstand an onslaught from an ancient vampire. If you wish to live *and* keep your bond a secret, you have much work to do. This is a hard world we exist in and if you want to be a part of it, you must be more focused upon your survival because no one else is."

A light knock on the door announced Iain's return. I smelled the food from behind the door.

"Chicken fingers?" I couldn't hide my disappointment. I didn't especially like chicken fingers. They were so boring, but I would eat anything if it made Miranda happy.

Her dark brows furrowed, "You smell that?"

James spoke up, back in control of himself. "Her senses are nearly as powerful as ours."

Miranda's eyes narrowed and she looked back at me. "What else has changed? You must be honest with me how far this has gone if you wish to avoid losing yourself entirely. The vampire is stronger than the human, trust me."

"That's not true," I whined childishly, "James has become more human, too." I regretted it as soon as I blurted the words out.

Miranda spun back to James, her voice deadly calm. "After the display in there, I have to wonder what else you have been keeping from me, James." She motioned for Iain to deposit his tray of food on the table beside me and leave.

His disappointment at being excused showed in his shoulders, he clearly wanted to stay and watch our drama unfold.

She noticed and growled at him over her shoulder. "Iain, leave now. Speak not a word of what you have heard or you will be punished. I will see to it personally."

He inclined his head and exited the room, closing the door behind him.

Miranda jabbed a finger at the tray, "Eat." I grabbed a chicken finger and took a bite, shocked at how hungry I was once I began to chew.

She pointed her chin at James. "Speak."

Fortunately, we were of like mind to let her in on some of our secrets. It had become a necessity to reach out and she was our only expert. "My humanity has been returning."

"Meaning?" She glanced briefly at Henry behind me. I hoped he wasn't in trouble for not sharing with her too.

"Meaning I experience more human emotions than I have in a long time. I am more empathetic to others as well, I am clearly getting that from Claire." He kept it short, trying to give away as little as necessary.

"Interesting," was all she said as she regarded each of us briefly. I felt a tickle as she brushed against my shields, testing the truth of what I was saying. She was doing the same to James, I would bet, given the stiff set of his shoulders.

I was feeling stronger and more like myself as I ate the second chicken finger, glad to have something to focus on that wasn't one of the three vampires in the room. I didn't mind the taste of blood in my mouth from the cut where her blow pushed my cheek into my teeth. My stomach clenched as I tried to push away the memory of how much blood I had tasted tonight. Fortunately for my sanity, it had not actually passed down my throat, though that was only a small consolation.

I felt a nudge in my mind. My eyes went straight to James who was staring at the ground. Following his lead, I looked back down at my plate and dunked my chicken in the honey mustard sauce before popping it into my mouth. He nudged again and I lowered my shields a little and felt him inside my head, then I heard him.

"Fake sick."

My acting skills had never been very good but in light of Miranda's belief that I was weak, I figured I might have an advantage. Plus, I was already on the verge of illness as it was; James' request wasn't much of a stretch.

Pushing my plate aside, I stood and spun to face Henry behind me putting my back to Miranda. I moved fast on purpose. Just as I spoke Henry's name, I rolled my eyes back into my head and let my legs crumple beneath me. I prayed I was far enough from the other furniture as I felt my body go down.

James, having anticipated the move, had rushed forward catching most of me before I hit the ground. "Miranda, Claire is ill. I would like to bring her back to the hotel to rest."

I could hear her doubt when she hesitantly gave her consent. "You *will* return tomorrow at dusk when the boy rises." Her tone softened. "Until then, take care of her. Remember her limitations. It is your responsibility as her mate and husband and I cannot risk my position by helping you publicly. I am sorry."

She sounded so sincere, I actually believed her. We both did.

Ch. 54

James carried me to the hallway and back up the stairs, I kept my eyes closed the whole time, glad to have him blocking the bulk of what went with the sounds I heard as we wove through the throng of feeding vampires. We reached the back of the pub where he set me down and I continued to hold his arm. It wasn't just for show, as I had been severely shaken by the events of the evening. I would be glad to be shut up in our hotel room away from all of this, pretending to be a normal couple.

Someone had called a cab. It was waiting for us by the time we reached the front door.

"The Howard," James told the cab driver and sat back, wrapping his arm around my shoulders. It felt like he needed it as much as I did.

We rode in silence to the hotel and went straight to our room. Right when he clicked the lock into place, I fell face first onto the bed with a groan.

I lay there for a while, listening to water run in the bathroom. I zoned out until James shook my shoulder gently some time later.

"What?" I was instantly alert and rolled over to sit up. "What's happening?"

James chuckled and sent a soothing bump to tell me everything was safe. "Relax, Claire. I wanted to know if you would join me in the tub."

A warm soak sounded great. It felt great, too, when I slid in the water. James slid in opposite me and we soaked until I was pruney. *He* didn't get pruney, a detail which I found completely unfair.

"Do you think Miranda is going to exploit us now that she knows more?" My eyes were closed against the bright overhead lights while I soaked.

"I believe she will use it to her advantage, yes. However, what we do have working in our favor is her greed. If she uses her knowledge too soon, others will find out about it and she might have to share us or bargain to keep us for herself. You might have noticed that our kind does not share well."

I snorted. No, they did *not* share well. But I wasn't so sure Miranda's motives were solely based on greed. The way she had opened up to us said a lot. It had planted a seed of trust within me, not enough to totally discount the alternative.

"I think she will keep it as her ace in the hole. We are safe until she needs us." James went on, he didn't sound upset at the prospect of being used as a bargaining chip in their political scrabbling.

"That doesn't bother you that we could have her hanging over our heads forever?" I opened my eyes to see his reaction.

He was staring down, flicking at the water and hiding his expression. "Of course it bothers me, but our options are limited. To go against the Court is to face exile and lose the protections they afford us. It is much the same as your government. It might not be perfect, but it is necessary for us to have any order at all in our society."

"How is exile bad? Aren't most vampires solitary anyway?" I watched the ripples in the water as he traced designs on my knee where it broke the surface.

"An exiled vampire is open to attack without consequence. He can be killed for property, vengeance or merely for entertainment. A Court of three has been in place for nearly fifteen hundred years and as long as we play by their rules, they guard us against anarchy within our ranks. These three in particular have only been in place for four hundred years or so and have kept the peace relatively well."

"How do the members turn over? Are there elections?" I giggled at the prospect of vampire campaigns. What kind of skeletons did *those* guys have in their closets? Literally.

James did not share my amusement. "As you can imagine, it is a highly sought after position affording significant power to its members. They are only replaced when they are killed and they are succeeded by a member agreed upon by the remaining Court members."

"Well that's very Roman. Isn't it pretty easy to bribe two members of the Court to guarantee your place and then kill off the one you can't or pick your least favorite thereby securing your own position?"

James cocked his head, a curious expression on his face. "For an empath, you have a very analytical way of looking at things. Is that you or is that me?"

Shifting uncomfortably, I answered his question honestly. "I am a very analytical person situationally, at least I used to be. How the two sides both fit inside me is beyond my understanding. Maybe there is something bigger out there I'm supposed to use it for. Lately I've been kind of speculating that," I shrugged self-consciously feeling the pink creep up my neck, "I guess that sounds kind of narcissistic doesn't it?"

"I don't think so. Who knows why we have what we do within us. For you, maybe the empathy came first and your analytical side was born of a need to have control over it. It's self-preservation; your ability to decipher what situations to avoid acts as your failsafe measure." James offered.

I stared at him, open-mouthed. He was astute, but that explanation was over the top Doctor Phil.

"What? I read."

"I guess you do. I'm not used to having people read my mind, though. That is the very thing I'd come up with."

"Well," he tipped his head, "it seems we both need to get used to being in each others' minds; this bond is getting stronger. I used to have to focus to find you. Now I can always feel you, right at the edge of my own thoughts."

"It's the same for me. You have always had this spot in my head, except now it's grown. As soon as I reach for you, you're there. Sometimes I don't even know I'm reaching, you're just right where I need you."

"Do you have to lower your shields or is the bond coming through the shielding for you?"

"I don't even consciously keep them up anymore. I have to think to *lower* them, now they are just so second nature to me." I held up a finger making a point. "I do lower them sometimes since it makes it easier. But the bond supercedes any shielding I have; I can't stop you from getting in any better than I could on day one." I was embarrassed to have to admit that Miranda was right, that my shielding was weak.

James withdrew from my thoughts and was focusing on something. Curious what he was doing, I watched his brows knit in concentration and then I felt something slam into my mind. It felt exactly like I would imagine getting electrocuted would and I jumped gasping in surprise.

Water sloshed, splashing James in the face. "What was that?"

James laughed, wicking water from his face with his long fingered hands. "There's nothing wrong with your shields."

I caught the twinkle in his eye before he ducked his head to hide the crooked grin that had cropped up. "Did you do that?" When he didn't answer but kept smiling, I kicked him. My foot found his butt cheek and fortunately, in the water I couldn't kick hard, because my foot felt like it had hit a bowling ball.

"Ow!" I straightened my leg to see it out of the water, checking for blood or a bone sticking out or some sign of injury to go with the stabbing pains.

James was instantly penitent. "Are you hurt?" He grabbed my foot and inspected it sympathetically.

"What are you sorry for, your butt being hard enough to break my bones?" I felt like an idiot for hurting myself. The bone didn't feel broken, but I was definitely going to have a monster bruise.

When he had completed his inspection of my foot, his hand slid up my ankle checking for "concussion injuries" he called them.

In the morning I asked James to borrow his cell phone to call back home. If we were going to keep traveling like this I might have to invest in a fancy phone like his instead of my stripped down model that couldn't even send a proper text.

"I have to call Stephen. I didn't last night what with the time difference, but he's probably up and out now. It's after lunch." After Tonya's news last night that Stephen was under investigation for Brian's disappearance, I had tried to think of some plausible scenario in which Brian might have disappeared without Stephen's involvement, something we could tell the police to make them leave him alone. The problem was, Brian was dead and Stephen had been in the

328

room when he was killed. There might be some sort of evidence tying him to the scene or Brian to him if the body turned up. He might not have been the killer, but I didn't think a police detective would believe for a moment that a vampire had killed Brian.

Stephen picked up after several rings. "Hey James."

"No, Stephen, it's me. Are you okay? Tonya told me about the investigation."

"Claire, you saw Tonya? Oh, right, at the thing. How did that go? Is Tara handling it okay?" He sounded tired.

"Yes, it went all right. We have to go back tonight when he wakes up. 'Rises' I guess they call it. Tara handled it about as well as could be expected. Tell me what's going on with you, though. I'm worried. Should I come home?"

James' head popped up from the table where he'd sat down with his laptop. It caught my interest only mildly. I was focused on the other end of the line.

Stephen sighed heavily. "So far no body, no crime. Right now they're investigating the possibility that he went to a party, drank too much and wandered off. Problem is the party story is sounding pretty thin, and rightfully so; he wasn't much of a partier. His sports always came first." His voice had turned bitter, my guess was an old argument was behind it. "They're asking where you two were since they know about the party at your house the Friday before he disappeared. They've questioned all of us already. Annika is laying low and running down some leads on the nightclub since the police don't know about her yet, we want to keep it that way."

I lowered my voice, forgetting for the moment that it made no difference. "Are you sure you're all right? Do you need me to come home to be with you? Because I can?"

329

Movement caught my eye again. James definitely had an opinion about me going home.

"No," he was slow to answer making me doubt his sincerity. "Do what you need to do there. I think it might be better for them to check things out here for a while before they talk to you. That will give them time to turn up everything and we'll be better able to gauge what they've got by their line of questioning. We'll know if we're going to have trouble."

"Stephen, has anything like this ever happened to you or your family before? You know, that involved the police?"

"Yes," he confessed unusually subdued, "when she was young Tara lost control and we had to go underground for a while. It wasn't so bad then, we were able to disappear a lot easier before computers and technology became an issue." Stephen was genuinely saddened at the idea they might have to walk away from their lives. Even I was able to figure that out without having to use my ability.

We talked a little more, mostly about what was going on with him and I filled him in on my tour of the University and our "normal" adventures in Edinburgh. Ten minutes later we hung up, agreeing to speak again in a few days for an update on Omar and the investigation, figuring the clan might be too busy with Tara to be counted on for information.

When I hung up, I looked over at James. I was frustrated at not being able to help my friend and scared I might lose him and his family if they had to go away. Irritable, I was more severe with James than I needed to be. "Is there something you need to say to me?"

Closing his laptop, he folded his hands over it entirely too calm and cool for my tastes. It fanned my annoyance. "Love, I need you here. With me." He continued softly.

"What do you mean you need me here? What do *I* have to do with this?" I assumed anything I was involved in was done when we'd met with Miranda.

"Who do you think is supposed to handle Omar when he rises? You can't leave because this is your first assignment from the Court and I need you."

"Oh my gosh. So this is it? We're really doing this, huh?" My heart fluttered with the mixture of excitement and fear flooding through me.

He was eyeing me closely to gauge my panic and I felt his familiar bump against my defenses. He was being polite by giving me the option of letting him in, which I didn't. "Are you sure you're comfortable with this?"

"I guess." I put on a brave face. "Who better to be my first one than someone I knew?" All of a sudden I had a very real need to get up and clear my head. I wondered if it was windy enough to need a coat.

James didn't move, his muted response stopped me cold. "Actually, it's harder if you knew them. It can be hard to see them so... different. They don't rise like their human selves. He will be more like an animal at first, purely interested in his physical needs. Sometimes it can be difficult to control them." Frowning, James rubbed the backs of his fingers. "His age is definitely going to be a factor. Not many children are turned, but those I've heard of have a harder time adjusting to the complications of being a young vampire and the impulse control. I'm not sure about Omar though, his life is such a mystery."

My curiosity piqued. "Did Tara give you any information about his past?"

"Not much," he shook his head. "All he remembers is that before Gaston found him a year ago, he was living on the street in Detroit.   He doesn't remember much else, just surviving."

"Poor kid.   He's had an awful time of it."   I compared his situation to Brian's.   He had parents to search for him, but they would never know the truth.   Which was worse?   "Do you think that means no one will come looking for him?"

"I doubt it. If no one has so far, no one will."

Deflated and feeling much older than nineteen, I sank back on the bed into a slouch. "I could use a tea or something."

"You need breakfast."

"I'm not hungry. I just want a tea."

He clucked his tongue teasingly. "You heard Miranda. Now that you're mine, you are *my* responsibility and I need to take proper care of your body."

"You certainly have been doing a good job of that." Sitting up a little straighter I gave him a flirty look over my shoulder.

Flashing his teeth, James seemed quite pleased with himself at the compliment. "Yes, but I have ignored some of your other needs.   We need to keep your strength up in the future."

It took a moment to push off the mild annoyance I felt at being handled again. In an effort to be mature, I tried to look at it as an education and defer to the "expert" for the present. "Fine, I'll have toast but that's it."

James set the laptop aside and rose, striding to the door in victory. He opened it and waved me through, bowing low while keeping his blue eyes on me, "Madame."

"*Mademoiselle*." I corrected him, breezing past. When his eyebrows went up in question I sniffed haughtily, not fully hiding my grin. "Don't be so sure of yourself. I haven't said 'I do' yet." It gave me a thrill to see the stutter in his confidence as I walked past him into the hall. It might be good for him to know he still had to work at it, I thought smugly.

Ch. 55

We didn't have to be back to the pub until dusk which afforded us some free time.

"I'd like to talk to the Andrews about Stephen, I feel like we should be doing something to help him. Do you know where they're staying?" I asked him when I finished breakfast, toast *and* a yogurt at his insistence, much to our server's entertainment.

He was surprisingly dismissive. "They're staying at Henry's flat here in town."

"Henry has a flat here? Why?" It was hard to think of him as the same boss I had met just months ago. Cosmopolitan, bad ass vampire Henry was so different from mild mannered, fatherly librarian Henry.

"Henry stepped in for Miranda for a brief period in the late 16th century at her request. When she was ready to resume her position twenty or so years later, he left. Miranda apparently told him she needed the time to handle some personal affairs. The arrangement was unique in that Henry gave it back without a fight. That had never happened before." James explained offhandedly, like it was no big deal.

I questioned what kind of personal affairs would have been so important to cause her to walk away from the power of being a member of the Court. I also wondered whether she would have killed him if Henry *hadn't* rescinded after her sabbatical. I was never going to be able to work for him again, people would start to wonder why I wouldn't look him in the eye. "So, they're staying there with him?"

"Yes, would you like to call over there? I have his number."

"I was thinking we could walk over, see them in person."

"It's raining." James pointed out.

"You won't melt." I chided, drawing a confounded look. "My Grandpa used to say that, 'You aren't that sweet, you won't melt.'"

James flashed his beautiful smile, his features relaxing for the most part with only a minor tightening around the eyes hinting at his tension. "I've never heard that one before." Then, serious again, he made his point. "You saw how things ended last night. I don't think it's a good idea for us to go."

"But even if Tara is angry, the rest of them aren't. Are they?" In my naiveté I presumed to know more than him and discounted his concern. "They'll be able to put that aside for Stephen's sake." Seeing his intention to dissuade me got my back up and I snapped. "Stephen was my first real friend and he's helped me a lot. Now *he* needs help. How can I not try?"

Without a word, James grabbed my coat and held it up for me to shrug into it. His resignation gave me no joy. I hoped he was wrong about our reception.

Ch. 56

Sparked by my introduction of Grampa's quip, we kept to colloquial sayings on the way to see the family, steering well clear of anything more volatile. Since James had lived for so long and in so many different places, I ran out long before him.

Our conversation had lulled us both into a false sense of peace when we reached Henry's flat ten minutes later, only mildly damp thanks to a short break in the weather. The flat was in an old, grey stone building with five steps up to the entrance, guarded by an ancient looking call box. James pushed the button marked Campbell. For such a dynamic being, it seemed peculiar to see his name on something so ordinary as an apartment security box. Like he didn't really live in this world.

A female voice, garbled by the mechanism, requested our identities and James declared us both. We were buzzed in after a long pregnant pause that had me instantly defensive of him. Tara should be thanking him for doing what he could to save the boy's life, not condemning him for it.

The box listed Henry's flat as number 20 and inside I counted four units per floor. With there being five floors of windows from street level, Henry's flat would be on the top floor.

We walked up the five flights of stairs in the dark, aged building while I wondered why Henry would live in such shoddy quarters. When we arrived at his door, James knocked softly and Tonya, not her sister, answered.

She didn't bother to smile, solemnly waving us inside. She might be upset, but still, she let us in. That had to be good, I thought optimistically. Coming from behind us she strode past to lean against the island in the kitchen where it looked like she'd been before our arrival.

Once in the unit, I gaped in disbelief. We had walked into a large great room. It was open and modern with tons of windows facing away from the street we'd entered on. The floors were polished concrete stained to a charcoal grey, the windows rose from the floor to the ceiling along the back wall. The long, pale grey flannel drapes remained closed because it was daylight was my assumption. In my imagination the view encompassed the entire city. There was a sleek, contemporary kitchen to my left, the living room in front of me and a long hallway to my right. I would guess the bedrooms were down the hallway.

Troy was in the kitchen with Tonya, standing at the stove. He neither turned nor spoke to us. A dishtowel was thrown over his shoulder and he was cooking, looking incredibly domestic. I couldn't readily identify the dish by smell, but I recognized the familiar scents of olive oil, shallots and shellfish.

Henry emerged from the hallway and addressed us. "It was not wise to come here with things so undecided, James. Tara is at the store; she will be back soon and you should not be here when she returns." He regarded us steadily before joining us, his demeanor solemn.

Not bothering to point out that *he* knew that we shouldn't have come, James defended himself. "The only alternative was to kill him. Is that really what she wanted? It wasn't what *he* wanted. When I asked him, he said he wanted to live. I have to honor that regardless of Tara's prejudices."

As if on cue, the front door opened and Tara walked in carrying a brown paper grocery bag. Her appearance shocked me. In less than a day she had aged twenty years. Her eyes were sunken, unwashed hair pulled back into a messy ponytail and her dark knit clothes lent her a slovenly, unkempt appearance. When she saw us, she glanced from me to James and her expression changed from melancholy to outrage in a heartbeat.

"How dare you come here," she snarled at us. Her eyes darted back to me as she spoke and made it clear that I had chosen my allegiances poorly.

Unable to comprehend her hatred, I jumped to point out her oversight as I saw it. "He saved Omar's life Tara. Omar *asked* him to. Why is everyone so angry with him?"

Tara was a big girl with no fat on her large frame. She had always intimidated me, and now as she focused her narrowed hazel eyes upon me, my heart ceased to function. The bag dropped from her hand and snarling, she hurled herself at me before the bag hit the floor.

The hair on the back of my neck went up and I watched, petrified, as Tara launched herself at me and the magic of her change charged the air. She was a mountain lion mid-leap with her teeth and claws directed at me, ears flat against her huge head.

Too fast for me to do anything else, I put my hands up to protect my face, bracing for the impact that never came. The cat was plucked sideways from the air and thrown down on the ground, hissing and yowling in frustration. James crouched over her, holding her body pinned to the ground, fangs out and looking scary as hell.

"Tara, James, that is enough." Henry's command stopped them instantly. "James, I think it best if you and Claire leave. My obligation is first to the clan and they wish to distance themselves right now. James if you need to discuss anything or see me before dusk, call. I will meet you elsewhere." He frowned down his nose at me severely. "Claire, this world is new to you and you should not be so quick to judge. Not everyone sees our existence as an option

338

favorable to death, especially for a child. Do *you* find the decision a simple one?"

Brusquely he reminded me of my place without mincing words or sparing my feelings. "I'm sorry Henry," I looked to Tara still in cat form lying at James' feet and twitching her tail angrily. "And Tara, maybe it's stupid of me, but I am still hoping it's all going to be okay."

Tonya laughed bitterly from the kitchen. "You are naïve, even for a human, Claire."

Impulsively I lashed back at her, my hold on myself was tenuous and unraveling fast under the strain; I could feel it. "Why, just because I want the people I love to be happy? I know how hard life can be," my voice cracked making me feel even more stupid, "especially when you're alone. I don't need to be eighty or however the hell old you all are to see that. I've *felt* the horrible things people are capable of. That cuts through a lot of the crap that takes most people years to figure out." My eyes stung. I bumped James letting him know I wanted to go.

Deferentially, James bowed to Henry. "Until this evening then." He put a hand on the door and I forced myself not to run out.

When we were back to the ground floor, I collapsed more than sat on the bottom step and lost it. Head in my hands, I wept like the silly fool that I was. I was grateful when I felt his arm wrap around my shoulders, guiding my head onto his chest as he lay back on the step.

"Is humankind so bad that you all have given up on us?"

James' hand stopped petting my hair. "What are you talking about?"

339

"All of them and you, not you, your kind, I've met are so... down on us humans. Is that what living so long brings, disgust with the rest of the world?"

"For many, yes." James' tone was matter of fact. "I've told you before, with age it is hard not to lose touch with one's humanity. When we become distant from humans, we lose sight of what makes you special. We see you only for your weaknesses."

I sat up to see his face. "What do *you* think makes us special? Why *do* you and Henry like humans? Why are you so ready to go to great lengths to defend us when it costs you so much? And why are *you* doing this for Omar? I know you didn't want to ever turn someone and now you have, why?"

Pointedly, he ignored the detail I'd unintentionally picked up when I'd been inside his head as he'd turned Omar. "What makes you so special, so unique and worth defending *are* your weaknesses. Your emotions and your passion are things that we lose with time. They give you your spark. Only the rare vampire can keep touch with his or her humanity. And I'm only partially doing this for Omar." He stroked my cheek.

I'd picked up on the fact that he was different; I was beginning to understand just how different he really was from the rest of his kind. "You've been able to keep yours."

"Henry and I have fought for humans because any genocide is wrong. And actually, I *was* losing touch with my humanity as well until recently." His fingers ran down my hand and touched the ring he'd given me. "It was your doing. Our bond has brought it back stronger than it has been in decades and for that I am eternally grateful. I had missed that part of my human life the most. It had always been a large part of who I was and I'd feared I was losing that." His face was so open I saw the rawness behind his declaration.

Embarrassed of his praise and not sure what to say, I squeezed his hand and held it so that when I regained my feet he came with me. "Come on," I sniffled, "I'll feel like an idiot if they come out and I'm here crying on their doorstep. I'll talk to them tonight when I see them."

His face clouded over.

"What?" I asked as we walked out to the steps down to the street.

He avoided my eyes and pretended to be interested in something off in the distance.

"What?" I prodded, growing frustrated.

Stopping, I pulled him up beside me and stood in front of him, forcing him to see me. "What aren't you telling me about tonight?"

He sighed and met my gaze, his eyes dark. "You can't be there tonight. It's too dangerous for a human to be there."

"Hmm." I rubbed my chin sarcastically, "If it's too dangerous how are we supposed to make this work?" I waited for him to return to the conversation about my turning.

"The first night is the most dangerous," he explained. "I will need your help tomorrow. I told you I would have to get his hunger under control if you are going to help and remain human."

"Help with what exactly? No one has ever said what it is I'm supposed to be doing. Why does it need to be *me* you work with?"

341

"You already know I need to teach him to shield himself if he has any abilities. He will be hypersensitive to any stimulation, including his own emotions like you have been lately." He felt compelled to remind me. "*You* will be able to project peace and calm to him and keep the sensitivity to a minimum while I work with him to learn to control himself. Do you remember what we did when we turned him?"

I nodded my head mutely, not wanting to talk about it; my cheek stung again as a reminder. "We will be able to help those with and without special abilities much quicker and more effectively than even Ursa and I were able. You will make them more capable of focusing and managing themselves until they can do it alone."

My girlish vanity was placated by the compliment that I was a better partner to him than his ex. I wouldn't admit it out loud and held my smile inside. "Well, I guess I have a solo night on the town then. Any recommendations for a good dinner?"

Ch. 57

James left just before dusk, asking me to be careful and to take a cab if I left the hotel. He would be tied up until sunrise, leaving me nearly a half of a day and all night to myself. It had honestly been the longest amount of time I had been alone for months. With the boldest of the anti-human faction nearly gone, I had a weekend pass and relished the freedom it offered.

It was far too early to go to dinner so I took a long, luxurious shower. By the time I was done, the entire bathroom was foggy and my skin was red. I followed it up by painting my toenails in a new coral pink color I hadn't had a chance to try yet.
When my nails were dry and my hair twisted up in a clip, I dressed myself in jeans and a light green wool sweater thick enough to handle the chilly dampness of the Scottish winter. I was looking out the window at the lights of the city, seeing that it was dry for the moment and decided a walk before dinner would be perfect. Grabbing my coat and room key, I wrapped my scarf around my neck and walked out to enjoy a night of freedom.

It was cold but not terribly so. It had been worse back home and, as James had pointed, out I was losing my sensitivity to the chill. Being in a reasonably upbeat mood I was able to take a philosophical view on the loss, there were worse things for me to get from my vampire.

The streets in New Town, the section of Edinburgh where the hotel was located, were thinning in the evening hours as people headed home or to work or whatever their daily routines demanded. For the time being, I enjoyed blending in with normal people and being one of the nameless masses with the bonus of not feeling a single person around me.

To be sure I wouldn't get lost, I walked in a large perimeter making all right turns. I knew I would be able to find my location with minimal effort, though I didn't pay any more attention to street signs or addresses than that. The shops around me were a blend of old and new and I liked looking at the buildings; they were different from what I was used to seeing in America.

Having moved around a lot with a military dad, I'd gotten to see much of the country and had become appreciative of architectural styles. New Town might have come along about the same time as my home country, however, the flavor of it was distinctly different and I was rapidly finding myself affected by the spell of its sights and sounds, even the smells of the bouquet of restaurants, cars and salt water wafting in from the sea.

It was in this simplistic trance of senses that I wandered the city for some time before I became aware that my nose was starting to run in the cold. Apparently my body *was* still affected by the cold, whether I could feel it or not. Drawn back to the present I started looking around for a pub or coffee shop I might want to go inside to warm my flesh. I would be thoroughly embarrassed if I went and got hypothermia wandering around like a dolt with an open coat and no hat in January.

My feet had taken me to Grassmarket Street where I noted the sign as I stopped and glanced around. There was an odd vibration I could feel on my skin and, thinking I was having trouble with the cold, I glanced at the store whose door I found myself in front of. It was a red storefront and gold-stenciled letters called Helios Fountain and had the welcoming look of a neighborhood bookstore, advertising a café in the back. The sign above the recessed door touted unique gifts, books and Vegan baked goods. Unable to resist, I had to go in.

Opening the thick red wooden door I heard the bell chime merrily and was greeted by a warm mix of smells that included old books, baked goods with a good amount of cinnamon in them and incense that left a sweetly thick residue on the inside of my nose and the back of my throat.

The older man behind the counter who greeted me with a warm "halloo," sported a shock of wild grey hair that looked suspiciously like a well abused brillo pad. His green turtleneck was rumpled, leading me to wonder if he had slept in it or just picked it up off the floor this morning. It struck me with an odd sense of nostalgia that this was what I used to want for myself. To live and work alone in someone else's bookstore, preferably in the back where I wouldn't have to see people. Now, I decided it looked very lonely.

I roamed the aisles perusing the eclectic gifts and saw an unusual shelf of jewelry. Seeing my interest, the shopkeeper came over to introduce the items. He noticed that I was looking at a very old pendant in particular. It was a triangle cast in what appeared to be pewter. Delicate knot work reminiscent of the type on my ring decorated the outside and in the middle were two interesting symbols touching.

Smiling an unflattering, unevenly spaced, partially toothy grin, he effused an undeniable enthusiasm and warmth.

"You have a good eye." He assured me, patting my arm. "This one is very old. Germanic, I believe. It was a pendant worn to welcome the blessings of the harvest and to invite fertility."

Instantly, I was drawn to his charismatic vibe I felt even through my defenses. "I don't need fertility." I smiled.

His eyes traveled to the ring on my finger and his face crinkled up as he cackled. "Newlywed, huh?" He waved his wrinkled hand at me dismissively. "Newlyweds always worry about babies. Don't worry, the timing's never right, they come when they come. Fertility can mean a great many things. Wealth, good luck, friendships," he raised a bushy brow, "love."

There was no chance of babies with James but a little good luck sounded like a welcome blessing. "What other charms do you have?" My eyes wandered the case this pendant had come out of.

The older shopkeeper was quietly muttering to himself as he handled the pendant. Glancing sideways at me, the gentleman said, "No others, this is the one you need. It's yours for twenty euros."

Pulling my wallet out of my coat pocket, I opened it up and pulled out my money to show him, "All I have is fifteen American dollars and I came in here to get a snack, sorry."

Waving a hand in good-natured defeat, he put the pendant back on the table and indicated the back of the store with a tip of his head. "Maybe next time. The café is in the back, pick a book and warm up. Stay as long as you'd like."

I thanked him, feeling the most normal I'd felt in a long time. "Any recommendations?" I waved toward the bookracks.

He furrowed his bristly black and gray brows, putting his hand to his temple as he thought. "What are your interests? An adventure, maybe some romance? Does the occult appeal to you? We have a very different selection than those chain bookstores. Come see." He touched my arm and I jumped at the static that shot through me. The old man must have thought he'd hurt me. I caught a glimpse of his troubled expression as he turned and disappeared into the tall shelves, trusting me to follow.

The majority of the titles we passed were foreign to me. He'd been telling the truth, none were what one would find at a standard bookstore and some even looked old and used.

Trying to appear nonchalant, I kept my eyes on the books stacked on the shelf nearest me as I asked, "You mentioned the occult, where's that section?"

He faltered half a step before he walked past me motioning me to follow. We angled back into a small nook and I was pointed to a tall but narrow bookshelf next to a window. A flash of movement at the window drew me up short. I watched the pedestrian and automobile traffic on the street for a minute before rolling my eyes at myself for being so jumpy. Someone wasn't *always* following me. I had to learn to relax or I was going to make myself crazy.

With an effort, I was able to redirect myself back to the gentleman and saw with chagrin that he was watching me again.
"I'm sorry, I thought I saw someone I recognized out there." I smiled weakly, flushing.

His dark, beady eyes burned with an intense inner fire I'd failed to notice prior. "Might I make a suggestion?" He wagged a finger in time, conducting music only he could hear.

Less adoring of the strange little man, I bobbed my head once. "Sure, that would be great."

He reached up and plucked an older book from the shelf near the top without even looking. "I think you will find this one suits your interests." He handed it to me, his thin claw-like hands clutching the book until I took it from him with no small amount of trepidation.

Feeling the cracked and faded leather cover, I examined it as I ran my fingertips over its rough texture. The cover was

347

dark leather and had been chewed by dog or caught in a grinder by the look of it. I thanked the man and walked back to find the aforementioned snack before perusing its contents.

Ch. 58

Black tea with cream and sugar and a slice of lemon cake in front of me, I opened the old book with no title. The cover held only a combination of sigils involving intricate knot work and symbols I didn't understand.

Flipping through the pages, I saw that the writing was very old type with "s" printed as "f." There was no publishing date in it, but I guessed it to be from the mid 1600's from the tiny amount I knew about printing. Tea nearly shot through my nose when what I was looking at suddenly made sense to me. This was a book of *spells*. The old man couldn't have known how perfectly suited to me the subject matter was. The specific section I'd flipped to was on protective amulets and spells. I was certainly finding myself in situations lately where even my shielding wasn't as effective as could be and no amount of shielding helped when I found myself surrounded by powerful ancient vampires. I could use some extra help.

I whipped my head up and out of the book, surveying the café and what I could see of the bookstore, expecting the old shopkeeper to be staring or laughing but he was nowhere in sight. The butterflies in my stomach fluttered away while I contemplated how a total stranger would know whose company I was keeping; I no longer believed in the possibility of random coincidence.

He wasn't all vampire I knew that. He didn't feel like one, yet he had to have some knowledge of them or of me to direct me to this particular book, right? Maybe he was a servant, although he hadn't felt like Brian. The potential for harm to come to me while here in the shop with the bell tinkling every now and again and the café girl close by was minimal, I thought, and I stayed in favor of reading the book and maybe learning something.

The girl behind the café counter was a short redhead in her mid-twenties and had the pleasant look of the fresh-faced girl next door. She hadn't given me a second glance so I figured my secret was safe from her.

I chewed on a mouthful of cake reading about protective charms, amulets and spells. There was a time in my life not too long ago when I would have mocked the book as a bit of new age hooey, but its age and feel lent to its authenticity. Plus my education in the past five months had taught me there were many things in our world I had no understanding of and should not be so quick to disbelieve.

I had finished the entire chapter when I went to take a sip of tea and noticed my cup was empty and I needed to use the restroom. I walked up for another and asked the counter girl if I could leave the book and cake while I used the facilities. She eyed me like I was from another planet and with a sweeping glance at the mostly unoccupied section said she'd keep an eye on them.

When I saw there was another customer who I hadn't noticed come in, I was more than a little surprised. I must have been very interested in my book, normally I would have seen or felt another presence. The customer was a nice looking man, probably in his late twenties with dark hair and as he glanced up at me, I saw blue eyes ringed with long black lashes. His lips curled into a mild smile, the kind you give a stranger to show you're friendly, no more. He was attractive though not enough to explain the small jolt I felt when he looked at me. I smiled politely back and hurried on to the restroom down the hall.

When I returned, my fellow customer did not look up from his book and I returned to my chapters on defensive magic. Again I was drawn in and had finished my cake and second cup of tea when a shadow fell over my pages. I'd felt him approach which kept me from spilling the tea I was lifting to my mouth when I saw him.

Glancing up, I saw the shopkeeper squinting at me, his expression softened when I gave him a brief hassled smile.

"Are you finding it to your liking?"

Forcing the suspicion out of my tone, I managed a kinder smile. "Yes, I am, actually. Thank you." Regardless of what I thought of the guy I recognized the fact that I wanted the book. "I didn't notice a price, is it for sale? I would really like to keep reading it."

"Will you be here in Edinburgh for long?" He moved closer to the chair opposite me where I had hung my coat, his hands rested on the chair back.

"Yes, I think I'll be here for at least another week." I thought it was safe to give him that.

"Why don't you borrow it then, but you must promise me that you will return it before you leave." His hands moved around on the front of my coat, stroking the fabric. I thought he was nervous, or at least quirky. Afraid I was staring and might make him uncomfortable, I lifted my gaze to his giving him a "sweep" in the process. He felt like any other human.

"I can't borrow this, it's too valuable. What if I damage it by accident?"

He gave a brief shake of his shaggy head, "You seem trustworthy. Bring it back when you're done." The hands on my coat gave it a final whack and he was gone, with nothing left to say.

I was left shaking my own head in disbelief. What a strange man and how unusually trusting. Again, I had to wonder, how did he know? He seemed to really want me to have this book right now. I wished we were alone in the café, I would have asked him how or what he knew about my situation.

Considering the worn leather exterior, I made up my mind. I put my coat on and bussed my own table, nodding a goodbye to the redhead who held up her hand in a distracted nod to my parting. Returning to my table, I scooped up my borrowed book and headed up front.

Right as I made it into clear view of the front counter, I heard the tinkling of the bell over the door again. In walked a heavyset couple sporting home dyed black hair, hers was spiked, his was long and greasy. They were engaged in a loud conversation with an accent so thick I had no hope of understanding.

I hung around in front of the store, spinning a round rack of postcards while I waited for the intuitive shopkeeper to return to the counter. He did come back from the section where he had directed them just a few minutes later looking expectant.

"Yes, Miss?" He gave no indication we'd spoken before.

Leaning in I whispered, "Why did you give me this book?"

So slightly I could barely see the movement, he shook his head. "You need a bag, yes I will just go and fetch one for you." He went behind the counter to hand me a plastic shopping bag, which I promptly slipped my book inside. Figuring he didn't want me to give him away to the couple, I went back to my spinning rack.

"Is that all, Miss?" His tone was final.

I stared at him behind the counter, eyeing him for some sign as to why the sudden dismissive behavior.

"Thank you for shopping. Good-bye, Miss. Do be careful walking alone." His eyes were tight when he gave me the nod that I was to leave and walked with a nervous hitch in his step back in the direction of the heavyset couple.

His message that I was excused was clear. I just didn't understand why or what had scared him. It had seemed to me he was frightened for me all at once. Perplexed and distracted, lost in my own head, I walked back out of the shop and onto the street.

I had walked out of the store so busy thinking about what had transpired in the bookstore that when I stopped on a street corner and surveyed my surroundings, I had no idea where I was.

The streets were empty, the sky had grown dark and the air was colder than it had been earlier. I wished I had kept enough money for a cab back to the hotel instead of buying that second cup of tea.

As if it would have told me anything I looked up at the road sign, Randolph Crescent. I had no idea where I was and didn't see any people around to ask, nor did I see anything familiar. It appeared the only option was to trudge until I found someone to ask or a public house of some sort.

Eyes open this time, I was growing more concerned that I was really lost and I started to worry about the neighborhood when I saw the cars parked on the curb growing more and more shoddy as I walked.

Taking that as a sign, I turned on my heel to walk back the other way and saw a man half a block up walking toward me. It was reassuring to see another soul except I had learned about lonely streets and strangers. I held my breath, intending to make a better threat assessment as he approached. As we drew closer, I began to recognize the brown leather coat that had been sitting next to him and his dark hair poking out from under a striped brown knit hat. When we were close enough for me to see the blue eyes and black lashes, my heart skipped a beat. Up until a few months ago, I might have ignored the meeting as pure happenstance. Now, I did not.

Keeping my eyes down, I decided to continue down the street without asking directions. He had other ideas.

"Hello." He spoke just as I was about to pass him. The sound of his voice stopped me dead in my tracks.

It resonated in my body, calling to me physically the way only one other had ever done. My body's traitorous reaction was second only to my mind's blurring of facts. I was willing to follow the man the instant he spoke.

Recognizing his magic as enchantment, I tried to swim back to clarity by calling to mind memories of who I was, *my* wants and needs. Static hummed in my head making it hard to concentrate, my feet stopped listening and halted, taking with them my chance of escape.

In a panic, I scanned everything in my immediate vicinity, pictured the street sign and threw open the marks in my head to broadcast an SOS to James. It was dark now and I knew he was tied up with Omar, but I had been through this too often to think that I could battle the supernatural if it became physical. I wasn't sure I could fight a mental battle with this one who was not a vampire but reeked of Lucas. I hoped my betrothed would send someone to help.

"Hi." I breathed back at him, willing myself to move forward and past him. Slowly, consciously fighting for every step, my feet moved except now he had changed direction and was walking with me. It was clear that I would not be able to run from him gauging from my body's magnetic reaction to him.

His smile confirmed what I already sensed in the flash of white teeth, no fangs. "A beautiful woman should not be alone in such a neighborhood as this one at night." The accent was not Scotttish, it was lighter and easier to understand, maybe from somewhere to the South. "Allow me to escort you home." His hand took firm hold of my elbow and guided me down the sidewalk, I hoped in the right direction to get me home.

We walked for about ten minutes while I lamely tried to push his influence from my mind to no avail. Two powers were fighting in my head; the lure of Lucas' power coming from the stranger and the static shorting out my mind making coherent thoughts nearly impossible. Seeing how jumbled I'd become, I was glad I had called to James when I did. I wasn't so sure I could do it now.

It was full dark. I was totally lost and being escorted somewhere other than the hotel, I realized when we turned down a darker street. Somewhere in my addled brain I chastised myself for being a fool, he'd never asked my destination, of course he couldn't be bringing me there. Halfway down the block the pressure on my elbow brought me to a halt and directed me toward the darkened door of an abandoned business.

While he was fumbling with the keys I recognized the danger I was in and tried to will myself backward, away from him and keep him from getting me through that door. I couldn't do it. In desperation, staring at the blackness and who knew what waiting for me on the other side of the door, I did what I *could* manage. I let my legs go limp, falling down on my butt on the sidewalk and refusing to move.

Several things happened all at once. The stranger's hand released my elbow and the power of his spell on me broke, allowing me to finally throw up my shields and push out the influence that was turning my brain to jelly. The static stopped as well and I felt my consciousness returning. The tawny cat that broke from the shadows ten yards up the street hissed and glared, the black tip of its tail visible as it twitched and writhed like a snake. I was overjoyed to have both shaken off the stranger's spell and have reinforcements.

Pushing myself up, I stepped away from him and brushed off my pants thinking I was going to have a nice bruise from the concrete by morning. I walked to the cat, the kink in my leg from landing on it working itself out in a few strides and put my hand in its fur, feeling the thickening of my shields when I touched her. With her, I was confident enough to face the blue eyed man. At first touch I knew the cat was Tonya, I recognized her feel as being the same as when she was in her human form.

"Who are you and what do you want?" I asked him in a shaking voice.

He stared entranced at the cat beside me. "Is that yours?"

I looked down and she glanced up, blinked and returned her eyes to the stranger.

"I asked you a question." Ignoring him, I stayed on the offensive.

Entranced, he gawked at the cat. "No one sent me. I saw you in the shop, when you left I followed. I wanted to help." The toneless delivery smacked of a thrall. James had told me about a vampire's ability to insert commands and thoughts into someone's head and I suspected I knew who had done so to this guy.

"Why?"

The stranger finally looked up at me, his gaze too intimate for comfort and I "heard" Lucas. "I felt drawn to your magick. Do you not feel it as well?"

I felt a bump and again the desire to be with him started to creep into my consciousness. I lowered my shields without thinking and started to take a step toward the alluring stranger, static buzzing low in my head and growing louder.

My fingers pulled away from Tonya's fur and she growled a warning.

I felt my hair rise and knew the cat was using magick to counter the effects of the enchantment and whatever else I was feeling. It didn't break the stranger's spell entirely, although it lifted enough to clear my head and make me step back to touch her fur. When I touched her, I felt his spell once again push back to the periphery and the static dissipate.

"No, I don't." I answered his query rebelliously.

The stranger's eyes swept from the cat to me and back. He continued to stare at her, fascinated. "I just wanted to talk to you."

"Then talk." The threatening route wasn't helping. I knew we had to talk to him and find out more about what Lucas was up to and that it was too dangerous to let him stay on the loose. I also knew there was no way I could manage that on my own.

Reflecting, I looked down at Tonya wishing I could hear her in my head like I could with James. She stared at me and switched her tail, equally frustrated.

"What should we do with this guy? Is he pure human?"

She nodded.

"Do we bring him back with us?"

She paused, tail switching as she thought it through. Finally, she nodded in agreement.

"I have to bring him back alone, don't I? You don't have any clothes or anything." Glancing down, I cursed the inadequate length of my coat. It wouldn't cover her past her hip.

Nodding again, she rolled her eyes at the stupid human.

Embarrassed to admit my weakness, I leaned down and mumbled at her knowing I had to. "I can't be alone with him."
She glanced up and regarded me steadily. I watched the hazel eyes, so human in their examination, her tail switched absently and her ears flicked several times. She chirruped a strange sound and pushed her face into my hand, rubbing her cheek on my hand as loving as a house cat.

My heart leapt. "You're coming with me?" I fought the urge to hug her furry neck, her kindness would *not* extend that far.

She chirruped again.

"How are you going to get into the hotel?"

She looked at me and gave a sneeze that sounded a lot like "oh, please."

"Fine, but I was just wondering if you were going to walk in as a cat or as a naked woman. I don't know which way works better for you."

"Excuse me, 'he' would like to know where you are taking 'him'." Came the soured voice from the momentarily neglected "prisoner." Catching the look the cat gave him, he put his hands up, "Don't get me wrong, I love the idea of seeing you as a naked woman but I was supposed to..." He stopped himself sensing he'd given something away.

Whirling, I narrowed my eyes at him and heard a growl rising from beside me. "*What* were you supposed to do?"

Seeing that he didn't intend to answer, I pushed trying to project trust to him.

He bowed his head, frowning with his attentions turned inward. Comprehension broke over his features. "You're like the other one."

My insides churned. "What other one?"

Staring intently, he gave me a thorough visual inspection before answering; the polished facade was swiftly falling away, leaving behind the rougher individual underneath. Lucas' charm was getting harder to see which was good for me. "You aren't the same as him, but what you do," he tapped his temple, "feels like what he does."

"Who?" I held my breath.

He crinkled his face, searching the memory whose exact details continued to elude him. "The tall blonde guy."

My stomach tightened and I felt my skin crawl. "What did he want?"

"He said he wanted to see you." Apparently back to himself, the blue eyed stranger scoped the street up one end then down the other. "He should be here soon."

"He wanted to see me?" I thought *I* was dense. "You think that this is how normal people see each other? Stalking and abducting a woman off the street?" I rolled my eyes. "Why would he need *you* to do *this* if he was on the up and up?" Despite the fact that of all people I understood how Lucas could mess up one's mind, I was finding it hard not to get mad at this guy. More than likely it had something to do with the relief I was feeling at being alive and not being captured. Again.

Having vented some of the anger clouding my lucidity, I caught a discrepancy in what this stranger was saying. He knew when someone was messing with his head so he was sensitive and yet he had no shielding, like I was. It was possible he didn't know what he was, but Lucas had and that brought up another point, how he had he gotten Lucas' ability to Enchant. Henry or James would know.

Turning to Tonya, I hated to divulge another failing so soon but had to admit that I was indeed lost and would need her help finding my way back to the hotel.

She was not impressed and whisked past me, head held high as she cut across the street. Glad she was leading, I followed and so did the stranger. He even hurried to catch up with her when I lagged behind.

Ch. 59

Several times on the long walk back to the hotel I felt the stranger, who'd introduced himself as Donovan, try to Enchant me. Unfortunately for me, he still had Lucas' power flowing through him and was trying to use it. Fortunately I had found that when I first sensed it, if I firmed up my shield and put my hand on Tonya, I could keep it down to a dull roar and limit the buzzing of static accompanying each wave of attack coming from Donovan.

Our strange little party walked right up to the rear door of The Howard at the valet podium and entered the building unseen, the valet being off duty for the night. We walked up the back stairs, only having to duck back into the stairwell once when a butler picking up a pair of trousers for pressing nearly bumped into us coming out on our floor.

The cat raced back in and up a flight when the door had opened and the butler greeted us in a friendly manner, remembering me awkwardly by name. It hadn't escaped his notice that I wasn't with the same man I had checked in with. My cheeks pinked at the blow to my reputation. Safely inside our room, I locked the door and lay against it feeling the adrenaline ooze out of me, leaving me weak and exhausted.

Our cat friend disappeared into the bathroom and I felt the tingle on my arms indicating she was changing forms. At first, I panicked thinking I was about to see more of my friend than I wanted. Then I remembered the complimentary bathrobe on the back of the door in there. I knew Tonya would easily fit in the long, loose robe that had pooled around my feet when I'd tried it.

"What did you buy at the shop?" Donovan asked, pointing to my bag and rubbing his arms. He must have felt the magic on his skin as well, except he didn't know it's source.

361

Stepping away from the door, I smoothed the bag protectively over the book and setting it on a chair. "It's just a book about astrology. You know, Leos and Libras and all that."

At that moment, Tonya walked out of the bathroom wearing nothing but a bathrobe and looking scandalously tousled. Donovan noticed, of course. His mouth hung open and I was feeling his desire slamming against my shields. Thankfully, my defenses were back up to speed or things could have gotten X-rated fast.

"Wow," was all he could manage. A real thinker without Lucas' help; I rolled my eyes.

Tonya was watching him closely, I had never seen her receptive to a man's charms and was baffled when she didn't snub him in her usual aloof fashion. He was attractive, I got that, but where was the draw? I figured it would take someone pretty special to get to her. What if he tried to use her to get to us like Brian had done to Stephen?

Thinking of Stephen again, I felt torn between my duties here and at home. It was hard to see it as just a missing persons case when we didn't know what Bradley or Gaston did with the body, we didn't know if we should worry about it turning up and Stephen facing murder charges.

"Hey, Tonya, do you have a phone that will call back home? I owe Stephen a call." The need to hear his voice tugged at me.

She lowered her gaze and waved her hands over the borrowed robe, pointing out what should have been obvious. "Claire, I didn't come here with anything."

Blushing, thinking of her leaving her clothes somewhere I realized I didn't know if she would have a way of getting them back. "Tonya I'm sorry, I didn't even think about that. I can replace whatever you had to leave."

Tonya waved me off. "No, Troy has everything. We were together when James got the call."

She and I were of like minds not wanting to disclose too much in front of Donovan, his tie to Lucas still being unclear. Hearing where she'd been made me feel a little less guilty for having hijacked her evening; she would have been eager to escape the vampire scene.

"What are you?" Donovan asked Tonya. His eyes glowed in his reverence, not the least bit fearful.

Alarmed, I looked at Tonya who was unaffected by his question. When I considered it, I realized she had probably had to answer this very question more than once. With a chill, I grasped that she might not be planning to let him live so it didn't matter what he learned tonight. He wouldn't prove to be a threat to her secrecy if she so chose.

"I am blessed with dual forms," Tonya spoke proudly. She was pleased with her life, unlike some who considered it a curse.

Donovan continued to ogle her. It was starting to get creepy. "Have you ever made anyone like you?"

"No." She shot down the request we could both sense coming before he could ask.

Her openness confirmed for me that Donovan wouldn't last the night. Still it didn't explain why she was downright chatty with him. I'd never seen Tonya so, I daresay, friendly.

I didn't want to be around the guy while he looked at her like that and knew me staying with him wasn't an option. "I'm going downstairs for a while. Let me know when you're done visiting." I announced and recovered my book from the chair. They barely acknowledged my departure.

Ch. 60

For the remainder of the evening until the restaurant closed at eleven, I sat at a table and read my book. Afterward, I moved to the lobby at the invitation of the desk clerk. He saw that I didn't want to go back upstairs and very politely offered for me to continue reading on one of the chairs and even had a butler bring a snack of tea and finger sandwiches at one o'clock. It was the same butler who'd had the trousers earlier. My cheeks flamed red. Who knew what he thought was going on with the comings and goings in that room.

At some point in the wee hours waiting for Tonya, I had fallen asleep in the chair and was awakened from a deep sleep by a familiar voice in my ear questioning why I had come downstairs. He sounded annoyed, thinking Tonya was being difficult and had driven me from our room. Picking me up while he continued with his irritated muttering, James asked several times what had happened to elicit my call that night. The pull of sleep and steady rumbling of his voice worked against him and I barely managed a sleepy "hello," preferring the pleasant half sleep I found myself in.

James carried me through the halls quickly and easily, unlocking the door one handed without so much as a decipherable fumble. I'd failed to tell him about Donovan so, needless to say, he was surprised when he pushed the door open with his foot and saw two bodies in our bed. The arms that had so gently been cradling me tightened and brought me fully awake with a squeak.

I admired the discipline it took for him to wait for the door to close behind him before asking Tonya what "the hell" she thought she was doing in our bed with the "threat" he had sent her to "neutralize."

Tonya sat up, unfazed and answered that she had done her job, he was no longer a threat. Poor Donovan didn't seem to understand what was going on, although he was ready to defend his "date."

Sitting up, he put an arm around Tonya's shoulders. It was hard not to laugh at the idea of her needing protection from him. "Your bed? Sorry buddy, the girls agreed we could have the room for the night so you two will have to go somewhere else." Donovan declared.

Being in such close proximity, I heard James' warning hiss before Donovan possibly could have. Stepping in to prevent unnecessary bloodshed I put a hand on James' chest, whispering as quickly as I could to explain that I had indeed left the room to them, though in my defense they were just talking when I'd left. It was perfectly natural that he would have assumed the room belonged to Tonya and me, none of James' clothes or personal effects were out and he certainly didn't have a shave kit in the bathroom.

We backed out of the room, the door closing behind us while I went on to explain everything else I could remember. James put me down at my request and I held his arm keeping my mouth close to his ear for privacy sake. I went on to confirm that Donovan knew what Tonya was but I didn't think he knew about any of the others. When I began to explain what Donovan had done and said and that Lucas was behind it. James' anger flared fresh and with a growl he tried to turn and go back to the room, which I was pretty sure would not end well for Donovan.

Again, I stopped James from doing physical harm to our new acquaintance by appealing to his newly recovered human emotions. "I don't think he knows what he's doing. At least I'm not sure he does it on purpose. And he thinks I'm friendly with Lucas, so I don't think he's a bad guy. Unless he's a really good liar, but he honestly doesn't seem smart enough. Is there a way Lucas could have given him some of his mojo?"

The tension was broken when James laughed at that, his features lightening. "Mojo?" Then, shaking his head, he talked while he mused for a while about the possibilities. "Lucas' powers are special because of his special split nature. I cannot give my powers to a normal human, but I can share them with you to some extent only because of your ability. I will speak to Miranda or Anton about the possibilities. They are some of the eldest and best able to remember the special talents of Elves." He cocked his head, eyes softening as he took in my groggy, sleep-mussed appearance. I tried to smooth my hair, becoming self-conscious under his inspection. "You need to sleep." James pointed out gently. He sounded distracted.

Threat to the human gone, my eagerness to hear about his night took over. "James, how did it go? Did Omar do okay?"

James' eyes pinched at the corners. "Yes, he's fully turned, but his youth has complicated the transition as we had feared. He will take some time to acclimate." I could tell he was disturbed by some aspect of the change, but I was too afraid to ask and he wasn't letting me see.

Putting my hand on his arm, I asked him indirectly. "Do you think he'll be alright? What about Tara?"

James failed to hide his wince at the mention of Tara's name and knew that he had to tell me something. "She insisted on being there when he awakened tonight, even though Henry and I both advised her not to. You might have picked up on the animosity between the weres and vampires."

I nodded, gripped both by fear and fascination.

367

"We are both top predators and can be territorial, which is why our kind rarely mixes with theirs."

"Did something happen?" In equal parts I wanted to know and cover my ears.

James rubbed a hand over his eyes and sighed. "Omar rose confused and hungry. Tara was eager and did not heed our warnings. When she got too close the boy attacked her. Her injuries are severe but she will recover." His abrupt laugh sounded harsh in the silent hall. "Gabriel was a tremendous help in controlling the boy. He can completely dominate someone, I've never seen anything like it. Lucas even lent a hand in calming Omar a few times before he had to leave." He stopped, making the connection between Lucas' early departure and my evening's excitement.

My breath caught at mention of Lucas. It didn't go unnoticed. "No, the two of you will not be close to each other again if I have a say in the matter."

I wasn't going to argue with him. Consciously choosing to want someone else would be one thing. Having someone manufacture desire in me was entirely another.

"You're tired." He pointed out again, fishing in his pocket. Pulling out his phone, he made two quick calls while gently putting his arm around my back and pulling me toward him.

I lay my head on his chest and closed my eyes for a minute when I felt my legs go out from under me again. If I weren't so drained, a novelty I was crediting to something Donovan had done, I would have been annoyed.

"I can walk, you know." I managed to point out purely for the sake of my pride.

He laughed. "Yes, but I would like to get to Henry's before the sun rises and we cannot do that if we wait for you to shuffle there."

"I thought we weren't welcome." The prospect of a fight with any of the cats tonight was beyond my scope.

"Tara is not in any position to argue right now and it is one of her own clanswomen who has put you in this situation." James was defiant. "I would say it is only fair that they put us up since the hotel is full and I am not going to waste all night searching for a replacement."

I saw no reason to argue, and I let him carry me without any further argument. We arrived in the lobby and he called a cab. Standing outside in the cool air without a coat, I shivered. I always got cold when I was tired. I savored the reminder that some of me was still left, though less and less when I really looked.

James slipped his wool coat off, draping it over my shoulders while we waited. Before too long the cab arrived and we rode in silence to Henry's flat. My head rolled against his shoulder on the ride over. Fighting Lucas' influence had taken a heavy toll and it was becoming apparent I was not going to hold up much longer.

We were buzzed up without argument and when the door opened the smell hit me. "Is that blood?" I wrinkled my nose.

James stiffened against me but didn't answer. He walked me to one of the bedrooms down the hallway. I was so tired I did no further investigation into the blood smell nor did I look around. Normally the fact that I was in one of Henry's homes would have had me excited to at least check out signs of who he was.

As it was, I fell asleep before James had gotten his shoes off to lie beside me.

Ch. 61

In my dream we were in a cave, just Omar and me. Omar was covered in blood and was crouched over what must have at one time been human, only now lay as an unrecognizable heap of meat. He glared at me, nothing but hunger in his young eyes and I tried to run. The cave became a confused maze of stone as I ran and I could not find an escape, each turn brought me face to face with another cold wall of rock. At my last turn I reached a dead end and waited, helpless, for Omar to turn the corner. Only it was Lucas who came to me. Approaching with a predatory gaze he held me with his hypnotic green eyes and musical voice saying, "I can bring you more pleasure than you have ever known." When he reached me, he brought me willingly into his possessive embrace and kissed me just before he sank his fangs deep in my chest, chewing his way through my body.

I awoke with a start, aware that I was alone in bed and very much still physically affected by my dream and not just with fear, I was glad James wasn't here to have to explain myself. He was right that Lucas' enchantment would always call to me. Drawing upon my meditation experience, I calmed myself before rising to dress and explore the flat.

My room for the night had been the first of two rooms in the hall on one side and when I opened the door I noticed the blood smell coming from the last of the two rooms opposite me. Knowing through the same heightened sense of smell that alerted me to the blood that it was Tara, didn't stop me from entering.

Quietly I turned the knob and pushed the door open far enough to see her in bed across the small room. Tara's sun kissed golden flesh was pale and waxy. Her hair and part of her face were hidden by bandages wrapped around her head and the blanket pulled down to her waist exposed even more bandages wrapped about her torso and arms.

Her eyes opened when I drew closer and she watched me approach, eyes flat with pain. She closed them before I could speak and I assumed she wanted me to leave, so I took a step back only to hear her formerly strong voice call out raspy and weak. "He's a monster, Claire."

"He didn't mean to do it Tara. He'll get better with time." I went to her, putting my palm lightly on the hand resting on top of the blanket. I wasn't sure where else I could touch that wouldn't hurt.

"They are *all* monsters, Claire. They are all selfish, murderous creatures. Their only interests are their own needs and no one is safe when they're with them."

With a pang I understood whom she meant. "How can you say that? James is selfless. He's dedicated himself to helping others. He's given *me* a life and a future where I had none before. He helps Henry whenever your clan calls him, even though he could easily walk away. James wants to help people." Hearing my rising pitch I took a breath and went on more calmly. "That's all he was trying to do for Omar. He was trying to give him a future. A monster wouldn't do that, a monster would have killed him already."

"He did kill him." Tara closed her eyes and either fell asleep or pretended to, leaving me no further recourse for her accusations. How could she hate vampires when they were so heavily involved with them? Thinking back to the first night I had met them, I had been in Tara's house and when Henry and James approached, the Andrews had been upset. Not the least of whom had been Tara, angry that they had dared come to her house.

I felt a touch at my back. "How can she hate you so much?"

"She does not hate us nor does she hold us in high regard." James' response was deliberate and he picked his words carefully. "She has been with us long enough to see our darker side."

Unconvinced, I turned to face him. "But I have seen you put your life in her hands. You've fought together. How can you do that if you know she doesn't trust you or even like you?"

"She is bound to Henry through her family. She cannot break that bond as much as she wishes she could. When Henry calls the family to help us, they must obey and vice versa. He is a kind Master, but he is still their Master."

"Is ours going to be that way as well? I *must* obey you when you command?" Miranda's allusion to the same revisited me. If that was her reality, I saw Tara's animosity in a new light. I had lived with no control over myself and it wasn't a life.

James was hesitant to answer. At first I took it as an affirmative, yet his response surprised me. "We have seen marks compel only the human to obey before, but ours are different. They are equal. I am not so sure I could command you. Nor am I certain I could disobey you."

My jaw dropped. "*You* might have to obey *me*?" The concept that I would have power over someone so much stronger floored me.

"Come on, let's leave her to rest." We backed out of the room to allow Tara some necessary rest.

"How long will it take for her to heal?" I asked as we walked down the hallway.

"Her injuries were severe, but fortunately we were able to stop him before he severed anything significant. She will be mobile within the next few days."

I shook my head in wonder. It was amazing how quickly everyone in my family could heal, even me. Good thing, considering the violence we found ourselves constantly immersed in.

"Could I use your phone? I wanted to call Stephen and see how things are going with the investigation and I owe him a call anyway to give him an update."

James handed me his phone without comment and kissed my head as he walked past me to join Henry. Our host had been seated in the living room when we entered and I waved as I dialed.

"Hello?" Stephen answered and I could hear a lot of noise in the background.

"Hi Stephen, it's Claire. How are you?"

"Hi honey." His use of a pet name, something he'd never done and I hoped wouldn't do again, alerted me to trouble. Then he lowered his voice so that it would be inaudible to most humans. "I was going to call you. I'm waiting at the police station to speak to the lead detective so I don't have a lot of time, but I wanted to let you know something I found out."

"Should we worry that you're meeting with the police?" I felt my pulse jump fearing for his freedom.

"No, they're just fishing right now. Don't come home yet." He read my mind. "I think it would be best if you let things cool down before you came back. Let's face it, the less time you spend with them, the better."

"You think I'll mess up and blow it don't you?" It was hard not to be offended, it was also hard not to see the truth in it.

"Not exactly, but you aren't going to be the best one to withstand a fishing expedition with an experienced detective."

Only a fool would argue and I was trying so hard to graduate from that distinction. "Okay fine. Didn't you say you found something out?"

"Yes. Just before she disappeared, Annika researched the deed filed with the city on the club here in town and found out Bradley had a silent partner not listed on the main deed. When they had some work done a few years ago, a second name was listed on the permit. He was a front man for a corporation going by the name of Nightshade Holdings, LLC. Maybe you could look into it from there?"

I agreed I would and then before we could discuss anything else, Stephen announced the arrival of the detective and disconnected.

When I was off, I joined the other two in the living room and repeated what I had learned. Neither of them had ever heard of Nightshade Holdings and we all agreed it was worth investigating. It was likely those were the very partners involved in his other dealings as well.
"You know, Stephen says we don't need to come home to help him with the investigation, although I wonder if he's just saying that. Do you think we should go home? He said the police are waiting to interview us." I looked to them for direction, this being new for me.

Henry offered his opinion first. "I think that we should wait for some of the commotion to die down. Let the police sit on the case and let it grow cold. By the time they speak to us when we come home, they will be buried under myriad other cases and won't have the time or manpower to continue to devote to a cold case." He rolled a shoulder unconcerned. "At that age people go missing all the time."

James agreed and I saw the sensibility of his plan if not the coldness. I know it should have bothered me from a human level, hiding the death of one of my own kind. At the same time I couldn't feel bad for Brian, he'd brought his fate upon himself as well as the suffering of a number of others, me included. So, although I felt badly for his parents, I knew Brian's disappearance might forever remain unsolved.

"What do you mean? How long is working with Omar going to take? You were only going to be with Ursa for a few days when you were there for Annika."

He fidgeted nervously with his hands, "Claire, Omar is going to take longer than Annika. Annika, had tremendous self-control already and was mature for her age. It doesn't worry me that she's gone off to be by herself already, from what I've seen she can handle it as long as she doesn't let herself get too thirsty. Omar is a child. He has been living on the street most of his life running half wild, *and* he's been mishandled by the very kind he is now surrounded by, making his case far more complicated. He is not very accepting of his new existence."

"Well," I asked, genuinely curious, "if he can't handle people around him for the foreseeable future, how am *I* going to help him?"

There was a definite "look" that passed between Henry and James clenching my throat and chest. I wondered if I was too young for a heart attack. "What is it?" My voice was flat, waiting.

"I had an idea last night that might work in this case." James spoke slowly, watching my reaction guardedly. "We think we have figured out a way that would allow you and I to work together without getting you near him until he's safe. We might be able to use it for other cases as well if it works this time. It would give me more time to control their thirst before bringing you physically close to them."

I caught on, feeding from his excitement. "The bond? You want me to monitor and project through the bond from a distance?"

James was animated, buoyant at my ready acceptance. "Exactly. If you can, we can avoid having to risk your safety or turning you. I think we can mimic what we did when we turned him and you can be in an adjoining room safely out of reach."

I thought about it for a minute, watching James and Henry. James was years younger in his relief. That combined with the array of emotions I'd seen recently gave me a taste of what he must have been like as a human. It cooled my temper over having to stay here longer to watch him so excited over his discovery, liberated from the weight of his collection of years.

"I'm willing to try if you are." It was certainly a more appealing option than being turned or getting chewed up like Tara. "How long do you honestly think this is going to take? Stephen and you both are talking like we are going to be here all month. Is that right?"

"Claire, Omar is a special case and we aren't sure exactly how long he will take. We must be prepared to spend some extra time on him."

Out of the corner of my eye I caught James rubbing at the back of his finger and subconsciously I felt my anxiety ratchet up at the appearance of his nervous twitch.

"Tara has asked us to watch out for his future and I am compelled to comply. It is possible we will finish early, but we could also be here for the entire month."

"But we only have five days; you heard Anton."

Soberly he nodded without taking his eyes from mine, they were dark, mirroring my trepidation. "The Court wants him destroyed if there is any hint of his ability left after five days, you are right. I have only that small amount of time to teach him to shield and protect himself should there be any small bit of it that has survived. There is also the fact that we will be doing this under the noses of our ruling body. We must be prepared for anything."

"You're going to lie to the Court? Isn't that a death wish?" Blinking, I waited for some reaction from one of them to their suicidal plan. At least James had the good sense to be nervous.

Henry remained unaffected; we could be making a grocery list by his attitude. "We will endeavor not to lie or, if we must, I hope that Anton will be the one interviewing, not Miranda. If the two of you can do your jobs, it won't be a lie that the boy is no longer a danger to our kind. It will take some fast work by both of you to bring him up to speed on shielding very quickly. After that, we hope to take him home with Tara where we can control who he comes into contact with. His removal from here might make him easier to work with because he finds it so stressful, which is what I believe is making him so reactionary. We are familiar to him and James is, after all, his creator. It is expected for the two to remain close for some time while James instructs him and guides him the only issue being they may want it to happen here." Henry tipped his head and flashed a cool grin. "You should be pleased the case may run longer. It will pay better."

"What?"

James blinked and, becoming conscious of his nervous tell, put his hands on his legs. "The position with the Court is a paying position. You will be compensated for your time." He was hesitant to go on, knowing I wasn't going to be pleased. "You know you will most likely have to spend a lot of time here in Europe. This being the area of our greatest populations we are called here most often. School is going to have to wait."

Fighting the initial surge of frustration, I watched my life pass from one Master to another. My ability, James and our bond and now the Court, any illusion that I might have control over my future was a farce. Any time they called I would be expected to drop everything. I bristled at the prospect.

Henry surprised me with a greater degree of sensitivity than I thought possible. "Why don't the two of you go back to the hotel? I have recalled Tonya and she will bring the human with her for my review. I understand he has some special talents?"

I blushed without meaning to and Henry mumbled interestedly, "I see it is true." James glowered, causing Henry to actually laugh. It was the first I had heard his laugh and I liked it. It made him seem more like the Henry I felt comfortable being around, not the scary one. I guess I had to start seeing some positives, this was going to be my life like it or not.

Ch. 62

We headed back to the hotel, picking up a warm savory scone and a tea on the way. The scone was incredible, filled with spinach and chunks of ham. I would have enjoyed it more if I hadn't been moping.

My happy tummy and I got in to the hotel and stopped at the front desk with James as he asked room service for a full linen change. Without missing a beat, the desk clerk assured us that when our friends left that morning, they had sent housekeeping and the job was already done.

Thankfully, we did not have to wait before going straight up and confirming that all was as it should be. I noticed that the book I had been reading the night before, and had thrown down on the chair beside the door in my haste to keep James from killing Donovan, was still on the chair.

I exclaimed joyfully when I saw that the book hadn't been damaged or tampered with. "I don't know how I would have replaced that."

"Where did you get that?" He was checking out the book over my shoulder.

Running my hands protectively over the warm leather I told him about my evening before I'd met Donovan. "It's a great little place and the shopkeeper was a funny little old guy. He recommended this book to me and when I started flipping through it, I saw it was perfect for me. He wanted me to buy a pendant for good luck too. It was like he knew what I was involved in. He was kind of weird, but not in a bad way." I was rambling, not entirely paying attention to what I was saying. "I checked him and he's human but he was so intuitive I wasn't sure at first. I think he owns the place, Helios Fountain. Neat name, huh?"

James had been pulling out a change of clothes from the armoire and made a noise bringing me back to him. He turned and I saw the curious look on his face. "Helios Fountain?"

"Yes, that was where I met Donovan." I must have neglected to give him the shop's name this morning or last night, whenever it was. It hadn't seemed an important part of the story.

"Was he an older man with a young woman in the store? Both of them uncannily perceptive? She has red hair?"

"*He* was, I didn't talk to her except to order from the café and ask about the restroom, but she did have red hair. Why, do you know them?"

He was visibly agitated. "I heard about the father a long time ago when I lived here and only recently heard about the girl. She is supposed to be following in her father's footsteps, learning to be a witch."

"A witch? You can't be serious." My reality was under constant revision. "Is everyone I meet something else? Something that isn't supposed to exist?"

"Not all, but now that you are looking for it, you will find it's far more common than you think." He passed into the bathroom and I heard the water turn on.

I sighed. "You read my mind. Only I couldn't decide between getting another hour or two of sleep first or heading straight into the tub."

Moving smoothly to where I stood, James helped me to shrug off my coat and scarf. "I got messy last night, I was hoping you would join me." He grasped the bottom of my shirt to pull it off. I was exhausted from having just a few hours worth of sleep but when his fingers brushed the sensitive skin on my stomach I wrestled with my options.

He grinned crookedly at me when he said he wasn't trying to lure me to bed. He was just trying to be helpful. He seemed genuine in his explanation and I was already letting him help so I relaxed and went with it. Before I knew it, I was stepping into a hot tub with James sliding in across from me. I knew I was truly tired when the sight of him didn't cause me to pounce. James actually looked self-conscious when I chuckled at my thoughts. I reassured him that I was laughing at myself and he was somewhat mollified.

We talked about life in general, places we had both lived. I had lived more places in the States, he had lived more places abroad. He agreed the next time we were in San Diego or Ocala he would let me take him sightseeing since he'd never been to either, but only at night though. They were both very sunny locales.

"What's that on the floor?" He was facing the open bathroom door and there was something catching the morning light coming in the window. It was small and metallic, lying on the floor in front of the closet where James had undressed me.

Craning my neck and leaning out of the tub to see, I knew instantly what it was and who had given it to me. "He really wanted me to have that at the store." I mumbled confused. "I don't know how he got it on me."

"Who? The witch?"

I nodded my head. "It's the pendant I was looking at in the shop, but I couldn't afford it *and* get a snack, so I refused it." As it dawned on me, I gave a little snort. "He came to visit with me while I read in the café. He was touching my coat and must have slid it into my pocket. I'll have to return it when I bring back the book."

382

We both dried off and James, finishing first, went over to see the metallic object, a towel wrapped around his waist. His hand reached toward it and I felt that strange static again right before I saw a huge arc of glowing white electricity cross between the pendent and his hand, throwing him backward into the wall with a crack. Tossing my towel aside I ran to him as he was picking himself up off the floor, glaring furiously at the object on the floor.

"That's an amulet." He watched me carefully as he asked, "What exactly did you tell him about yourself?"

"Nothing." I was sure of it. "He made all the assumptions, I didn't say anything but that I was going to be here for a week."

We got dressed and I put the amulet in my pants pocket as far away from James as possible.

"It is strange that Donovan caught up with you in a bookstore belonging to a powerful and well known witch. How did you decide on *this* store?" James was thoughtful as he picked up the book and flipped through it growing more concerned.

"I don't know, it just seemed right at the time."

"Hmm." He gave me a quick glance and then back to the book. "He recommended this one to you? You didn't tell him you wanted anything of this nature?" James was still flipping through the book, more slowly now, scanning the contents carefully.

I answered hesitantly, feeling my pulse quicken as my tension escalated. "He asked what type of book and mentioned the occult. I tried not to be obvious when I asked for it." Frowning I tried to remember why I'd made my request. "I'm not sure why I wanted it. He pulled this one off of the shelf without trying any others and told me to borrow it while I was here in town. He wouldn't let me buy it. You know, we started at the pendant, I mean amulet, before he loaned me the book and he wanted me to buy *that*. He even dropped the price for me but I told him I had only enough for my snack. He said the amulet was old Germanic and good for fertility and luck."

He put down the book. "Could I see that again? Just put it on the bed," he added quickly, holding out a hand meant to keep me at a distance as long as I held the offending object.

I pulled it out and set it on the bed. He leaned in and kept his hands behind his back while he studied it. After examining the two symbols on the triangle shaped amulet for a few moments, James was ready to kill.

"That sneaky bastard. I'd heard rumors about him and his motives." His lips were tight and I saw his fangs growing in his anger. "I'm surprised no one's killed him yet."

"What does it mean? Was he lying?" I couldn't imagine the quirky little man inspiring such a reaction.

"Those symbols are called runes. Put together they are charms against the likes of me. He meant to separate you from me. Did you tell him anything about any of us?"

Shaking my head, I answered him. "No, he did see my ring and called me a newlywed. He just kept looking at me like he knew me."

"Let's go meet your new friend," he suggested, pulling on his coat.
I was already maneuvering into my own.

Ch. 63

The cab ride was short. We were at the bookstore within minutes and the shopkeeper greeted us at the door. I wasn't sure he was going to let us in from the way his eyes bugged out at James' unexpected presence, but after a few nervous glances at James and me, he stepped aside and allowed us to enter.

"Alan Brightmore?" James extended his hand. "James Thomas."

Embarrassed, I realized he'd been able to deduce so much of me and I hadn't even picked up his name.

He eyed James' hand suspiciously, slowly accepting it in a handshake. Immediately upon James' hand closing around his, Alan cried out and tried to retract his hand to no avail. I watched James look down at the shorter man to catch his eye, Alan fought to avoid his gaze.

With a hint of a self-satisfied smile on his lips, James released him. "You know what I am, Alan. And now, I know what you are." The ice in his tone gave me goose bumps.

Alan startled and glanced up at him, catching himself just before their eyes met. "I've never met one of your kind in person. What do I call you?"

"James is fine. Claire told me about your guidance with the book and amulet yesterday. I thought I might come by to thank you, you were so helpful."

His eyes widened, his hands coming up defensively. "I didn't mean to interfere. She smelled of your kind of magic and I wanted to help her. I didn't know she was *yours*.

Please extend my apologies to the Court. I never would have…"

James threw back his head and laughed. "Don't worry. I don't work in the Guard anymore. I am only here to protect *my* interests."

That got both the shopkeeper and my attentions. I couldn't believe James was saying this in front of a human. Witches were apparently considered "in the know."

When he saw my reaction, James elaborated. "Alan has been on our radar for quite some time, given the circles he runs in. He knows about us and has been involved in some ugly cleanups," Alan paled at the mention and I could only imagine, "though we have never made direct contact." His hand slid down to mine and he squeezed it gently. "His interfering in our relationship has inspired me to put a face with the name."

"You aren't going to hurt him, are you?"

"No, although he was incorrect in his assumptions, he *was* trying to help you. How can I fault him for that?"

Alan was wagging his head back and forth between the two of us. "I've never heard of such a thing. She has her wits about her in your presence. She is more than a thrall or a servant. How can that be?"

"It happens on occasion that our kinds cross paths and remain together for a time." James waved off any further inquiries. "There are questions I have for *you*, Alan. Can we speak freely here?" James glanced about the store seeing that there were no other customers.

"We were having a slow day, it's Sunday. We were going to close up a little early. I'll have my daughter, Davina lock up now. No one will mind." He called out in another language,

Gaelic maybe, and the redhead from yesterday came up, watchful of the two of us.

Studying us carefully, Davina approached frowning. Alan gave her a reassuring shake of his head telling her we were okay and asking her to start closing the place up. "Yes Da. Could you give me your keys to lock up when I'm done?" She sheepishly cast her eyes to her shoes. "I've left mine somewhere."

"Hmm, again? Couldn't have been that boy's flat I suppose? You have to be more careful with the keys Davina, we have locks for a reason." Alan wasn't pleased with his daughter's choice if I read his tone correctly. He handed her the keys he fished out of his pocket.

"Yes Da." Davina took them and went up to lock the door, glancing back over her shoulder at James. Alan waved her off again, signaling she needn't worry. He led us to the back of the store and to a door on the wall of the café I hadn't noticed yesterday. It was painted to blend in, the handle was inset. It led upstairs to a flat full of as many books as the store below. The eclectic mix of furniture and rugs lent it the look and feel of a traveler's treasure trove, warm and well loved.

"Please, have a seat. I'll make us some tea." Alan disappeared down a narrow hallway straight ahead, leading to the kitchen that had to be over the front counter below.

I was perusing the leather bound, ancient looking books on the shelf nearest the hall when James approached me from behind. His hands slid around my waist, his lips tickled my ear as he spoke softly to me.

"Alan is a witch with a gift, he senses people's destinies. Funny how he thought you needed protection from me. It makes one question what he thought would be your destiny." He nuzzled my ear and kissed my neck.

I would have turned, though I honestly didn't want him to stop. "I don't wonder; I know what my destiny is. I'm in this with you until the end, whenever that might be."

His body went hard and I wondered what I said wrong as he withdrew his hands. I turned to face him, examining his expression for clues and seeing him wrestling his emotions under control.

"What did I say?" I was genuinely confused at his reaction.

"Do you worry your life will end too soon with me?"

"We're supposed to be together, you know that." I had started to say more, to explain that a short life with him beat a long life with no one, which is what I would have had. Just as I began, Alan entered the room carrying a tray with a teapot and service for three.

"Here we are," he said as he sat down, seemingly oblivious to what he had walked into. "I apologize, I was not prepared for company and don't have any biscuits or such to feed you. If you'd like, I can fetch some from the shop."

Before I glanced over at Alan, I saw James' brow furrowed as he fidgeted with his hands. I wasn't sure I could hold down a cup of tea as my stomach started to flip anxiously, he was bleeding over into me and I was having a hard time holding both sets of nerves down.

The sound of tea being poured was background noise as well as Alan chattering about something inconsequential. Suddenly, whatever he was saying was important to me as I felt James riveted upon our host. I tried to concentrate on what I was hearing.

James reacted so strongly to Alan's words that he was completely focused and still, facing him with black eyes. He waved off the tea offered to him. Alan had obviously forgotten that vampires do not take food or drink.

"I thought you had not seen my kind before. Our messages were always sent by human courier."

Alan took a sip of his tea. "He wasn't exactly a vampire; he was a human who smelled of vampire. A servant I supposed, like I thought Claire was."

"When was this that he came here and what did he want?" James' focus was intense. I felt him close down the nerves that had plagued me and my mind was once again my own.

Sensing something amiss by James' intensity, Alan put down his teacup. "It was just about a week ago, after the New Year. He wanted to know what I had on psychic bonds. You know, telepathy between a few select people. I sold him the only book I had on the subject and he was on his way."

"What did he look like? Did he pay with a credit card or give you his name?"

Alan closed his eyes, picturing the customer. "It was an unusual request, so specific. He didn't seem the type so I remembered him better than I should. He was a middle aged man, American like your Claire here. He was perfectly average, brown hair maybe, average build, nothing special at all. But I do think he paid with a credit card. If you give me a few days I can track down his slip and get a name for you."

"Yes, do. And I would like a copy of the book you sold to him if you could order another." James walked toward the staircase suddenly in a hurry to be off. "Claire, are you ready? We have business to attend."

Confused and not just about what I had heard transpire between James and Alan, I rose to exit with James. Alan followed us out and unlocked the door. He paused and I took the amulet from my pocket, trying to hand it to him.

Waving me off, he spoke firmly. "You *do* need this. Maybe not for him, but you need it." I felt him press it back into my palm, folding my fingers around it, his eyes glassy. "Guard yourself well, Claire. These are dangerous times for us all." Blinking life back into his eyes, he tried to smile. "Take care of yourself."

Impulsively, I threw my arms around him. "You too Alan." He blustered, but I felt him hug back before he stepped away from me. James stood at the door with it held open, watching me. Alan was blushing as he waved, closing the door.

Ch. 64

James took the lead on the way back to the hotel. Taking the most direct route it still took a half hour, giving me plenty of time to think. I followed James for a block, lagging behind, sending the clear message that I wanted space. I didn't understand his mention of destinies at Alan's shop. How could he question our being together at this point? What the hell had set him off this time? If it was the question of my giving things up, or him feeling bad about putting me in dangerous situations, I was going to scream. I thought we'd settled that.

We walked in our room and shut the door. No sooner had the latch clicked into place then James' phone rang.

"You have *got* to be kidding me." I muttered, tired of the constant interruptions.

"Yes?" He listened and immediately motioned for me to put my coat back on just as I was shaking it down my arms.

I rolled my eyes and he promptly ignored me, turning his back. The snub got my back up and I stewed while I waited for him to hang up.

As soon as he hung up, he started talking without allowing me an opening. "Henry has requested that we return. He has Tonya and Donovan there and he wants to meet before Omar is available for the night." Speaking in monotone, he gave nothing away, nor did he meet my eyes. I was having difficulty gauging his mood without either.

"Wait a minute." I stopped mid coat shrug. "Aren't we going to talk about whatever that was back there?"

"I don't think we have time. Henry is waiting." James was busily concentrating on his phone.

Fed up, I reached out and snatched his phone. "I don't care what Henry wants. I want to know what that was back there." I forced my face in front of his. "The details don't matter, the simple fact is that I would rather die tomorrow with you than live forever alone. If that doesn't prove anything, I don't know what will."

James' serene façade fell away and I watched his muscles stiffen, knowing if I touched him now he would feel like steel under a thin cotton shirt. His eyes were nearly black though his fangs were still holstered. "I don't doubt that we're meant to be together." His expression turned tortured. "But *why*? Do you never wonder *why* we are together? *Why* a human and a vampire are bonded as we are? What caused *this* to be our destiny?" James paced the room agitated, his eyes were wide and I could almost see his nostrils flaring.

My hushed answer was an effort to settle him down. It was never good when he was this worked up. "Again you're talking about destiny. It doesn't matter. So much happens that I don't understand in this life, especially lately. And in the end, none of it matters. We love each other, we're bonded; let's accept that."

Coming to a halt in front of me, James took my hand and led me to the bed where he motioned for me to sit beside him. I considered being stubborn then thought better of it and sat down.

"When I touched him, I saw why Alan was worried about your destiny. That's why he gave you the amulet and the book."

I started to sigh and roll my eyes in exasperation, only James squeezed my hand and I stopped to hear him out.

"I could see his vision of your destiny." James got back to his feet and paced, once again unable to contain his distress. "You were underground and you were dying." He stopped with his back to me and I could feel him struggling for control. "You were covered in blood and I held you in my arms. Your blood was on my hands and in my mouth. I could taste it." He refused to turn around and look at me.

Speechless, I sat on the edge of the bed waiting for what I knew was coming next.

James hung his head in despair. "Claire, he saw me kill you. Bond or no, how can I condemn you to that? How can I keep you with me knowing you will die at my hand?"

Ch. 65

James was in a hurry to avoid any further discussions about destiny and my mortality, so we were buzzing in at Henry's within ten minutes. I didn't object.

Upon arrival, I noticed Tara wasn't in sight and I no longer smelled blood. I hoped that meant she was healing. Tonya and Donovan sat on the white couch in the living room, Henry stood behind Tonya, a hand resting easily on her shoulder.

When Henry spoke his words were shockingly aimed at me. "Claire, we need your assistance." I felt my heart speed up. I didn't want the extra responsibility right now. Cutting a sideways glance at James, I saw that he was fidgeting; he knew something. Of course he did, I thought snidely. Henry raised his hand indicating that I should wait for him to finish before freaking out. "As you are aware, James is busy with the boy's transition."

Still keeping secrets from the newcomer, I had the presence of mind to notice.

"However, Donovan also requires guidance with his abilities." He nodded at the top of the uncomfortable man's head; Tonya patted his leg, reassuring him.

From his expression I was guessing he wasn't entirely certain about any of this. Vaguely, I could remember when I was in his shoes, finding out the monsters were real. Poor Donovan, I thought. There was a stinging rebuff at the sentiment in my head which I chose not to dignify with a response.

"If you could handle it while James is otherwise occupied, I would consider it a great favor."

What could I say? "Okay. I can try."

"No she can't." James tried to overrule.

"Why? Don't you think I can do it alone?" I glared at him, this was only the latest in offenses this evening.

He kept his eyes on Henry, speaking through a tight jaw. "Do you remember his ability and its effect on you? Are you better prepared than you were just last night to work with him for hours on end, even after you get tired? Alone?"

I hadn't thought too hard about the realities of it, but maintained that I could handle it. I had already figured out, all by myself, that if I kept on my toes and caught him before he really threw out his ability I could stop him from affecting me.

Squaring my shoulders and focusing solely on Henry, I accepted. "I would be more than happy to help. Where and when do we start?"

"You will accompany us to the pub tonight and Charles has graciously offered to let us use his rooms. I would like to be available in case you have any trouble."

"No! She can't go to the Court." James' resolve hardened and I wasn't the only one who noticed.

Henry was growing visibly perturbed with James' protests and I sensed a confrontation on the horizon. "James, if she says she is ready, then she is ready. You must allow her to try to train one. A human is much safer than Omar, even you must admit that."

Unlike Henry, I understood the biggest reason behind James' stubbornness and jumped in. "It isn't the job Henry, it's the place. It's a long story. Maybe we could stay here? If that's okay with you?"

Henry lifted a brow at James in expectation of further protests, except James was silent, only lifting a hand to wave off his right to argue. Henry nodded once again, looking satisfied, "Yes Claire. If you are comfortable being alone with him, I have no objections to you working here."

Tonya spoke up from the couch. "I would like to stay."

Her acceptance of Donovan again struck me as odd. I wondered if it was real or if he had used his taste of Enchantment to draw her to him.

"No Tonya." Henry tapped his fingers on her shoulder. "With Tara out of commission I will require your help with the boy should he start to come around. When he starts to come back to his senses it is possible he will panic and require someone non-vampire who can take a little more damage than a human." Henry reminded her.

"Should I come back when James leaves at dusk?" I asked.

Henry confirmed that that was exactly what he was hoping for, excusing himself to check on Tara. I excused myself as well and felt rather than heard James behind me. His frustration was flying off of him in palpable bolts making me very uncomfortable as I waited for him to blow up. And as much as I didn't want to admit it, I thought he might have had a point for concern.

Once we were on the street, James hailed a cab and we rode back to our room in silence. The storm didn't break until I sat down hard on the couch in the sitting room facing James at the door, waiting for it.

His lips were tight and I could barely hear him when he spoke. "Why are you doing this? What do you hope to prove?"

"Who says I'm trying to prove anything?"

"You know you aren't ready to do this alone. You should have said no. I can work with him during the daytime when Omar rests."

Now it was my turn to be angry and I stood up, fists clenched at my sides. "I'm not ready? Then tell me how I am supposed to work with a vampire with no self-control if I can't even handle a human. At least Donovan won't attack me."

"Not for your blood."

When I realized his real motivation for trying to keep me away from Donovan I was livid. "You will deny me the opportunity to practice on a relatively safe student just because you're worried I'll go and kiss him? You're ridiculous. Do you know that?"

He closed the distance between us in two long strides and took hold of my arms in his hands. His grip was firm but not bruising, so I knew he still had control of himself, though it felt pretty tenuous. He vibrated on my periphery. James' eyes were black and his fangs were starting to show against his lips as he got more upset.

"Claire, I could handle a kiss and I think you could too. I don't think that is what this character has in mind. I can feel his pull on you. What if he takes advantage of you or drags you off to Lucas? Can you fight a full grown man if he decides to pick you up and carry you off?"

I refused to give in to his line of thinking. "James, did you not see him with Tonya? I think now that Lucas' charm is wearing off, he's ruled by his wanting her more than me. And don't worry, you can trust me not to leave here with him." Taking a deep breath, I made a conscious effort to lower my voice and force him to listen. "I figured out how to shield from him. He just took me by surprise the first time, that's all. Now I'm ready for him."

397

"Really?" That got his attention. I felt his grip on me loosen.

"Mmm hmm, all I have to do is have my defenses up ahead of time and not lower them at all. Even to sweep."

He looked confused.

"You know I do that. I lower every few minutes to 'look' for people. And vampires." I added. "It's a habit I've gotten into since we seem to attract trouble. I like to see it coming."

From his surprise I could tell he hadn't known that. His lips twitched and a smile played at his mouth, now gone back to a more human shape without fangs behind them. "I've underestimated you again." As he said it, I watched his expression change. He was thinking about Alan's vision, I could tell.

Taking his hand in mine, I waited for him to look at me. "Listen, this is my life too. I know you want to protect me and that's flattering. But look at what we've done, what *I've* done. I can take care of myself too and you need to start believing that. I *chose* this life and you cannot change that or we'll both hate you for it. No matter what the end looks like, I want it to be with you."

Midnight eyes met my own and I saw that he was torn between what he wanted and what he feared most; that it would be his hand that would bring about my demise.

"You warned me once that your kind are covetous and possessive and I deal with that pretty well. Sometimes I even like it. But if we are going to work together, you are going to have to let me spread my wings. There's no point giving me a job you won't let me do."

He didn't look convinced although he did make an effort to look contrite. "I will do my best, even if it goes against my nature."

Sensing victory, I allowed a gracious smile. "You told me yourself you were regaining your humanity. What better way to test it?"

I thought I felt his chest rumble when he pulled me into him.

Ch. 66

Late that afternoon, while night fell around us, we rode to Henry's flat holding hands in silence.

Trying to make small talk, I commented on our transportation situation. "All of these cab rides have to be adding up."

James eagerly picked up the thread. "You know, I sold my other car and have been thinking about getting a second again since we are a two person household now. Maybe we could rent a car for the rest of our stay. It would be a good opportunity to try out a few different models."

"Sure, but I don't want to drive in the city here. Maybe out in the country where it's less crowded." The narrow roads were confusing to even walk on, I was never sure which way to look first before crossing.

James had an affinity for cars, I'd felt it when we'd first connected. The conversation succeeded in distracting him, something I was grateful for. "Do you have any particular cars you have had your eye on?"

That caught me by surprise. "What, you mean you want *me* to choose?"

He shifted his shoulders against the back cushion to face me. "Claire, you're going to be my wife soon and I would like for us to have a second car. You can help choose unless you would prefer to take the Audi and I will get the new car." He finished with the hint of a taunt in his tone, trying to goad me with the threat of a hand me down even, if it was still nicer than anything I planned on getting for myself, ever.

"I like the sound of that." I touched his leg.

"What part?"

"The wife part. I like it."

He leaned in to kiss me. "You know, we have never discussed a date."

I felt my stomach flip. "No, we haven't. I was thinking we would need to work around your travel schedule. If we did it this year, that is." I didn't know how long a typical engagement was and nothing about us was typical, leaving me no clue what to expect. Any time was okay with me, I'd made my decision already so making it official was easy.

Sitting back and looking straight ahead, he tried to appear unconcerned. I felt him concealing his nerves. "I was thinking it might be nice to have it in France. Surprise your parents while they are there for their anniversary. Everyone I would invite is already here in Scotland, it would be an easy trip there and back."

My mouth fell open. "James, that's a week away! How could we get ready in time?"

The side of his mouth twisted into a sly smile. "You worry about your dress and I can manage the rest. I know people." The date being so soon took care of one of my secret fears; that I would die before becoming his wife. After our previous scares and my looming inaugural training with Omar, I thought that was a very real fear. And if anything were to happen, I wanted to know that I had been tied to him totally in both of our worlds, that people would know we'd meant something to each other in a way they could understand.

"Is that a yes?"

Nodding excitedly and smiling, I felt the idea take hold. "Should we tell my parents?"

"I don't know." He grinned. "A surprise might be fun, what do you think?"

On an emotional high and reflecting on the fact that I might have the only vampire in existence to call something "fun" that didn't involve blood sport, we arrived at Henry's flat and buzzed in. Tonya greeted me anxiously at the door.

"Can I talk to you?" Her mood dragged me back to the ground.

"Sure." I followed her to the last bedroom down the hall. She entered first, waiting for me to follow and closing the door behind me.

"What's up?" I asked when we got inside, already having a pretty good idea who, if not what, we were going to discuss.

Tonya was uncharacteristically fretful, rubbing her palms on her thighs. "I want you to do something for me."

I was starting to answer yes when she put up her hand out to stop me.

"Before you answer, you might want to know what it is. I'm not sure what your moral position on the subject might be."

Making a show of sitting down on the edge of the bed and crossing my arms, I waited for her to explain.

"You know Donovan knows too much."

Worried at the change in direction from where I thought this was going, I pursed my lips letting my air out slowly in a toneless whistle. "Is Henry going to erase his memory or…?" I couldn't say the other option out loud.

"It depends. First you have to find out if it's his ability or all Lucas. If it's innate, Henry will want us to train him and he's fine, provided he respects the rules." She blushed and added uncertainly, "And while you're deciphering him versus the vampire, I wondered if you could find out if he's bespelled me or not."

"Tonya, can you not block him out?" I'd always assumed she had an ability like the others, the concept that she was unguarded from psychic attack was incredible.

Easing back from the door, Tonya eyed me cautiously, gauging how trustworthy I was. "I'm not like the rest of my family, I don't have an ability. Henry has done his best to teach me to protect myself but without the gateway of an ability my defenses are seriously limited and, as you might have noticed," she dropped her gaze to mine, "Donovan's charm is hard to refuse."

It was my turn to be uncomfortable. I settled for a mumbled agreement, ducking my eyes and flushing pink.

"So you can do it?" When I glanced back at her, she was once again the confident beauty, no signs of insecurity whatsoever.

"Be happy to." I assured her. With the initial shock ebbing, I felt a certain sense of pride to be of some help to her. I'd never thought there was anything *I* might be able to do better than her.

Together we returned to the front room and Henry and Donovan barely glanced at us, they were deep in conversation while James watched me closely. I sent him a warm feeling that I was no longer angry and gave him a shake of the head to tell him not to worry.

Henry finished with Donovan. "Tonya, are you ready then?"

Casting a last furtive glance at me, she walked up to Henry and said that she was. A curious shadow rolled across

Henry's face and then it was smooth again by the time Tonya joined him at the entrance.

James had been milling with the others beside the couch and leaned forward to whisper something to Donovan. Even with my borrowed hearing, I couldn't make out anything more than a mumble. When James leaned back I saw a flash of his fangs and I could see from the way Donovan paled and gulped that he saw them as well.

"Understand?"

Donovan nodded.

"Dusk is upon us, let's be off." Henry looked at me, "Claire, if anything goes wrong, you need to call." His expression was severe as he added, "By any means at your disposal."

James kissed me, squeezing my hand. "Call me if things get too intense. Don't be foolish, please. I want you to be careful with him." He moved so that his lips were on my ear, "Don't leave with him, I'm begging you. We were lucky last time."

"I'll be careful," I assured him and squeezed his hand back.

The door closed behind them and Donovan and I were alone, staring at each other.

Immediately I felt him bump against my shields, currently running at full blast.

Angrily, I pointed at him. "Let's set some ground rules. You are here so I can figure out if you get to stick around. If you want to have a long, happy life there will be no more of that."

He raised an eyebrow arrogantly, "Or what? You'll tell your boyfriend?"

Clearly not used to being rejected by women, I observed with a sigh, he was going to be a pain in the ass. "I don't need James' help dealing with you. You're weak and I can handle anything you've got." I tapped my temple exuding the best bravado I could muster. He couldn't see me as shakable, not again.

"I was doing alright before you had reinforcements. I think your boyfriend knows it and that's why he doesn't want you alone with me. Henry thinks the blonde guy did some sort of magick on me and I can't do anything myself, but he's wrong."

His insight took me by surprise. He didn't seem that smart honestly, maybe he did have something more to him after all. Clicking through what I knew from my limited exposure to these kinds of things, and as impressionable as he had proven to be thus far, I thought maybe he was open to others' abilities. A channeler like me. There was one way to find out.

"What about Tonya? If you like her you'll want to control yourself or that will end painfully for you. Have you seen her claws?" I raised an eyebrow at him.

Donovan blanched at the mention of her claws and maddeningly came back with more of his annoying swagger. "I can handle the lady. She liked me just fine last night, or did you miss that part?" He leered. "Want to try it yourself or are you scared you'd like it better than what you've got?"

"You are a cocky bastard; has anyone ever told you that?" Typical pretty boy, he thought he was God's gift to women. I remembered "feeling" guys like him in school and the poor girls they bedded purely for conquest. Not a one meant anything. Fleetingly, I felt bad for Tonya.

He shook his prideful head, his undaunted confidence nauseating. "It's not cocky if it's true. You can't tell me you aren't tempted." He bumped me again.

Ignoring his ineffective efforts at psychic seduction, I pushed back and smirked at the stunned expression that rewarded me. "I'm not."

"Let's get started." I led the way around to sit.

His eyes tracked me, his arrogance giving way to wariness.

I motioned for him to sit on the couch. Still eyeing me from under those long dark lashes, he moved cautiously to the couch and sat. Positioning myself close enough that I could reach, I sat beside him.

"I'm going to see what the blonde guy did, that's all." It was mostly true. Gently, I lay my hand on his forearm and pushed my way in.

He had no shielding to speak of to stop me and I slid easily into his psyche, mimicking what I'd felt James do.
Sensing my entry, he pulled away from me. "I'm not letting you into my head. No way!"

Doing my best impression of one of my no-nonsense professors, I glared at him sternly. I doubted it would make a difference. It was hard to be imposing when you are at least five inches shorter than your opposition and a girl he obviously had no respect for.

"I don't know what you people are doing; no chick is worth this." He started to stand up. "I'm out of here."

The situation was getting out of control fast. I couldn't fail on my first try. Panicking, I threw out the first thing that came to mind. "If you walk out of here what makes you think Henry won't come find you?"

406

The bluff worked, Donovan shifted nervously and stammered. "Fine, we can play pretend. It doesn't matter anyway."

Relieved, I could breathe again. I waited for him to sit down.

After he sat back down, I put my hand back on his arm. "I want you to think about why you followed me last night."

"Why?" He screwed up his face.

"Because that's how this works." I could see that he was not going to be an easy subject to convince. If he wouldn't believe in the metaphysical, I would try more proven science. "Think of this like an EKG. I want to see how your body reacts when we compare how you feel about what the blonde guy asked you to do and what you chose to do."

Blowing out a lungful of air, he laid back against the cushions. "Whatever makes you happy Doc."

When I slipped into his head my eyes flicked to his and caught the tremor he tried to hide. Object as he would, Donovan knew there was something to what I was doing. I was willing to bet he had a few "incidents" in his history that were beyond scientific explanation.

"Think about last night." I reminded him gently.

The first thing that jumped to his mind was the part of the night that came after we'd met and I had to fight the urge to jump out or ask him to stop. I'd promised Tonya. The first thing that struck me was that Donovan was amazed he'd been able to bed her, gone was the swagger he'd been so willing to throw around. It looked like I wasn't the only one faking confidence.

Satisfied that he'd had nothing but honest motives with Tonya and not wanting to have any more information about her sex life, I pulled back with a chuckle.

"You're going backward. I need to see *earlier* in the night, not that."

Donovan actually blushed and averted his eyes before he came back with a less convincing version of his asinine façade. "You said you wanted to compare, I was just giving you a taste of what it *could* be like."

"Thanks for that," I said flatly, "now can you think about when you followed me?"

He let the smug expression fade and I watched confusion play at his features; frowning and hanging his head, he eventually shook it and looked back up. The distress in his eyes wasn't feigned. "I don't remember much, just that he told me to go get a friend of his. I don't remember following you or anything you said I did. Not until Tonya showed up."

Knowing James would be furious, I did the only thing I could think of to dig deeper. "This is important Donovan, I need you to close your eyes and just picture the blonde guy. Can you do that?"

A hint of fear sparked in his eyes and I rubbed his arm where my hand rested. "Don't worry, nothing's going to happen. I just need to see if he did anything to you, but I need you to find him in there for me first. It's like a phone book, I can call for you but I need you to turn the pages." Breaking it down helped and he closed his eyes while I waited.

In a few minutes he found him. Lucas had picked Donovan out at a coffee shop that afternoon and set him on me. He'd come into the shop when I did and trailed me out. The feel of Lucas' power had faded in Donovan but it spiked when I tapped into Donovan's memory of the confrontation on the street. Again I felt the power of his Enchantment tugging at me, only this time I'd been ready and slammed the door shut on it and yanked my hand off of his arm.

Smoothing my shirt when I stood, I walked around the couch into the kitchen. "Would you like a glass of water or something?" I needed one.

"Sure. Do you think he has anything stronger?" Donovan craned his neck to see me over the back of the couch. He looked pale, the memory had troubled him as well.

"I don't know, I'll look."

Pouring myself a glass of water, I let my mind wander over what I had learned from Donovan. When I was in his head I didn't see any signs that Lucas' influence would remain. Already it was fading; I'd been able to shut him out faster, something I wouldn't have been able to do last night.

"Wow, I hope you like beer. Pick your flavor." Henry had a plethora of beers in his fridge and since I couldn't celebrate my success with a drink, I was glad he could.

"Does he have any Brooker's? I'm a local boy, I was raised on the stuff."

"Yep." I grabbed one and dug in the drawers until I found a bottle opener. Carrying the opened beer to the couch in one hand with my water in the other, I sat down in the chair opposite him.

I watched him rapidly pour half of his pint down his throat while formulating my plan of attack. "Donovan, you have a special ability. I watched the way you reacted when you felt me in your head. You're sensitive to other people's abilities; maybe things like this thing with the blonde guy have happened before?" I opened the door for him to admit it to me and to himself.

His reaction wasn't the one I expected. His eyes grew wary and he took another gulp of his beer. "That's not special, that's mental."

I was right, he was aware that he was different, like me. That might make him easier to explain things to. "You're not mental, you have what my friends call an ability or a talent."

Donovan rolled his eyes and stared straight ahead, beer resting on his thigh. He looked like all he was missing was a football game. Soccer here, I suppose.

"I wouldn't have believed it either if the same thing hadn't happened to me." His eyes shifted toward me then back. I had his attention. "Sometimes I would feel things that I shouldn't be feeling." Letting him in on what I'd gone through seemed fitting. "Like watching tv in the living room and all of a sudden being really sad, crying out loud kind of sad when I'd been watching something that wasn't." I recalled the day my Mom had lost a close friend. She'd gotten the call when I was watching a rerun of the A-team. "Then you learn the person in the next room is heartbroken and you're picking up on it."

Donovan took another long drink before resting his bottle on his leg; he started picking at the label. "Yeah, it's happened once or twice. The last time was a year or so ago at the Highland Games. A bunch of us went up to watch and have a good time. I went into the pub to get a round and this big guy, big and strange like that Lucas fellow, caught up with me coming out of the pub and pulled me aside. He asked me to go with him and talk to this other guy in a different pub." His nail scraped faster on the foil label.

"Afterward, all I could think was I was a nutter to go with him. I don't remember going but I must've because when I could think again, I was walking away from town covered in blood. I don't know where it came from, just that it was on

410

me and I didn't know if I'd done something awful to someone." The poor guy paled at the memory, his hands shook and unable to hide it he shook the beer harder showing me it was empty.

I got up to grab him another.

"I never told anyone what happened, I told my friends I met a girl in the pub, that that's where I went. I watched the news for weeks waiting for word of what happened. I never heard anything."

I watched him drink, letting him make peace with his new reality. It made sense that other vampires, maybe even weres or witches, *anybody* with sensitivities like James' could find him and use him if they wanted to. James said he could scout for it if he tried.

That brought up an interesting question, why hadn't James sensed Donovan's ability? I deliberated the details of their two meetings. James had been upset and feeling overprotective of me both times, but that shouldn't have blocked his sensing of Donovan. James was good, he'd been doing this for years and I was sure not all of the times had been under ideal conditions. I would have to ask James when he returned.

"I can help you eliminate those black out incidents with a little training. How would you feel about that?"

Thoughtful, he set down his half empty bottle on the coffee table and shifted so that he was facing me. "I'd like that. I don't want to have to do what everyone else wants all the time." His honesty gave me another glimpse at what was behind his bravado and I thought maybe I could see what it was Tonya found charming after all.

I gave one brief nod and slid forward in my seat. "Shall we then?"

Donovan was worried but he was willing. He held out his hands to me, a little shaky at first, and we went to work.

Ch. 67

Not long after dawn I awoke, feeling another presence in the living room where Donovan and I had fallen asleep only a few hours before. Donovan lay stretched out on the couch, his arms thrown over his head. I was curled up in the chair.

As soon as I opened my eyes I saw James standing in front of my perch, his face a blank mask. Smiling sleepily at him, I pushed the fog of sleep off of me and sat up, my hand was completely numb. "How did it go last night?" I asked him, running one hand through my hair, trying to make sense of the wavy mess and shaking the other hand to regain blood flow.

He made a show of trying to look stern. "Why don't you tell me?"

"You know full well nothing happened." I scoffed at his charade. "You would have known it when it did and you would have smelled it on us when you walked in." I doubted we could keep our bond closed if one of us was having sex with someone else. The heightened state would blow them wide open. I know it did for us.

Crouching down, he kissed my nose. "I am so proud of you."

"How about you?" I blushed and hurried to deflect the focus off of me. "Is Omar improving?"

James looked over at my student. "Can I buy you a cup of tea?"

We walked down half a block to an all night café catering to internet junkies and gamers. There were still a few stragglers left from the night before. Finding a small table in the corner, we settled in and I sipped at a hot tea feeling it shake the rest of the cobwebs from my mind.

"You first," I encouraged.

He was going to argue until I pursed my lips obstinately and he shrugged. "Omar is improving. He was more sensible and we were able to discuss what was happening to him."

"How did he take it, being one of the enemy so to speak?"

James was conservative in his pleasure. "Actually, I was surprised. He took it better than expected, he was happy." I felt my eyes pop out and he continued, tempering my surprise. "At first he was upset, he broke some furniture *and* somebody's arm, but when I explained that we were only visiting and would return to Minneapolis and Tara soon he was much more manageable. He isn't as concerned with being one of us as being around us."

That made a weird sort of sense. "So you told him he was going home? Is that the right thing to do considering it's too soon to tell? Speaking of which, have you seen any indication of his ability? Is it gone?"

He was unhappy at that, his lips tightened only the tiniest bit. "It's too soon, he's still too wild. Maybe tomorrow we'll start to see something if it's going to present itself." James eyed me curiously, "And you? How did your first session with the gigolo go?"

Choking on my tea I reached for my napkin, laughing. "He has no idea what he's doing. He's actually kind of sweet, I can see why Tonya likes him."

"What does that mean?" James went still, his low voice threatening enough to get the attention of the few people in the café. He did look incredibly intimidating, even to me.

414

My temper flared right back. "Can you *please* get past this jealousy thing with him? I'm trying to share what I learned with you and I need your input. So if you can focus, I would greatly appreciate it."

"Go on." He still looked angry, although he had toned down the ominous demeanor.

I went on to explain what I'd found in my exploration. He was as interested as I was when I related Donovan's story of what happened with the blackout involving the pub and another vampire. "Is he sensitive like you? He's not exactly channeling which is what I first thought." My options were limited to the abilities I knew existed, and that wasn't many.

"No, he's not like either one of us." I watched the familiar line between his brows telling me he was thinking. "He could be a dummy."

"You're being petty." I pointed out. "He might not be smart but you don't have to belittle him."

James' teeth flashed and he touched my hand. "I meant a dummy as in an extra that can be 'charged' with an ability and used accordingly. That would seem to fit."

"Why can't you figure him out? It should be easy for you." All of a sudden I realized that was the second part of my assignment, James *couldn't* sense him.

He was equally perplexed. "That's why I think he's a dummy. When the charge wears off he's back to a blank slate; it leaves no trace of itself. I'd be curious to see if he picked up anything from you after last night or if he can only carry one charge at a time."

Hearing that Donovan did have an inherent ability I wanted to know his fate. "I'm assuming he will be allowed to keep his memory? Do we want him to know the full extent of his ability? If he knew some of the stuff he could do with the right charge he'd be unbearable to live with, wouldn't he?"

James watched our server refill my teacup and waited until he left to answer, he sounded bored. "Yes, he will be able to keep his memory, but like the witch, he will have limited contact with our world. I think the best approach with him would be to explain his ability as a weakness. Something he should guard himself against in the future and try to keep hidden. The fewer of my kind who know about him the better for everyone involved. A man as arrogant and vain as Donovan won't want to think of himself as weak. He'll do what he needs to protect himself and we won't have to worry about him."

Gawking at James, I was astounded by his deviousness. "How can you do that? That kind of information can be destructive to someone like him. He isn't a complete jerk, I actually think he's a decent guy."

His eyes darkened in an instant. "I don't like you defending him. Are you *sure* he didn't Enchant you?"

"You can be a real ass," I snapped back, stood abruptly and stalked out of the café. It was a long walk home, and I fully intended to make it by myself. I was several blocks away when he made his presence known to me by walking heavily so that I could hear his footsteps on the pavement.

Knowing I was being hypersensitive and juvenile, I sped up and he let me stride away, letting me fume. The possessive, jealous vampire bit was getting on my nerves and the shot about not being able to keep myself free of my student's influences stung more than it ought. I had a moment of clarity and thought things might be shifting again within our connection. It might be time to visit Miranda again and find out how much further our bond had evolved. The thought made me sick to my stomach.

Because I was in front and not paying much attention to what was ahead of me, but rather who was behind me and what was in my head, I failed to notice the two men waiting in the narrow alleyway at the edge of the next building.

The taller of the two stepped out and grabbed me around the waist with one hand while his other went across my mouth and he pulled me into the early morning shadows. The shorter and bulkier of the two had a knife I would normally call small, but under the circumstances it looked gigantic.

Short One demanded, "Give me your money." His thick Scottish brogue made him nearly impossible to understand. I didn't do anything.

The taller one had an excitable look about him that I guessed was chemically enhanced. I'd seen a flash of his gray patchwork teeth when he grabbed me cementing my opinion. Meth or crack was my guess from what little I knew about their effects. "You can give it to us or we take it." His sour breath nearly knocked me flat.

"Let her go." James commanded coldly from the mouth of the alley.

His command had no effect on either assailant, however, instead of sharing my astonishment, James only got angrier. Tall One gripped me harder making it hard to breathe and I squeaked when he jammed me into his side. I gagged when I sucked in a nose full of his stink from so close. Short One faced James, his knife held out in front. "Move on buddy, this is between my girlfriend and me."

From my vantage point I could only see James' face and the back of Short One's greasy, brown head. I had seen James go vampire a few times, it still sent unpleasant thrills of terror through my body.

From the curses and shouts I heard from Tall One and Short One, I deduced they felt the same. The only difference being my fear was unfounded and theirs was very real. Tall One shifted his hand and James' black eyes followed. In his excited, nasal voice my unwashed captor shouted. "Come closer and I'll snap her neck. I'm serious, I'll do it." His threat lost some fire when his voice cracked.

My eyes were waiting for his movement and yet I missed it, seeing only the effect. One minute I was choking, the next I was free, and sucking huge gulps of air into my lungs. The sudden release left me wobbling off balance and I spun loose. Out of the corner of my eye I saw the tall corpse slide down the wall behind us, his eyes open and lifeless.

Short One moved shockingly fast for a human, whirling and slashing with his knife in my face. My body reacted on its own, swaying back to avoid the slash and I stepped in when the knife passed my face grabbing the man's thick forearm in my hands and slamming it into my raised knee. The knife clattered to the ground and without missing a beat, I stepped back, still holding his arm, feeling it twist with me and snapped his elbow with mine. Screaming, he cradled the top of his bent arm against his side.

I reeled backward, eyes bulging at the sight of the violence I'd done without any conscious thought. I did nothing but blink when the Short One came for me again, murder in his eyes.

James lunged from beside me to kick Short One and he flew into the other wall a few feet away with a sickening thud. He too slid to the ground, broken and lifeless.

Gathering my limp form against his side, James strode briskly out of the alley, slowing only when a red light stopped us at the curb. We reached the hotel in record time and upon arrival in our room, he released me and I sank down on the bed debating whether I was going to be sick.

I began to shake and felt cold all over. The memory of the hollow popping sound of his elbow dislocating and bones cracking haunted me. James turned on the electric kettle and I heard him open the door to the mini fridge. Something cold was placed in my hand and I was ordered to drink.

I did what I was told and spluttered when the whiskey burned my throat. "I can't drink this!" My mouth was on fire and throat threatening to close around the bruising I already felt forming.

James was calmly mopping the blood off his already healing side as he reasoned with me. He threw his shirt in the garbage, headed I was sure for a dumpster a few blocks over like our like deposit from the other night. "It will help you with the shock and calm you down."

"Yeah, but it tastes terrible. What about what Miranda said?"

"You aren't going anywhere for the next few hours." His cool hand smoothed my wild hair and he sat down next to me. "I'm sorry you had to see that. It's hard for me to control my nature when it comes to you. I hadn't meant to kill them." His thumb brushed my cheek. "You handled yourself well."

The fact that two men were dead because they had chosen me to accost that morning didn't bother me. Now that I was safe and no longer had a knife to my throat, I felt the shock subsiding as well. It could have been the whiskey but I was concerned this life was chipping away at my humanity.

I smiled weakly at James, staring into his blue eyes, still dark as he worked to calm himself. "I was you back there."

James avoided my eyes. He knew how I felt about losing myself to him. And he wouldn't admit it, but I had felt his fear that if I lost my humanity so would he.

"How could they ignore your command?" I had to give myself another thing to think about. "These attacks aren't random, are they?"

"They were human which means they were thralls, humans temporarily under a vampire's control. Only a thrall already under another vampire's control can ignore a command. You're right that these attacks are specifically targeted. The question is who is behind them."

I yawned, tired now that we were safe and the adrenaline had worn off. He kissed my head and lay back, pulling me down with him. Curling up against him, I put my head on his chest and tried to think of nothing at all but this. This was safe; this was easy. For a short time I slept.

A little while later while I was in the shower I heard him talking on his phone. I could tell from his tone it was nothing so I let the words flow past me unheeded when I came out to get dressed. James suggested we get out of the city, head north to a small fishing village that served a good piece of fish and had a marina he wanted to show me. Besides, he owed his editor a story and he could get what he needed in a matter of hours.

We went down to the lobby and I, fully expecting to hail a cab, took our normal path to the front door. I was surprised when James steered me, pulling my hand toward the back door and stopping at the valet's station.

The valet, a leggy brunette with an appraising eye for James' physique had been expecting him. "It's on its way now, Mr. Thomas."

A sleek black Mercedes coupe pulled up and the other valet stepped out, motioning for us to get in. Glancing over at James, I saw his smug smile before he slid in. The valet closed the door on me and I looked over, waiting for the explanation even though I could feel that he wasn't going to tell me the truth.

Staring straight ahead, he put the car in gear and said simply, "It's costing a fortune for us to cab everywhere." The side of his mouth twitched. He wasn't lying necessarily, he was playing.

Sitting back in the buttery leather seat, I didn't put up much of a fight. After the last two skirmishes on the street, I knew he was being protective, although it was hard to be self-righteous when I was warm and comfortable listening to the engine purr in such a luxurious car. "Yeah, this feels cost effective."

Out of the corner of my eye I saw him smile as we pulled out onto the street to head out of town. "It's more practical than the Ferrari."

Ch. 68

While we had been out experiencing a wonderfully safe and injury free day, James had received a call from Alan Brightmore, the shopkeeper *I* now counted as an ally. He had bad news on the credit card. It had been stolen and the fee not paid, the credit card company was going to call his store to alert him to the fact. As to the book, he'd found the title and was working to get a copy.

At two the phone rang again; it was Anton letting us know that I would be expected that night. Anton blew off James' concerns about my safety saying Omar's thirst was "manageable" and should cause no further delays. Anton disconnected before James could argue that "manageable" meant nothing. If Omar got away from James and bit me, he could easily frenzy and things could go too far very fast. Gulping, I stared at my marinara, no longer hungry.

At dusk, I went with James to the Court. I was armed with a utilitarian dagger for protection. It wasn't much to look at but it was small and flat and lay on the inside of my leg without hurting me, and it was made of pure silver. James would be in untold trouble if any other vampires knew he had given it to me but he was beside himself that he had to bring me underground. He wouldn't take no for an answer. When I took the blade, James made me promise to use it on anyone that threatened my safety. Even him. I refused, but he wouldn't relent.

"I'm serious, Claire, you have to think of yourself tonight. Don't hesitate to use it." Giving up arguing, I took it and fixed it to my leg, knowing in my heart there was nothing that could bring me to end his existence.

We arrived at Frankenstein's Pub just as the sun was setting behind the overcast sky in a brilliant display of pinks, roses and purples. I loved Scotland's winter. It was milder than home and overcast often. James virtually never wore his sunglasses and the sunsets over the water were awe inspiring. Watching this one, I wondered if it would be my last.

We ran the gauntlet upstairs; it was some sort of battle of the bands and things were wilder than usual. Our usual escort, Rose, nodded in deference to me when she saw us together in the waiting room. The three members of the Court were waiting in one of the rooms down the hall to the left of the thrones in the reception hall.

I had never been down that side before and saw that there were indeed two rooms. One for each Charles and Anton, I was guessing, since Miranda's was the only one on the opposite side.

The room itself was relatively sparse for furnishings, but well stocked in arms. Scanning the room, I saw swords on the wall, guns in a case to the side and a bearskin rug in front of a leather couch to the other side of the room. I guessed this to be Anton's room. Charles' would have rugs and soft furnishings even without the need to use them.

"Welcome," Anton stepped forward, his bristling demeanor contradictory to his courtesy. "James, we need the boy's education to move forward. It is not safe to allow him to walk among us without knowing if he retains the ability to harm any of our number."

Charles and Miranda watched James and Anton face off, the tension between them palpable. I wondered what had happened to take the general dislike they had for each other and turn it into the outright loathing I saw now.

"I have come to do as you've ordered, however, I do *not* believe he is ready for this." James couldn't be openly hostile to his superior without consequence, but he was riding the line.

A knock at the door interrupted the tense confrontation. "Enter," Charles called out. The door opened and a short black vampire led Omar inside.

"He has fed," spoke the black vampire before turning on his heel and exiting the room.

Omar's appearance had me speechless. As a human he had been darker complexioned and timid. His newly paled pallor was the easiest change to absorb, especially given the fact that he'd just fed, bringing his color the closest to human he would ever get again. More difficult to swallow was his agitated state, apparent in his constantly shifting black eyes, extended fangs and angry glare that kept landing on me. James was right, Omar was little more than an animal.

My hand sought James' and I gripped it as tightly as I could, keeping my face blank. My mind went to the dagger hidden beneath my short black dress. "Let's go to work." I flinched when my voice cracked and hoped no one noticed. I couldn't stand here and have him stare at me any longer. Work would be a welcome distraction.

"Claire will need to work from one of the other rooms; Omar is not ready for a human to be so close." James spoke to the members of the Court respectfully but firmly.

Anton waved his hand, not giving the request any consideration before denying it. "That is not necessary. The proceedings are best held in the open for all to witness lest there be any dishonesty."

"Dishonesty? *We're* not the ones trying to pull a fast one." The words jumped from my mouth before I could think. James' hand squeezed mine hard enough to shut me up, too late.

Anton was in my face in the next breath, his hand closing around my neck. The pressure of his steely hand was excruciating on my already bruised throat. I struggled against him, trying in vain to loosen his grip. He struck a blow across my face hard enough to make my nose and mouth explode with blood. "You would do well to know your place, *human*," he sneered. "Your bond might intrigue my colleague but it holds no fascination for me and affords you no leniency in my quarters."

James knew he couldn't attack Anton or we would all be killed; Anton knew it, too. But his need to protect me was making him wild. I felt his frustration sear through my head a second before he lost control, blew the marks wide open, and flooded me with his rage.

A vampire's anger is a breathtaking thing. They have the capacity for tremendous patience *and* terrible damage. I felt James' anger sweep through my being as Anton choked me out, my vision fading from the lack of oxygen my mind and body were screaming for.

Instinctively, my hand shot out and gripped Anton's wrist, squeezing it hard enough to make the bones pop. At once his hand, now useless, released my throat and I fell to my knees gasping raggedly for breath. Each lungful I took tore at my raw and swollen throat. Charles had taken Omar down; he had the writhing vampire, struggling to get at me, trapped lying on his stomach with the portly ruler kneeling on his back. The door opened and the vampire who had brought him in dragged the hungry Omar out.

I watched Anton examine his wrist with clinical coolness. James retrieved me, pulling me back with him to retreat to a chair only a fast dash from the door.

James watched my eyes roll, feeling my escalating panic while I found it more and more challenging to breathe. Tissue swelled in my esophagus, threatening to cut off my air supply. I was already choking on my own blood now clotting in my mouth and nose.

425

Miranda whirled on Anton, chastising him for his behavior. I admired her political skill as she pointed out it was the vampire who had attacked Anton and not the human through the bond they shared. The human could not be punished for a wrong she did not commit. Bravo Miranda, James carried a higher value to them and they would be less likely to harm him.

The air could no longer get past my damaged airway. James was in front of my eyes, fading out and I was vaguely aware of his growing sense of dread before my eyes rolled back into my head and I passed out.

Ch. 69

Coming back to myself I realized I was drinking; I was so thirsty! I was sucking hard, trying to swallow as much of the warm liquid as possible. Each swallow made my throat hurt less and I began to taste the metallic flavor in my mouth. As soon as I realized what it was, I stopped drinking, turning my face away.

Vision restored, I saw that I was in Miranda's quarters on the chaise and, as a courtesy, forced myself to swallow the residual blood in my mouth. James sat beside me. His shirtsleeve rolled up to his elbow exposed the wrist I'd been drinking from, his tongue swept over the wound to close it. I could see that he was on edge.

I felt him bump my shields. Opening up, I heard him.

Don't talk. They'll hear. It's bad.

My pulse quickened and he leaned down to kiss my lips, his tongue flicked a stray drop of blood off of my cheek. Raising my hand to my face, I felt that it had been washed clean. My lips were tender but the swelling was already going down.

Interested in learning what I could, I cast out. I swept for Miranda, knowing I could find her easily, being most familiar with her.

She was nearby, arguing heatedly with the other two. I could hear them if I concentrated hard, really straining my nearly vampire hearing.

Miranda continued to argue that James had struck using my body to break Anton's arm. Wow, I hadn't realized I had broken it. I wasn't sorry.

Anton was contending that I had to be killed immediately before I caused any further corruption to a valued member of the Court. I assumed he meant James, even if Anton himself didn't value him. He was making the point that I was a wild card he didn't want in this Court.

Charles was less decisive, although he sounded like he tended to agree that I should be spared. He didn't like or dislike me, he merely argued that I was harmless. I'd take that over hated, even if it was patronizing.

I caught James' eyes, he saw that I was listening and didn't need interpretation. Watching him give me a reassuring grin, I couldn't return it. I knew if they killed me they would have to kill him, too, and I couldn't let that happen. If it came to that, I had to come up with a backup plan, something that would at least save him. No matter what happened here, he had to survive. Not only because I loved him, but so many things rested on him. Without him, who could transition the new vampires? Without him, who would help Henry stop a war? No, James had to live.

Needing privacy, I firmed up the membrane between us and pushed him out. Predictably he felt it and I saw the line between his eyes. Shaking my head, I signaled to the voices in the other chamber. His frown lines deepened. The voices next door bought me time to think.

I had reached my own decision just as the door to Miranda's quarters opened and they came to announce they had reached a consensus.

"James, Claire. Rise." Charles was formal in his address.

This couldn't be good. Anton stood beside him, fuming with his wrist straightened and laying limp at his side. A vampire's bones took nearly a full day to knit as opposed to their faster healing tissue.

428

We stood, the infusion of James' blood coursed through me, giving me a temporary lift in strength and clarity. Added to my other enhancements it made me nearly as quick and sharp as a young vampire.

"We have reached an impasse in our debate over your fate. It is unclear which of you intended to harm Anton. James, as you are aware, attacking a member of this Court is grounds for punishment. Claire, a human attack is grounds for death. As we cannot be certain which one of you was behind the attack, we are unable to competently assess a punishment."

I wasn't sure if we were being spared or not, I got ready to make good on my plan to bring the punishment down on my own head when Anton chimed in.

"As we are at a stalemate, we will withhold judgment until after you have finished with the boy. If you prove to be valuable, this Court will be lenient." Anton looked smug. I had always known he was a snake. My memory went back to Bradley's last words that the Court was torn on the subject of protecting humans and that we would be punished. My guess as to who hated humans was easy.

As a matter of fact, it was hard to believe Anton *hadn't* had this in mind when he'd provoked James by striking me and drawing blood in front of Omar, putting him into frenzy.

"Bring the boy." Anton spoke loud enough for the door to open and Iain to enter, holding Omar's arm tightly.

Iain made eye contact with me and flicked his green gone dark eyes to the boy's face. Following, I examined the boy's face and saw what he meant. Omar was thirsty; he was eyeing me eagerly, fangs fully extended.

Smelling blood, I looked down at the front of my dress and saw my blood was still drying. I knew then that Anton wasn't intending to let me walk out of here tonight even if we succeeded. No matter, James would live and that knowledge allowed me to remain functional, if a little shaky. "Let's go to work." I said again and looked to James for agreement.

Though he appeared worried by my behavior and closed mind, he gave me a nod and I knew he was ready.

Our audience only bothered me for a minute before I was entirely absorbed in my task. Sending out my mind, I found Omar easily.

Once I had the feel of him I tried to alter his emotions, using mine for a guide. Tapping my favorite memory of my dad, I projected my feelings into James' head. The boy's reaction was intense and immediate.

I had been warned that a newly turned vampire had stronger sensations than older vampires, though I had never seen their quicker reflexes. Before anyone could stop him, Omar had bowled me over and was on top of me. His fangs deep in my shoulder, had been deflected from my throat only by my last minute spin when I'd seen him leap.

The impact of being knocked down on the cold, hard stone floor with a vampire, no matter how small, lying on top of me was enough to knock the wind out of me. However, I had just fed from James and was strong enough to push his lighter body off of me and thrust him at James.

James grabbed hold of Omar's flying body, pinning his arms to his sides and held him while we went on to work hard, trying to break into his mind. At every turn he deflected us as we desperately tried every avenue we could think of. The boy was toughened from a hard life.

Trying to find smoother entry, I pushed in and dug for some form of a positive experience to latch on to, something that had made him happy. I stopped digging in the past and went nearer to the present. That was where I found it. Tara. Tara's house was his happy place. He loved the safety he felt in his room at her home.

Triumphant, I touched on his memory of Tara and combined it with my happiest feelings. Some of which also included Tara. Within minutes, Omar calmed visibly enough that James loosed his grip, though he did not release the boy entirely.

When Omar stopped struggling, James was able to talk to him. He kept his voice soothing, like he was speaking to a frightened animal, which I was guessing wasn't far from the truth.

"Omar, as we discussed last night, the sooner you learn to control yourself the sooner you leave here and go home. I need you to focus now and stop trying to attack Claire. You remember her. She was the one who saved you from that place, she's friends with Tara."

Omar's wild eyes were growing sensible. His mouth moved, his fangs making it hard for him to speak.

"Sorry Claire." His eyes kept flicking down to the front of my dress and the blood I knew was tempting him.

I half laughed, half cried. We were doing it. We were slowly bringing Omar around. I let my hopes rise thinking we might actually be able to save him.

"That's okay, I know this is hard."

"I miss Tara. Can she come to visit?" He sounded homesick.

Shooting James a furtive glance, I saw him shake his head once. Omar didn't remember the attack. That was good. He couldn't handle that right now.

"Soon Omar." I answered his query. "Let's get you functional first."

Together we worked for a few hours and he showed great progress in developing his shields. A couple of times, I felt a tickle in my head coming from Omar that I couldn't identify and felt fear flutter in my stomach as I speculated what it might be. His ability had survived and I was feeling him trying it on James.

After Omar's concentration was noticeably disintegrating, we called it quits just before daybreak. We agreed we would return at the next evening's sunset and were excused. Miranda gave me a wrap to wear over my dress since mine was covered in blood and would be hard to make it home in unnoticed.

We stopped in the pub above, now closed to all but vampire visitors leaving the Court. James had three huge drinks and pointed out I had also not eaten for some time. I ordered a light dinner and barely tasted the food while I ate in an exhausted fog before driving back to the hotel.

Ch. 70

I didn't open my eyes until well after noon the next day. That didn't leave much time before we had to go back to work.

James seemed guardedly pleased by our progress although his expression went blank when I asked him to confirm my fears about the "tickle" I felt the night before.

"He still has it, doesn't he?" I asked, feeling my heart sink.

James nodded. "It could have changed, it feels different. I'm waiting to find out what's changed before saying anything."

I realized why he didn't know exactly how it had changed. "It's gotten stronger; it affects humans now. I felt it."

At that, James snapped his fingers and smiled broadly. "That explains it."

"I don't understand. You act like it's a good thing that he's twice as dangerous now."

"No, he is twice as *valuable* now." Going on to explain excitedly, "It has changed because it isn't directed at vampires anymore, I don't feel anything from him. Now he can control *humans*, not vampires." He was beaming, "He's safe."

I felt the relief spread through us both. It had worked. Now we just had to convince the Court.

Ch. 71

We spent the afternoon in our room. I didn't have the energy to go out. We had lunch brought up for me and got ready in time to head down to the car at sunset; my knife once again accessible on my leg, just in case. James' insisted.

"Do you like the car?" James asked lightly, making small talk on the way across the George IV Bridge.

I smiled at him. "I can't decide which of your two cars is the nicest car I've ever been in."

Chuckling he answered, "I like being comfortable. Are you saying you consider this the other car then?"

"I like it but I'm not a big car nut, so I guess as far as I'm concerned you can decide. What else did you have lined up for our trial period?" I tried to sound like I knew what I was doing when buying a car. "Were you thinking another luxury car or a sports car since you sold the Ferrari?" I joked.

"I was thinking an Aston Martin if we wanted a sports car to see if you liked the power and handling. Otherwise, BMW makes a fine sedan or if you want something more prestigious we could go with a Bentley or Rolls Royce. Whatever you want."

Eyeing him to see if he was kidding, I saw that he was only partially joking. "You would seriously buy a $300,000 car if I wanted you to?" My conservative upbringing squelched the thought of such an extravagance.

James pulled his gaze from the road to look at me. "When you have an eternity to make it back, what's spending a little money?"

"So you would buy me anything?"

He nodded.

"A vacation home in the Hamptons?"

"Done," he replied, staring at the road without flinching.

"An island in the South Pacific?"

"Not a problem." The corner of his mouth twitched.

"All of the above?"

"Where do I sign?"

"Exactly how much money do you have, can I ask?"

He flashed me a grin. "Of course you can ask. It's half yours in less than a week." He told me and I was glad he was driving. I would have crashed.

"Are you kidding?"

"Does it change anything?" His gaze flickered over nervously.

"No. Does it change anything that I don't care?"

His hand reached over to take mine and he gave a gentle squeeze. "No, I knew you wouldn't."

We pulled up to the pub and James found a parking spot conveniently close to the front door. It seemed the vampires Glamoured the best spots so they could avoid walking. How convenient. I might be tempted to see if James could do that this winter back home when it was 30 below and I had to go grocery shopping.

We went to the bar for a drink before heading below.

Amani was working the bar again. I tried to get James to head to a table before she noticed us, but she was faster.

"Hello, if it isn't the happy couple. What can I get for you?" She was doing a better job of hiding her fangs than her claws.

James ordered our drinks, his usual and a ginger ale for me. When Amani brought them smiling smugly, I saw she was prepared to harass me again. Sighing, I braced for it but then James stepped in.

Signaling her with a finger to come close, he leaned in to whisper in her ear. She must have thought he was going to share something good with her, because she leaned in, smiling and narrowed her eyes at me.

"Amani, you and I both know I hold a secret that could have you locked in a coffin for a very long time. Back off of Claire and I will keep your secret. Otherwise, I will have no problem sharing it with the wrong people."

Amani's eyes widened and she briskly walked down the bar to take another order from a party dressed in costume, something the Pub tended to encourage. We enjoyed our drinks in peace.

When we were walking down the hall out of earshot, I dared to ask. "What did she do?"

Keeping his eyes forward James said, "You know who really killed JFK?"

I froze, my mouth open in absolute disbelief. "You're kidding!"

He laughed. "Actually, I am. But it sounds better than she killed an important vampire whom you've never heard of under questionable circumstances."

Swinging my hand to playfully slap his chest, I knew it was a mistake before I made contact. "Damn!" I swore as I felt the bone in my right pinky give way.

Gently, he took my hand in his and examined it. "Just a minute," he said and walked back to the bar returning a minute later with a bag of ice.

I reached for it and held it to my hand, feeling like an idiot once again.

"Claire, please stop hitting me. You're lucky it's just a finger, it could have been your hand." He kissed the top of my head while I marched on feeling idiotic.

Ch. 72

Rose glanced at my hand and saw me flush. I was grateful she didn't ask.

I wasn't so lucky when we met in Miranda's quarters and Anton laughed, referring to me as "stupid and breakable," again wondering out loud why someone didn't just drain me and get it over with. James fought hard not to tear him apart. Anton was pushing James publicly now, why? What did he stand to gain with an open fight?

Omar entered the room, pulling me instantly out of my thoughts.

Tonight's Omar was a very different vampire than last night's. He was still visibly tense and on edge, his eyes darting about the room, but he was much more in control of himself.

"Good evening Omar." James welcomed him first, testing. "You look well tonight."

"Thanks. I've been working really hard so I can go home soon."

He was a little boy just wanting to go home. I felt sympathy for the poor boy, deciding we had to get him out of here before he had a breakdown from the stress.

We went straight to work again and Omar did better than expected, even coming close enough to touch me with no significant changes in his concentration. Anton was unable to fault his progress.

"It has been long enough James. Does the boy still have his ability intact? Is he a danger to vampires?" Charles asked when we took a break at midnight.

I kept my reaction hidden as best as possible, turning to face James and watch his expression as he reported to the Court.

"We have been teaching control and testing his boundaries. Omar has been an excellent student and I am certain he is ready to go home if you approve."

Miranda was suspicious. "James you are aware no one is to go home until we are certain he will not harm any of our kind."

"Miranda, I can guarantee that Omar will never harm a vampire with his ability."

"Can you promise that?" No one could question her meaning. If James were wrong, he would bear the responsibility and subsequent punishment.

James met her eyes for a moment before answering with certainty. "Yes. His ability has shifted focus."

The three ancients of the Court went quiet and I felt the atmosphere change as they prepared to attack if necessary.

I fought to keep my breath even and my heartbeat close to normal.

Sure of himself James added, "His ability has transferred to humans and no longer affects vampires. He is safe and may be of some use in the future as he ages and gains control of himself."

Miranda silently surveyed our trio for a long time. Finally, she made up her mind and called Iain, who apparently did not have either abilities or shielding. A cursory "touch" when he came in and I confirmed just that.

"Omar, tell Iain to attack me." She ordered the very thing Omar had been doing to wipe out Henry's friends in

Milwaukee.

Frightened, Omar whipped around to James who only nodded that he should do as he was told.

The boy closed his eyes and concentrated, I imagined he would have been sweating if he was able. Everyone was staring and after a minute when Iain was clearly not affected, Miranda turned to us, visibly pleased while Anton glowered.

Charles addressed us. "You may leave, but remember you are personally responsible for the boy and his actions. Any transgressions on his part against our kind shall cost you dearly."

James accepted the terms of Omar's release and the three of us left together as quickly as possible, escorting Omar home to Tara. A quick call to Henry updating him let us ask how Tara was doing.

"She is up and around and doing well. We can fly tomorrow should we choose." Henry answered James.

"I think the sooner the better." James told Henry about the repeated attacks on us by humans and thralls and Anton's mysteriously reckless behavior. Henry agreed Edinburgh would not be safe for us for a while.

Ch. 74

When we reached the hotel, James made our travel plans, wanting to get as much distance between Omar and the Court as possible. Tonya didn't want to go; she was going to stay and "help" Donovan settle into life with an ability he had to hide.

With Omar being so young and light sensitive, we had to time our flight to get him in and out in the dark, although since it was winter and nights were long, we arranged it easily. He flew in a coffin in the cargo hold. At my horrified expression, James pointed out this is how they had been functioning for decades. Again, I found a need to adjust my perception of the world around me. Not all coffins contained real corpses.

I was shaking my head when he came in to the bedroom after he hung up with the airline.

"What's wrong?" James asked, curious of my reaction. "Don't you want to leave?"

"No, I'd been looking forward to going to France for a few days. I know it sounds dumb, but I was still hoping to see my parents and stay a little longer. I like it here." I shrugged off the disappointment, reminding myself time didn't matter. "That's okay, maybe we can come back after you get Omar settled."

Lying on the bed beside me, he threw his arm over my waist and pulled me close to him. "Claire, I made flight arrangements for us to go to France tomorrow. I think we can safely stay for a week before returning home. What do you think? Omar will be safe with Tara and Henry watching out for him."

Feeling a bubble in my chest, I rolled over to face James. "Really? We don't have to go home yet? I can't wait to see my parents."

He was smiling when he kissed me. "What about that other thing we are going to do there? Are you excited about that?"

"Very." I kissed him back. "I hoped it wasn't being postponed." He shot me a look like that would never happen.

"So tell me what you have planned for us?" Contrary to most girls, I had the luxury of never having had a wedding fantasy. Anything with him would be perfect.

"How do you feel about boats?" James pulled back to watch my face.

"What kind of boat?"

He explained what he'd set up.

"Did you plan all of this?" I didn't know what to say. It sounded perfect. It was small, intimate and included all of my favorite people. Well, I thought sadly of Stephen stuck back home with a detective hounding him, almost all of my favorites.

Shaking his head at the misplaced approval, James admitted, "Tonya has been a great help."

"Next time I see her, I'll have to thank her." My head was spinning. I was going to see my parents, and be a married woman all within a few days. "Oh my gosh!" I sat up with a start.

"What?" James put his hand on my shoulder.

"A dress! The one thing I was supposed to do and I haven't done it. There's no way I'll have one in a few days." I felt silly for worrying about something so trivial.

"Tonya mentioned a dress shop there; she could pull some strings with the owner." He wiggled his eyebrows, "Money opens all doors." I knew he was teasing and stopped myself from a swat, settling for a kiss instead.

Flicking a brow at my display of self-control, James kissed me back then did it again. I lost my clothes somewhere along the way, feeling for the first time in a long time that we were in control of our destinies.

I thought again of destiny as I lay in James' arms while my heart slowed from our exertions. I laughed out loud, wriggling in my excitement.

"James, Alan was right!"

His grip tightened and I squeaked. "What do you mean he was right?"

"He was right only he was wrong. We were underground, that was true, only the blood you tasted wasn't drawn by you nor was the blood on me. You brought me *back*. You *saved* me."

I could feel the relief flood through him when he realized the truth in what I said. The terrible destiny he had seen for me had been fulfilled, only it wasn't terrible and it was passed. I had lived because of him.

We lay without speaking until I drifted off, his hand tracing faint patterns in my arm. It seemed only minutes later when I opened my eyes to see the sun coming up over the ancient skyline of Edinburgh. Stretching luxuriously, I remembered with a twinge that my little finger was hurt, but it barely felt stiff upon further exploration. It would most likely be better

443

by nightfall. Grunting in amazement, I was again in awe at the magick of my bond with James.

Becoming aware that I was alone in the bed, I sat up and glanced around the room. Seeing no sign of James, I swung my legs over the side and walked around to the door. He wasn't in the sitting room either and I was starting to wonder when I saw a note sticking to my purse on the bench by the entryway.

Dear Claire-

I've gone to take care of something, I will be back soon. Think of what you want to do with your last remaining days of freedom.

Love Always,
James

At first I was confused by his reference to my freedom and then I remembered the wedding. What did I want to do with my last few days of freedom? Sappily, I realized all of the things I wanted to do were things I could do after I was married since they all included my husband to be. What a hopeless case I am, I thought happily.

Room service brought breakfast: fresh fruit, a croissant and tea. While I waited for my tea to steep I called and made arrangements to meet Tonya later at a dress shop. She swore she would handle everything.

I was still wearing my comfy clothes, reading when I heard the lock click in the door and James walked in. I felt my stomach flutter when I watched him enter the room. His short, black coat was wet with melted snow and he ran his hand through his hair to wick off some residual moisture leaving his dark hair smoothed off his face.

"Where did you go?" I asked him lazily from the couch.

Striding over, he chuckled and kissed my head. "Enjoying your alone time I see."

"Mmm, hmm." I marked my page with a scrap of an old plane ticket and craned my head upward to see him. He looked like he had a secret and I raised an eyebrow in question.

"If I can bother you to get dressed and brave the elements, I would like to show you something."

I was intrigued by the contained enthusiasm I felt coming off of him. Shooting him curious glances several times, I dressed in a pair of jeans and a warm sweater.

"Ready?" He asked, putting out his arm for me.

I nodded and put my hand on his arm, letting him lead me to the car.

We drove out of town a dozen miles into the countryside when we pulled off onto a narrow, twisting gravel road. At a seemingly random flat spot where the trees gave way to the fields, James stopped the car and got out. Before I could open my door he had it open and had reached for my hand.

I stood on a picturesque flat site surrounded by rolling hills and overlooking the river below us.

"What is this?" I turned toward James, completely without a clue what I was looking at.

He remained motionless next to me for so long I wondered if he was going to answer at all. I watched the river while I resigned myself to wait. The peace of the place transferred itself to me and I felt something wonderful. Serenity.

"I told you I focus only on one life at a time." He reached for my hand. "But this is a place that I keep coming back to.

I wanted to share it with you. When I first left the Guard, I was unhappy with myself for the things I had done for them. Isolation was something I needed. I craved it." He pointed to the trees behind us and I saw what remained of a small stone foundation at the base of the forest. "This was an oasis for me when I needed one, my house was right there. It has always been a good place for me; it reminds me of my home when I was a child in Canada. When I need peace, I come here."

I looked up at him and he squeezed my hand continuing to watch the river.

"I wanted you to see it."

My heart swelled. I knew I would never know everything about James and his many lifetimes, but I knew *him*. And that was enough.

The End

Acknowledgements

Empath was my first book and I've been so blown away by the way it has touched people. First books are always the closest to our hearts and no matter how many more stories I pull out of this head of mine, I think the story of James and Claire will always be my favorite.

So thank you to everyone who has been a part of this experience from Leslie, the first person to say, "You got a book there," through the editors, graphic designers, and "sweepers" who helped put the final touches on these third editions. My family has been more than patient and I'm so lucky to have them and their support as well as my friends. Ann and Lynn I love that you come to the signings and promise never to read my work.

Most of all I would like to thank everyone who buys a book regardless of the author. You let us keep doing what we love and that is truly a gift.

www.ingramcontent.com/pod-product-compliance
Lightning Source LLC
Chambersburg PA
CBHW021120260626
47169CB00005B/1375